# A CROWDED MARRIAGE

There are already three people in artist Imogen Cameron's marriage—herself, her husband, Alex, and their nine-year-old son, Rufus—and that's just the way she likes it. But all that's about to change...

When the Camerons hit dire financial straits they are forced to move out of their London home and accept an offer from Eleanor Latimer of a rent-free cottage on her country estate. Ordinarily, the offer of a free home in the country is not to be sniffed at but, as Eleanor just happens to be Alex's beautiful, rich and frankly flirtatious ex, Imogen is very sniffy indeed.

Once installed in the less than idyllic Shepherd's Cottage, Imogen's life is suddenly full to bursting with surly locals, psychotic chickens, a maddening headmaster, mountains of manure, a bossy vet, and of course Eleanor, who seems to be permanently at Alex's side. As far as Imogen's concerned, this...well, this is just silly, someone's going to have to go. The question is who?

# A CROWDED MARRIAGE

## Catherine Alliott

**WINDSOR**
**PARAGON**

First published 2006
by
Headline Review
This Large Print edition published 2007
by
BBC Audiobooks Ltd by arrangement with
Headline Publishing Group

Hardcover  ISBN: 978 1 405 61802 1
Softcover    ISBN: 978 1 405 61803 8

British Library Cataloguing in Publication Data available

Printed and bound in Great Britain by
Antony Rowe Ltd., Chippenham, Wiltshire

For the Gwynns, with love.

# CHAPTER ONE

By the time the suicide victim had been cleared from the Piccadilly Line and normal service had resumed, I was, inevitably and irrevocably, half an hour late. As the train lurched out of the tunnel where it had slumbered peacefully the while and picked up speed—quite alarming speed actually, and wobbling precariously, as if perhaps a shoe or some garment was still in its path—I glanced feverishly at my watch. Half-past one. Half-past one! I went hot. I mean, naturally my heart went out to the deceased man—or woman even; we hadn't been told the gender, just a rather macabre announcement over the Tannoy about a 'person on the line'—but why did it have to be my line? Why not the Jubilee or the Bakerloo? Why, with unerring accuracy, did the severely depressed have to pick the blue one—for the second time this year? It was almost as if they saw me coming. Saw me happily applying the eyeliner and the lip gloss in my bathroom, chuckling away to Terry Wogan, merrily swapping grubby trainers for a pair of high heels, putting on my good suede jacket for a foray into the West End and thought—yikes, if *she's* getting out and about, if *she's* having a good time, that's it, I'm out of here, I'm toast—and hurled themselves into the path of an oncoming train.

Which is an extremely selfish and uncharitable reaction to a truly tragic event, Imogen Cameron, I told myself severely as I got off at the next stop and hurried up the escalator. Sorry, God. I raised my eyes sheepishly to heaven. Even as I did, though, I

1

knew I was cutting a secret deal with Him. Knew I was admitting to being a guilty sinner in return for Him making it go well with the guy I was about to meet and oh, sorry, God *again*, but oh Christ—I was going to be so *late*!

I raced out of the tube entrance and down Piccadilly in the direction of Albemarle Street. Late, for my first meeting—first *lunch*, nay—with anyone who'd ever shown even the remotest interest in my work: a gallery owner, no less, who'd casually mentioned exhibiting my paintings in a private view and who'd offered to buy me lunch, discuss terms, but who, under the circumstances—I glanced at my watch again—had probably got bored of waiting and scarpered. In desperation I hitched up my skirt, clutched my handbag to my chest and for all the world like Dame Kelly Holmes sprinting for the line, jutted out my chin and hurtled through the pinstripes.

I'd met him at Kate's last week, at a seriously smart drinks party surrounded by her fearfully social friends. There'd been buckets of pink champagne sloshing around, and since Alex and I were on an economy drive and only knocked back the cheapest plonk these days, I'd got stuck in. By the time Kate sashayed up with the gallery owner, introducing me as 'my artist friend across the street who does the most *fab*ulous paintings', I was practically seeing double. She'd then proceeded to lure him into her study—simultaneously tugging me along with her—to admire a rather hectic oil she had loyally hanging above her desk. Not one of my best.

'Yes . . .' He'd peered closely, then, as if that sort of proximity was a bit alarming, stepped back

2

sharply. He flicked back his floppy chestnut waves and nodded contemplatively. 'Yes, it's charming. It has a certain naïve simplicity'—or was it a simple naïvety?—'that one doesn't always come across these days, but which, personally, I embrace.'

He'd turned from the picture to look me up and down in a practised manner, taking in my wild blonde hair and flushed cheeks. I was delighted to hear he embraced simplicity as there was plenty more where that came from, and I beamed back drunkenly.

'Tell me, do you exhibit a lot?'

I didn't, not ever. Well, not unless you counted that time in a pub in Parsons Green where me and three other painter friends had paid for the upstairs room ourselves and only our mothers had turned up, and once in a converted church in the country where I'd put the wrong day on the flyers so no one came at all, and was about to tell him as much when Kate chipped in, 'Yes, quite a lot, don't you, Imo? But not so much recently. Not since that carping critic in *The Times* burbled on about the possibility of over-exposure.'

She took a drag of her cigarette and blew the smoke out over his head as I regarded her in abject amazement. That she could *tell* such flagrant lies, standing there in her Chanel dress and her Mikimoto pearls, but then Kate hadn't just been named Most Promising Newcomer at the Chelsea Players Theatre, her very upmarket am-dram group, for nothing, and continued to smile her sweet patron-of-the-arts smile and fix him with her baby-blue eyes. He buckled under the pressure, swept back his waves and turned to the painting again.

3

'Yes, well, critics are a loathsome bunch,' he growled. 'Don't know their arses from their elbows, and certainly don't know talent when it hits them in the face. I should know,' he added bitterly. He drew himself up importantly and slipped a hand into the inside pocket of his tastefully distressed corduroy jacket.

'Casper Villiers,' he purred, pressing a card into my hand, his dark eyes smouldering into mine. 'Let's do lunch. I'm planning a mixed media exhibition in the summer, and I need an abstract artist. Say Tuesday, one o'clock at the Markham? Bring your portfolio.'

And off he sauntered, just pausing to shoot me another hot stare over his shoulder as he relieved a passing waiter of a glass of Kate's excellent champagne. I hadn't liked to tell him that the 'abstract' art before him was in fact an extremely figurative hay cart in an extremely figurative barley field and that I didn't even possess a portfolio, I'd just felt my knees buckle.

'Seriously influential,' Kate hissed in my ear. 'Knows literally everyone in the art world and can pull all sorts of strings. Rather cute too, don't you think?'

'Very!' I gasped back as, at that moment, my husband had sauntered up, looking amused, but never proprietary.

'Pulled?' Alex enquired.

'Hope so,' I gushed back happily. 'He's a gallery owner, in Cork Street. He liked Kate's picture and he wants to look at the rest of my work. At—you know—my portfolio.'

'Terrific!' He had the good grace not to question the existence of that particular work of fiction.

4

'About time too. I was wondering when my artist wife was going to be discovered and I could plump for early retirement. I'm looking forward to adopting Kept Man status. Oh, and incidentally, you can tell him from me, we don't want any of that fifty per cent commission nonsense either. It's ten per cent at the most, and if he's not interested, it'll be back to the Saatchis for us.'

'Us?'

'Well, obviously as your manager I'll be taking a close interest in all financial arrangements.' He waggled his eyebrows and twiddled an imaginary moustache.

I laughed, but could tell he was pleased, which thrilled me. Recently I'd started to get rather despondent about my so-called work and its lack of remuneration, and wondered if I shouldn't retrain as an illustrator or something. Something to get a few much-needed pennies into the Cameron coffers, something to make me feel like a useful working mother now Rufus was at school full time. It had begun to seem grossly self-indulgent to shut myself away in the attic with my oils, a broom handle wedging the door shut, yelling, 'I'm on the phone!' to all-comers, producing paintings that no one except me had the slightest interest in. I'd even dutifully gone out and bought some watercolours and a sketch book with which to capture Paula the Pit Pony or Gloria the Glow-worm, but my heart wasn't in it, and in no time at all I'd found myself throwing on my overalls and squaring up to one of my huge canvases again. Casper Villiers' invitation, then, was the life-line I needed. A boost to morale that had been far too long in coming.

As I hurried along the dusty West End

pavements, my progress impeded by ludicrously high heels—I'd decided against the struggling-artist look since Kate had implied I was so successful the general public was in danger of being saturated by my talents—I tried to drive from my mind the summer exhibition he'd referred to. It was an increasingly pressing fantasy. The opening night: a private view on a warm evening, friends and family spilling out of the gallery on to the pavement, chattering excitedly, clutching champagne flutes; Alex looking heavenly in a biscuit linen jacket, stroking back his silky blond hair; my mother elegant in flowing taupe, my father . . . oh God, Dad, in that black leather jacket and cowboy boots. I moved smartly on. The press then: cameras flashing, lenses trained on my canvas in the window, my latest life drawing perhaps, that I'd rather pretentiously entitled *Nude in South London* (or as my sister, Hannah, had snorted *Bollocks in Brixton*), and then my name in discreet grey lettering on the window: 'Imogen Cameron—Solo Exhibition'. No. No, that wasn't right because he'd said it was to be a mixed exhibition, and golly, not necessarily with me in the mix since he'd only seen one picture.

To broaden his knowledge, I'd spent the whole of last week feverishly photographing the rest of my paintings and arranging the prints in a leather portfolio—hideously expensive but worth the outlay, I'd reasoned—which I now clasped in my hot little hand, along with a couple of small oils, which I was sure he'd like, in a carrier bag. If only he was still there! If only he hadn't got bored with waiting and—oh, hello—here we are, the Markham. And I'd almost shot straight past! I gave a cursory glance to the rather grand pillars that heralded the entrance to a white stuccoed restaurant and hastened on in. As I pushed through the glass double doors I emerged into a sort of panelled lobby. Luckily there was a girl behind a desk directing traffic.

'I'm meeting a Mr Villiers,' I breathed, peering anxiously through the door to the restaurant. 'But I'm terribly late and he might well have—oh! Oh no, he hasn't, there he is.' And I was off, waving aside her attempt to escort me, and bustling through the packed dining room, weaving around tables with a 'Sorry, oh, *sorry*,' as I jogged a media type's crumpled linen elbow, misdirecting a forkful of risotto, intent on the solitary figure in the corner.

'I *do* apologise,' I began breathlessly as he got up to greet me, looking much younger than I remembered and much better-looking. His chestnut waves flopped attractively into his dark eyes and his smile was wide and welcoming as he took my hand. 'You see, there was this wretched suicide on the line—well, no, sounds awful, not wretched, although obviously for him, but—'

'Couldn't matter less,' he interrupted smoothly. 'I was late myself. I've only been here five minutes. Drink?' He gestured to a bottle in an ice bucket. 'I took the liberty of ordering some champagne, but if you'd prefer something else?'

'Oh! No, how marvellous.'

I sat down and reached for my glass eagerly, taking a greedy sip. Well, glug, actually. God, I was thirsty. I put it down thoughtfully. Steady, Imogen. Don't want to get disastrously pissed and start showing him your appendix scar or your cellulite,

7

do you? Just . . . take it easy. But that was a good sign surely? Champagne? You didn't expend that sort of outlay unless you were interested?

I crossed my legs in a businesslike manner and smoothed down my skirt with fluttering hands. I was horribly nervous, I realised. 'And, um, obviously I've brought along my Portaloo,' I glanced down at it, propped up by my chair. No, hang on . . .

'Portfolio?'

'That's it.' I flushed. *Shit.*

'Only I'm pretty sure this place is fully equipped on the sanitary front,' he laughed.

'Yes, bound to be, ha *ha*! Oh, and plus, I've brought along a couple of small oils, but I don't know if you want to eat first or . . . ?'

'Oh, eat first, definitely. Plenty of time for all that.' He grinned, and twinkled at me as he flicked out his napkin.

Ah, right. A bit of chatting and flirting were in order first. Well, fine, I could do that. Could flirt my little socks off, if need be. Still smarting from my faux pas I managed to flick my own napkin out and twinkle back, then, taking the quickest route to any man's heart, plunged in and asked him all about himself.

Casper rolled over like a dream: he leaned back in his chair, stuck his legs out in front of him and launched expansively into 'My Glittering yet Thwarted Career,' whilst I leaned in, captivated, eyes wide, murmuring, 'Really?' or, 'Gosh, how marvellous,' then later, 'How dreadful!' when we got to the thwarted bit. It transpired Casper had been the most promising student at St Martin's and a close contender for the Turner Prize, but his

8

ideas had been cruelly stolen by jealous, inferior rivals. He'd reluctantly given up his dream of becoming an artist and opened a gallery instead, which was a tremendous success, and he now enjoyed great acclaim as a talent spotter.

'Benji Riley-Smith, Peter De Cazzolet—you name them, I've discovered them,' he murmured confidentially, leaning right back in his chair. He was practically horizontal now, chin level with the table.

'Really?'

I hadn't heard of any of them and could hardly make out what he was saying he was so far away from me.

'Casian Fartmaker, Barty Bugger-Me—' (I was lip-reading now so I may have got that wrong) he shrugged modestly—'I've been, well, shall we say, instrumental in their success?'

'Yes, let's,' I breathed, sneaking a look at my watch under the table. I mean, granted this paean of self-congratulatory praise was being delivered with plenty of smouldering looks and lashings of champagne over a fashionable monkfish apiece, which was all very pleasant, but time was marching on. I had to pick Rufus up from school at three thirty and Casper still hadn't looked at my work.

'So. You're a friend of Kate's,' he said, lurching forward suddenly. He propped his elbows on the table, laced his fingers over the fish he'd hardly touched, and fixed me with his dark eyes. 'She's kept you very quiet.'

I'd been leaning right in to listen to his monologue so our noses were practically touching now. 'Has she?' I inched back, hopefully not too obviously. 'Oh, well, I suppose I haven't known her that long. Only since she moved to Putney a few years ago. We've been there a while.'

'We?'

'My husband and I. And my son, Rufus. He's nine.'

'Ah.' There was something deeply disinterested in this monosyllable and I could feel his attention wandering.

'But Kate's lovely, isn't she?' I rushed on. 'Sebastian too. They're great mates of ours. How do you know them?'

Nice one, Imogen. Back to him.

'Oh, Kate knows everyone,' he said airily, and as he turned to wave down a passing wine waiter, I thought that, to an extent, this was true. Or to be more precise, everyone knew Kate.

Married to an eminent surgeon and with her very own designer label and boutique in the Fulham Road, Kate was one who attracted others. If I hadn't liked her so much I'd have envied her horribly—beautiful, fun, but kind too, and terribly self-effacing. I'd heard about her long before I'd met her. 'Oh, you *must* know the Barringtons,' people said when Kate and Sebastian moved to Hastoe Avenue. 'They live across the road from you. *Every*one knows Kate.' Well, I certainly knew their house. Huge, red brick and imposing and on the right side of the Avenue (south-facing gardens and off-street parking), it was as hard to miss as our modest little semi opposite (north-facing pocket handkerchiefs and parking in the street) was easy to. And I knew the girl they meant too. Had seen her sailing off to work, blonde hair flying, calling out last-minute instructions to the nanny, and then returning from the school run later, hordes of gorgeous blonde children in the back of a gleaming four-wheel drive. I'd seen her in the evening too, going out to dinner with her husband, waving to the children at their bedroom windows, swathed in cashmere and pearls, long legs flashing out of a tiny skirt. But I hadn't met her, and might not have done either, had she not knocked on my door one Monday morning looking wild-eyed and desperate.

'Have you got a hacksaw?' she'd blurted urgently.

'A hacksaw?' I blinked.

'Yes, only Orlando's got his head stuck in the banisters, and I remember seeing you sawing up some boards in your front garden.'

'Oh!'

My painting boards. Cheaper than canvas, but sometimes too big and unwieldy to fit in my easel, so requiring surgery.

'Oh, yes, I have. Hang on!'

I ran up two flights of stairs and seized it from my studio, then together, we'd dashed across the road.

The Barringtons' hall was about the size of a hockey pitch and had a grand sweeping staircase, up which marched hundreds of very expensive-looking balusters. Orlando's face was going a nasty shade of purple between the top two so I hastened up with my saw, but as I hacked away close to his left ear with Kate shouting, 'It's either that or his neck!' I rather hoped Dr Barrington didn't decide to leave his operating theatre early and come home to see me sawing his son out like some flaky magician. Orlando emerged unscathed, but causing wilful damage to a listed house left me in

11

serious need of a sharpener. Since it was only ten in the morning Kate had hastened to her Present Cupboard and produced—oh splendid—we'd bonded over a box of Lindor chocolates.

Yes, everyone liked Kate, and it seemed my young gallery owner was no exception. He'd long been an admirer, meeting her first at St Martin's where she'd designed shirts and he'd painted landscapes and . . . oh, he still painted landscapes, did he? . . . Really? . . . still dabbled in oils, and—oh Lord, we were back to him again.

'Even now,' he confided over clasped hands, sotto voce, 'when people come in to buy a Hodgson, or a Parnell, but find them too expensive, I say—hold on a minute,' he raised a finger expressively, 'you might be interested in a little-known artist I have out the back here, and then I take them out and show them one of mine, and do you know, they very often buy.'

'How fascinating! Without knowing it's you?' I asked breathlessly but without the slightest interest. I really *did* have to collect Rufus soon.

'Oh, no, I never let on.'

He winked and I looked suitably impressed and little womanish, but—oh, *please*, perhaps over a coffee, could we look at my work? Find out when this wretched exhibition was?

'So . . . coffee?'

I beamed. Finally. 'Please!'

'And shall we take it upstairs? Where it's more comfortable?'

Oh, even better. Clearly there was some sit-soft area, a lounge or something, where we could spread the pictures out, stand up and view them around us.

'Good idea.' I was on my feet.

In retrospect I suppose I did notice a flicker of surprise pass over his eyes; a faint startle, perhaps, at my alacrity, but he soon recovered. His face was naturally pink from all that champagne—either that or a rush of excitement at the prospect of seeing my work—and I let him guide me, his hand perhaps a touch too solicitous on my back, through the restaurant and back to the front desk.

He was talking nineteen to the dozen now, rather nervously in fact, about the new Turner Whistler exhibition, and it occurred to me this might be quite a big moment for him. A young star in the making? The new Tracey Emin perhaps, with him as my mentor? My Svengali? I smiled and nodded indulgently at his prattle, although I did pause to wonder why we were getting in a lift. That struck me as odd. Up it glided and on he chattered, smoothing back his waves and laughing too loudly and then, as the doors slid open, he ushered me out into a long corridor. A long, wallpapered corridor, with pink carpet at our feet, and lots of oak-panelled doors on either side. He walked me down it, rummaging in his trouser pocket, jingling loose change, but it was only when we passed a girl with a mop and bucket that it struck me . . . that this was a hotel. And that the jingling in his pocket was not coins, but keys, which he was bringing out even now, and fitting into a door with the number fifteen on it.

I gave a jolt of horror. Blood surged up my neck and face and to other extremities I didn't even know could flush. I stood there, aghast. Casper gently pushed open the door to reveal an enormous double bed with a bright red quilt in the

13

middle of a dimly lit room. The curtains were drawn, and there was another bottle of champagne in the corner in an ice bucket. I half expected soft music to drift from the speakers, petals to float down from the ceiling. The bed seemed to be getting bigger, flashing alarmingly at me like the pack shot in an early TV commercial. As I gazed in disbelief, the saliva dried in my mouth.

'Shall we?' Casper murmured, indicating we should move on in.

'Oh—I . . .'

'We can spread your paintings out on the bed.'

I panicked. And for one awful moment, was tempted. Tempted to believe the fiction: to go right on in—perhaps wedging the door open with my foot, I thought wildly—that's my foot on the end of my elastic cartoon leg—whilst my elastic cartoon arm flung open the curtains or dragged that passing maid in for moral support—but in the very next moment it came to me with absolute clarity that if I set foot in that room, I had also to be sure I could survive a leap from a third-floor window. Either that or be prepared—when I emerged via a more conventional exit, shouting rape—for critics to suggest that by entering such an obvious seduction suite, I had Willing Accomplice writ large on my forehead. I turned. Took a deep breath.

'There's . . . been a misunderstanding.'

His smile wavered for a second. 'I'm sorry?'

'Yes, you see, I had no idea this was a hotel. I was in such a terrible rush to get here I didn't pause to look. I thought it was just a restaurant, and when you said coffee upstairs, I assumed you meant in a bar or something. I had no idea you

14

meant . . .' I trailed off, gesturing helplessly at the bed.

'Oh! Right,' he said shortly.

I saw his expression change from one of incredulity that I could have misunderstood him, to one of anger that I could have embarrassed us both so. For a moment, I thought he was going to hit me. Then he did something far worse. His face buckled and he ran a despairing hand through his hair.

'This isn't me,' he said softly. 'This is so not the sort of thing I do.'

Oh Lord. I swallowed.

'Look,' I began, 'it's fine, honestly. You don't have to explain.'

'My wife and I—well, we've split up. Recently, if you must know.'

Must I? I hadn't asked, had I?

'We—we're having a trial separation.'

'Right,' I whispered. I looked longingly down the corridor, to the lift, to freedom.

'But it's not permanent,' he said defiantly, as if perhaps I'd suggested otherwise.

'No, no,' I assured him quickly. 'I'm sure it's not.'

'And God knows I loathe it, *loathe* it. Seeing the kids only at weekends, not living at home, all that crap. But—well, I've got to get on with it, you see, and I get so lonely, and I'm staying here, at this hotel, while we sort things out, and I thought— well, we were getting on so well downstairs, so I thought—'

'It's an easy mistake to make,' I said quickly. 'And my fault too. I expect I missed the signs. The signals. Forget it. And now I really must be—'

'And when you said, "Let's go and look at my etchings,"' he looked at me accusingly, 'I thought—well, I assumed . . .'

Did I? God, *stupid* Imo. 'Yes, yes, I do see.' I blushed hotly.

'And the thing is, she's seeing someone else, I think. In fact I know she is.'

His eyes, to my horror, filled with tears. I had a terrific urge to be in the Scilly Isles. On a little boat, perhaps, bobbing around the bay. I glanced around wildly. Where was that passing maid? Surely her shoulder to cry on would be more appropriate? More absorbent?

'Someone younger than me,' he blurted out, 'her personal trainer, such a cliché!'

Younger? Younger than Casper? How young could they get?

'He's Spanish, called Jesus, would you believe it, probably performs miracles, probably takes her to heaven and back,' he said bitterly. 'He's certainly been spreading more than the word. I expect he's hung like a stallion too—probably has to sling it over his shoulder when he gets out of bed.'

I gazed around. *H-e-l-p.*

He pinched the bridge of his nose with thumb and forefinger to quell the tears. 'He's twenty-four,' he gasped, 'with the body of an eighteen-year-old! The children call him Jeez. They ride on his back at the local swimming pool, he can do handstands on the bottom. Apparently he can make his ears waggle without touching them. Heaven knows what else he can waggle. With my wife! My Charlotte!' At this his voice broke and his shoulders gave a mighty shudder.

I stared at him aghast. He was struggling for

16

composure but seemed to be losing the battle. I hesitated, but only for a moment, then plunged my hand into my bag for my mobile. I quickly punched out a number.

Casper leaped back in fear, his eyes wide with terror. 'What are you doing?' he squeaked. 'Are you ringing the police?'

'No,' I sighed resignedly, 'I'm ringing my son's school. I'm going to ask them to put him into after-school club and then I'm going to ask my neighbour to collect him for me.'

'Oh!'

I put a hand on Casper's shoulder and swivelled him around in the direction of the lift.

'You, meanwhile, will come with me and together we'll find that sit-soft bar I've been fantasising about all lunch time. You will have a brandy and I will have a coffee, and whilst we sup our respective beverages you can tell me all about your wife and her scheming, faithless ways, and all about the dastardly Jesus too. On seconds thoughts,' I muttered as I marched him off down the corridor, hobbling a bit now in my heels, mobile clamped to my ear, 'I think I'll have a brandy too.'

## CHAPTER TWO

'Oh God, I'm so sorry!' Kate wailed, hurrying through from the kitchen to put a mug of tea on the coffee table in front of me.

'Why should you be sorry?'

'Because it's all my fault! I thought he was going

17

to sign you up for the Cork Street equivalent of the Summer Exhibition, not try to molest you, then weep all over you.'

'I suppose I should be flattered,' I mused, sitting up a bit in the squashy pink sofa in her conservatory and sipping my tea in a dazed fashion. 'I can't remember the last time a man other than my husband even tried to hold my hand, let alone have sex with me. Unless you count the deputy head at the school carol concert last year.'

'The deputy head tried to have sex with you?'

'No, tried to hold my hand. I was miles away and hadn't realised we'd been urged to greet our neighbours with the sign of peace. Nearly slapped him.'

Kate snorted. 'Very Christian. But I'm surprised at young Casper,' she said thoughtfully, sinking into the sofa beside me. 'He's always had an eye for the girls, but I wouldn't have thought he'd try it on with you as blatantly as that. I shall ring him later. Have words with him.'

'No, don't,' I said quickly. 'It was a complete misunderstanding and, actually, probably my fault too. And anyway, he's miserable and lonely.'

'I suppose,' she said doubtfully, sipping her tea.

'Although hopefully after two brandies and a thorough character assassination of Jesus of Barcelona, he's feeling a bit better now.'

'Jesus of who?'

'Barcelona. The personal trainer. The Latin Lothario who's taking his wife to the Promised Land on a regular basis.'

'Oh God,' she groaned. 'You really got the works.'

I laughed hollowly. 'Oh, I've sat through more

18

photos of Barnaby and Archie, aged eighteen months and three years respectively, than I have of my own child.'

Kate made a face. 'Sad.'

'Very.'

We were quiet a moment. Kate narrowed her eyes thoughtfully at the Welsh dresser opposite. 'Does Alex carry around pictures like that in his wallet?'

'What, of me and Rufus? No, does Sebastian?'

'No!'

We regarded each other in silent outrage.

'Actually,' I conceded, 'I think I've always found it a bit cheesy. Those men with pictures of the wife and kids on the desk—what's that all about? In case they forget what they look like by the time they get to work? Or to announce to the office they've got a happy marriage?'

'The latter probably, and you're right, it's an insecurity. I mean, look what happened to Casper. He had the pictures and his wife went out shagging.'

'Yes, and then he tried to redress the balance, although I must say, I think his current strategy of picking up middle-aged women in hotel restaurants is deeply flawed. I'm not convinced that's going to make her drop her square-jawed hunk and come running back.'

'I agree. I mean,' she added quickly, 'about him picking up women, not the middle-aged bit.'

'Thanks,' I said gratefully.

She cradled her mug and shifted round in her seat to eye me wickedly over it. 'And you weren't in the least bit tempted? Casper's rather attractive in a loose-limbed, puppyish sort of way.'

'Not remotely. Too wet behind the ears for my tastes and, as you know, I go for the older man. I don't want a puppy.'

'Which is not just for Christmas.'

'Well, quite. I'd have to throw sticks and get house-training. Anyway,' I added, 'I hadn't shaved my legs.'

'Ah. Now we get to the nub of it.'

We giggled.

'Quite nice to say no, though,' I reflected, resting my head back in the soft, damask cushions and gazing up at the ceiling. 'I'd forgotten what it was like to be sexually propositioned and turn a man down.'

Kate shot me a quizzical look but I didn't elaborate. There was a time and a place for such confidences and six o'clock on a Wednesday afternoon with four small children running about, some with bigger ears than others, was not one of them.

'Thank you for collecting Rufus for me,' I said, watching my son on his hands and knees in his grey school uniform on the conservatory floor, as he assembled a Playmobil fort with Orlando, whilst Tabitha and Laura, Kate's daughters, who were enjoying an exeat from boarding school, painted each other's toe nails with rapt absorption. Not for the first time I reflected that daughters would have been nice. Would still be nice.

'Oh, it was no trouble. Orlando was in after-school club anyway because I suddenly realised we're at the opera tonight and I wouldn't have time to wash my hair, so I quickly shot to the hairdresser's.'

I smiled into my tea, marvelling at the disparity

20

of our lives. My son was in after-school club because I was desperately trying to earn a few pennies by flogging my pictures whilst Kate's was there because she'd been indulging in a luxury I'd never experienced and probably never would. Not whilst I could stick my head under a shower for free.

I gazed out of the sunny conservatory, a natural extension of her enormous vaulted kitchen beautifully furnished with free-standing oak cupboards and hand-painted Swedish linen presses, to the billowing garden beyond; well over half an acre and possibly the largest London garden I'd ever seen. When I'd first stood at these windows and gaped at the view, I'd been staggered. I couldn't even see the bottom of it. An initial sweep of lawn complete with croquet hoops gave way to an apple orchard and longer grass, then beyond that, in the middle distance, something that looked remarkably like a bluebell wood. It was like being in Wiltshire, rather than West London, and I'd said as much.

'Ah, but you see, that's where my heart is,' Kate had confided with a smile as she'd joined me that day at the window, arms folded. 'In the depths of the country, preferably on a horse. But I have to make do with pretending I'm there in this *rus in urbe* extravaganza.'

'I wouldn't mind making do with this,' I'd gawped.

'I know, neither would most people. I'm spoiled. But it's a sad fact of life, my friend, that however much you have, you want more. Or something different, at least.'

When I knew her better I realised she seriously

21

minded about living in London. But Sebastian was a cardiovascular surgeon at the Wellington and needed to live within a certain radius of his hospital in case they needed him, so that was that. They'd tried owning a country cottage in Norfolk, but Sebastian found it almost impossible to get there on a Friday night and Kate hadn't wanted to be there without him. 'I'm rather like the Queen Mother in the Blitz,' she'd quipped. 'If the King isn't leaving neither am I, and if I'm not leaving, neither are the children.' So they'd sold the Norfolk cottage, and sold their Knightsbridge house too, moving from Montpelier Square to leafy Putney as a sort of compromise. And actually, once inside, you'd be forgiven for thinking you really were in a country house. Faded chintzes on the sofas, heavy oil paintings of dead ducks and partridges on the walls, and antique furniture on the polished wooden boards all contrived to preserve the illusion. There were even rabbits in a hutch in the garden and Kate was threatening a Shetland pony.

'There's plenty of space,' she'd said excitedly, dragging me down to the orchard one day, 'and if I scooped the poop to keep the pong at bay, Sebastian would be none the wiser. He never comes down here, anyway.'

'He might see it from the bedroom window,' I said doubtfully.

'I'll tell him it's a big dog.'

'What, the Hound of Putney Common?'

'Why not?'

I smiled to myself now as I gathered up my son's belongings—book bag, lunch box, PE kit—and attempted to prise him away from the joys of

Orlando's toy box with its mountains of Lego and remote-control cars, and back to his own, less exciting quarters with no sisters, bantams or ponies. But as I told him the other day as he'd dragged his heels from this very same kitchen, other people's houses were always more attractive, and Orlando probably felt the same about Rufus's house. Rufus had turned contemptuous eyes on me.

'Come on, Rufus.' I beamed down at him now.

'We're going?' The eyes he turned on me now were anguished. 'Aren't we staying for tea?'

My son had yet to enter polite society.

'No, darling,' I said quickly before Kate could offer, 'because Daddy's coming home early tonight so we can all have supper together. That's nice, isn't it?'

Not as nice, clearly, as stopping here with Orlando and Laura and Tabitha and sitting around the huge tea table whilst Sandra, the nanny, produced tiny sandwiches with crusts off and meringues in the shape of white mice and melon balls—*melon balls!*—for pudding; whilst at home, Mummy hacked a doorstep off a loaf and frizbee'd a Jaffa cake at him. But he was an obedient child and I could do a lot with my eyes.

'Alex is coming home early for a change?' Kate got up to show us out. 'That's nice.'

'Well, relatively,' I said nervously, following her down the black-and-white-tiled hallway. 'I mean, relatively early, not relatively nice. Nine o'clock rather than ten o'clock, probably.'

She grimaced. 'Tell him from me to break the habit of a lifetime and make it back for bath time for once. Really bust a gut.'

23

I laughed, but was aware of a whiff of disapproval in Kate's tone. A suggestion that Alex's after-work socialising—even though it was client-oriented and he loathed it—was excessive and at odds with family life. But then as Alex had pointed out as he'd flopped down exhausted on the sofa the other night, his handsome face racked with tiredness, tie askew, fresh from yet another city cocktail party, it was all very well for Sebastian. His clients were all horizontal and anaesthetised by the end of his working day; there was no chance of one of them sitting up and saying brightly, 'Mine's a pint.' 'And anyway,' he'd observed sourly, rubbing the side of his face and yawning widely, 'we can't all save lives for a living.'

I think Alex was fond of our new best friends, but found them a little worthy for his tastes. An 'homme sérieux' was how he described Sebastian, adding, 'That man's never dropped a bollock in his life.'

'Meaning?'

'He can't let go. Never has a drink and let's his hair down. What's he afraid of? That he'll make a prat of himself? So what?'

'Well, he may be an homme sérieux, but he's also a fairly grand fromage,' I'd replied archly, thinking personally, I wouldn't mind a little less bollock-dropping around here. Always the last to leave a party, always the life and soul, Alex was the ultimate bon viveur; but then, he would argue, it went with the territory. As a mergers and acquisitions specialist at Weinberg and Parsons, his job was to drum up new business and schmooze clients, and you couldn't do that on a glass of tomato juice and a face like a wet weekend, now

24

could you?

Rufus and I said our goodbyes to Kate and walked across the road. As I let us into the little semi with the Queen Anne door and the pretty stained-glass fanlight, the mess hit me. The house had originally sported a long thin entrance hall but it was dark and gloomy, so Alex and I had knocked the wall through into the adjacent sitting room. The net effect was that you walked straight into one largish, slightly less gloomy room, but straight into clutter. My response—which should have been to stoop and scoop the toys and clothes as I went, like a cotton picker—was to step gingerly over it all, whilst Rufus's was to run straight through to the only other downstairs room, the kitchen. As I neatly sidestepped a basket of laundry, I thought wistfully of Sandra across the road, but at the moment I couldn't even justify a cleaner, let alone a nanny. I followed Rufus to the kitchen, where he'd hopped up on to the counter and had got the bread out of the bin. He was hacking away fairly adeptly with a knife.

'Hey, what about having supper with Daddy?'

'Oh.' He paused, mid-slice. 'I thought you were just making that up to be like the Barringtons. I didn't know we really were.'

I laughed and dumped his book bag on the table. 'You're too shrewd for your own good, Rufus Cameron. Come here, I'll do it.' I took the knife from him.

'What's shrewd?'

'Um . . . knowing, I suppose.'

I cut the bread, spread it with peanut butter and folded it into a sandwich for him. He took it and bit into it, still none the wiser. But it was true, I thought, as I watched him sitting on the counter, munching away, swinging his legs in his shorts and grey socks and drumming his heels against the cupboard door, this was a very knowing child. One who tuned into my moods very acutely: who knew when his mother was happy or sad, pensive or nervous. My beautiful boy, with his auburn curls and deep chocolate-brown eyes: edible, clever. One of the things that had astonished me about having a child was that feeling of him being an extension of oneself, another organ pumping away. I wondered if other mothers felt that way. Since I had only one child, I had nothing to compare him with. Sometimes I wondered if our bond was too strong; if I should step back a bit, let out the umbilical cord. Alex said I mollycoddled him, but then Rufus and his father . . . I licked some peanut butter from my finger and turned to put the bread back in the bin. I shut it with a brisk snap. And to be fair, Rufus wasn't altogether the son Alex had expected.

'Throw a ball at him and he ducks!' Alex had complained after a disastrous trip to the park when the pair of them had returned looking mutinous. 'He needs to toughen up a bit, be more of a lad.' He tossed the rugby ball on to the sofa and flopped down crossly beside it, still in his coat, whilst Rufus ran upstairs.

'He's nine, Alex. You want him sinking pints and singing rugby songs?'

'No, but I don't think he should be doing this, either. I mean what's this all about?' He'd plucked a piece of tapestry Mum had given Rufus from behind a sofa cushion and waved it at me.

'It's just a bit of sewing,' I'd said, snatching it

angrily. 'What's wrong with that?' Though I myself had wondered guiltily about Rufus taking it into school.

'Are you sure you want to take that, darling?' I'd said, eyeing him nervously one morning as he packed the sewing in his bag. 'I mean, when will you have time to do it?'

'Oh, I do it at break,' he'd said calmly. 'When the other boys are playing football.'

'Right,' I'd breathed. 'But don't they think that's . . . you know . . . odd?'

He'd shrugged. 'I don't know. Is it?'

'No! No, of course not.'

I'm ashamed to say, though, that the following morning, when he went to look for it and couldn't find it, it was at the bottom of my underwear drawer. And I was relieved, when I went to pick him up later, to find him in the thick of a card game with his great mates Arthur and Torquil, a couple of embryonic professors from recorder group.

'A sensitive, musical child,' his teacher had smiled at Alex and me one parents' evening as we'd sat facing her like giants on tiny Lilliputian chairs; 'but not a shrinking violet by any means. Oh, no, he can hold his own in class discussions. He's got it up here.' She'd tapped her head and I'd glowed proudly. 'Why, only the other day on our nature walk he was telling us the difference between a buttercup and a celandine, and then went on to identify a cowslip for us. He's definitely our wild flower expert!'

I couldn't look at Alex.

Now, though, Rufus was settling down with his peanut butter sandwich and his yo-yo in front of

*The Simpsons*, which surely was what any other nine-year-old boy who'd already spent an hour in after-school club and another at a friend's house would be doing? Aside from sitting down to a proper cooked tea with vegetables, of course.

I hovered in the doorway. 'No homework, Rufus?'

'Only reading, and I've already done it.' He kept his eyes on Bart and Marge.

'Right.' Probably finished the book, if I knew Rufus.

'I've finished the book.'

I smiled. 'Well done, darling.'

He turned. 'Mum, go. We don't need quality time every night and I've had a play with friends so I've done the interactive bit, and there's protein in the peanuts and fibre in the bread, and I promise I'll have an apple for pudding, so go.'

Spooky, this child.

'Well, I might just pop up for half an hour, if you're sure.'

'Course.' He turned back to the television. 'And if the phone goes I won't say you're painting, I'll say you're in the middle of turning out the treacle tart, OK?'

I grinned and picked my way through the debris to the stairs. This was a reference to being accosted at the school gates one morning by Ursula Moncrief, class rep and all-round terrifying professional mother, who, flanked by a couple of flunkeys, had said accusingly, 'I rang last night about your contribution to the Harvest Festival, and Rufus said you were upstairs painting!'

From her tone Rufus might just as well have said I was upstairs flaying a couple of naked rent boys,

28

tied up with satsumas in their mouths.

'Um, well, yes, I do occasionally,' I'd stammered, as a wave of disapproval rippled around the Ursula camp. 'Most nights, actually,' I added bravely.

'So where's Rufus?'

'Well, he's . . . downstairs. Doing his homework,' I added quickly.

More teeth sucking at this, because of course I should be down there with him, strapped into my pinny, frying fishcakes, and ready to spin round and help him spell 'alligator', if need be.

'Tell them to fuck off!' Alex had roared helpfully when I'd reported back.

I didn't, but was grateful for his support. Alex had little truck with the mummy mafia, having seen it all before with Lucy and Miranda, his daughters from his first marriage, now sixteen and fourteen respectively. His views on school-gate mothers— 'a load of frustrated, overqualified women channelling their thwarted careers into overstimulated children'—were trenchant, and possibly true. Nevertheless, I was easily cowed, and these days Rufus and I were more circumspect about my whereabouts. The treacle tart ruse seemed to work.

Yes, the girls. It was probably time they came to visit again, I thought nervously as I mounted the stairs. My heart began to pound at the thought and I clutched the banister.

Lucy and Miranda lived with their mother, a stunningly beautiful woman called Tilly, who, after the divorce, had gone to America. When we were first married and the girls were younger, I'd hardly seen them at all because Alex often had business in the States and visited them when he was there. Last year, however, now that they were teenagers, they'd crossed the pond alone, to stay with us in London. It hadn't been the most auspicious visit. They were possibly the most beautiful, long-limbed, self-possessed, scary creatures I'd ever encountered, with their low-slung Miss Sixty jeans and Ugg boots and yards of silky dark hair. I remember coming back from Tesco one afternoon, laden with shopping, to find both of them draped across Alex on the sofa, two pairs of long legs over his knees, the room in darkness, curtains drawn as they watched a movie. Instinctively, I'd said, 'Oh— sorry.'

Lucy had mocked me with her eyes. 'Why are you sorry?'

I blushed. 'Well, I just meant . . .' I laughed gaily. 'I felt like I'd intruded!'

'Bit late for that, isn't it?'

I remember my face burning as I went through to the kitchen to unpack my shopping. It wasn't even a justified remark. Their parents' marriage had been over long before I came along.

Alex had come up behind me and put his arms around me as I unpacked.

'She doesn't mean it,' he whispered in my ear. 'She's just a kid.'

I turned round in his arms. 'I know, but . . . Alex, doesn't she know about Eleanor?' I searched his face.

He shrugged and looked away. 'I guess not. Eleanor's her godmother, Imo. She adores her. I can't tell her that.'

'But surely Tilly's told her? Told her what happened?'

He shook his head. 'I doubt it. Tilly's far too proud.'

Right. So I took the rap. I was The Other Woman who'd broken up the happy home. And he was right, why dig up the past? But it just seemed so unfair, and sometimes I wanted to say to them, 'It wasn't me, you know! Ask your precious godmother all about it!' But that would hurt them even more, and Alex was right: they'd been through enough.

And I'd try harder with them next time, I thought, going on up the next flight of stairs and opening the studio door. Make more of an effort. Take them both shopping on the King's Road perhaps, although the very idea brought me out in a muck sweat. What, hold up belts and scarves as potential purchases as their eyes ridiculed my choices? I scuttled across to my paints in panic. My paints. In this tiny, north-facing, and therefore perfect, room, which was my sanctuary, my retreat. Here I could unwind. Be me.

Under the slanting dormer window that looked on to the street, an old pine table was covered in paint tubes, rags, drawing pads, books, pencils and my palette, almost an art form in itself it was so stiff with paint. The heady, oily aroma hit me as I stood over it, making me beautifully woozy for a second. I turned. The room was chaotic, but only to the uninitiated: I knew where everything was. Stacked on the floor around the walls were my canvases, or, more recently, boards, painted in my swirling, free style, lots of them—I was nothing if not prolific—and in the middle of the room, my easel, with a half-finished painting in it. I pretended to ignore it as I went past to get my

31

smock from the back of the door, a common trick, snubbing it, as if I wasn't terribly interested, but even before I'd thrown on my old lab technician's coat and squeezed some paint on the palette, my eye was drawn. It was a stubble field in winter: a grey, chilly scene, and since Putney didn't throw up many stubble fields, I had a photo of one propped up behind it.

'Isn't that cheating?' Kate had asked in astonishment on a rare visit to my sanctum. This was not an uncommon reaction, but still one that surprised me.

'Why? I'm painting from a photograph, not another work of art. How is that cheating?'

She'd made a 'suppose so' face, but I was aware people still felt it wasn't quite right. A bit rum. I wasn't actually *in* that field, feeling that light, those shadows. But then again, punters liked country landscapes on their Fulham walls and the odd one or two I'd sold so far had all been executed thus. Needs must.

As I took a brush from a jar of turps and wiped it on a rag, I spotted Kate emerging from her house opposite. She came down the path, looking supremely elegant in a little black jacket, short pink skirt, and kitten heels, and slid into a waiting taxi at the kerb. It purred off, bound for Sheekey's, where Sebastian was meeting her for a little pre-opera supper, whilst meanwhile Sandra bathed the children and read them bedtime stories. I smiled. Other people's lives. I turned back to the easel. Now. That beech tree in the corner—surely the sun shouldn't be filtering through the branches quite so fiercely?

I was just getting to grips with the sky, fussing

32

about its greyness and adding a touch of Prussian Blue amongst the swirling clouds to darken it, when a head came round the door.

'Oh! Rufus. You startled me.'

'There's nothing on, so I'm going to bed.'

'Already? But you haven't had a bath or anything yet.'

'It's ten o'clock, Mum. When are we going to get Sky?'

'Is it?' I glanced at my watch, horrified. 'God, so it is. You should have been in bed ages ago. Come on, chop chop.'

Guilt making me brisk, I put my brush down and hustled him off to his room and into his pyjamas, muttering darkly as if it was *his* fault, for heaven's sake. How would this child turn out with such a distracted mother? I quickly made his bed and plumped up his pillow. No need to draw the curtains as they hadn't been opened. As I kissed him good night and turned out his light, I remembered Kate telling me about a house she'd picked Tabitha up from, where upstairs she'd found unmade beds, loos that hadn't been flushed, closed curtains, and knickers with skid marks on the floor. I went hot as I nipped to the bathroom to flush the loo and pick up yesterday's pants. Not for the first time, I decided, my painting had got out of hand. Instead of heading back to my studio where I knew I could stay until midnight, I went determinedly downstairs, did the washing up, tidied the sitting room, turned off all the lights, then headed on up to bed. An early night for once, I decided. And then when Alex came home, well, maybe . . .

I had a quick shower and got into bed, loving the

33

feeling of my warm, tingling body under the cool duvet. The street outside was quiet now with only a distant roar of traffic in the background. I tried to stay awake for Alex but was aware of my eyelids growing heavier. At some point I stirred as a taxi drew up and rumbled outside. I listened for Alex's tread, but it was Kate and Sebastian, paying the driver, and then Kate's voice as Sandra came to the door, asking her how the children had been, what time they'd gone to bed; then silence.

Sometime later, Alex crept in beside me.

'Sorry, darling,' he whispered. 'Did I wake you?'

'No, it's fine,' I murmured sleepily. 'I wanted to wait up for you. How was your evening?'

He groaned. 'Averagely ghastly, thanks. I suggested a light supper in a wine bar, thinking I'd get away with just one course, but the Cronin brothers were over from the States and wanted to be shown some traditional English fare. We ended up in Simpson's, having roast beef and Yorkshire pudding. I think I'm about a stone heavier.'

I smiled and rolled over to hug him from behind, my cheek on his back. 'Well, you don't feel it.' I nestled up to him and ran my hand up his bare thigh.

'Humph,' he grunted.

'Poor you,' I murmured softly, still stroking his leg. 'Perhaps you need to wind down?'

He sighed. 'If I wasn't so exhausted, that's exactly what I'd like to do. But I'm shattered tonight, Imo.'

My eyelashes brushed his back. 'You're right,' I agreed. 'It's late and I'm pretty tired too.' I rolled back on to my side of the bed.

Ten minutes later I was aware of my husband's

rhythmic breathing beside me; of faint catches in his nose and throat as he exhaled. The land of Nod had claimed him. It took me a while longer, though. My eyes were wide and staring in the dark for quite some time. Eventually, though, I did fall asleep.

## CHAPTER THREE

The following morning Alex put his lips to my ear.

'Guess who's downstairs.'

'Hmm? What? Who is it?' I opened my eyes blearily. He was standing over me in his dressing gown, a broad grin on his face, cup of tea in hand. He put it down beside me.

'Your mo-ther!' he sang.

'Oh God,' I groaned. 'You're kidding.'

'Nope. Apparently we're all going to this match of Rufus's this afternoon, a nice big family outing. I for one can hardly wait. Please tell me your sister's coming too?' His eyes widened in mock appeal.

'Of course she's not,' I snapped, 'and the match isn't till three, so what the hell's Mum doing here at seven? How did she get here?'

'She cycled, apparently. Waved goodbye to her neighbours in Belgravia and trilled, "Just off to the country!" before peddling down to rural Putney for the night.'

'She's staying?'

'Well, she seems to have an awful lot of carrier bags with her if she's not, but I haven't questioned her too closely.'

I swung my legs over the side of the bed. 'Oh Lord. And where's Rufus?'

'Downstairs having a passive cigarette with her.'

I giggled. 'Probably in heaven.' I pulled on my dressing gown.

'Oh, he is. There's undoubtedly a note of high excitement in the air, but I took the liberty of opening a window on their little soirée. It smells like a brewery already.'

'She's not had a drink!'

'Not yet, just the Gauloise, but she tells me in France she always has a café Calva for breakfast and that in Provençal society it's rude not to.'

'Yes, well, she's in South London society now so she can jolly well have PG Tips and lump it.' I tied my dressing-gown cord smartly and took a slurp of my own tea. 'How are you, anyway?' I eyed my husband over the mug rim. 'After your night on the tiles?'

'God, hardly.' He sat down heavily on the end of the bed. 'Americans are very clean-cut these days. Gone are the days of lining up bottles of Chablis and taking them to some lap-dancing club—thank God. No, it was a Club Soda apiece and then they bustled back to the Waldorf.'

'But you got the deal?'

'Who knows, Imo, who knows.' He rubbed the side of his face wearily. 'They were kind enough to let it slip at the end of the evening that they were seeing two other firms, though.'

'Ah.'

My husband nonchalantly swept back his blond hair from his high forehead and straightened his back in his navy dressing gown, but his blue eyes were troubled and I knew better than to ask more.

36

Alex had been specifically employed at Weinberg and Parsons to drum up new business and, so far, the only business being done was old.

'It's the same all over,' I soothed, 'you said so yourself. The City's in turmoil, no one's having an easy time of it. But it'll get better, you'll see. These things go in waves.'

'In my case with a wave byebye.'

'Oh, don't be ridiculous,' I said staunchly. 'Your glass is always half empty.'

'Either that or I've got the wrong glass. But you're right, things go in cycles, so who knows? Anyway, meanwhile you'd better get downstairs before your mother cleans Rufus out of pocket money.'

'Gee-gees?'

'No, cards today.'

'Ah.'

I picked up my mug and hastened downstairs: through the sitting room, which was indeed knee-deep with bulging carrier bags, and into the kitchen, where . . . oh, I see.

The air was heavy with cigarette smoke, but through the fug, perched on stools either side of the breakfast bar, I could make out Mum and Rufus, three cards apiece, re-enacting a scene from *The Sting*.

'Twist,' said Mum tersely. 'Twist again . . . Twist . . . Stick.'

'You can't stick,' pointed out Rufus. 'You're bust.'

'No I'm not.'

'Yes you are, look—ten, nine and three is twenty-two. It's pay twenty-ones.' He reached across and took her coins.

'Morning, Mum.' I eyed her beadily. 'You're early.'

'Oh, not really, darling,' she said in her gravelly voice, dealing out the cards again. 'When you get to my age you only need a few hours' sleep—ask Margaret Thatcher. I've been up since five. Dealer takes all.'

'You were dealer last time,' Rufus reminded her.

Mum eyed him defiantly, opened her mouth to object, then shut it again and handed him the pack.

'She cheats,' Rufus observed to me, without rancour, as he dealt.

'I know, I grew up with her,' I said, reaching in the cupboard above their heads for the cereal packets. 'I'd check her sleeves, if I were you, and if she scratches her ankle, check inside her shoes. Rufus, what have you had to eat?'

'Granny bought me a *pain au chocolat*. I don't want any cereal.'

'Oh, fair enough. Mum? Cup of tea?'

'Please, since there's nothing stronger.'

'Well, you can have Earl Grey?'

'I think I had him in the seventies, darling,' she drawled. 'Conceited little aristo, as I recall. Twist . . . twist . . . damn!' She threw down her cards.

She really minded about winning, I thought, watching her with a smile. And, of course, that was why Rufus enjoyed it so much. He knew her mind was on the job as much as his was. She wasn't indulging or patronising him—oh, no, she was after his pocket money. She'd take it gleefully too, only handing it back grudgingly when he won it back off her next week. I watched as she scrutinised Rufus's shuffle, perched straight-backed on her stool, slim and elegant in a cream jacket with the sleeves pushed up to reveal tanned arms and bangles, khaki cargo trousers, lots of beads, a cigarette poised in jewelled fingers, her fading red hair piled loosely on her head and stuck about with combs. Always stylish, her clothes now had a French flavour as she'd spent much of the last ten years at her house in the South of France. Her story was she'd moved there for the weather, and she certainly got that in her idyllic sun-baked stone farmhouse just outside Aix, but my sister, Hannah, and I privately thought she'd gone abroad to get over losing Dad to Marjorie Ryan. Why she was back now, swapping the glorious colours and scents of a Provençal spring for the rainy streets of Belgravia was a mystery to us, but she seemed happy enough in the little flat she'd rented and loved spending time with Rufus. I secretly wondered if it had occurred to her, as she paced her olive grove, smoking her Gauloise and narrowing her eyes into the evening sun, that he might be the only grandson she was going to have and she didn't want to miss him growing up.

'The match isn't until three o'clock, you know,' I told her, putting on the kettle.

'I know, but I thought I'd have a go at your garden. My bank, pay twenty-ones.'

'Oh, Mum, would you?' I swung round gratefully. 'It's such a mess and I just haven't had a chance to get out there.'

'Of course you haven't, you're far too busy,' she said loyally.

I glowed. My mother, unlike my sister, was one of the few people who didn't think that because my art was unremunerated, it was a waste of time.

'I sold one last week, you know,' I said, pouring

39

myself a glass of orange juice.

'I know. Alex told me. But I don't think you charged nearly enough.'

'She didn't,' said Alex, coming in and doing up his cufflinks. 'And it was one of the big jobbies; should have gone for twice the price.'

'I don't actually charge for the amount of paint used or the size of the canvas,' I countered, although I was rather enjoying being buoyed up and discussed like a budding Picasso with a couple of agents. 'It's not like selling tomatoes.'

'Well, make sure you get some decent prices out of that gallery chappie Kate recommended. When are you meeting him?' He went next door to collect his overcoat and briefcase, glancing at his watch. 'Shit, I'm late.'

'I have met him,' I said, following him in so Rufus couldn't hear. 'Turned out he was only after my body after all.'

He swung around at the front door in astonishment. 'You're kidding.'

'Is that so extraordinary?'

'Well, no, of course not, but blimey,' he boggled. 'Bloody cheek!' he spluttered. He gazed at me a moment, then shook his head bemused and reached for his briefcase. 'No dice on the paintings then?'

'No dice,' I agreed, amused that it hadn't occurred to him to ask if I was still intact. Unraped, as it were. I opened the door for him. 'So no injection into the Cameron finances just yet, I'm afraid. You must go darling, while at least one of us has a job. We'll see you this afternoon.' He looked blank as he stepped outside. 'At the match.'

'Oh, the match! God, wouldn't miss that for the

40

world.' He popped his head back and yelled down to the kitchen, 'What position are you playing, Rufus?'

There was a pause. 'I'm playing rugby.'

'Yes, but what position?'

'I dunno.'

'Well, give them hell!'

Another pause. 'Who?'

Alex and I exchanged smiles. He kissed me. 'See you on the touchline.'

As I shut the door and made to go up and get changed, noting that, as ever, Rufus was already in his uniform ready to go, I reflected on what it had taken to get us to this touchline position. To be proudly sallying forth, *en famille*, to watch our son in a rugby match. Being in a team—any sort of team—had not remotely flickered on Rufus's radar until the day when the lists had gone up in the school hall for the nine and under A and B squads, with Rufus's name on neither. I'd scanned them avidly when I'd collected him, along with a clutch of similarly eagle-eyed mothers. Even Arthur and Torquil had made the B team, it being such a tiny school, but not my son. I'd felt my blood pressure rise, felt fury mounting.

'Never mind, darling,' I'd muttered, hurrying him away from the group of exultant mothers.

'What?' He looked blank.

'Not getting in the team.'

'Oh. That.'

'Don't you mind?'

He shrugged. 'Not really.'

I drove home very fast. Too fast. They'd written him off. Written him off at nine—how dare they! And Alex would be so disappointed, I thought with

41

a lurch. We wouldn't tell him, I resolved quickly. But he'd find out, I reasoned even more quickly. Sebastian would tell him Orlando was in the team. My hands felt sweaty on the wheel. I glanced at my apathetic son beside me.

'Rufus, don't you like rugby?' I said crossly.

'It's OK.'

'So, if you were in the team, that would be OK too?'

He shrugged. 'I suppose.' He turned. 'I'm not very good at it, though, Mum.'

'Well, that's hardly surprising, is it?' I shrieked. 'You haven't been given a chance!'

The following morning I strode into school and ran the games master to ground in the long corridor. He was in his tracksuit, pinning up another list, this time for the Colts.

'Mr O'Callaghan, Rufus seems to be the only boy in his year not in a rugby team—is that fair?' As I said it, I nearly cried. Honestly nearly sobbed. Keep breathing, keep breathing.

Mr O'Callaghan turned and frowned. 'He's not the only one, Mrs Cameron. There's Magnus Pritchard.'

'Magnus Pritchard has a broken leg!' I yelped. 'OK,' I said, trying to keep my voice steady, 'he's the only boy with two legs not in a rugby team!' For one surreal moment I felt Pete and Dud's one-legged Tarzan sketch coming on.

Mr O'Callaghan fiddled nervously with his whistle. 'Well, the list stands for Wednesday's match, I'm afraid, but I'll see what I can do for next week, OK? It obviously has to be entirely on merit, though.'

'Oh, obviously,' I'd purred obsequiously, and I'd

42

scurried away, hugging my precious secret to me. Next week. Next week he'd be in.

The whole of that week I'd prayed to God, to Allah, to anyone who was listening, to give strength to Mr O'Callaghan's pen; to empower him to write Rufus Cameron, in bold letters on the nine and under B list.

The following Monday Rufus and I hastened into the school together. By now even Rufus had caught my excitement and had admitted last night, albeit with rocketing sugar levels after three Ribenas—the closest I could get to getting him pissed—that he'd actually quite like to be in the team. His disappointment was all the more acute, therefore, when he realised he wasn't.

'I'm not there,' he said, his eyes quicker than mine.

I couldn't speak I was so angry.

'I'm in again!' came a voice from behind, and I turned to see Orlando, his face wreathed in smiles.

'Oh, well done, darling.' Kate's eyes scanned the list. I wanted to hit her. Wanted to hit my best friend hard in the mouth.

'Not you, Rufus?' she frowned. 'That can't be right, surely?'

'Of course it's not right!' I said in a shrill, unnatural voice.

Kate looked startled. 'Oh, well, maybe next week,' she murmured.

'No,' I said breathing hard through clenched teeth. 'No, this week.' And I strode off towards the staff room.

I'm not very proud of what happened next. Kate, to this day, swears I pushed Mr O'Callaghan into the PE cupboard, locked the door and threatened to take all my clothes off, but of course that's nonsense. What really happened was that I saw Mr O'Callaghan already in*side* the PE equipment room—cupboard, Kate insists, snorting—followed him in, shut the door, and rationally asked him to reconsider. I do remember seeing the naked fear in his eyes as he backed into a pile of clattering hockey sticks whimpering something like, 'Help me!'—I expect I misheard—but I have no idea why the top button of my shirt came undone nor why he was seen running, wild-eyed from the cupboard, grabbing a pen from a passing child and writing 'Rufus Cameron' in large, shaky letters at the bottom of the B team list.

I sighed as I mounted the stairs to my bedroom now and peeled off my dressing gown. Hell certainly hath no fury like a woman whose child has been scorned, but I wondered, if Rufus wasn't an only child, if I'd feel everything so keenly. Feel his disappointments like serpent's teeth, his tiny triumphs like Olympic achievements. If I could share my emotions out between some siblings, would they dilute, or would I just emote even more until I became one gigantic emotion? I didn't know, because as yet it hadn't happened and however much I cupped my hands around my mouth and hollered, 'Come in, Cameron minor, your time is up,' nobody showed. Obviously I knew I had to do more than holler, but sometimes I wondered if Alex did.

I had a shower and dried myself slowly, keeping an eye on my reflection in the long mirror. My figure still wasn't bad—at least I hadn't completely gone to pot like Hannah—but those thighs could definitely be slimmer. I really ought to lose a few

44

pounds but I worried that dieting affected fertility and I couldn't help thinking that if I ate well, a big fat baby would follow. And it suited my face too, I thought. What was it they said? After thirty, you choose between your face or your bottom. Well, I'd made my choice, and Alex approved too. 'It suits you,' he'd murmur in bed when he held me close. 'You're voluptuous, Imo, not like those terrible stick-insect women.' Not like his first wife, I knew he meant, but part of me longed to be like Tilly and her daughters: tall, dark and reed thin, not round and blonde and obvious.

'Are you going to paint today?' Mum called up from the bottom of the stairs.

'Yes, why?' I abandoned my reflection and reached quickly for my bra and pants.

'Well, I'll take Rufus to school if you like, then get out in the garden.'

'Oh, Mum, would you?'

'Course.'

I rifled in my drawer for a top, but as my hand closed on one, I went cold. I ran to the top of the stairs.

'Mum, make him hold your hand, won't you? And he has to be taken right to the gates. Don't let him tell you he can walk from the corner.'

My mother shot me a withering look as she hustled Rufus out of the front door. 'We're cycling. See you later.'

Cycling! The front door slammed on my open mouth. I stood there, horrified. Rufus had only ever cycled in the park, never on a busy road. She couldn't mean it. I ran to the bedroom window. Sure enough the pair of them were walking bikes down the path, and as Mum hopped aboard and led the way, Rufus pedalled after her, wobbling wildly, no helmet. I struggled with the window latch: it wouldn't open. I hammered: it wouldn't break. Terrified, I ran downstairs, flung open the front door and was on the point of yelling, 'STOP!' when I realised that was guaranteed to send him under the wheels of that passing juggernaut. I stifled my scream and made myself watch as he peddled alongside it. He did it rather beautifully. Much steadier now, and in a straight line behind his granny. As they disappeared around the corner, the postman delivering to next door gave me an odd look. It took me a moment to realise I was in my bra and pants. I hastened back inside and shut the door. God, what was wrong with me? I plunged my fingers into my hair. I seemed to veer from flagrant neglect and tossing Rufus a crust at tea time, to suffocating the poor child, never letting him out of my sight, and running down the street after him with no clothes on.

'You're an obsessive,' Alex would say, non-judgementally. 'You're either obsessed with your painting, or your child, but the two are mutually exclusive.'

'Is that wrong?' I'd asked anxiously.

'Of course it's not wrong, it's you.'

And actually, Mum was such a breath of fresh air, I thought as I went slowly back upstairs. She gave Rufus his head, let him have a bit of slack, just as she had done with Hannah and me. When we were young, she was forever saying things like, 'Don't go to school today, darlings. Let's go round London on the top of a double-decker,' or, 'Fancy motoring to Haydock to catch the one thirty?' Yes, it was lovely for him to have such a free-spirited

46

granny, and lovely for me too to have her help. How very spoiling, for example, to be able to lock myself away in my studio all day while she revamped my garden. What a treat!

Of course, I should have known better. After all, I've known her thirty-four years.

Later that day, as we stood together on a windy school playing field amongst other shivering parents, waiting for Rufus and his team to materialise and for Alex to appear from work, we exchanged furious whispers. At least, mine were furious.

'I'm not being a bore,' I hissed, 'I'm not even an avid horticulturist, I just think it defeats the object of a garden!'

'Nonsense, darling, it's terribly low maintenance. Frightfully economical too.'

'Yes, but it's not real!'

'But you wouldn't have known that, would you? When you came out, you thought it was marvellous.'

I gazed at her helplessly, her grey eyes wide under her dashing suede hat. It was true, I'd emerged from my studio at midday feeling woozy and sated—my usual euphoric state after four blissful hours at the canvas—secure in the knowledge that I'd slapped some good paint today and knocked a recalcitrant seascape into shape, to find my mother outside, surrounded by empty carrier bags, seemingly planting the last of her goodies, and had fairly marvelled at the sight that met my eyes. Gone was the tired strip of pale brown lawn surrounded by depressing darker brown beds, and instead, a gloriously tasteful green and white garden frothed around a patch of soft

47

emerald lawn. Well, I say soft. It was only when I bent to stroke my new grass and fondle the nodding ferns in my border that it hit me: it was all fake. I was standing in a silk and plastic paradise, the whole thing a fabulous fabrication, with not one petal, leaf, or blade of grass real at all.

'You never have to water it or prune it, and it never wilts or dies—what more could you ask for? It works beautifully in my little roof terrace at Wilton Crescent.'

'But you can't even smell it!'

My mother's eyes widened as she puffed away on her Gauloise in the wind. 'Oh, you can, darling, you can get scented sprays. Just blast it on first thing in the morning. I've got lavender and fresh pine.'

'What, like a frigging lavatory?'

'No, I bought them in Harrods; they're the real thing. I'll get you one if you like. Honestly, you are ungrateful, Imogen, after all my hard work. Ooh, look, here they come. Come on, Rufus!'

She clapped her gloved hands together excitedly as sure enough, twenty-two little boys came running on to the pitch in white shorts and red or blue rugger shirts, looking fit to burst with pride. My heart nearly burst too when I saw Rufus, beaming widely, chest out, little legs pumping. I waved madly, and forgot for one moment my mother's breathtaking presumption to take it upon herself to replace my garden, sad though it was, with a bogus reproduction, a seasonal nightmare complete with white roses and snowdrops all blooming at the same time, for heaven's sake. Alex would freak!

Where was Alex, incidentally? He was cutting it

48

very fine. I looked around anxiously, but saw only Mr O'Callaghan running on to the pitch. A palpable frisson rippled around the assembled mothers. Mr O'Callaghan was tall, blond and rugged, but just a little too white-eyelashed for my tastes: what Mum would call a near miss. He jogged about the pitch importantly and shouted instructions, wearing very short white shorts.

Kate came up behind me wrapped in scarves. She found my ear. 'I think Mr O'Callaghan's shorts could go up an inch, don't you?'

I giggled. 'Got to take your thrills where you can.'

'Absolutely, why d'you think we've all come to watch? Look at Ursula Moncrief, her tongue's practically on the floor.'

'She's always sucking up to him,' I muttered as we watched her trot on to the pitch in stupid high heels to ask him something.

'Oh, Mr O'Callaghan,' mimicked Kate, 'shall I keep score?'

'Oh, Mr O'Callaghan, shall I hold your balls?'

We cackled like two frustrated housewives.

'It's those great big rosy thighs of his,' muttered Kate as we watched him bounce around. 'That's what does it.'

'Well, I wish he'd stop flashing them and get this show on the road. My hands are frozen.'

'Mine too. Shall we rub them on Mr O'Callaghan's thighs at half-time?'

'He'd probably love that; not sure about Orlando, though. You know my mum, don't you?'

She did, and they kissed and exclaimed delightedly, and before long were admiring each other's cashmere, recommending expensive restaurants to each other and comparing the efficacy of their cleaners. I had absolutely nothing to contribute to this conversation so I kept my eyes firmly on the game.

It set off at a breakneck pace and I held my breath, waiting excitedly for Rufus to get the ball, to race heroically down the pitch and score a try whilst the *Chariots of Fire* soundtrack played in my head. It didn't take long to realise that wasn't going to happen. The pack raged up and down the field with lots of red-faced little boys scrabbling and shoving for the ball, but Rufus seemed to regard it as more of a spectator sport. If the action came down his end he danced around the scrum excitedly, offering shrill advice, but dodged the ball neatly if it came his way. If the action was up the other end, he stood pensively, staring into space with his hands behind his back like Prince Charles, only occasionally seeming to remember where he was and jump about a bit.

'He's skipping,' Mum muttered to me.

'I know,' I groaned, watching as he skipped happily after the pack when it came towards him. 'Rufus, run!' I hollered.

He smiled, waved at me, and skipped even faster.

I pulled my hat down over my eyes. 'I can't watch.'

'You don't have to,' Mum informed me. 'He's off the pitch now.'

'What!' I squeaked indignantly, pushing my hat up. Fully expecting to see Mr O'Callaghan sending him off and bringing on a reserve, which I'd naturally object to in the strongest possible terms, I glanced around wildly. 'Where?'

'Over there. Stroking a dog.'

Sure enough Rufus had taken time out to crouch down amongst some bemused parents on the touchline and stroke a spaniel. I daren't yell at him for fear of alerting Mr O'Callaghan, but as I watched, wide-eyed, I saw him move on from the spaniel to chat to a woman with a baby. He really was the Prince of Wales now, on a royal walkabout, chatting to the crowds.

The match finally ended at 22–14 to us, no thanks at all to my son, who didn't touch the ball once.

As the boys shouted their three cheers for each side and we all clapped like mad, I decided perhaps it was just as well Alex hadn't made it. He'd have been mortified. Inwardly, though, I was fuming. Where the hell was he? I'd tried his mobile all through the game and it had been switched off. Perhaps I'd try the office again. I finally managed to get through to Judith, his secretary, who said in a rather strained voice that she thought he'd gone home. Someone had rung, she said, and he'd taken the call and gone.

'Gone home? What, not to the school?'

'I don't think so.'

'He was supposed to meet us here.'

'Oh.'

'So—hang on, Judith, who called?'

'I'm not sure, because it went straight through to his private line.'

'Yes, but I'm the only one who rings through on that line, aren't I?'

'Um, I'm not sure.'

She sounded uncomfortable. Suddenly I went cold. My heart stopped, and then it began to

51

pound on again. I switched off my phone and turned to Mum, who was showing Kate some earrings she'd bought in Venice.

'They're glass, you see, not stones at all. Terribly clever.'

'Mum, Rufus has to have a shower and then a quick match tea. Could you possibly wait for him and bring him back?'

'Yes of course. Why, darling, where are you going?'

'I just want to go and find Alex.'

Mum looked surprised at being charged with so important a duty and I could sense Kate's eyes on me too, but in a moment I'd gone. I tucked my chin in against the wind and walked quickly across the playing fields, found my car in the car park, and seconds later was reversing out of the playground far too fast. I raced down the backstreets of Putney, clipping wing mirrors with a passing taxi and haring round bends. As I turned the corner into our road, my eyes scanned the line of parked cars. I couldn't see it; couldn't see the horribly familiar dark green Land Cruiser, so I told myself I was being stupid. I parked and walked quickly up my path, forcing myself not to run, but my heart was racing as I got my key out of my bag.

As I let myself in the house, I saw the coat immediately. It was thrown casually over the back of the sofa: dark blue velvet with snappy brass buttons, and a handbag and some keys were on the hall table. From the kitchen I could hear voices, laughter. As I went through the sitting room to the kitchen, willing myself to be calm, I saw them through the French windows in the garden together. They each had a glass of champagne in hand, and Alex was throwing back his head and laughing at something she'd said. He turned as he saw me approach and I saw the light in his eyes.

'Oh, hello, darling, look who's here. Isn't it marvellous? It's Eleanor!'

## CHAPTER FOUR

When I first met Alex he was married to Tilly. The fact that the marriage came unstuck, though, was nothing to do with me. It was 1995, and I'd just returned from Florence where I'd spent a happy year as a post-graduate studying portraiture and sculpture under Signor Ranaldez at the Conte San Trada Academy. I was going out with a sweet Italian boy called Paolo, a fellow art student, and now I was back in London conducting a rather complicated long-distance relationship with him. We wrote and telephoned constantly, and the idea was that I'd go back and see him in the summer and he'd come to England in the autumn. Life, in the main then, was rosy. Money, however, was tight, and in order to pay my rent in Clapham where I shared a house with three fellow painters, I took a job as a secretary in the City. Just for a few months, I reasoned, then I'd have enough to rent a studio and set myself up properly as an artist. The offices I'd resigned myself to working in short term were in Ludgate Circus, and Alex Cameron was my boss.

From day one, when he swept down the corridor, coat flying, pushing his blond hair out of his blue eyes and calling, 'Morning, Maria!' as he

53

passed my desk, I had a feeling my plans were scuppered.

He stopped, just a few paces away, swung round, and did a double take.

'You're not Maria.'

'No, I'm Imogen Townshend. I'm a temp.'

'Of course you are!' He clapped a hand to his forehead. 'It's all coming back to me. And actually, you're nothing like Maria. You're not . . .' he made a bump over his stomach with his hand, 'you know.'

'Pregnant?'

'That's it.'

I grinned. 'Hope not.'

He laughed. 'Yes, that would get tongues wagging, wouldn't it? If all my secretaries got pregnant one after another. I'd have to claim there was something in the water. Coffee-making skills in order?'

'Perfectly.'

'Good, because I've got a meeting in ten minutes and I could badly do with something strong and black before I face the Powers That Be in the boardroom.'

And off he went. And likewise, off I scurried like a good little corporate secretary, thinking how I'd much rather be wielding a paintbrush than a percolator, but that actually, if I was going to be skivvying for someone, he might as well be as decorative as this.

He got more decorative. Two months passed and Maria had her baby and then decided she couldn't possibly leave it with the nanny in Sevenoaks and could someone please stay on a bit longer, like for ever, and look after Alex and her spider plants? I promised to water them and stay for as long as it took Alex to find a permanent secretary. And so the interviewing process began. Alex would chat to the prospective secretaries first, then hand them over to me, the idea being that I'd explain the job in a little more detail. One particularly foxy blonde came out of his office with her eyes shining.

'He's heaven,' she breathed as I showed her where the photocopier was. 'Surprised you get any work done at all!'

I showed her to the lift.

'I thought she was fine,' remarked Alex later, as he signed some letters I'd put in front of him.

I smiled thinly. 'Lazy.'

He looked up surprised. 'Oh? How can you tell?'

'Trust me, it's the eyes.'

It was the same with the next one. 'Too timid.' And the next one. 'Too tall.'

'Too tall?' Alex said, startled.

'She couldn't get her legs under the desk; she was like a giraffe. You don't want to have to buy her a new desk, do you?'

'Er, no. No, I suppose not.'

The next one was too simpering, the next too tidy, and it was at that point, when I was running out of insults, that I realised I was in trouble. I had to make a decision. I couldn't possibly stay on as a temporary secretary for ever. I had to become a permanent one. I rang the agency to cancel the flow of interviewees and broke the news to Alex. He was delighted.

My friends back in Clapham, however, threw up their hands in horror. When would I paint? Draw? What about my art? My mother was aghast—a *sec*retary, after all that studying, with all that talent! My father, not a man to get involved, even put in his two pennyworth—'You're barking mad, girl!'—but by now I was beyond reason. I'd already written a long letter to Paolo explaining that I wouldn't be coming out in the summer due to family commitments, but a week later, I wrote another one, telling him I'd met someone else. I didn't mention that the man in question had no idea, that my feelings were unrequited, and that he was in fact married. Neither did I mention that I satisfied myself with admiring him from afar and salivating through a glass door with 'A. Cameron' written on it. Details.

And anyway, it wasn't always from afar. Occasionally our fingers would touch as I handed him a file, and sometimes, sometimes he'd stand over me as I typed, then lean across and point at my screen, inadvertently brushing my shoulder. Occasionally, too, when we were in the lift together, he'd put his hand solicitously on my back to guide me out first, as I'm sure he'd done with Maria, but I bet she didn't gasp and stumble back against the buttons, sending the lift plummeting to the basement. Once, we actually got stuck in the lift together. We weren't alone—there were a couple of other people making polite chitchat until Bill the janitor released us—but I was the only one to emerge short of breath, clutching the furniture. Yes, I was in love. Painfully and properly, and it was the first time it had ever happened. I couldn't keep it a secret either. I had terrible mentionitis, and hardly a day went by when his name wasn't dropped—'Alex said this', or 'Alex thinks that'. My family were on to it like vultures, and, after a hasty pow-wow, my sister, Hannah, was sent up from the country as emissary to make me see reason. She took me out to lunch and then insisted on coming back and meeting Alex. Happily, he was in a meeting, but I showed her his office instead.

'This is his desk,' I said reverentially, tenderly squaring up some papers on it. 'And this is his lamp. It's an Anglepoise.'

'Yes, I can see that,' she snapped impatiently. 'Why are you stroking it?'

'I'm not.' I snatched my hand away.

'I bet you stroke that too,' she jeered, jerking her head at his coat hanging on the back of the door.

'Don't be ridiculous,' I spluttered.

I didn't tell her I was beyond that. I was sniffing it.

'A banker!' My mother hooted when I went out to see her in France; she laughed throatily as she stood at the stove making a *bouillabaisse*, spilling ash in it then stirring it in, pretending it was pepper. 'You'll be telling me he's got a Porsche next.'

He had, but I couldn't tell her that. My family were arty, bohemian—Hannah was a potter, my father an actor—bankers and their Porsches were anathema to them. They'd expected me to rock up with a floppy-haired poet one day, someone with a healthy distain for materialism, a garret in Islington and a cat called Ibsen, not a thrusting young executive who lived in Chelsea and got his thrills from playing the money markets. And the worst of it was, I knew it was hopeless. He was married to Tilly—a gorgeous, languid ex-model of a creature—had two young daughters, and lived

57

happily with his perfect family in a dear little house in Flood Street.

Occasionally, when they were going to the theatre or a drinks party, Tilly would come into the office to meet him from work. Doe-eyed and with limbs like Bambi, she'd pass my desk with a shy smile and a friendly hello, then, after tapping softly on the glass door opposite, would flash an even wider smile at her husband and go in. I'd watch through the glass, manically chewing a pencil down to the lead, as he stood up and kissed her, clearly pleased to see her, and she'd sink down into his sofa to quickly paint her nails, or ring the nanny, while he finished some work. Ten minutes later they'd sail out again, laughing and chatting and I'd watch them go with a frozen smile, feeling like Cinderella as I called a cheery, 'Have a good evening!'—picking bits of lead from my mouth.

Then I'd slump back in my chair and wish my life wasn't like this. What had happened? Three months ago I'd been a promising young artist with an amusing set of friends and a sweet Italian boyfriend, and now, here I was, a suicidal secretary in Ludgate Circus, miserably turning the lights off in my boss's office, looking at the styrofoam cup he'd chucked in the bin and willing myself not to pick it up and drink from it. What was going on?

I knew I should leave. My painting was suffering—let's face it, I hardly painted at all these days—but every time I tried, I couldn't go through with it. The thought of not seeing him every day, not taking in his post, not typing up his letters and taking them in for him to sign, his blue eyes glancing up as I came through the door, his face creasing into a smile—or what was worse, imagining it creasing up for someone *else*—brought me out in a muck sweat and sent me scurrying back to my desk again.

And then, a little over a year down the line—yes, I know, a whole year—something, and I couldn't quite put my finger on it, something changed. Alex seemed distracted and upset, and Tilly, when she rang and asked to be put through to him, sounded tense. Curt, even. She rang less and less, and one day, came in solely, it seemed, to have a blazing row with him. I couldn't hear what was said, but her voice was shrill and quivering. When she'd gone I turned to Jenny, a fellow secretary who worked for a senior partner. She'd looked at me in amazement.

'Oh, yes, didn't you know? He's been having an affair. Tilly caught him out and she's livid. I think they might be splitting up.'

I sat there staring at her, speechless. Alex? My Alex? Having an *affair*? No, it was too preposterous. I felt the blood drain from my face. Felt sick. My insides shrinking. How? It was outrageous. Why, I was so close to him, kept his diary, knew his every move, I'd have *not*iced. I made my lips move, unaware of what they were saying. Surely no one at work?

'No, no one here,' Jenny assured me. 'And I only know because I know someone who knows her. It's an old family friend, Tilly's friend too, in fact. Eleanor Latimer.'

'Eleanor Latimer!' I shrieked.

Eleanor Latimer was indeed a good friend, a *great* friend, who'd grown up with Alex in the country, and whose husband was a friend of Alex's, and whose children got on well with Alex's, and whom they went skiing with every Easter, and to Tuscany in the summer. I knew. I booked the tickets. Organised the villas, the hotel rooms. I was the indispensable personal secretary about whom Eleanor raved, apparently—'Lucky you, Alex, having someone like Imogen as your right-hand girl!' Why, I'd even met her when she'd come in with her husband once, some frightfully grand titled chap, tall, lean and consumptive-looking in a covert coat, and met her again when she'd popped in on her own to have lunch with Alex . . . Lunch with Alex. Why didn't I think? But I hadn't, because, well, she was an old family friend, so why shouldn't they have lunch together? And she was so jolly and nice, so chatty—not shy like Tilly, but matey, with her curly brown hair and merry eyes and laughing mouth. She'd perched on the edge of my desk and confided that it was Tilly's birthday soon, and that Alex wanted to buy her some stuffy Georgian decanter, but she'd come in to persuade him to go to Cassandra Goad in Sloane Street.

'Tilly doesn't want a ship's decanter for heaven's sake,' she'd chortled. 'She wants something sparkling in her ears!'

'Are you ganging up on me?' Alex had come out of his office, smiling.

'Imogen was just agreeing with me,' she laughed, winking at me. 'You need to get your wife something she can wear, not pour the port with.'

I gaped at Jenny. Eleanor Latimer. Eleanor *Latimer*!

'How long?' I whispered.

She shrugged. 'Don't know. Not my business. Doesn't surprise me, though. Obviously got his brains between his legs, like most men.' Jenny's

Pete had been caught recently with his trousers down and her views on men were uncompromising and trenchant. She sniffed and stalked off to the photocopier.

I'd walked home that night; all the way to Clapham. It took two hours in the pouring rain. That he could do such a thing. That he could transfer his affections, have an affair with another woman, and for it not to be me! The sense of betrayal was almost too much to bear. My heart felt like a shrivelled leaf fluttering in my chest, as if someone had reached in and squeezed it dry. I'd leave, I thought as I trudged up the steps to my front door, soaked to the skin: leave now. I'd hand in my notice in the morning. Yes, first thing.

And I'd really meant to do it, but the following morning, as I arrived, Alex called me into his office and shut the door behind him. His face was ashen as he paced about the room; he was distraught. He wanted to talk to me as a friend, he said, as someone he could trust; someone he knew wouldn't blab to the senior partners, who, it being an American bank, took a very dim view of anything immoral, anything untoward: he wanted my counsel. Tilly had thrown him out. He was staying in a hotel in Bayswater. It was all over between him and Tilly, had been for a long time, oh—he sat down on the sofa beside me and sighed—a *long* time, Imogen. After the second baby was born, she'd . . . well, you know. Lost interest. Become so wrapped up in the children, he'd felt excluded. And Eleanor—well, of course he adored Eleanor, always had done, he'd grown up with her. Should have married her really, but she'd married Piers, with his title, and his house in

Tite Street and one day, his inheritance, Stockley. But he, Alex, had *always* loved her, and when Tilly had been so cold and remote and they, he and Eleanor, were together so often on holidays, or shooting weekends, well, they just couldn't help themselves, do you see? His blue eyes had appealed to me.

I'd swallowed hard. Had it been going on a while?

No, not very long, and it didn't happen often, because they hated themselves so terribly afterwards.

'And will she leave Piers for you? Is that what's going to happen?' I asked, half of me hating him for loving her and not me, and half of me ridiculously thrilled to be sitting here beside him on his sofa, listening to his confidences, our hands almost touching, hearing such intimate secrets. I was so close I could have reached a hand inside his jacket and felt his heart beating.

'No,' he said in despair, looking down at his hands. Those hands I knew so well, had scrutinised so minutely. 'No, that won't happen. She's too devoted to her children, her family. She won't break up the home. She won't leave Piers.'

'But, you and Tilly . . . ?'

'I can't go back to Tilly now.' He raised anguished eyes to me. 'I don't love her, Imogen. Not properly, and how could anything be the same after this?'

'Would she have you?' I ventured.

'I think . . . she would. Yes, she would. But . . .' He shook his head. Gazed bleakly into space. 'It's no good. I can't pretend to patch something up if there's nothing there any more. Can't live a lie.'

'Not even for the girls?'

He shook his head sadly. 'Not even for the girls.'

He got up and walked to the window, his hands in his trouser pockets, his back to me; broad shoulders hunched in his pale blue shirt as he looked out at the cold grey morning. Which was where he was, of course: out in the cold. Out in a hotel in Bayswater, without Tilly and his children, and without Eleanor, who was distraught, according to Alex; torn between him and Piers, in turmoil; but had sensibly, in Alex's opinion—and how he wished he could emulate her—gone back to her family. And Piers had been none the wiser. He'd been oblivious to what was going on, away on business a lot, tied up in his work.

'But what will you do?' I'd asked.

'Me?' Alex turned back from the window. 'Oh, I'll be fine. I've said I'll let Tilly stay on in the house for as long as she wants. I'll find a flat somewhere. Putney, maybe, near the Common. I've always liked it round there.'

And he did. He took out a mortgage on a tiny ground-floor flat in Putney, and in time, Eleanor and her family moved out of London to the big house in Buckinghamshire—Piers's widowed mother evidently deciding this was the moment to get round inheritance tax and move into the Dower House, enabling Eleanor, Piers and their children to move into Stockley and breathe new life into it. She was a shrewd old bird, by all accounts, and I secretly wondered if she knew the lie of the land and was putting a sensible distance between her daughter-in-law and Alex. Getting her out of London. (Sensible was a word that cropped up a lot in those days, as if the two families had just been sorting out furniture and chattels, not broken hearts.)

So Eleanor had a project, something to focus on, to get her teeth into. Stockley needed completely revamping, Alex would tell me on the odd occasion we had a drink together after work, it hadn't been touched since the seventies, and the wiring was a deathtrap. Eleanor had quite a job on her hands, he said; just what she needed. 'Drink up, Imogen. If we're quick we'll get another one in.'

And I did drink up, and ate up too, when Alex and I shared the odd wine-bar supper together. Well, he was lonely—only that gloomy little flat to go back to, and rather less money to spend with his wealthy friends now that he was supporting two households—and he seemed to enjoy my company. Positively sought me out at the end of the day.

Time passed, and eventually, of course, the inevitable happened. It was one of those evenings when we'd had a quick supper after work, and then I'd gone back to advise him on the décor of his flat in Putney, which, I'd assured him, didn't have to be all white and minimalist just because it was a bachelor pad. A nice bank of book shelves across that blank wall in the sitting room, for example, wouldn't go amiss—books always warmed a room up—and in the bedroom, why, that huge expanse of magnolia just cried out for a set of Beardsley prints. Here, I demonstrated, with a sweep of my hand; over the bed . . .

Did I think about getting pregnant? Did I deliberately not mention the fact that I wasn't on the pill, or neglect to ask him to use a condom? No. Not deliberately, but then, it was the last thing on my mind. The only thing on my mind, right then, was that finally, *finally,* this heavenly man was here in my arms, all mine, where, after all the to-ing and fro-ing, he rightly belonged. I was ecstatic. Incredibly, indescribably, heart-soaringly, ecstatic. And so was he. If a little surprised. It felt so natural, so right, he told me afterwards with wide astonished eyes as we lay there, naked together in bed. He'd been so blind, he hadn't seen what was so manifestly right in front of him all along, and was amazed that I had.

'You knew?' He propped himself up on one elbow in the dark, the better to look down at me. 'You knew this might happen one day?'

'I've loved you pretty much from the word go.' I admitted in an extremely uncool manner. But why not, I reasoned. Better to frighten him off now, if frightened he was going to be, than have it all come out later on. No more games, no more pretending: this was me; upfront, honest. Take it or leave it.

And he took it. He was flabbergasted, staggered, but also, I think, incredibly touched and flattered, and rather humbled that I'd kept it so quiet, never let him see I was besotted, never got pissed at an office party and propositioned him.

'So you never knew?' I asked him, lying there in the dark, looking up at his face, stroking the crook of his arm. 'Never suspected?'

'Had no idea,' he admitted. 'And why would I? I mean, it occurred to me often to wonder why you were working for me, this beautiful girl with her flowing blond hair, who everyone assures me paints like a dream and speaks fluent Italian. And of course I loved having you sitting outside my office—what man wouldn't? A pearl amongst all those Southend secretaries who pour into Ludgate Circus every day, all those Sharons, and there I was, with this stunning, talented, highly educated girl; but it never occurred to me that . . . well, I'm fifteen years older than you, and you're so . . .' He hesitated. 'I always thought I was out of your league.'

'And I thought I was out of yours.'

We'd gazed at each other in the darkness. The realisation of what could have been, had I known more about his personal life, known that the physical side of his marriage was over years ago, and had he known about my feelings for him, crept up on us. We exchanged bemused smiles.

'And Eleanor?' I asked hesitantly.

He sighed, stroked my hair. 'Eleanor was there at the time. She filled a gap. I'll always be very fond of her, but . . . well, we're just friends. Always will be.'

I smiled into the handsome open face beside me as he lay back on the pillow, and conveniently forgot how he'd said, almost in tears in his office, not so long ago, how much he loved her. How, if he couldn't have her, he didn't want Tilly either. I stretched out my hand and stroked his cheek. He took hold of my finger and kissed the tip of it.

'Stay with me, Imogen?' he said softly.

And I did. I moved into his flat and brought all my ramshackle worldly goods with me: a vanload of paintings and books and folksy cushions and a terrible exploding wicker chair. But when I discovered I was pregnant, I moved out again.

I'd done the test with shaking hands, sitting there on the side of the bath, watching in horror as the thin blue line appeared. I did it again in disbelief, but it came back even stronger than ever. I packed my bags and hastened them down the path to the car. I'd taken the day off work, pleading sickness, so I left Alex a note on the table saying that he was right, the age gap *was* too great, too insurmountable, and that I was going back to Italy, to Florence, to paint.

Instead I went to Clapham, where my friends welcomed me back with wonderment, but with open arms. At ten o'clock that evening, however, he appeared on the doorstep, eyes hollow and dark, arms hanging limply at his sides. Clarissa and Philippe, covered in paint, melted into their bedrooms.

'What's going on?' he whispered brokenly, raising his arms and letting them fall. 'What are you doing to me?'

I'd gazed at him, and had almost managed to go through with it. Then I said: 'I'm pregnant.'

He didn't flinch for a second. 'And your point is?'

'M-my point is,' I stammered, 'that I'm going to keep it. But I don't want to trap you. Don't want you to feel that you have to in any way be with us, or help bring the child up, or—' Whatever other selfless, magnanimous utterances were going to gush from my lips were halted, however, as he crossed the room, took me in his arms, and stopped my mouth with his kisses.

'Marry me,' he whispered urgently, his eyes scanning my face. 'Marry me, Imo, and have the baby and let's be together for ever.'

I'd like to tell you I gave it some thought, took time to consider, weighed it up a bit, but who am I trying to kid? My heart didn't even miss a beat; in fact it fairly somersaulted.

'Yes,' I whispered, equally urgently back as his eyes shone into mine. 'Yes, let's do that.'

And so my happiness was complete. Mum, Dad, and even Hannah came round to the fact once they'd realised it was a *fait accompli*, and Alex and I moved from the tiny flat in Brunswick Gardens—stretching our finances to the limit now that half went to his other family—to the semi round the corner in Hastoe Avenue, where we live now. I had a heavenly time doing it up, getting a friend in architectural salvage to knock the sitting-room wall down, splashing lots of creamy paint about and stencilling boldly, and positively breezed through my pregnancy.

One Monday morning, when I'd returned from visiting my mother in France, Alex took me up to the attic. Gone was the dusty, cavernous loft space filled with piles of suitcases and cobwebby old furniture, and instead, I found myself walking into an empty white room, floorboards painted pale grey, exposed beams likewise, with a sheet shrouding what appeared be a cross in the middle of it.

'My God, what's this?'

I stared around in wonder, marvelling at the steep sloping ceiling, the pine table set just so under the window; under the north light.

'It's a studio,' Alex told me. He whipped the sheet off the cross with a flourish like a magician, and revealed my easel, a blank canvas already screwed into it. His eyes burned into mine, full of love.

'Paint,' he urged me. 'Paint.'

And I did. All through my pregnancy: great splashes of colour, huge billowing skies, windswept cornfields with poppies—joyful, instinctive paintings, which seemed to flow out of me, sitting on a stool in the final months when standing became too much for me. I'd never been so happy.

And then, one day, about two weeks before I was due, I was strolling around Peter Jones, looking at the changing mats, wondering which Moses basket to get, fingering the tiny soft vests and wondering if it would be tempting fate to get a few of those now, when I walked from the baby department into the lift—and straight into Tilly.

We were both shocked to see each other. But the door had slid shut, and there we were, the two of us, alone. She looked at my huge stomach, my Moses basket, then up at my eyes. If she knew, which she probably did, it was still, clearly, a terrible shock. I was appalled. Couldn't speak. And all credit to her that she did. She licked her lips and managed a faint smile.

'Imogen.'

'Tilly!' I gasped.

I felt my face burn, felt my whole body flush, and desperately looked away: at the buttons of the lift, at the floor. We travelled down to the ground in silence. As I got out and made to hurry away, eyes down, she put a hand on my arm.

'Good luck. You'll need it.'

I looked up, startled, and saw, not bitterness in her eyes, but pity, almost. I was about to hasten away, when I turned back, defiantly.

'What d'you mean?'

She seemed about to shrug and move on, but then gave an odd little smile.

'In all my married life, Imogen, only one person made me want to behave like a victim. Only one person made me want to reach for the kohl pencil, outline my eyes in black, raise them theatrically to camera and whisper, "There are three of us in this marriage." I think you know who I mean. So good luck. As I say, you'll need it.'

And then she went on her way; weaving through the shelves of china and glass, skirting the spiral staircase, and out of the main doors into the square.

## CHAPTER FIVE

'Eleanor.' I forced a smile and made my way out through the French windows to the garden. 'How lovely, but what on earth—'

'I came up for lunch with a girlfriend and called Alex just on the off chance.' She came towards me, smiling broadly and holding out both hands, taking mine in hers. 'I have to practically drive past your front door to get back to Stockley and I thought, oh God, let's give it a go, they might just be in— and here you both are! Wasn't that lucky?'

'Terribly,' I agreed, as her proffered cheek brushed mine. 'But, Alex,' I turned, fuming inwardly, my voice unsteady, 'you were supposed to be at the match. Rufus was playing and you said—'

'My fault entirely.' Eleanor held up her palms to stem my flow. 'Alex said he was going to watch Rufus and had just literally popped back here to get changed and I promised faithfully to be with

70

him in ten minutes so we could go together—I was dying to see my godson in action—but bloody traffic! I was half an hour getting out of the Brompton Road!'

'Sorry, darling,' Alex looked sheepish. 'You know I really wanted to come, but poor Els got held up and I hung on and hung on, and of course by the time she got here it was too late. How did he do?'

'Brilliantly.'

Alex passed me a glass of champagne. I was so angry I nearly knocked it back in one.

'Did he?' He brightened. 'Good lad. What, really in the thick of it?'

'Oh, totally.'

I took another gulp and regarded Eleanor, standing before me. She was wearing a soft suede jacket and pale yellow Capri trousers with a crisp white shirt. Her brown curls were discreetly highlighted these days and swept back from her face, tucked behind her ears, showing off her fine cheekbones and startling, slanting hazel eyes. The passage of time had been kind to Eleanor; she was still very beautiful. In fact, if anything I decided, she was better-looking now than when I'd first met her. More polished, more expensive, but then, I thought uncharitably, it was easy to look good when you didn't have to lift a finger. I shouldn't think Eleanor had made her bed for years, let alone drawn a curtain.

'Well, good for Rufus,' she was saying in her husky voice. 'I didn't think he was the sporty type!'

'Oh, he's pretty much an all-rounder,' I lied.

'Just like my Theo. Piers and I were only saying the other night what an infuriating child he is. It doesn't matter if it's the classroom or the playing field—he can't seem to put a foot wrong!'

From what I remembered of her youngest, I rather agreed. He *was* an infuriating child, horribly competitive and out to win at any cost. He'd given Rufus a nasty Chinese burn when he'd beaten him at chess the last time we'd stayed at Stockley.

'I went to watch him play at Ludgrove last week, and he got four tries!'

'Four!' Alex spluttered with wide, overimpressed eyes. Pillock. I wanted to hit him. He turned back to me. 'Did Rufus get any?'

'Yes, he got five.'

'Five!' He looked astonished, as well he might.

'More champagne, Eleanor?' I reached for the bottle and calmly filled her glass. 'Although,' I went on, 'what on earth we're doing standing in a chilly garden on a Wednesday afternoon drinking champagne, Lord only knows!'

I laughed gaily, and as I topped up Alex's glass, I noticed he'd managed to change out of his suit and was in cords and a jumper. Had he changed while she was here, I wondered feverishly? And were they so familiar with each other that she'd followed him into the bedroom and perched on the edge of the bed, chatting as he stripped down to his boxers? Oh, stop it, Imogen, you're absurd.

I put the bottle down on the bench. He was looking particularly handsome today too, I thought, as he swept his hair off his brow. The worry that recently pretty much constantly etched his face had been replaced with a flushed glow, which could be the drink, or could be the company, I thought wretchedly.

'I'll tell you why we're drinking this,' he began

72

portentously, raising his glass and looking remarkably pleased with himself. 'It's all rather marvellous, actually.'

Oh God, it always was, wasn't it, when she was around? Suddenly his entire vocabulary changed and everything was frightfully marvellous or terrifically jolly, and I felt like a drag and a bore beside her eternal upper-class optimism. I tried not to look mutinous as he turned to her, a slight smile playing on his lips.

'Shall I tell her, or will you?'

As they stood smiling at one another, eyes shining, for one surreal moment I thought it could have been a betrothed couple, about to tell the happy news to some ageing parent. I caught my breath as she touched his sleeve with her fingertips.

'You.'

He turned to me, and I just managed, heroically, to stop myself from throwing my drink at him.

'Eleanor's offered us a cottage.'

'A cottage?' I was momentarily nonplussed.

'Yes, at Stockley. She's got one vacant at the moment, and she says we can use it. Isn't that wonderful?'

'Well, it's . . . terribly kind . . .' My mind was whirring. A cottage. At Stockley. Jesus. 'You mean . . .' I stalled for time, 'for the summer? For a holiday?'

'Oh, no, not just for the summer, for as long as you like. And to be honest, you'd be doing me a favour by taking it,' Eleanor was saying. 'The place is empty and has been for some time, so it needs quite a bit of work. Alex said he wouldn't mind doing that—nothing structural, only decorating—

but I'd much rather have it inhabited than be constantly worried about the gypsies getting hold of it. They're a *night*mare round us at the moment. Ruthie Greyshot had them in one of her barns and they claimed they were sitting tenants. She couldn't get them out!'

'Yes, but,' I licked my lips, 'couldn't you let it out to tenants? Properly? I don't know if Alex has misled you, but we couldn't possibly afford to—'

'Oh, no, I don't want any money for it. If I let it out properly I'd have to do it up, and I can't be fagged with that. No, I promise you, you'd be doing me a favour just by occupying it.'

'Isn't that marvellous?' said Alex. 'A place in the country, where Rufus can run wild and play in the woods and dam streams, and you can grow vegetables and paint—just like you've always wanted!'

It was true, I had always wanted it, and if it had been anywhere else I'd have leaped at it. Fallen on my knees in gratitude.

'Where exactly is it?' My voice was tight, ungracious, awful. Eleanor looked anxious now, sensing perhaps that I felt boxed in.

'It's on the edge of the home farm, a tiny little detached cottage called Shepherd's Cottage. And years ago that's exactly what it was: the shepherd's place. But a row of terraced cottages were built later for the farm hands. I promise you it's minute, Imogen, absolutely tiny, nothing flashy at all. I think we've even still got a few animals down there. Piers will probably task you off to keep an eye on them. That's how much you'd be doing us a favour.'

'No trouble at all,' gushed my husband.

I straightened my shoulders and cranked up a smile. 'How lovely, Eleanor, and of course we'll think about it. We'll discuss it later, won't we, darling?'

'Oh, but what is there to dis—'

'Yes, of course,' broke in Eleanor hastily. 'You'll need to talk about it. But the offer's there if you want it. So!' she said with some finality as if that was that for the moment. 'I was just admiring your garden, Imogen. What a triumph!'

I clenched my teeth. 'Yes, well, I'm afraid my mother's a bit of a loose cannon these days. She gets carried away.'

'Oh, but I think it's terrific,' she enthused, bending down to finger a rose. '*So* realistic, and just think, you never have to water it or dead-head it or anything!'

'Quite.'

'I really think it's a must for Stockley,' she mused. 'Just one little patch, next to the knot garden—terribly amusing and frightfully disconcerting. Imagine all the old dears' faces when we're open for the public: "Oh, look, a *Maximus pergalitor*, Mabel—oh heavens, it's plastic!"'

Alex threw back his head and roared.

'Can't you just see their faces?' she appealed to him. 'With any luck they'll be so appalled we'll be inundated with letters of complaint from Disgusted of Tunbridge Wells, and then we'll be boycotted and Piers will never make me open the gardens again!'

They enjoyed this hugely and laughed gustily. Why couldn't I join in? Why did I always force myself to adopt this sour position, like some

75

lemon-sucking killjoy, someone I didn't recognise, didn't like? I knew Eleanor always hoped she could jolly me out of it, but somehow, the laughter got stuck in my throat.

'Oh, and here she is!' she cried, glancing through the house as the front door opened. 'The creator, the designer—the *artiste*! How marvellous!'

My mother came down the hall with Rufus beside her.

'Daddy!' Rufus ran through the kitchen and jumped into Alex's arms.

'Hello, rugby boy!'

'Daddy, I was in the team and you were supposed to come and watch!'

'I know, and I'm sorry, but you obviously didn't need me, Rufus. Five tries!'

Rufus drew back in his arms, perplexed. 'What?'

'Bath time now, darling,' I broke in hurriedly, prising him from his father's arms. 'Quickly, say hello to Eleanor, and then straight upstairs. I can see you need a good soak after that match. Look at your knees! Come on, chop chop.'

'But I had a shower,' he was saying as I seized his hand and hastened him away, giving Eleanor only a millisecond to ruffle his hair and congratulate him.

'Mummy, after the match, I had a—'

'Come along, darling!'

We were up those stairs with a bath running in moments.

'I *did* have a shower, Mummy,' he said as I kicked the bathroom door shut behind us.

'I know, Rufus, but humour me and have a bath too.'

Something in my voice made him catch my eye. He looked alarmed, but didn't question my logic as he began to peel his clothes off. The tiny bathroom window overlooked the garden, and above the running taps, I could hear Eleanor greeting my mother like a long-lost buddy. She must have met her all of three times, but Mum, of course, loved it.

'Celia, this is inspired!' Eleanor was enthusing gustily. 'I was just saying to Imogen that I'd like one at Stockley. Really razz up the tourists!'

Mum puffed delightedly on her ciggie and bent down beside Eleanor to show off the faux foliage, whilst Alex looked on indulgently, putting in his amused contribution occasionally. I bet he wouldn't have done that if I'd shown him, I thought savagely, turning off the taps with some force. I bet he'd say, 'Don't be absurd, Imogen. This garden's ridiculous. Your mother's a perfect menace!' But because Eleanor admired it—oh, no, all at once it was delightful.

'Mummy, why did you tell Daddy I scored five tries?'

Rufus was standing before me in the bath, naked and ankle-deep in water, trusting brown eyes on me. Faintly fearful ones, too. It was on the tip of my tongue to come clean and say, 'Because I wanted to out-try that poisonous Theo Latimer who scored four last week,' but knowing he'd feel crushed and inadequate, instead I said brightly, 'Because you so nearly did, darling. You were so close to the line and really instrumental in setting them up. And, after all, your team did score five, and you're part of that team, aren't you?'

He considered this for a moment. Then his eyes brightened. 'Yes. Yes, I suppose so. It was a team effort, wasn't it?'

'Of course it was, darling,' I scrubbed his already clean knees vigorously. 'Of course it was. A team effort.'

*       *       *

When I came down, Mum and Eleanor had gone. Mum had shouted a cheery toodle-oo up the stairs and I'd cheerio'd back, but Eleanor had obviously passed her goodbyes through Alex. He was in the kitchen, putting the champagne glasses in the sink and throwing the bottle in the bin. It was chilly now, with the French windows still ajar; the sun had disappeared behind the clouds.

'Eleanor's gone?' I said casually, throwing Rufus's pristine rugby kit quickly into the washing machine as I passed and pulling my cardigan around me as I hastened to shut the French doors.

'She had to dash off. Wanted to miss the traffic.'

'Ah.'

'But she sent tons of love.'

I smiled as I reached up to turn the mortise key. He was repeating exactly what she would have said in her husky voice. 'Tons of love to Imogen.'

'We must think about her offer,' I said lightly as I breezed around the kitchen, plucking some dead flowers from a jar and tossing them in the bin, turning on a lamp as I passed and flicking on the radio. 'It's very kind of her, but I can't quite see what's in it for her!' Except to have my husband on her doorstep morning, noon and night, I thought feverishly, chucking yesterday's newspaper into the recycling pile.

'Well, in return, we do the place up. That's the

78

idea. And it's more than kind, actually,' he said in a strained voice. 'It's a life-saver.'

I glanced round from tipping powder in the drawer of the washing machine. 'What d'you mean?'

'I've . . . actually had quite a lot of time to think about this, Imo. She rang me a week ago and offered it.'

I turned around to face him properly; put the powder down.

This. *This* was what I hated. *So* much. I gripped the top of the washing machine behind me. The secret collaboration, the two of them whispering away together, without Piers and me involved. Ooh! I turned back and slammed the powder drawer shut.

'Right,' I said lightly, bending down and busily setting the dial. 'Why didn't you say?'

'Because I needed to mull it over in my own mind. Needed to think it through. But, the thing is, Imo, I really think we ought to move down there. Permanently.'

I swung around and stared at him incredulously, mouth open. 'Move down there? What, leave London? This house? For some crummy country cottage on the Latimers' estate? Oh, don't be ridiculous!'

I stared at him. He'd sat down now, at the kitchen table. His face was pale, but determined. His hands clasped before him.

'Imogen, we have no choice.'

'What d'you mean, we have no choice?' My voice was shrill, fearful. He looked so . . . peculiar.

He made a helpless gesture. 'The bills, the mortgage, everything. The overdraft . . . Imo, we're

79

so overdrawn the bank won't let me have any more. And if we moved down there, we could let this place out. Think of the money we'd save. I could commute—we'd be fine.'

I stared at him in horror. He meant it. He really meant it. I pulled out a chair and sat down slowly opposite him. We were silent a while.

'Alex, things can't be that bad. You're exaggerating.'

'I'm not exaggerating,' he said, giving a false bark of a laugh. 'Wish I was. Things are—' he flicked a quick, nervous tongue over his lips—'well, they're pretty fucking hopeless, actually.'

His eyes slid past me to look out of the window. I went cold. Alex's eyes never slid about like that.

'Have you lost your job?'

I had a sudden awful vision of him pretending to go to work all this time, as I'd heard people did: putting on a suit and tie and going off to sit in some ghastly steamy café somewhere, desperately ringing headhunters on his mobile. His eyes came back to me.

'No, I haven't lost my job. But . . .' he hesitated, 'well, I've had a warning.'

'Oh God.' My hand went to my mouth.

'No bonuses will be given to anyone in my department this year, and apparently, if we don't "shift our asses and get some new business in"— well . . .' He shrugged his shoulders despairingly. 'Who knows?'

'Oh, darling, you will!' I reached across the table and took his clenched hands. Shook some life into them. 'You will get some business; you said the other day it was only a matter of time!'

Normally he'd nod, agree, sigh and move on, set

about making supper with me perhaps, but he just sat there. He looked shaken. Responsible. For his family. For their plummeting fortunes. Suddenly I felt ashamed. How long had he been living with this? Worrying he was going to get fired, not telling me?

'Everything's going to be fine, you'll see. Things will pick up.'

He shrugged. 'Maybe. And meanwhile?'

'Meanwhile, well, meanwhile we'll think about it. About . . . Eleanor's offer.' I swallowed. 'Golly, this isn't something that can be decided overnight, Alex. There are all sorts of things to consider, to throw into the equation. What about Rufus? What about his friends, his school—'

'There's a little local school he could go to near Stockley. It's a church school—free. And he'd probably get a place. I've already checked.'

'You've already . . .' I stared. My mouth dried. He was serious. Deadly serious.

'But . . . he loves Carrington House. All his friends . . .'

'He'll make new friends down there, Imo, and we can't afford Carrington House any more. Even if we decide to stay in London, he'll have to go to a state school.'

'A state school!' My blood froze. What—where they sniffed glue and beat up the teachers? Over my dead body. Not my sweet, precious Rufus.

'And move somewhere smaller. We could still stay in Putney, but it would have to be a flat. A maisonette, maybe.'

I got up from the table and went to the French windows, clutching the tops of my arms, my heart pounding. What, in the area where everyone knew

81

us, so everyone knew we'd gone down, not up? When everyone was moving to bigger houses with bigger gardens, the Camerons went smaller? With Rufus at a state school where he'd be bullied and picked on? I gazed out at the neighbour's wisteria tumbling prettily over the garden wall. He knew he'd got me. Knew I was cornered. But turning to look at him now, I knew how much that pained him too. The sadness in his eyes was not pretty to watch. I turned back to the window; rested my forehead on the cold glass. Tilly had got quite a decent divorce settlement from Alex. In his guilt, he'd been generous. They'd sold the family home eventually, but she'd got the lion's share of the capital, and of course he paid for Lucy and Miranda's schooling. There was no talk of them leaving their private American schools, I noticed. I dug my nails hard into the palm of my hand. But I'd known all this when I'd married him. Known he would always support another family, and that I had to be happy with what was left. And I was— very happy—as long as I had him. And it wasn't as if I contributed anything, either. Wasn't as if I had a proper job.

When I looked round again, he was at the far end of the kitchen, at the sink, his back to me. His hands were deep in his pockets and his shoulders sagged in his blue jumper. It struck me, for the first time, that he looked older. I had a sudden flashback to how he'd looked striding down that corridor at Weinberg and Parsons all those years ago; so dashing and handsome, coat streaming out, blond hair flying. I took a deep breath and went across to him. I put my arms around him from behind and rested my head on his back. He didn't turn, but stayed staring bleakly into the stainless steel depths.

I sometimes wondered if Alex ever missed the life he'd had. The house in Flood Street, the glamorous social life, the restaurants every night, the opera. As I held him, I felt his disappointment at the way things had turned out permeate through him. It cut me like a knife. He didn't want to be bailed out by old friends. He didn't want to be shamed into accepting charity, and Eleanor had done it in such a way that it didn't seem like that. We'd be doing *her* a favour. As usual, she came out of this shiny and bright, a far, far nicer person than I was, who just wanted to hold on to the trappings of my life, to be like Kate across the road, with my child's private school blazer and cap hanging in the hall and my occasional girly lunches and the odd invitation to charity balls, when in fact—we were out of our depth. Alex had clearly known it for some time, and I . . . well, I'd known too, but I suppose I'd been fooling myself. Clinging to the wreckage. I swallowed hard and squeezed him tight. And actually, I could cope with anything, except his sadness.

'We'll sleep on it, darling, hmm?' I whispered, my voice, when it came, surprisingly croaky. 'We'll see.'


## CHAPTER SIX

Kate dropped the frozen packet and a million petits pois shot, like tiny green missiles, to every corner of her kitchen. She turned, her face shocked.

'You're not.'

I nodded miserably. 'We have to, Kate. We've been through it so many times now. Unearthed every unpaid bill, every final reminder, every threatening letter. I tell you, it's not a pretty sight.'

It wasn't. Alex and I both suffered from brown envelope syndrome, my policy being to ignore them and pretend I'd open them later, but I was horrified to discover he'd gone one step further and popped them under sofa cushions. We'd decorated the kitchen table with them last night, sat down opposite each other, and forced ourselves to face reality.

'Yes, but this is so drastic. Moving out! Things will improve, surely?'

I took a deep breath and prepared to take on the role of my husband, the executioner, as Kate played me, the condemned: pleading, arguing, imploring for a stay of sentence. I shook my head as I'd been taught. 'Apparently not. This is the second year running he hasn't had a bonus, Kate, and it's not just him either,' I added loyally. 'The whole of the City's in chaos. People are losing their jobs left, right and centre. And as far as the house is concerned, if we don't jump now, we might be pushed,' I said, echoing the master's voice.

'What, you mean the bailiffs?' She gazed at me without blinking.

I shrugged. 'Who knows? I mean I agree, I thought they only appeared in Dickensian costume dramas, but apparently they still exist—just look a bit different these days. Ford Mondeos and jangling bling, as opposed to tailcoats and top hats.'

Kate sat down unsteadily opposite me at the table. She looked stricken. I hoped she wasn't going to cry, because if she did, I surely would too.

'I can't bear it.'

I nodded miserably. 'I know. Neither can I.'

She rested her arms limply on the table and gazed at me, her huge, baby-blue eyes filling up. I looked out of the window, in real trouble now. We both knew how much it meant to have a mate across the road to pop over and confide in, to have a laugh, a coffee, a piece of chocolate, to cheerfully character assassinate a few mothers at school, to have such instant gratification literally on each other's doorstep, but it was more than that. Recently, Kate and I had become very close. I knew things about her that I have a feeling no one else did, and she knew things about me I certainly wouldn't have told anyone else. I think she'd found it easy to confide in me because I didn't mix with her elevated social set and wasn't likely to spill any beans, and I . . . well, I just liked her. What had started as a convenient friendship to do mainly with proximity had blossomed into something rare and precious to do with compatibility.

She got up quickly from the table to save us both from a nasty scene and went for the dustpan and brush in the broom cupboard.

'Bloody peas,' she muttered, brushing them rather ineptly into the pan. She threw them in the bin.

'You've thrown the dustpan in too,' I commented.

'What? Oh.' She retrieved it absently and slung it in the cupboard. Then she turned and folded her arms, regarding me beadily like someone looking into the eye of a storm.

'I can't help feeling you're panicking. That this is crisis management.'

'Oh, we are,' I agreed. 'And it is. A crisis, I mean. And if we have any chance of saving ourselves we have to move fast. We're going under here, Kate, sinking well below the surface. Eleanor's offer is a lifeline.'

'Eleanor,' she spat, opening the fridge door to get some salad out for lunch. 'I thought you couldn't bear her! Thought you reckoned she still had her claws into Alex and was just waiting for her chance to pounce. Well, now you're offering it to her on a plate!' She tossed a cucumber and a pepper on a chopping board. 'She'll be all over him like a rash!'

'I think I've overreacted,' I mumbled, chewing a fingernail. 'In fact, I'm sure I have. Eleanor, is, in actual fact, a very sweet person.'

'Bollocks,' Kate scoffed, chopping up the cucumber with alarming zeal. 'Last week you told me she was a conniving hussy who'd married for money and was regretting it on a daily basis. You told me she was thoroughly disillusioned with chinless Piers and looking for some extracurricular action with her eyes firmly on your husband!'

'I did not,' I spluttered, colouring up. 'I mean— I—I certainly remember saying that if you marry money you pay for it, but I'm pretty sure I was generalising. I really don't think for one moment she's after Alex.'

Kate turned and waved her knife dangerously at me. 'You said, the last time you went to stay with them, she practically got her tits out at the dinner table. You said it was a black tie event for

86

twenty with a magician doing the after-dinner entertainment and she might just as well have done the juggling herself.'

'*Did* I?' I was horrified. 'God, how awful. I'm such a cow. No, no, she looked lovely that evening. Just a bit—you know. Chilly.'

'And you said that when you walked into the billiards room after coffee she was bending over the table with Alex bending over behind her showing her how to pot the red. You reckoned he'd have been potting something else if you'd come in two minutes later.'

'Yes, but I misinterpreted that,' I said quickly. 'Alex explained to me in the car on the way home, it's a bit of a running joke with them. He's always tried to teach her billiards, ever since they were little, and she's always been hopeless.'

'Ever since they were little,' Kate scoffed. 'Ever since they were little and he was the land agent's son and she was the farmer's daughter and they went to Pony Club together and grew up in each other's houses. He plays on that as if that excuses their overfamiliarity.' She stopped suddenly. Saw my face. Went a bit pink. 'Sorry. That was out of order. I didn't mean . . . well, I'm sure you're right. You misinterpreted it. And I'm just upset.'

I got up and we met in the middle of the kitchen, hugged each other tight.

'I'm upset too, Kate; can't *bear* the thought of going. Can't bear it. And I hate the thought of being beholden to her too.'

She drew back sharply and looked at me. 'Oh, I wouldn't take it rent free.'

'We're not going to,' I said quickly. 'Alex would have, but I made him ring a local estate agent and find out what the going rate was for renting a dilapidated cottage round there. It's peanuts, actually, but Alex has written to Piers saying it's a terribly generous offer, blah blah blah, but we'll only accept if they let us pay rent. I do have some pride.'

'Quite right,' she said, fishing a tissue out of her sleeve and blowing her nose loudly. She went back to butchering the cucumber. 'And what about your house? Number forty-two?' She jerked her head over the road.

'We're not going to sell it, we're going to rent it out.' I perched on the edge of the table. 'Alex wanted to sell, but I've talked him out of it. We're getting a stonking great rent for it, incidentally, so who knows? In a year or so, when we're back on our feet, maybe we can move back? Come back to London.'

Kate smiled down knowingly at her red pepper and chopped away in silence. 'You won't,' she said eventually. 'No one ever comes back. Once they've gone, they realise how much better life is out there. And aside from the fact that I'll miss you like hell, I think that's what's upsetting me so much. The fact that I'll still be in sodding London with my successful husband and my vast sums of money, and you'll be in a little cottage in the country with roses round the door and a veggie patch at the back and a few chickens in the yard. Heaven.' She sighed. 'What's it called—Rose Cottage? The Orchard? Go on, make me drool.'

'Shepherd's Cottage.'

'*Shep*herd's Cottage,' she breathed, putting her knife down for a moment and gazing straight ahead. 'Even better. More kudos, less chocolate box. With baby lambs gambolling on the hillside behind you and trout glistening and leaping in the brook? Typical!' She brought the knife down with such force that half the red pepper leaped off her board in alarm. I picked it up and she gouged away at the seeds inside it like a Shakespearean henchman going for Gloucester's eyes. I gulped.

'Well, you'll come down and see us, of course. Spend weekends, and we'll come up here. You know, to dinner, the theatre . . .'

Even as I said it, though, I knew it wouldn't happen. Knew that, whilst Kate would be blissfully happy mucking in with the steam stripper and the Polyfilla on a Saturday morning before munching a ham roll on a back doorstep, Sebastian, after a hard week at the operating table, could probably think of better things to do. Likewise, theatre trips would be unlikely to feature in the Camerons' social calendar for obvious financial reasons. The truth was that our lives, which up to now had been so intrinsically woven, so intricately stitched together, were going to be pulled apart with alarming ease. A relationship that had taken many hours of coffee drinking, school running, scooping up of each other's children and cooking of kitchen suppers to perfect, was to be shelved in moments.

Kate dredged up a great sigh from her L. K. Bennetts. 'Of course we'll see each other. Of course. I'll come down for the day in the school holidays and bring the children, and you'll pop up here occasionally when you're in town, but . . . it'll be different. It'll be the end of an era. The end of . . . old ways.'

We exchanged sad little smiles, and might have exchanged another hug, but Kate sensibly picked up her knife and began paring again in a more measured, slightly less manic way. 'But a new start for you, my friend, which is just what you need. What you both need. Time to move on.'

That evening I told Rufus, who was much more stoic and phlegmatic than I'd imagined. He mulled it over for an hour or two without saying very much, but then, later that evening, came to find me in my bedroom.

'Where will I go to school?' he demanded, raising huge brown eyes to me in the mirror. He was sitting at my kidney-shaped dressing table, swivelling on the stool and playing with old lipsticks in my drawer, twisting them up and down while I changed the sheets behind him.

'Oh, Rufus, you'll love it. It's a dear little church school in the village, much smaller and cosier than Carrington House, and it's got a fantastic reputation.'

I'd steeled myself to ring Eleanor a couple of days ago and she'd instantly raved about it and given me the headmaster's number.

'Everyone says it's a brilliant school,' she'd gushed down the phone. 'All the local children go, and Vera's children adore it.'

'Vera?'

'My daily.'

'Ah.'

'And the head's great, apparently,' she'd rushed on. 'He's new, really dynamic, really turned the school around. Terribly charming too, I gather.'

He must have been having an off day when I rang.

'This term? No, I'm not convinced I can. We're full to bursting.'

I'd explained that my husband had already telephoned and secured, I'd been led to believe, a place for Rufus.

'Oh, yes, I remember now. I did speak to your husband. But it was all very hypothetical. I certainly didn't promise anything.'

Oh, splendid.

'Um, I'm a friend of Eleanor Latimer's,' I breathed shamelessly, perhaps hoping that by dropping the local nob, he, in turn, would drop everything.

'Are you indeed?' he'd barked back. 'Yes, well, you can tell her from me that the next time her dogs crap all over my playground I'll bloody shoot them.'

'Right, will do,' I'd quaked. 'But in the meantime . . . ?'

'In the meantime, leave it with me. I'll see what I can do.' And the line had gone dead.

A week later I'd received a curt missive via email informing me that since a child's father in Year Five had tragically been killed in a combine-harvesting accident, the family were moving away and there was now a place for my son. Dead man's shoes, I thought, reading it in horror. Heavens, was this the sort of place we were going to? Did people fall into combines as a matter of course, skin rabbits with their teeth and pop ferrets down their trousers before they went shopping?

'A church school?' Rufus turned to face me from the dressing table. 'What—you mean it's in a church?'

'No, sausage, it's run by the Church. Which makes it, well . . .' I shook a pillow into its case, smiling, 'Christian. Caring. Nice.'

In my mind's eye I imagined a chubby, smiley vicar in a billowing cassock sweeping into the little wooden schoolroom and beaming kindly down at the rows of rosy-cheeked children sitting cross-legged before him, delivering a homily about how *all* God's creatures were precious, and then blessing them before they ran out into the fields to play, the little girls with pigtails flying to skip and spin hoops, and the boys to damn streams and look for frogs.

'Do they still have Dib Dabs in the country?'

'Of course they do. You'll buy them at the village shop.'

Now Rufus and a couple of the aforementioned apple-cheeked boys were stretching up over a counter, conkers hanging from their pockets, to hand their pennies over to a dear little currant bun of a lady, who was beaming widely and taking down a glass jar full of pear drops.

'But you know, Rufus,' I regarded him kindly, 'the pace is slightly slower in the country. You might find it's all humbugs and catapults rather than Dib Dabs and Game Boys.'

'Oh.' He looked disappointed. 'What's a humbug?'

'A humbug is a slimy bastard who says one thing and then does something entirely different,' snarled Alex, sweeping into the bedroom and flinging his briefcase on a chair. 'See my boss on this subject.' He wrenched angrily at his tie.

'Golly, you're early. Good day?' I hazarded nervously.

'Reasonably diabolical, thanks. Roger Bartwell has taken over my Hedges and Butler account. I hope the brakes on his new BMW fail and he dies in a heap of twisted metal in excruciating agony. Crash and burn, that's what I say, crash and burn. Put Mummy's lipstick down, Rufus.'

'She said I could.' Rufus dabbed experimentally at his lip.

'I don't mind,' I said indulgently.

'YES, WELL I DO!' Alex roared, shooting me a look. Rufus dropped the lipstick and glared at his father.

A silence ensued as Alex changed out of his suit. He took off his jacket and tie while I smoothed down the bottom sheet and plumped the pillows.

'We'll be near Aunt Hannah, won't we?' Rufus hazarded at length. He'd surreptitiously picked up the lipstick again and was twiddling it furtively, under cover, in the drawer. If this comment was designed to get back at his father, it certainly worked.

'Yes, that's the downside of this little venture,' Alex snapped, sitting on the bed and taking his shoes off. He hurled one across the room. 'Your bloody sister!'

'And Uncle Eddie,' Rufus reminded him brightly. 'I like Uncle Eddie.'

This caused Alex to hurl his other shoe. 'Eddie!' He groaned, flopping back dramatically on the bed, arms out like a starfish. 'With his bloody balls!'

Rufus and I giggled.

Hannah, my elder and much more forthright sister, had married Eddie Sidebottom many years ago when they'd met at a commune in Istanbul. Hannah, in those days, was a right-on leftie with a heart that bled all over the place and a social conscience she was determined to dump

93

somewhere. She traipsed around the world looking for causes, desperate to revolt against the bourgeois, middle-class upbringing she'd never had, and irritated beyond belief that she hadn't. That we lived in bohemian Highgate and my father was an actor and not an accountant, and my mother, far from being a blue-rinse Tory, wafted round in beads, pulling distractedly on her ciggie, not knowing what day it was, was a source of constant annoyance to Hannah. It irked her that no one noticed her rebellion. In fact, when she came back from the commune, Mum asked if she'd had a nice time in Cornwall.

'Cornwall? I've been to Istanbul!'

'Oh, I thought you said Cornwall. And who's this?' She smiled.

'This is Eddie. We're getting married.' Hannah squared her shoulders defiantly.

'That's nice,' said Mum, adjusting her new Bo Derek wig in the mirror. 'Is he a taxi driver?'

'No, why?'

'You get a lot of taxi drivers in Istanbul.' She'd looked at Hannah in surprise, as if she should know this. 'Pity,' she murmured, leaning in to the mirror to check her teeth for lipstick. 'We're very short of taxi drivers round here. Poor Bertie Featherstone waited two hours outside the Arts Club the other night.'

Eddie was in fact a teacher from Wigan, and was as different in his laid-back, laissez-faire way from Hannah—who could be chippy and bossy—as was possible to be. He was tall and shy, with long grey hair—even at twenty-three—and delightfully charming: a gracious Sergeant Wilson to Hannah's terrierlike Captain Mainwaring. He deferred to her at all times, called her 'my little angel', and clearly thought the sun shone out of her kaftan. We definitely thought it shone out of his, and when they duly got married and settled down to what Mum and I regarded as a giggle-makingly bourgeois, unrebellious life in a semi in East Sheen, we were delighted. They both taught at the local poly—Hannah, art, and Eddie, English—and Hannah got fatter and Eddie's hair got shorter and whiter, but other than that, nothing changed. The move to the country came some years later when they decided to get away from the rat race, buy a cottage, teach locally and, of course, have loads of children. They achieved all of the above effortlessly, but sadly, no children. After years of trying and some lengthy, invasive, expensive investigation, it was discovered that they were both culpable and they decided to give up. They were surprisingly philosophical about their infertility, discussing it at length with all-comers, with Hannah, in typically robust style, balking at nothing.

'My vagina's too acidic,' she informed the entire family over a pub lunch one Sunday when we'd gathered to meet Dad's latest girlfriend—Mum included. 'And even if I douche it with yoghurt on a regular basis, which, frankly, defies gravity and makes a terrible mess,' (the female members of the group winced and crossed their legs) 'it's still not going to create a conducive enough environment.'

Samantha, Dad's latest squeeze, appeared to be choking on her scampi.

'And the thing is, Eddie's sperm are terribly lazy,' she confided loudly as Eddie nodded sagely into his pineapple juice. 'Even if he saves them all

95

up for about a month and then lets them go in one massive ejaculation, they still can't make it up my cervix.'

Visions of Eddie, roaming around the countryside with a scrotum fit to burst for weeks on end, staggering in and out of work with his mighty cargo, and then finally waddling up the stairs to the bedroom and discharging it like a mammoth tsunami, sprang inconveniently to mind, over the Scotch eggs.

'You could always use a syringe,' offered Mum, brightly.

Hannah made a gormless face. 'We've told you. We don't want IVF.'

'No, I meant to get the yoghurt up.'

There was a short silence as our little group digested this.

At length Dad sighed, patted Eddie sympathetically on the shoulder, and tottered off to the bar to get another round in. 'Bad luck, laddie,' he muttered as he went.

But Eddie didn't mind. As a self-confessed hypochondriac, there was nothing he liked better than discussing his bodily functions, and he viewed his lack of fecundity with resigned fatalism.

'I knew it,' he'd say, hunched over his empty glass, a maudlin look in his eyes. 'I just knew it. It's hereditary. I blame my father.'

'How can infertility be hereditary?' asked Alex. 'Your father had you, didn't he?'

'Yes, but then look what happened to him. I'm on to the next stage already, you see. I'm one step ahead. It's all in the balls.'

Eddie's father, also a hypochondriac, had had the last laugh when he'd died suddenly of testicular cancer. Eddie was convinced it was only a matter of time for him, and according to Hannah, inspected his balls on an almost daily basis.

'And not always in private,' she hissed. 'We were on a train the other day. He looked like a pervert fiddling away under his overcoat!'

'I felt a twinge,' said Eddie, unrepentantly.

Recently, though, only a regular checkup at the doctor's would pacify him. Eddie's doctor, a mild-mannered, old-style practitioner, who'd seen it all before and was already overfamiliar with Eddie's twinges and pangs, was happy enough to oblige. Once a month, Eddie went to the surgery, dropped his trousers, and Dr Williams had a rummage. They discussed the weather and the Test at Headingly and Freddie Flintoff's spin bowling, and then Dr Williams would sit up, declare that Eddie's bollocks were in peak condition, and send him on his way. This happy relationship only foundered when, one morning, quite unexpectedly, Eddie found himself dropping his trousers for a Dr Earnshaw.

'Where's Dr Williams?' Eddie asked in panic, clutching at his belt.

'He's on a sabbatical,' Dr Earnshaw replied smoothly, sucking the end of her pencil and eyeing him over the top of her glasses. 'Drop your trousers, please.'

Eddie's testicular cancer improved dramatically after that, with Eddie declaring his twinges far less frequent. Unfortunately they didn't take long to relocate and were now in the vicinity of his chest, just below his ribcage. Very close to his heart.

'He won't have a bath with the door shut any more,' Hannah hissed furiously down the phone to me, 'in case he has a heart attack!'

Neurotic about his health he might be, but to Rufus, Eddie was simply a joyous uncle: an uncle who always had time for him, who played chess with him endlessly, took him bird watching, taught him to distinguish a pigeon's egg from a plover's, and more importantly, let him play with his blood pressure machine.

'That's it, lad, pump it up . . . now sit back and relax. Watch the dial.'

'Can't I jig about a bit?'

'Can do, but it'll register off the scale, like.'

Some energetic dancing would ensue, which, sure enough, sent Rufus's reading through the roof, and then Eddie, unable to resist, would indulge in some break dancing, which he was particularly good at, and they'd compare coronaries.

'Will we be quite close to Hannah and Eddie?' asked Rufus, spinning round fast on the stool now, using his fingertips on the dressing table to propel himself.

'Too close,' muttered Alex, throwing his socks in the laundry basket and unbuttoning his shirt as he headed for the shower. 'Don't do that, Rufus, you'll break it.'

'What?' Rufus glanced after him.

'Yes, nice and close, darling,' I said quickly as Alex disappeared.

After a moment, though, his head popped back around the door. 'You're changing the sheets again? I thought you'd only just done that!'

'I dropped some tea on them this morning,' I lied, colouring up and busying myself with the poppers on the duvet cover. For some reason my husband found clean sheets incredibly provocative and, in the old days, couldn't resist ravaging me on them.

'Oh. Right. What's for supper?'

'I bought a couple of fillet steaks. And *Four Weddings* is on again later. I thought we might watch that when Rufus has gone to bed.'

Alex rubbed the side of his face and yawned widely. 'I'm a bit knackered actually, Imo. I'll probably just watch a bit of footy in the kitchen and then turn in, but you watch your film.' And off he padded to the shower. Then he called out as an afterthought, 'I'll have that steak, though.'

## CHAPTER SEVEN

'Bye, then.'

I looked damply at Kate and walked into her arms. We stood clutching each other in her sunny front garden opposite my house. My old house, I should say, which, less than a month ago the estate agent had walked around sucking his teeth at, opining that it would be 'a tricky one to shift, Mrs Cameron,' but then miraculously, had shifted it in days. An American couple, he'd rung to say breathlessly, were desperate to move in, the husband's job having already started over here, his wife in the States champing at the bit to come across and get the children into schools. Could they move in in two weeks' time? Well, what could I say? They were offering a jaw-dropping amount for six months' furnished accommodation, and although we'd planned to take our furniture with us, Shepherd's Cottage had apparently got all the basics—beds, sofas, tables and chairs—so, as Eleanor said, letting it out furnished was actually a bit of a blessing.

'Perfect,' she'd declared to me down the phone. 'So you don't have to cart all your stuff down or put it into storage, and you can be here next week!'

Yes, perfect I thought as I held on to Kate under her magnolia tree and promised, in a choked voice, to ring soon. Out of the corner of my eye I saw Rufus and Orlando sheepishly kicking gravel, unsure how to handle this.

'Bye,' muttered Orlando eventually, thrusting his hands in his pockets and addressing his shoes.

'Bye,' agreed Rufus. He picked up a stone and threw it at a tree for composure.

Alex and Sebastian were doing slightly better, pumping each other's hands in a good-humoured, matey fashion. They'd got along well enough and had shared a few bottles of claret over the years, but they probably wouldn't give each other another thought and were merely going through the motions, aware that their wives were in trouble.

'We'll speak soon,' I sniffed, drawing back and fishing a hanky out of my pocket.

Kate nodded mutely, her face pale and stoical, but tears were spilling down my cheeks now. Alex came over to extract me before we were awash.

'Bye, Kate.' He squeezed her shoulders affectionately and gave her a kiss, before disentangling me and leading me away. 'Come on, darling,' he said gently.

'Wait,' I croaked, wiping my nose with my sleeve. 'I haven't said goodbye to Sebastian.'

I was in real trouble now, and Sebastian took

the brunt of it.

'Oh God, I'll miss you so much!' I released a gaspy sob into his cashmere pullover, clinging on for dear life. Sebastian was tall and spare, and if you believed Alex, had a fence post inserted rectally. He wasn't really the sort of man you slobbered over.

'I love you both so much!' I cried, hanging on tight.

He patted my back, awkwardly. 'Come back and see us soon!' he said with forced jollity, which made me realise he wouldn't be coming to see *us*. Sobered me up, rather. With Alex's help I managed to peel myself away, blow my nose, and with a last buckled smile at Kate, who had her arms tightly folded, lips compressed, got in the car beside Alex.

A trailer was attached to the back of our car, carrying most of our belongings, but the Volvo was nevertheless crammed to the gunwales with the immediate trappings of our lives. Our very much London lives, I thought sadly, glancing round at the cappuccino maker and the Cath Kidston bed linen piled high in the back, where Rufus had to clamber in now, beside boxes of carefully packed John Pawson porcelain and Villeroy and Boch brushed steel. We may be poor, but we were stylishly poor. No doubt it would be all Boden and Le Creuset in the country, I thought miserably.

Alex let out the handbrake, and in another moment we were away, Rufus hanging out of the window, all inhibitions gone now, shouting, 'Bye! Bye!' to Orlando, who was running along the pavement beside us, seeing how long he could keep up. Alex drove slowly, letting Orlando keep pace for a bit, then speeded up when we got to the end of the road. Orlando stood and waved madly, and as I watched him in the wing mirror, it struck me as a painfully poignant tableau: a little boy waving goodbye to his mate across the road, whom he'd never be as close to ever again. I was ambushed by tears, and sensibly, Alex didn't attempt to console me. He let the torrent run its course, which was well on the way to the M4.

At length, though, we hit the motorway and I dried up. Rufus was listening to *Harry Potter* on his headphones, oblivious to his mother's snivelling, and Alex slipped in a CD: Bach's cello concerto, full of pain and longing, didn't help enormously, but next up was a frisky little Mozart number, which was cheering. And actually, the further we drove, the better I felt. The lull of the music and the purr of the engine was soothing and I wondered, perhaps, if we shouldn't move to Scotland? I'd surely be a new woman by the time we got there.

By exit 8 I was tapping my foot and humming merrily, and it was only when we hit the B roads ten minutes later that I remembered what we were doing here and felt sick. I sat up in my seat and looked apprehensively out of the window.

'I'd forgotten how rural it was,' I commented as lush spring meadows flashed by in a haze of emerald green. 'Are you sure this is only Buckinghamshire? Not Herefordshire?'

'Quite sure.'

'And it's still commutable?'

'An hour and a quarter door to door, Piers assures me.'

'Piers. And how would he know? How often

does he trouble the London underground, I wonder?'

'His tailor's in Savile Row, apparently. He's having a few suits made at the moment.'

'What, plus fours and gaiters?'

Alex smiled thinly and I remembered that whilst my husband could joke about my friends and their fence posts, it wasn't always so funny when I joked about his.

We purred through the Latimers' village. My village, I thought, looking around with interest, Little Harrington. It wasn't exactly picturesque, no duck pond or village green or creeper-covered pub, just a ribbon of featureless houses running alongside the roadside built in the local pale grey stone and plunging off occasionally into side streets, but it had . . . well, it had integrity, I decided staunchly. Oh, and look, a village shop! Well, OK, a Spar. It flashed past in lurid green and orange. There didn't seem to be anyone about, though. Putney High Street would be buzzing by now; where was everyone? And what was the Little Harrington look, I wondered? Ah, there was a woman of about my age. Overcoat, bare legs and trainers. Right.

Didn't Eleanor get lonely, I wondered nervously as the car plunged into semidarkness and we began our ascent through some woods, climbing to the top of the hill to where Stockley sat, in a commanding position overlooking the valley. My stomach began to churn.

'We're on Latimer land now,' Alex informed me grandly. 'These are Stockley's woods.'

Stockley's woods. So they owned them. I wasn't quite sure where I stood *vis-à-vis* owning woods.

103

Weren't they—you know—God's? Look at all those trees. *More* trees. How many trees did a person need? But no neighbours. Not even a simple peasant, doffing his cap and carrying his sandwiches in a hanky on a stick. A deer startled at our car, making Alex and me jump, then leaped back into the woods again.

When the trees parted and Stockley came into view, I decided solitude had its compensations. I'd forgotten how beautiful it was. It was large, but not overly high and mighty, more long and low and very symmetrical, with crumbling stone pillars either side of the white front door. Its pretty Queen Anne windows looked out like benign eyes, and the sun glanced off its mellow stone façade. I could quite see why Eleanor had fallen in love with it. The fact that Piers came with it was just a minor inconvenience, I imagined. We swept on past the gates with its little lodge house, and my head swivelled back in surprise.

'We're not going in?'

'Not yet. I thought we'd go to our place first, don't you think? She's left a key out for us. Under a pot.'

'Oh. Fine.'

Alex, as usual, was party to more arrangements than I was but I was determined not to be piqued.

'And you know where the cottage is?' I asked pleasantly.

'Just down this lane, apparently. Then left down a track.'

'There's a track!' cried Rufus, and Alex obediently swung the wheel and we lurched through a gap in the hedgerow. Rufus took off his seat belt and leaned forward excitedly between us.

'And there's the house, look!' He pointed as, sure enough, after we'd rattled over a couple of cattle grids and snaked down a chalky zigzag track, it came into view. A tiny whitewashed cottage with a grey slate roof crouching, or perhaps cringing, in the fold of some hills, which rose up to the woods beyond. The cottage was flanked by a small square yard, a barn full of hay, and acres and acres of wide open space.

'Looks like a farm,' Rufus commented excitedly.

'Perhaps it once was,' I agreed. 'It's tiny, though, isn't it?' I said nervously.

'These cottages can be awfully deceptive,' Alex informed me as we got out. 'Perhaps it's bigger inside.'

It could have been pretty, I decided, as we waded through knee-high grass to get to it, but it had a forlorn, decrepit look: the green paint on the front door was peeling and the windows were equally distressed. The small front garden, such as it was, was just a jumble of nettles and ragwort. My heart sank, knowing I had a husband who would neither notice nor care. The back garden, as I've said, was a yard. With a stinking manure heap parked centrally. I swallowed and glanced at Alex, who was standing and nodding appreciatively, hands on hips, eyes narrowed, like a man who's Come Home. Like a man who's missed the smell of the new-mown hay and the call of the wood pigeon, but I knew better. Alex's late father might have called himself a land agent but he was, in fact, an estate agent and the family had lived firmly In Town. The only Pony Club activity Alex had participated in was snogging at dances.

Next to the front garden was a field, which

appeared to be inhabited.

'Cows!' yelled Rufus excitedly, running to the fence to see.

'Bulls, actually, darling,' I said, looking at their huge horns with horror. 'Rather a lot of them, too. Fancy putting them all together in one field? Surely they'll fight?'

We regarded the bovine group, who raised their heads and stopped their rhythmic chewing to stare opaquely back.

'Oh, I'm sure they're friendly,' said Alex jovially, and reached tentatively over the fence to pat one. It mooed loudly and a tongue the size of a salmon enveloped Alex's hand.

'Christ!' He snatched his hand back. 'Tried to bite me!' He looked at me in horror, clutching his fingers.

'And sheep! Look at all the sheep!' Rufus was running to an adjacent field and jumping on the fence in excitement.

'You can get a terrible disease from sheep,' Alex said as we followed nervously at a distance. 'Eddie told me.'

'Eddie,' I scoffed. 'What does he know about sheep? And as Hannah pointed out, you do actually have to fondle them to get it. Have to get really quite intimate, and with the best will in the world I don't think there's any danger of— RUFUS, DON'T TOUCH THEM!'

'Look, Mum, little lambs!'

'Yes, but you mustn't touch!' I rather bravely scaled the fence to rescue my son from the jaws of a tiny white lamb. 'Not without gloves. Now come on, let's go and see the cottage.'

Alex had already deserted the bucolic scene for

the relative safety of the front doorstep. 'I've found the pot, but there's no key,' he informed us, lifting a dirty terracotta pot gingerly in his fingertips like exhibit A. A couple of beetles scuttled to safety.

'Perhaps she meant round the back.'

We traipsed round to another peeling green door, but there wasn't even a pot by this one. Just that manure heap. Alex frowned.

'Right. Well, I suppose we'll have to go up to the house. She must have forgotten.'

'*Completely* forgotten,' I squealed, barely disguising the note of triumph in my voice.

As we made for the car, though, a cry went up behind us.

'Mum, I'm in! The window was open.'

We swung round and, sure enough, Rufus was hanging out of a downstairs window, grinning from ear to ear.

'Oh, well *done*, darling!'

We hastened back, full of renewed optimism as he ran to open the door. The optimism was short-lived, however, as we found ourselves stepping into what was indeed, a very deceptive cottage. It was even smaller than it looked from the outside. There was a tiny sitting room—or parlour, perhaps, since there was definitely a Dickensian feel to all this—an even smaller everything-else-room with a table and four chairs, a cupboard-sized kitchen, and upstairs, two bedrooms and a bathroom you surely wouldn't want to linger in on account of the distressed sanitary ware. I looked at the cracked basin in dismay. Everything, from the banisters, to the sticks of rudimentary furniture, to the window ledges, I discovered, running my finger along them, was covered in a thick layer of dust. I set my mouth firmly and came back downstairs. I've often thought that a child's presence can have a very civilising effect and this was one of those moments. Rather than reaching for the nearest chair and hurling it at him, I merely flashed my husband a look that went beyond hatred and hissed, 'Marvellous. Absolutely marvellous.'

'Well, it's certainly got potential,' he was saying foolishly, jangling coins in his trouser pocket as he bent to peer out of the sitting-room window. 'Terrific views too.'

I treated both these comments with the contempt they deserved and swept past him to the kitchen.

'I know we're not parting with much money here, Alex, but common courtesy dictates that you at least sweep the kitchen floor or put some milk in the fridge. Look at this!' I threw open a cupboard and something grey and furry fled. We shrieked and clutched each other.

'You said it would be habitable,' I breathed. 'If I'd known it was going to be like this I'd have come down last week and sorted it out!'

The fact was I'd meant to, I really had, but packing up in London had taken every spare moment of my time and actually, every ounce of emotion.

'Cold Comfort Farm,' I seethed, opening one filthy cupboard after another and slamming doors shut. 'Look at the dirt. Look at it!' I was behaving rather badly now, but even as I stormed around, I knew my anger was misdirected. I couldn't really give a monkey's about the size of the rooms or the dust—which, let's face it, in a place this size wouldn't take long to shift. What was depressing me, what was *really* depressing me, was that it was glaringly apparent that there was nowhere to paint. Three bedrooms. I'd been promised three bedrooms! Could Rufus possibly sleep on a sofa bed downstairs, I wondered feverishly? Or could I paint downstairs and we just wouldn't have a sitting room? No, of course not, Imogen, don't be so selfish. No, I thought going through to the sitting room, chewing my thumbnail, no, I'd just have to put my career on hold. Golly, plenty of women did, didn't they, I thought miserably. And anyway—I went to the window and rubbed the filthy pane with a fingertip—it wasn't as if I had much of a career to hold in the first place, was it?

'Let's go and find Eleanor,' said Alex, rubbing his hands together decisively as if that would solve everything. As if a few more rooms and luxury en suite bathrooms would miraculously appear.

'I think perhaps you're right,' he added cleverly as he ducked under the door frame on the way out. 'We should have gone to find her in the first place. Shouldn't have arrived unannounced.'

I nodded wordlessly, not trusting myself to speak, following him out to the car. And of course, he'd be in London most of the time, I thought as we waded back through the long grass, while Rufus and I were down here. He wouldn't be back before dark, and then at the weekends he'd no doubt find any excuse to be up at the big house, fishing for trout with Piers, flirting in the kitchen with Eleanor, whilst muggins here set traps for the mice and got to grips with the rising damp. And actually, that was where he'd seen himself all along, I thought with a sudden flash of realisation. Not in

Shepherd's Cottage at all. Oh, he'd imagined he might *sleep* here occasionally, partake of the odd breakfast, but most of the time he'd be up there, helping Piers select cigars from the walnut humidor, or fine wines from the cellar, or in the pale yellow drawing room, helpfully pouring pre-lunch gin and tonics for the corporate shooting parties, leaning against the marble mantel, looking gorgeous, being terribly charming, glass in hand . . . an asset to any house party. Eleanor would introduce him as her oldest friend and everyone would purr and coo and say how lucky she was to have him close by, and the men would find him affable and amusing and the women privately admire his good looks and there'd be much laughter and bonhomie, and then the phone would go and Eleanor would carefully put her hand over the mouthpiece.

'Alex, darling,' she'd make a face, 'it's Imogen. She wants to know if you're coming back for lunch.'

Alex would sigh and roll his eyes and . . . oooh! My blood came to such a rolling boil as I slammed the car door shut I thought my head might pop off. I should never have agreed to this, *never*!

'Where's Rufus?' said Alex as he got in beside me.

We glanced around as, at that moment, a shriek went up.

'MUMMY!'

We got out as one and dashed back, our tempers forgotten. Together we raced round the side of the house to find Rufus, by the back door, surrounded by a huge posse of aggressive-looking chickens. There must have been at least forty of them. He gazed at us, wide-eyed.

'Every time I move, they move with me!' he shrieked.

'Right,' I breathed, heart pounding. 'Don't panic. What we'll do is—*oh!*'

In another moment they'd left Rufus and rushed to surround me, attaching themselves firmly to my legs, pushing and clucking menacingly. I clutched a drainpipe and nearly fainted with fear.

Rufus ran to his father and hid behind him.

'Move slowly,' commanded my husband from behind the safety of the dustbin lid he'd commandeered as a shield. 'Don't make any sudden movements!'

I half shut my eyes and gingerly took a step, but they swarmed with me, cackling horribly.

'H-e-lp!' I whimpered, feeling like Tippi Hedren in *The Birds*. '*Help me!*'

'Wait there,' cried Alex. 'We'll get the car.' Still brandishing the dustbin lid, they raced off, whilst I, petrified, stood rooted to the spot, glancing down at the sea of feathers, beaks and beady eyes that surrounded me. Oh dear God, there were hundreds of them, *hundreds,* and actually—I gazed in terror—these weren't chickens at all! Chickens were brown and smooth and comforting, but these were strange fluffy creatures with furry heads and very sharp, curved beaks. Were they wild, I wondered? Had I stumbled across some rare and prehistoric breed? Some hawk with spiky hair? The last of the Mohawkans?

Moments later the car roared round the side of the cottage and through the open yard gate, screeching to a halt in a cloud of dust and chicken shit. The door flew open like something out of

*The Sweeney*.

'Come on!' yelled Alex in seventies cop mode. 'Run for it!'

'Run, Mummy!' urged Rufus.

I shut my eyes, summoned up every ounce of courage—and legged it, half expecting to hear brittle bones and webbed feet snapping beneath my kitten heels, but beyond caring. The birds ran with me, stretching out their necks and running with wide-apart legs under their feathered skirts, like fat ladies running for a bus. But I was faster. I threw myself in the car, heart pounding, and slammed the door shut, wondering if I'd decapitated anything. Alex performed a dizzy-making handbrake turn and we flew off.

We didn't speak for a few moments.

'This isn't going to work,' I finally gasped when I'd checked for headless chickens. 'This isn't going to work at all!'

Alex patted my knee. 'Nonsense,' he soothed, 'it'll be fine. It'll all work out, you'll see. Come on, we'll go up to the house the back way.'

The back way? I swung round, confused as we went past the cottage and plunged further down the track. His local knowledge was clearly more intimate than mine, which only added to my irritation.

'How come you know this way?' I snapped, still trying to get my breath. 'I thought you hadn't been to the cottage before?'

'Oh, I remember now, we came down here when I was shooting with Piers in the autumn. The second drive was down this way. It's where I shot that partridge. You couldn't come, remember?'

Oh, yes, that weekend. The shooting party. The

112

one I'd dreaded, but had been absolutely determined to go to, come hell or high water, but not, as it turned out, a high temperature. Rufus had got chickenpox the day before, so after weeks of quizzing Kate on shooting etiquette and raiding her country wardrobe and spending a small fortune on a hat in Lock's, which she'd convinced me would be an investment, I'd fallen at the last hurdle and had to watch Alex drive off on his own, a vision in Lovat green. Well, there'd be plenty more of those weekends, I thought grimly as we drew up at Stockley's back door. Plenty more opportunities to wear the bloody hat. I say 'back door', but most people would be overjoyed to have it at the front: it was large, black and heavy with lots of brass knobs on, and ranged about it were Wellington boots in all colours and sizes, evidence of generations of Latimers traipsing through.

'Hi there!' sang out Alex, pushing on through, and of course he was right. Good friends shouldn't go to the front, ringing bells and making the dogs bark and giving their friends the added nuisance of walking ten minutes from the west wing, only to find the door's warped through lack of use and yelling, 'Go round the back!' to the pesky visitors, but nevertheless, I envied him his confidence. I followed him down the flagstoned back passage and the dogs came wagging and pushing their noses into my crutch, but other than that, there were precious few signs of life.

'He-lloo!' yodelled Alex again, sticking his head round the kitchen door. It was the sort of kitchen I'd dreamed about in my shallower moments. Huge, high-ceilinged and baronial, with the ubiquitous Aga at one end and an open fireplace at the other, over which a stag's head presided, complete with a cigarette stuck in its mouth in a we-may-be-grand-but-gosh-we-can-laugh-at-ourselves sort of way. In front of the fire stood two high-backed armchairs, for all the world like his and hers thrones, and in a corner, a faded squashy sofa where the dogs hopped back to now to curl up and resume their slumber. Along one wall was an ancient oak dresser dripping with willow-pattern plates, and by the French windows, a long oak refectory table adorned with artfully arranged terracotta pots. Kate would have passed out with jealousy. Having recently seen my new kitchen, I wanted to torch it.

'No one about,' commented Alex needlessly. 'Tell you what, I'll head down to the front hall and you check out the playroom.'

The playroom was about three rooms further back on the left; past the butler's pantry and the gun room, deep in the bowels of the intimate family side. I opened my mouth to protest that I'd quite like to stick together and not be discovered snooping round Eleanor's house on my own, but Rufus, at the mention of a playroom, had already zoomed off, tail up, sniffing for toys. I sighed and made to follow him, as Alex turned and walked, quite quickly as I recall, in the opposite direction, towards the green baize door and the more formal side of the house. Before he reached the door, however, we heard shouts coming from that direction, but from upstairs. Voices raised in anger. I turned back in surprise, as Alex's step quickened and he disappeared. I made to follow him, clip-clopping down the flagstones in my heels, pushing through the baize door, from where I was afforded a view of the main front hall, dark, echoing and oak panelled with a sweeping Jacobean staircase. As my eyes adjusted to the gloom, I was just in time to see Eleanor run lightly down the stairs, barefoot in jeans and a white T-shirt, her face stained with tears, and fly into Alex's arms as he stood at the bottom.

'Oh, Alex darling,' she cried in a choked little voice, 'thank God you've come. Thank God!'

## CHAPTER EIGHT

Don't ask me what possessed me to give them a moment. To stand there in the gloom where I knew they couldn't see me, and watch as his arms encircled her waist and his fair head bent over her dark one. I think the answer is that I just froze. Alex thought I'd gone after Rufus to the playroom; Eleanor didn't know I was there. They perceived themselves to be entirely and exquisitely alone. As she lifted her face to his, though, I felt scared. Lost my bottle. I didn't want to know what came next. I turned and exited quietly back via the green baize door, then barged back through it again, noisily, giving a loud, enigmatic cough. The two of them sprang apart like deflecting magnets.

'Imogen!' Eleanor regarded me in horror, wiping her wet face with the back of her hand. 'Oh—I thought . . .' she glanced up at Alex in confusion. 'I thought you'd come alone.'

This struck me as a remarkably obtuse thing to say. What, alone already? Just like that? Without giving it a couple of months, say, to rent us asunder?

'Why?' I didn't recognise my voice. It was harsh, rasping.

'Well, you're not due till tomorrow so I assumed Alex had just popped down to look at the cottage, get the lie of the land.' She'd recovered her composure now and was gazing at me wide-eyed. 'But no—no, that's fine. If you've both come to look, that's marvellous. It's just I haven't had a chance to get in there yet, and it's filthy, I'm afraid, so—'

'Tomorrow?' Alex interrupted, surprised. 'That's when you expected us?'

'Yes, the twenty-fifth.'

'That's right—Sunday. Look, it's in my diary.' I rummaged in my bag, still smarting, but determined she wouldn't get the better of me on this one. I drew it out. 'Here, Sunday, to Stockley.' I pointed to where I'd written.

'But *Monday* is the twenty-fifth,' said Alex, peering over my shoulder as it simultaneously dawned on me. I flushed to my roots.

'Oh, darling, you idiot!' Alex laughed. It was said affectionately, but he was clearly annoyed.

'Well, never mind,' Eleanor said quickly. 'It doesn't matter at all. It's lovely that you're here. I'm afraid the cottage is uninhabitable tonight, though, I've got Vera and her girls going in tomorrow to scrub it from top to bottom. Don't go and look at it yet. I'll die!'

'We've already seen it,' laughed Alex.

'Oh, *no!*' she shrieked, and both hands flew to cover her mouth. 'How *embarrassing*. You must think I'm dreadful!'

'Not at all,' I muttered, still horrified that I

could have cocked up so comprehensively. We were a day early. Shit. How could I have got it so wrong?

'But actually, that's perfect,' Eleanor was saying. 'You can stay here tonight, in much more comfort, and then tomorrow you can have more of a say in which furniture you want. There's some terrible old stuff in there at the moment, but Piers's mother has a barnful of pieces she doesn't want from when she moved to the Dower House: lots of nice sofas and chairs you can take your pick from. Oh, Piers, look who's here. Isn't it marvellous?'

Piers, in a flat cap, Viyella shirt and corduroy trousers, and with his head slightly bowed in the manner of a very tall man constantly anticipating a low doorway, came through from the back passage, holding two bottles of wine in each hand. I was surprised. Somehow I'd assumed he'd been upstairs with Eleanor, involved in that shouting match, having some sort of domestic with his wife. Who had she been shouting at, then? One of the children? Would they make her cry? I glanced quickly upstairs.

'Marvellous,' agreed Piers, coming forward with impeccable manners, sweeping off his cap and stooping to kiss me and pump Alex's hand. 'I saw your car outside, actually, and assumed as much.'

'I'm so sorry,' I faltered, still pink. 'I don't know how I managed to get the dates so wrong. Hopeless of me . . .' Even as I was stammering my apologies I noticed Piers clocking Eleanor's tear-stained face and then saw Alex seeing him notice. One way or another a lot of thought processes were going on here with not much to do with the fact that we were a day early.

'I'll get Vera to lay another couple of places at dinner then, shall I?' Piers went on lightly. 'I was just off to decant the port.'

'Oh—yes, of course.' Eleanor looked flustered suddenly. 'I'm so sorry, we're going to submit you to a ghastly black-tie dinner tonight.' She grimaced. 'That's your penance, I'm afraid. But actually, it's perfect. You can meet all our neighbours in one fell swoop—or all *your* neighbours, should I say!'

'Oh God—you're having a party. No, we couldn't possibly—'

'Of course you can. It couldn't matter less,' Piers boomed. 'The more the merrier, in fact.'

'Particularly with the motley crew we've got coming this evening,' Eleanor said with feeling. 'It's a bit of a duty party, and some of them definitely need diluting. It'll give you some idea of what you're getting yourselves into. You might wish you'd never come!'

'But—I haven't got anything to wear,' I stammered. 'I left a case of evening clothes with my neighbour. I was going to pick them up later. Why don't Alex and I just go to the pub?' I said desperately. 'We could maybe leave Rufus here with Theo and—'

'Nonsense, I won't hear of it,' said Piers. 'I've got a spare dinner jacket Alex can wear and I'm sure Eleanor can find you something to fit, can't you, darling?'

'To fit' was an unfortunate phrase, and I could feel everyone wondering how the fuller-figured Imogen, without the assistance of a crowbar and a jar of Swarfega, would ever fit into one of Eleanor's teeny-weeny dresses, but Eleanor was all fluttery hands and assurances.

'Of course I can. In fact—I have the very thing. Come with me, Imogen.'

She seized my hand and, in a moment, was bounding up the stairs with me in tow.

'Oh, but I'd better check on Rufus, I haven't seen him since—'

'He's in the playroom,' Piers informed me, striding under the staircase towards the dining room. 'I saw him as I came through, happy as a sand boy with Theo's train set. You girls go and play. Alex, come and help me decant this port, would you? It's a Fonseca '66, rather a good one, I think. My father laid it down aeons ago and I'm slightly concerned that if we don't drink it soon it'll be vinegar . . .'

And so it was, that moments later, whilst my husband spookily acted out the decanting-wine-with-Piers scene I'd so recently envisaged, I found myself in Eleanor's enormous chintzy bedroom being squeezed, like a very pale fat sausage, into a red velvet dress the size of a napkin.

'It's not actually velvet, you see, it's velour, so it stretches,' Eleanor assured me, panting with the exertion of doing up the side zip as I held my arm aloft. Embarrassingly, my pits needed a shave and I wasn't convinced they were terribly fragrant after loading the car and the journey. 'It's one size, and it really does fit anyone. My sister wore it last Christmas, and she's the size of a house.'

Oh, marvellous.

'There!' She stood back in triumph as I regarded myself in the long mirror.

My hands instantly went to cover my cleavage. The dress was very low cut, so low you could practically see my tummy button, and as I spilled voluptuously over the top, my hips splayed out even more voluptuously at the bottom. My hand scrambled in horror for the zip.

'Oh, no, I couldn't possibly wear this.'

'Nonsense, it's perfect. Honestly, Imogen, you look terrific. You should wear dresses like this more often, and look, I've got these amazing bra cups that you just slip in and attach with glue so you don't have any straps.'

She was producing a couple of black triangles but I'd already scrambled out.

'No, no, honestly.'

'Or you can just put Sellotape over your nipples so they don't stand out like organ stops. I've done that before.'

Lordy.

'Um, maybe some trousers . . .'

'Well . . .' she crossed doubtfully to her wardrobe. 'These Joseph ones are Lycra, so maybe . . .' I snatched them gratefully but of course it was wildly optimistic: I could hardly get them over my thighs. I did manage—stupidly, and just to prove a point—to do the top button up, but not the zip, and then turned and pretended to view my bottom in the mirror.

'Mmm, not sure,' I gasped, for gasp was all I could do. Then of course I couldn't get the wretched things off.

Eleanor kindly turned away and pretended to tidy her drawers as I struggled, finally flopping back on her four-poster bed to peel them off with sweaty palms. She kept up a constant chatter to hide my blushes, but as she rooted around yet again in her wardrobe and I sat on the side of her bed in my undies, I wondered, wretchedly, what on earth I was doing here? Scrambling into her clothes, which were too small for me; borrowing her cottage, which was too small for her. Who was the fool?

'The red,' she said decisively, whipping out the velour number again. 'With these fantastic M&S grippy pants that hold all your bits in. Hang on, they're around somewhere . . .' She was rummaging again.

'*I have . . . the pants!*' I squeaked with feeling. Christ, I wasn't going to borrow those too!

She sensed the defiance in my voice and turned quickly. 'Look, I'm sorry you've been landed with this wretched party,' she said anxiously, 'and I'm sorry you saw the cottage in such a dreadful state, but I just know everything's going to be fine. You'll love it here, really you will. I'll make sure of it.'

Her eyes were wide and appealing, and actually this should have been my moment. My moment to say, yes, OK, I'm sure I will love it, but tell me, why were you crying just now, Eleanor? And why did you fall on my husband's neck and gaze adoringly into his eyes, and why do I always get the feeling you're after him, and why should I believe you're not when you wrecked his marriage to Tilly, pretended to be her friend, and then stole him from her? But I didn't. Perhaps because I didn't want to know the answers, and perhaps because I knew that by my coming down here and accepting her hospitality, she held all the cards and I held none.

Six months, I told myself grimly as I stalked off to the sumptuous spare room she'd directed me to, clutching the red dress and a pair of high heels;

six months was precisely how long our house was let for and that was precisely how long we'd stay. No longer. This was a short sabbatical to refresh our finances; a couple of terms out of school for Rufus, and then we'd be on our way; back in time for him to start the new school year back at prep school in September, and back to our old house too. And I'd tell Alex as much tonight, I resolved as I padded through the thickly carpeted bedroom to the bathroom. I turned on the taps and seized the bottle of Jo Malone placed considerately by the side of the bath. Sloshed a dollop in. Yes, I'd tell him just as soon as we had a moment together; before supper.

Well, naturally that moment didn't arise, because while I was having a bath, Alex was in one of the many other bathrooms this huge house boasted, having a shower, and evidently changing there too, because when he finally popped his head round the bathroom door saying he was going downstairs and did I want him to wait for me, he was in his dinner jacket. I had my toothbrush in my mouth and a mouthful of froth, and by the time I'd rinsed, swallowed and yelled, 'Yes I bloody do!' he'd gone.

By the time I'd put on my make-up and settled a highly over-excited Rufus into Theo's room amidst much giggling and talk of farting, and then summoned all my courage for the descent down the vast sweeping staircase, it was getting late. The red dress, ably assisted by my very own grippy knickers and the two bra cups—a feat of engineering that relied worryingly on something called body-glue—actually didn't look too bad. I caught a glimpse of myself in the long mirror halfway down the stairs. Rather obvious, of course, a voluptuous blonde in a skimpy red dress, but as long as I ate precisely nothing, I decided, and didn't turn round too quickly and knock anyone out with my jiggling bosoms, I'd be fine. I wobbled downstairs, breathing in hard.

Quite a few guests had arrived and gathered in the beautiful yellow drawing room with the ornate plaster ceiling, and Piers was buzzing around being mine host, getting drinks. They were mostly middle-aged, these neighbours—and by neighbours I knew we were talking people who lived in the same county and not next door—the women formidable, statuesque, with well-upholstered bosoms and lots of powder and jewellery, and the husbands, mainly ruddy-faced with paunches and dandruffy shoulders. They were standing in little clutches, braying loudly and shrieking with laughter, obviously terribly familiar with one another. One much younger man, with flashy dark looks and black curls that hung over his collar, was standing apart on his own, sipping a whisky. His head was cocked contemplatively as he regarded the spines of the books in the shelves. His head didn't move, but his eyes tracked right to look at me as I came in; they roved up and down as he mentally undressed me, which, since I was only wearing a napkin, didn't take long. When he'd finished he straightened up and his face lit up as if to say—ooh, good, a trollop. I flushed hotly and ignored his grin.

My eyes darted instead to—ah, yes, there they were. By the fireplace. Eleanor was leaning on one end of the ornate Adam mantel in a simple black sheath dress and pearls, whilst Alex propped up the other, supremely elegant in a borrowed dinner jacket, which, he being tall and slim like Piers, fitted like a glove. He was flicking back his fair hair as he laughed at something Eleanor said, and he looked so at home, so absolutely as if he belonged here, it almost took my breath away.

I fumbled in my bag for an uncharacteristic cigarette. Would Piers even notice if Alex moved *in* here, I wondered? If he sat with them at breakfast, strolled round the garden with them admiring the roses as a threesome, crawled into bed with them at night? The smoke hit my lungs and I suppressed a cough. It occurred to me that there might even be some grand plan going on. Perhaps the Latimer marriage was cold and loveless? Perhaps he beat her? Perhaps Piers had affairs. Maybe he was glad to have another man around; maybe it took the heat off him, or maybe, I thought wildly, he was secretly gay? Maybe he'd fathered his children and now wanted to be let off the leash? My mind whirled with possibilities and what with the very tight pants and the cigarette, I felt quite faint. It took me a moment to realise Piers was at my elbow, offering me a glass of champagne.

'Oh. Thank you.'

'That's quite a dress, Imogen,' he murmured, his eyes roaming over me appreciatively.

'Thanks. It's Eleanor's.'

'Is it? Well, it doesn't look like that on her. I'd have remembered.'

Right. Perhaps not gay. Perhaps very straight, so perhaps I could have an affair with him? That would be neat, wouldn't it? If a little yuk-a-roo.

'Sorry to be boring, Imogen, but we're a bit of a non-smoking house. It's Mummy, I'm afraid.'

'Oh. Sorry.' I looked around wildly for somewhere to put it out, and for Piers's mother, who was no doubt already fixing me with a steely glare.

'Oh, finish it now you've lit it. She's not here tonight. No, I just meant for future reference. Tell you what, come and meet Robert and Pamela Ferrers. They're terribly nice. Farmers.'

Farmers, right. By that I knew he meant landowners. Gentry. Probably the High Sheriff and his wife. He guided me across to a tall, thin couple in the corner.

'This is Imogen, Alex's wife. They're taking Shepherd's Cottage,' Piers was saying.

Alex's wife. Always Alex's wife, never Imogen Cameron, she's a wonderful artist, you must see her paintings. Oh, stop it, Imogen. Stop carping.

Pamela was haughty and imperious-looking with a hawklike nose down which she peered from her great height. I instantly warmed to her though when she affected a mock cockney accent.

' 'Ello, luv, I'm Pamela.'

'Ooh, 'ello, pet, I'm Imogen!' I grinned.

'You settlin' in nicely, then?'

I gulped. Flushed to my roots. Shit. She spoke like that. Except it wasn't a cockney accent, it was a strong West Country accent. Her husband was watching me closely. Piers looked aghast.

'Y-yeah. We are.'

'Tha's nice. Tha's a grand little cottage you got therre. A peach of a place, my Barb always says, don't you, Barb?'

Bob didn't answer. He was staring at me.

'Ooh, it's that orright,' I faltered, reddening under his gaze. 'A—a peach!' Oh, that the ground

125

would swallow me up. I knew, though, that if I wasn't to offend her, or her beady-eyed husband, I had to continue in this bucolic vein. All night, if need be.

'Tha's lovely soil you got down there,' Pamela was saying sagely, tapping my arm. 'Drains well an' all. Lovely an' loamy.'

'Mmm . . . ooh, it is. Loamy!'

She looked rather quizzical, hopefully puzzled by lack of small talk and not my peculiar accent. Oh God, please don't let her ask me where I was from. Could I bluff my way, agriculturally speaking, through my humble rural origins on some smallholding in Somerset, perhaps? Or was she au fait with every smallholding there was from here to Land's End? Knew every farmer and their straw-chewing daughters? Weren't they all related, these people? Or was that Norfolk? Piers, happily, was alive to the pitfalls, and was steering me away, saving my bacon.

'And you haven't met the Middletons either,' he said loudly, walking me across the room to a new set of faces.

'Thank you,' I whispered. 'So much.'

'My pleasure,' he growled. 'Now this is Tom and Sandra Middleton. More tenant farmers.'

'Got it,' I breathed as the Middletons broke off their conversation to smile interestedly. *Tenant* farmers. The real McCoy. Not landowning gentry stalking around waving shooting sticks and barking orders, but proper, rustic folk, getting their hands dirty. Sandra Middleton, petite and pretty, smiled and extended her hand.

'Hi.'

My fingers still clenched my cigarette, which had

gone out ages ago and was now a dead butt. I looked around wildly for an ashtray but there wasn't one, so I popped it in my open handbag.

'Hi,' I grinned, and took her hand.

'Ah, more fellow soil tillers!' said Tom cheerfully as I shook hands with him too. Piers had moved on to greet some late arrivals coming through the door, both about ninety and on two sticks apiece. Where was his wife while all this meeting and greeting was going on? Still propping up the fireplace with my husband, no doubt.

Tom had to repeat his opening gambit.

'Hmm? Oh, no, we're not farmers,' I laughed. 'We've just taken one of the cottages for a few months. We're going back to London in September,' I added firmly.

'Oh, really?' Tom looked surprised, but Sandra, clearly delighted to have first crack at some new blood, was busily filling me in on her role as helper at the local playgroup. Anxious not to make any more blunders, I found myself blithely agreeing that I might well come in to help the little ones with their reading, and maybe even take charge of the Show and Tell table, until Sandra was practically hyperventilating with excitement. Suddenly she rested a cool hand on my arm.

'God, you're smoking.'

'I know, I've already been told off by Piers, but someone else is too.' The man with the curls I'd secretly christened Heathcliff was puffing away by the open French window. I caught his eye and glanced away quickly.

'No, your bag.'

I glanced down, and saw to my horror that the little straw bag on my arm was on fire. Smoke was pouring from it and flames were even now licking the bamboo handle.

'Oh!'

Instinctively I shook it off. It smouldered brightly on the carpet. 'Oh God—quick!'

In one swift movement, a man's arm reached across, picked up the handle, and flicked it deftly into the fire, between Eleanor and Alex's legs. I remember their faces, turning as one, in horror.

'What the hell . . . ?' Alex looked aghast.

'Oh God, I'm so sorry!'

'Anything precious in there?' Tom Middleton was jabbing at the burning bag with a poker. A bit of a crowd had gathered.

'No, just a lipstick, but—oh God, Eleanor, your carpet!'

All heads swivelled like a Wimbledon crowd to look at the nasty dark patch in the Persian rug.

'Oh, I wouldn't worry about that. It's ancient.' She tripped lightly across and rubbed it with her toe. 'It's only singed. Adds character. And look, I can flip this one over it.' She deftly pulled a smaller fireside rug to cover the burn. 'There. He'll be none the wiser.' She glanced across at Piers who, happily, was still busy with the octogenarians. 'It'll be our secret,' she giggled. 'Anyway, I've never really liked it.'

Alex was by my side now. 'What the hell are you up to?' he hissed.

'I put a cigarette butt in my bag. It obviously hadn't quite gone out.'

'Obviously! Why didn't you find an ashtray?'

'Because there wasn't one. And I would have thrown it in the fire,' I snarled suddenly, 'but you and Eleanor were hogging it!'

128

'Oh, for heaven's sake,' he snapped, 'don't be so childish. Come on, we're going in to dinner.'

Seething quietly we walked silently together into the dining room, following the flow. It was a beautiful room, the walls hung with dark red silk and ancestral portraits, and tonight, lit entirely by candles, which shimmered in a sea of polished mahogany and silver and white roses. There were appreciative murmurs all round as we were shown to our seats, and I had the feeling people felt rather honoured to be here. I remembered Eleanor saying something about a duty party.

It looked for a moment as if I had Piers on my right and the old man on two sticks on my left, but suddenly I saw Eleanor dart across to the twinkly-eyed gypsy, nod and whisper conspiratorially in my direction. In a moment the old boy had been spirited away, and in his place was Heathcliff. Irritated, I pulled my chair out, ignoring his attempt to do it for me, watching as Eleanor nipped back and directed Alex to sit next to her. She winked at me and I gave her a tight smile back. Oh, you think it's that easy, don't you? I thought as she turned to whisper something to Alex. Put the local stud on Imogen's right and she'll be happy. Meanwhile you can flirt your little socks off with my husband.

As I sat down I realised the pants were a big mistake. They were clearly made of cast iron and, as such, wouldn't bend. I caught my breath. Damn. I'd only ever worn them to a drinks party before.

'Pat Flaherty,' said my neighbour with a flashing smile, putting out his hand. His dark eyes glittered.

'Imogen Cameron,' I murmured, briefly taking his fingers before turning smartly to Piers, but not before I'd caught the surprise in his dark eyes and then a snort of laughter as I resolutely turned my back on him.

'So good of you to have us here,' I smiled ingratiatingly at my host, realising with horror, as I crossed my legs, that this ghastly dress was split to the thigh. It gave Pat whatever-his-name-was a bird's-eye view. Out of the corner of my eye I saw him twisting his head to get a better look. I plucked my napkin from my side plate, spread it over my leg and leaned forward.

'Well, terribly good of you to look after all the animals,' Piers brayed, spraying crumbs as he devoured his bread roll in the manner of a man who hasn't seen food for days.

'Not at all,' I murmured, aware that a pair of eyes were roving down my bare back now.

'What?' I came to, suddenly. 'What animals?'

'Well, only the ones down at your place, obviously. The main herd are taken care of by Ron, my farm manager, but we've always kept a few down at the cottage.'

It came to me in a flash that this was what Alex had cannily glossed over when he'd mentioned 'keeping an eye on the animals'. What he'd agreed with Piers and Eleanor—as no doubt part of our rent—and why he'd gone a bit pale when he'd seen the bulls. We were looking after them.

'You want us to feed the bulls?' I breathed.

Piers threw back his head and roared with laughter. I heard my other neighbour stifle a laugh too. Didn't he have anyone else to talk to?

'They're not bulls, they're Longhorns,' he explained. 'Terribly tame and very sweet-natured. We've always bred them here. Got a few exotic

130

sheep too.'

Visions of bellydancing sheep sprang, confusingly, to mind.

'Oh. Right. And what do they eat, these Longhorns?'

'Four bales of hay a day as a rule,' he said airily, 'which you just pop in the roundels for them. It's all in the barn. Butter?'

'Oh. Thanks.' I took a knob. Well, that didn't sound too taxing. 'And the sheep?' I enquired nonchalantly, as if feeding sheep was something I did in my sleep.

'The sheep are just on grass, which is where the cows will be soon. It's just taking its time to come through. You don't have to bother with them. The ewes are lambing, of course, but we've never had a problem with Jacobs. Won't be asking you to stick your hand up any twats, if that's what you're worrying about—ha ha!'

'Ha ha, no, quite.' My eyes bulged in horror as I lunged for my wine glass.

'Obviously the silkies need corn in the morning and then Layers Pellets at night, but nothing more than that.'

He was talking a foreign language now. What the hell was he on about?

'I'm not much of a fan myself. Prefer a good old Black Rock pullet, but Mummy's always liked them. Frightfully good sitters. Prolific layers too.'

'Oh—the chickens!'

'That's it. Silkies. Exotic breed.' He looked at me doubtfully. 'I say, are you sure you can manage? Only I can ask Ron to give a hand if not.'

'No, no.' I straightened my back, and my resolve. If Alex had said we could do it then we bloody well could. 'I'll be fine. My, um, aunt farms, actually.'

'Really?' He looked surprised.

'Yes. Aunt . . .' I looked around wildly. A portrait of a woman who looked a bit like the queen hung opposite me. 'Elizabeth.'

'Right. Whereabouts?'

'Whereabouts?'

'Yes, where does she farm?'

I paused. Gave this some thought. 'America.' Somewhere far away. Far, far away.

'Ah. What does she farm?'

Yes, what *did* she farm, Imogen, this mythical American aunt of yours? Fields of billowing corn sprang to mind, like the ones in *The Waltons*, or *The Little House on the Prairie*, but I couldn't think what animals she might have. Then I remembered a chap called Bill, who I was pretty sure dabbled in farming.

'Buffalo.'

Piers looked astonished, as well he might. Golly, were they wild? I wasn't sure.

'Buffalo! Oh well, you'll be fine with our little herd then,' he mused, as happily, our starters arrived, causing something of a diversion. Piers contemplated his plate solemnly. 'Ah yes, of course,' he said abruptly. 'Mozzarella.'

I looked down at my own starter. 'No, feta, I think.' I speared a bit of cheese.

He turned to me astonished. 'Greek buffalo?'

I stared at him, at a loss. Greek buffalo? What the devil was this man talking about? Was he on drugs? Happily his attention was attracted at that moment by his other neighbour, a toothy woman in maroon silk, who wanted to know what sort of martingale he hunted in.

'Sounds like a plucky little woman, your aunt,' said a low, lilting voice in my ear. I turned to find a pair of dark eyes twinkling at me. 'Cheese making's the devil of a job.'

I regarded him imperiously. 'I'm sorry?'

'Your aunt Lizzie. With the buffalo herd.'

'Don't be ridiculous, you don't farm buffalo for cheese,' I spluttered, 'you farm them for—for meat.'

His eyes widened. 'I didn't know that. Like moose?'

I looked into his wide brown eyes. Was he mocking me? Did Americans farm moose? I wasn't sure. His voice had a strong Irish lilt to it.

'Yes,' I said decisively reaching for my glass. 'Just like moose.'

God, these pants were tight. I'd only had a glass of champagne and picked at my starter and they were killing me. Was I going to pass out? I slid down in my seat, trying to perch my bottom on the edge of the chair and straighten my body out a bit.

'Are you all right?'

'Yes, why?'

'You look rather uncomfortable.'

'Not in the slightest,' I snapped.

'And you seem to be coming adrift.' He gestured vaguely at my chest with his fork. I glanced down to see one of my black bra cups poking cheekily out of my cleavage.

'Shit!' Clutching my chest I dived under the table and tried to poke it back in, but the body-glue seemed to have lost its stick. In the end, in desperation, I had to pull it out, and then of course the other cup had to come out too. No handbag to stuff them in, so I sat on them. Face flaming, and making absolutely sure I didn't look at Pat, I turned back to Piers. Luckily he was offering to refill my glass.

'Oh, please.'

'After all, you're not driving.'

'No, quite!'

I was, though, nearly passing out with the pain in my nether regions, and it occurred to me that I might really faint. I had to get up. Piers was telling me about a horse that suffered from something called bog spavins as I slowly levered myself upright.

' . . . hocks look as clean as a whistle, but then, blow me, hack him out and he goes hopping lame! Everything all right?' Piers looked up, surprised.

'Yes, thanks. Might just nip to the loo, though.'

I had to get them off, that much was clear. Even if it meant everything bulged and spilled in a revolting manner, these pants had to go. I tottered painfully away.

The downstairs loo was occupied. I waited and waited, but clearly some dowager duchess was taking ages to spend a penny and then reorganise her petticoats. I glanced up the huge staircase. Could I face tottering up there? No. Instead I limped through the green baize door and down the back passage to the other loo.

'Won't be a mo!' sang out a fruity male voice as I rattled the handle.

Damn. Unable to bear it any longer, I went further on down the passage and out of the heavy back door by the boot room. The cool night air was welcome on my flushed cheeks and in a trice, I'd hitched up my dress and peeled the wretched things off. Ooh, the relief. I flicked up my dress and scratched my buttocks vigorously. Then I rolled the pants in a ball and glanced around furtively. No handbag, so—

'I should pop them in the azaleas,' came a voice out of the night.

I froze, horrified. 'Who's there?'

'Won't be the first time a pair of knickers has been found in the Latimers' garden. Or the last, I'd hazard.'

A wisp of smoke drifted up my nostrils, and at the same moment, I made out a dark figure in the shadows by the wood pile. My neighbour from dinner was leaning back against the logs, grinning delightedly, his teeth white in the darkness.

'I like a girl who takes her bra off at the table then nips out to take her knickers off too,' he drawled. 'Hadn't realised it was that sort of party. Things *are* looking up.'

'How dare you spy on me!' I gasped, horrified.

'Hardly spying. I was here first. Having a mid-course ciggie since the Latimers don't approve. I must say, I never expected to get mid-course entertainment too. What's next, the dress? Or are you going to set fire to yourself again?'

Suddenly I realised whose dinner-jacketed arm had shot across the room and flicked my bag in the fire, before melting into the crowd again.

'Although I have to tell you, if it *is* the dress, I'm not sure I can retain my sang-froid at the table. Not sure I can sit next to you making small talk if you're going to be wearing nothing but a smile and a pair of high heels.' A faraway look came into his eye. His face brightened. 'Actually, I'm willing to give it a go.'

'How dare you!'

He threw back his head and roared with laughter as I turned on my heel and stalked back inside. Clutching my pants, face flaming, I walked, head high, and with everything jiggling about a fair bit, down the passage and back into the dining room. As I neared the table I realised, with horror, my bra cups were still on my chair, for all the world to see. Oh, this was a *horrible* dinner party, I thought miserably as I added my pants to the sorry little pile and sat on them. A couple of women opposite exchanged raised eyebrows. *Horrible*.

Somehow I managed to get through the rest of the evening. I monopolised Piers during pudding, and only when politeness dictated that he turn to address a few comments to his other neighbour did I steel myself to turn to mine and deliver a few icy words about Peeping Toms. His chair was empty.

'He's pissed orf,' the woman on his left informed me loudly, and a trifle drunkenly. She leaned across his empty chair conspiratorially and rested a heavily jewelled hand on his seat. 'Knowing Pat, he's got some gel in the next parish keeping his bed warm.' She chuckled, showing very yellow teeth. 'Gone to give her a good seeing-to, no doubt!'

'Ah.' I smiled thinly. 'Yes, I might have known. You can always tell the type, can't you?'

She chuckled. 'You certainly can.' She picked at her horsy teeth distractedly. 'I hair you're hair for the duration?'

I blinked. 'Yes, we're hair—here, for about six months.' My head was aching with the effort of being part of *The Archers* cast one minute and a Noël Coward play the next. Luckily my toothy friend felt we'd exhausted all avenues of conversation, and with a brief nod, went back to her sorbet.

I glanced down the table to where Alex and Eleanor, heads close together, almost touching, were deep in conversation. Suddenly I felt very empty. Very alone.

A while later, during coffee in the drawing room, I slipped away. I didn't say good night to anyone, didn't break up the party, just stole upstairs and into the spare room, throwing the hateful dress on the floor and crawling into bed. As I lay there, staring at the ceiling, listening to the sound of the chatter and laughter drifting up from below, tears fell silently, sideways down my cheeks, soaking my pillow.

Sometime later, Alex crawled into bed beside me, smelling faintly of port, but I could smell her perfume too. He gathered me in his arms and kissed my cheek, then realised it was wet.

'Why are you crying?' he whispered.

'I . . . don't know,' I whispered back. 'I think I'm just tired.'

'Don't cry, Imo.' He kissed me full on the mouth, his body warm next to mine. He kissed me again, opening my mouth with his lips. 'Don't cry. It'll all be fine. I'll make it fine. You'll see.'

And then he made love to me: beautifully, gently and tenderly. And when, later, he rolled over with a deep sigh and went to sleep holding my hand, I realised my cheeks were wet again. This time, though, they were tears of relief.

# CHAPTER NINE

The following morning at breakfast, Eleanor apologised for the ghastliness of the evening.

'We do have to do these things periodically,' she grimaced, putting a rack of toast in front of me. 'Marmalade?'

'No, thanks.'

'And it was Sod's law that you were here, but at least it gave you a flavour of country life. In at the deep end and all that.'

'Absolutely,' I murmured, sipping my coffee and watching Rufus take the top off his boiled egg. Shafts of dusty sunlight were streaming through the huge sash windows on to the duck-egg-blue walls, skimming his auburn curls. Piers had taken Alex for a walk around the fields so Eleanor and I were alone with the boys.

'I rather enjoyed it, actually,' I lied.

I hadn't, on any level, but was still on air after last night. I felt ridiculously smug sitting here in her sunny kitchen, knowing that, after all her efforts, my husband had come up those stairs and made love to me. Of course it wasn't a victory— that would make me a very sad individual—but in my present state of mind, it was a secret to add to the other one I was hugging. We wouldn't be staying.

'Pat's amusing, isn't he?' she said lightly, packing Theo's book bag for school as he sat tapping his empty, upside-down eggshell and chanting a rhyme with Rufus. He was the youngest of her brood and, as such, had not yet been sent away.

'Mm, very,' I agreed.

'He's from Ireland, as you probably gathered. Single too. Split up with his wife last year. He's set a few hearts a-fluttering in the village, I can tell you!'

She waited, and I knew she was hoping I'd want more; lean forward over my coffee mug, and ask what he did, where he lived—but instead I leaned back and nodded out of the window at her garden.

'Fabulous daffodils, Eleanor. In fact the whole place is looking a picture. You must have a terrific gardener.'

She looked momentarily disappointed, then rallied.

'Dick? Yes, he's very good. He's Vera's husband, you know. They were here with Piers's parents. We inherited them. Ah, talk of the devil.'

At that moment, Vera and her army of helpers, three very solid-looking women in housecoats, bustled past the window up to the back door with buckets. We heard them clattering about and laughing as they came down the passage, then Vera stuck her head round.

'Morning, all!'

'Morning, Vera!' Eleanor sang.

'You want us to start down at Shepherd's Cottage then?'

'Please, and I think it'll take you most of the day. It's in a bit of a state, I'm afraid.'

'Right you are.' Vera grinned at me, revealing an unusual dental arrangement. 'Gather you came a day early, like. Couldn't wait to get in there, eh?' she cackled.

'Something like that,' I murmured.

139

'Must 'ave got the shock of your life when you saw it then. But don't worry, luv, I'll have it gleaming like a new pin in no time.'

I drained my coffee and got to my feet. 'I'll give you a hand. Alex has gone off with Piers, but Rufus and I could help out.'

'Ooh Lord, no, I wouldn't hear of it. Not in them nice London clothes. Tell you what, you come down 'bout tea time when we've finished, eh?' She let the door bang noisily behind her and disappeared with her cronies, still talking at the top of her voice.

'Do that, Imogen,' Eleanor advised me. 'Let Vera crack on, she'd much rather, and then you can spend the day with me,' she said happily. 'I've only got to take Theo to school and pick something up in the village. Then I thought we could go shopping and have lunch somewhere. There's a terrific new bistro in town I haven't tried yet.'

I smiled. 'I'd love to, but actually, I promised Hannah I'd have lunch with her today. She rang this morning, and they haven't seen Rufus for ages and he starts school the day after tomorrow. Mum's there too.'

Eleanor looked disappointed. 'Oh, yes, I forgot your sister lives round here.'

Eleanor knew everyone in the county but my sister and Eddie would not register on her social radar.

'Oh, well, maybe some other time?' She regarded me anxiously. 'I would so love us to be friends.' It was said with candour, and her hazel eyes were wide and hopeful, but I'd seen those eyes before, when she was advising Alex not to give Tilly a decanter, but a pair of earrings.

140

'That would be lovely,' I said pleasantly. 'But right now, if Vera's sure she's all right, I might get off and do a quick food shop. I gather there's a Tesco in town?'

'There's a Waitrose too. In fact I'm going that way myself, maybe I could—'

'No, no, don't worry, I'll find it.' I waved away her offer and, taking Rufus's hand, practically dragged him off his chair. 'I like to explore, feel my way around.'

How rude, I thought as we went outside to the car; how very rude of me indeed, but actually, this was all about self-preservation. Last night had shown me just how easily I could become a fly in a web, how easy it would be to be manipulated. I had to keep my wits about me, and if it was only for a few months, I could do that. I could do that easily.

When Rufus had stroked every horse's nose in the stable yard and tickled the sheepdog's tummy, we got in our car and purred down the front drive, admiring the mares and foals grazing behind the post-and-rail fencing as we went. At the stone entrance gates by the lodge, we turned left down the hill, through the woods and into the village. Clearly there'd been a downpour in the night but now the clouds had rolled back to reveal a glorious spring morning. Every cottage garden we passed was a riot of daffodils and primroses scattered with tiny raindrops glistening like glass beads. It went some way to taking the austerity off the stony faces of the houses, I thought, as I peered into darkened windows. I wondered how much Eleanor had to do with the village, as we purred on through it. Did she know many of the people here, or did she just sweep through it in her four-wheel drive on her

141

way to the hairdresser's?

'Is that where I'll get my humbugs?' asked Rufus, pointing.

'Er, possibly.' I looked doubtfully at the Spar.

'Can we go in?'

'Yes, why not? I'll get the newspaper.'

We parked on the forecourt and went inside.

'I thought you said there'd be a bell,' remarked Rufus.

'What?'

'Above the door. A tinkly one.'

'Oh. Sorry, darling.'

'You'll 'ave to move that,' a voice came from behind a copy of the *Daily Mirror*. 'I don't allow vehicles up against the window like that.' A woman behind the counter, with a tight perm and steel-rimmed glasses, lowered her newspaper. I glanced back at the car. It wasn't particularly close, but . . .

'OK, I'll move it. Chose some sweets, Rufus, and I'll be back.'

'And I don't allow unaccompanied children, neither. Not under the age of ten. There's a notice to that effect, just there.' She jabbed at a piece of paper above her head. 'Cause no end of trouble, they do.'

I regarded this charmless individual in her pink jogging suit.

'He's not unaccompanied. I'll be back just as soon as I've moved the car.'

'Even so, you can take 'im with you.' She rustled her paper again and I found myself looking at David Beckham on the back page.

'Right,' I muttered. 'Come on, Rufus.'

Silently we withdrew, reparked, then came back. Rufus chose some Polos—humbugs not appearing to be an option—and I picked up my *Daily Mail*. We approached the counter again. I flashed a wide smile as she took our things.

'I'm Imogen Cameron, by the way. We've just moved into the village. We're in one of the cottages on the Latimers' estate.'

A couple of old ladies by the freezer turned and stared. Pink Jogging Suit looked at us as if we'd just tucked some wine gums up our sleeves. She carried on ringing up her till.

'I expect you know them,' I said pleasantly. 'The Latimers.'

'Oh, yeah, we know the Latimers.' She caught the eye of one of the old biddies and they exchanged looks.

'Yes, well. I expect we'll be seeing more of each other. Rufus is going to the village school, so I'll probably pop in for my paper when I drop him off. And you are . . . ?'

She regarded me a long moment. 'I am what?'

'I mean, your name is . . . ?'

There was a weighty silence. I could feel myself going red. Rufus looked up at me anxiously.

'Mrs Mitchell,' she said eventually.

'Right,' I said faintly. 'Mrs Mitchell.'

As we left the shop I heard one of the old ladies say, '. . . and a packet of Rennies, please, Linda luv.'

'Linda. Her name's Linda,' Rufus said as we got back in the car.

'Evidently.'

We drove off in silence.

'Not particularly friendly,' he observed at length.

'No,' I agreed, thinking longingly of the lovely wise-cracking Khan brothers, Shied and Tac, who

143

ran the 7-Eleven at the end of our road in Putney. 'But then, they do say you have to live in a village for about three generations before you're accepted.'

'How long is three generations?'

'About a hundred and fifty years.'

He looked at me in horror.

'No, Rufus,' I assured him, 'we are not staying here for a hundred and fifty years.'

*  *  *

Having located Tesco and filled the boot of the car with groceries, we set off for Hannah's.

'Is Daddy meeting us there?' asked Rufus as we cruised into their village, or more accurately, their strip of ribbon development along a fast country road.

'No, Daddy's going into work today. Don't eat those sweets all at once, Rufus.'

'Is he?' He turned to me in surprise, his tongue poking through a Polo. 'I thought he went out walking with Piers.'

'Yes, but he's going in after that,' I said shortly. I too had assumed that he'd taken the day off and would be joining us for a jolly family day out, but apparently an urgent piece of work on his desk required his attention.

'But, Alex, you won't get there till mid-morning,' I'd said as he'd rung me at the cheese counter in Tesco. 'Is it worth it? You know, if you're going to do this commute properly, you need to get a really early start.'

'You're quite right, and in future I'll be on the seven fifteen, but I just thought, since it's our first morning, I'd have a leisurely start and pootle round the farm with Piers. Find out what I've let myself in for!'

What *I'd* let myself in for, you mean, I thought as I snapped my mobile shut and snatched up my piece of Dolcelatte. How was he going to feed a herd of cows from the City? And I couldn't help thinking this Urgent Piece of Work had only materialised when I'd told him where we were going today. My sister was not high on his list of priorities, and actually, he wasn't high on hers either. Hannah had never really got over her initial disapproval of Alex, and he in turn found her bossy and domineering. My husband liked his women pretty and compliant, and Hannah, these days, was neither.

We drew into the tarmac drive of their small, red-brick semi and I glanced up at the hermetically sealed double-glazed windows. It wasn't exactly the pretty thatched cottage with roses round the door they'd envisaged when they'd first moved out of London, but then rose-decked cottages came at a premium they hadn't envisaged either. A couple of teachers' salaries didn't go very far, and I knew they struggled to make ends meet. At least they looked out on to fields at the back, I thought, as I got out and gazed at the sheep-flecked meadow beyond, even if the traffic did zip past their noses at the front.

'Hi-ya!' I called through the letter box, knowing the bell had long since given up the ghost.

No response and the radio was blaring, so I pushed the door, which was on the latch, and went through to the narrow hallway. It was as cluttered as ever, and I tried to ignore the piles of books and

145

files and newspapers as I brushed past them, tried not to think of it all as evidence of Hannah being consciously scatty. Hannah wasn't scatty, she was supremely organised, and used to run a very tight ship, but these days it suited her to bustle around a chaotic house complaining she was far too busy to tidy up. I think a tidy house with nothing for her to do would have left her profoundly depressed. I did wonder Eddie didn't complain about the dust, though. A pile of what I sincerely hoped was jumble—old clothes, a bird cage, a wet suit, a couple of lamps and some more books—blocked my way to the sitting room, but I skirted round them to the kitchen, where Hannah was making fairy cakes in her Sea Scouts uniform, complete with scarf and toggle. The bright blue skirt and shirt were stretched tightly over her ample bosom and bottom, and it occurred to me she'd put on even more weight. She must be nudging fifteen stone, I thought, quietly shocked.

'Ah,' I smiled. 'Scouts today?'

'No, Eddie likes it,' she replied drily.

I giggled and gave her a kiss. She was still quick on the draw, even if she'd let herself go in other respects.

'Yes, quite right, Scouts today. We had a meeting this morning about the jumble sale, and Akela, can you believe it, likes everyone in uniform, even though the boys aren't there. How weird is that?'

'Very, but then again, give a man a whistle and a pair of shorts and he turns into a raving fascist. It's probably the only authority he commands in his sad little life.'

'Doesn't say much for my little life then, does

146

it?' she replied tartly.

'Oh, I didn't mean . . .' But she'd already bent down to embrace Rufus enthusiastically.

'Hello, angel,' she beamed. 'How are you?'

'Fine, thanks. Where's Eddie?' My son, not one for small talk, cut ruthlessly to the chase.

She laughed. 'Out in the garden with Granny. Your uncle has decided to dig a pond, and your grandmother is advising him, horticulturally speaking.'

'Cool. Can I go and see?'

But he'd already gone; out of the back door leaving it swinging on its hinges, and running down the lawn to the bottom of the garden, the soles of his trainers leaving dark imprints in the wet grass.

'A pond?' I moved closer to the window. 'I didn't think Eddie was interested in gardening.'

'He's not, usually, but he's got a thing about fish at the moment. Don't ask. Where's Alex, incidentally? I assumed you'd all be coming today?'

I watched as Rufus flew into Eddie's arms. Eddie swung him up and round in the air, laughing.

'Oh, he's gone into work. Giving the commute a trial run, but he was a bit late this morning because he went for a wander with Piers first.'

'Strolling round his new estate, eh?' she said with a wry smile. 'How's it going?'

I stuck my finger in the cake mixture and licked it. 'Well, stupidly we got here a day early. I got the dates muddled up, so we saw the cottage at its very worst, before it had been cleaned, and then had to go to a rather stuffy dinner party last night.'

'Oh Lord. Nightmare. What's it like?'

'The cottage? It's OK. I'll be fine for a bit.'

'A bit?' She turned, wooden spoon raised. 'I thought this was on a permanent basis?'

I stuck my finger in the mixture again, avoiding her eye. 'We'll see.'

She eyed me knowingly. 'I see. Cold feet already. How is Lady Muck?'

Hannah wanted no part of Eleanor's smart county set, who organised charity balls and played tennis and hunted, and referred to it snidely as 'filling in time between haircuts', but I think it rankled that she couldn't even turn the invitations down. After all, she was Alex's sister-in-law; an invitation to kitchen supper at the very least might have been forthcoming.

'She's fine,' I said lightly. 'She's been very sweet, actually.'

'Sweet,' she snorted. 'I've heard that before, and then I've heard that she turns very sour.'

'What d'you mean?'

'Sue Fountain told me. Eleanor was all over her when she wanted Theo to be in some gymkhana team that Sue organises, and then when she saw her at a party, she cut her dead.'

'Perhaps she didn't recognise her.'

'Nonsense, she'd been lobbying her morning, noon and night, banging on her door in the village, she knew exactly who she was. Val Harper said the same. Said she couldn't have been nicer when she wanted her to make some curtains for her right before Christmas, but then once she'd done them, she completely ignored her at the Carol Concert. She's not to be trusted.'

'That's a bit harsh. Just because someone's a bit fickle, doesn't mean they're not to be trusted.'

148

'Does in my book.'

'Trusted with what, anyway? What have you heard?' I said lightly.

Hannah turned. 'Well, nothing scandalous, if that's what you mean.'

'No, I didn't, I just meant—'

'No, Imo, I haven't got a clue about her private life. I'm sure she's got a blissfully happy marriage, and I'm equally sure,' she said flashing me a look, 'that you wouldn't be stupid enough to come down here with Alex if she hadn't. I do credit you with some intelligence, you know.'

I breathed in sharply. 'Yes, well, absolutely. I agree. And I think she and Piers *are* very happy. He's been terribly kind, actually.'

She gave me an arch look as she took her tray of buns to the oven. 'I think we both know the man's a complete prat,' she remarked, shutting the door with a bang. 'Come on,' straightening up, 'let's go and find the others.'

I followed her slowly down the garden path, biting my thumbnail. If Hannah was deliberately trying to feed my neurosis she was doing a very good job of it. She'd always known which buttons to press, but then I did tend to leave my buttons lying about a bit. I watched as she marched on thick calves down her lawn, huge hips swinging from side to side, every inch the formidable Scout mistress.

Mum and Eddie had their backs to me. They were standing by a rather muddy crater, showing Rufus the fish as he crouched down at the water's edge.

'Look, Mum.' He turned as I approached. 'They're enormous!'

I bent to look. 'Oh, yes, huge. And what fantastic water lilies!'

'Plastic,' beamed Mum proudly, puffing away like mad on a cigarette. 'All the greenery, the watercress—everything.'

'Yes, and the thing is,' Eddie was hopping uncomfortably from foot to foot in the mud, 'the fact that they're not real means the fish aren't getting the oxygen they need from them, and if they're not getting the oxygen, we aren't reaping the benefits of the photosynthesis which is so good for one. The whole thing's hopeless!' he wailed.

'Nonsense,' said Mum sharply. 'It just means it's much more attractive and you don't get all the nasty slimy green stuff you usually do with ponds.'

I made a sympathetic face as I greeted my brother-in-law. 'She'll be gone soon, Eddie, and then you can ship in as much oxygen-giving greenery as you like.'

'I'm sure he won't,' retorted Mum.

'Perhaps I'll have a mixture,' said Eddie diplomatically. 'How are you, Imogen?' He regarded me anxiously.

Knowing this wasn't just a social enquiry I gave a wan smile back. 'I've got a bit of a twinge, actually, Eddie. Right in the small of my back.' I gave it a rub.

Hypochondriacs, in my experience, fell into two camps. There were those who hated other people to be ill because it stole their thunder, and those who liked it on the grounds that if someone else had got something, statistically it reduced the chances of them getting it. Eddie fell into the latter category, and his day was made if you admitted to an ailment, so long as it wasn't catching.

150

'I find a little rubbing oil helps enormously,' he advised eagerly. 'And you're probably lying on much too soft a mattress. My mother suffered terribly from back pain, but a hard mattress really sorted her out.'

'It would take more than a hard mattress to sort your mother out,' remarked Hannah drily.

'How is your mother?' I asked, ignoring my sister.

Eddie's brow wrinkled. 'She's been falling over a lot lately. I'm rather worried about her. I'm thinking of getting her one of those bleeper things, you know, an alarm.'

'Oh, yes, I know. To put round your neck.'

'Like a noose?' murmured Hannah wistfully.

Eddie didn't rise. 'Come on, let's go to the pub. That's the plan, isn't it?'

'Ooh, yes.' Mum quickly stubbed her cigarette out and went hastily down the slippery mud bank.

'Why so keen?' I asked, eyeing her suspiciously. Mum liked a drink or six but much preferred a smart wine bar to a country pub.

'Your father's going to be there,' she confided, 'and he's bringing Dawn. You haven't met Dawn, have you?'

'Er, no.'

'Oh, she's marvellous, Imogen,' she breathed, taking my arm as I fell in step beside her. 'Your father met her in Curry's—she was senior sales assistant on washing machines and tumble dryers—but he's taken her away from all that, and now she wants to be a doctor.'

'Oh, right. Is she bright?'

'Breathtakingly stupid,' she chortled. 'Isn't it priceless? She's going to specialise in neurology,

151

apparently, and her mother—ooh, you must meet the mother.' She lit another cigarette, eyes sparkling.

'Must I?' I said nervously.

'Yes, they come as a package. Dawn never goes anywhere without her mother, a huge woman in a purple coat, who just sits, solidly, for hours on end without saying a word. She looks like Stephen Fry in drag. No one can remember her name, not even your father, and he's known her for three months so now it's too late to ask. Oh, they're terrific, darling.'

'Great,' I said uncomfortably as Hannah caught my eye.

It was marvellous that Mum could be so relaxed about Dad's girlfriends, and lovely that we could all still get together as a family, but the delight Mum took in her ex-husband making a fool of himself was sometimes discomforting. She hadn't always been so phlegmatic about his love life. When Dad had first gone off with Marjorie Ryan, a great family friend who used to share a house with us in France, and whom Mum had modelled Dior gowns with in the sixties, she was devastated. 'Heartbroken?' Kate had asked me once when I was telling her all about it. I'd hesitated. No, but then that wasn't Mum's style. She didn't shatter easily. Didn't crumble. I think she'd been relieved when he'd moved on to Audrey, a rather dumpy marketing executive with dozens of cats and none of Marjorie's style, had perked up tremendously when Audrey had been traded in for Michelle, a peroxide-blonde hygienist, and was positively enchanted by Dawn, the shelf-stacking embryonic neurosurgeon.

152

'She's obviously quite tough,' Kate had commented, and I suppose she was. I'd certainly never seen her cry. Her parents, my grandparents, had been killed in a car crash when she was four, and she'd been brought up by her godmother, a rather remote figure who bred Border Terriers in Northumberland. I think Mum—when she was allowed home from boarding school—was treated like one of the puppies; fed and watered, but otherwise expected to get on with it. As a result, she'd grown an extra layer of skin that was quite hard to penetrate. Conversely, though, she was very loving, and Hannah and I had enjoyed an idyllic childhood with plenty of nurturing and cuddles, a far cry from her own upbringing, and, one suspects, deliberately so.

As we all trooped off to the pub at the end of the road I watched her leading the way, supremely elegant in her floaty linen coat and long, aquamarine silk scarf, genuinely thrilled to be getting another peek at Dawn. I wished I'd inherited a few more of her genes; wished I wasn't so easily upset. I straightened my back as I held Rufus's hand along the busy road and resolved to be more like her.

We passed Hannah's local, an attractive whitewashed pub with leaded windows and lots of hanging baskets, and went on to a rather forbidding red-brick place called the Royal Oak. A couple of tough-looking teenagers were standing outside, smoking.

'Why are we going here?'

Hannah shrugged. 'Dad suggested it. God knows why. It's a dive.'

Happily it had a garden, albeit practically in the

car park, and we limbo-danced around the dustbins and beer barrels to get to it. Dad was already in situ, having commandeered a large wobbly table with benches and a brolly, and sure enough, beside him was a girl decidedly younger than me, I thought with a pang, and opposite her, a woman in a purple coat.

'Imogen darling,' boomed my father in his best John Gielgud voice, which is nothing like his native Welsh one, as he stood up to greet us. 'How simply wonderful.' He kissed us all, including Mum, and pumped Eddie's hand. 'Now, I don't think you've met Dawn yet, have you?'

'No, I haven't,' I agreed, smiling as I shook hands with the pasty-faced girl with too much eye make-up and artificially straightened dark hair.

'Hello.'

'Hi,' she muttered, avoiding my eyes.

'And her mother . . .' went on Dad, 'er . . .' He gestured hopelessly. I put out my hand but Dawn's mother was either consumed with shyness or hadn't heard. She clutched her handbag grimly and gazed past me, making no attempt to take my hand.

Dad rubbed his hands. 'Er, right. Now. Drinks, everyone?'

'I'll do it,' Eddie offered.

'Right you are, lad.' Dad beamed and sat down smartly, notoriously tight.

My father had been considered rather good-looking in his day: his piercing blue eyes and high cheekbones were quite startling, and he had a lot of dark hair, which Hannah and I were convinced he now dyed, but he was only about five foot eight and as such, suffered rather from small-man

154

syndrome. He never walked, always strutted importantly, head thrown back, very much the actor, sweeping his hair back from his brow and making grandiose, theatrical gestures with his hands. His acting career when we were young had mostly revolved around the theatre, but now it was more television-oriented he was becoming slightly better known. Recently he'd carved something of a niche for himself as the Attractive Older Man, and appeared regularly in a hospital soap opera, as well as having the odd cameo role in period dramas. Increasingly, Alex and I would be having supper, trays on our laps in front of the telly, and Alex would cry, 'There's your old man!' as Dad, hand on hip, would swagger into view in a powdered wig and gaiters, or sweep round a hospital corridor, white coat flying. He was always delivering lines like, 'I'm sorry, Mrs Brown, I'm afraid it's terminal,' whilst a dewy-eyed nurse looked on adoringly, or, 'Quick, man, saddle the horses!' as he swept out of a manor house in breeches. Sometimes he simply forgot he wasn't on screen and swaggered down Winslow High Street, where he'd recently bought a little terraced cottage, in much the same way. As he got up now to help Eddie with the tray, it seemed to me he swept an imaginary cloak over his shoulder first.

'How about some crisps, laddie?' he boomed.

'Oh, sorry, Martin, I'll get some.'

'No, no, these are on me,' Dad said loudly, brushing him aside and striding ostentatiously to the bar as if he were making some extravagant gesture. When Eddie had sat down and Dad was out of earshot, Mum turned innocent eyes on Dawn.

155

'I gather you're going to be a doctor?'

If Dawn found it odd to be lunching with her boyfriend's ex-wife she didn't show it. She sipped her Baileys nonchalantly and stared opaquely at Mum.

'Yeah, well, I was, only I can't now 'cos I haven't got biology GCSE, and the fing is they say you need that to go on to the next bit.'

Mum's brow puckered. 'Oh, what a shame. How very demanding of them. But then I suppose, if one is cutting people up, one should know the basics . . . ?'

'Yeah, I suppose, but the fing is it would take too long for me to do it now.'

'So what are you going to do instead?'

'I'm gonna be a beautician. Gonna go to college an' that. And I'm still helping people, aren't I? I reckon it's still health care?'

'Oh, very definitely,' Mum purred. 'In fact the girl who does my nails wears a white coat, which says a lot, doesn't it?'

'Yeah,' Dawn brightened. 'Yeah, it does.'

'I'd hazard you could even have a watch too.'

'Watch?'

'Yes, you know, hanging out of your top pocket.'

'Oh. Yeah!' Dawn looked enchanted and Mum winked at me but I ignored her, uncomfortable. When her sarcasm had been directed at Marjorie, an aspiring interior designer whose only work experience had been tarting up her own home in Fulham at vast expense in Colefax and Fowler, Hannah and I had chortled along with her, but Dawn was a bit of a soft target. I turned to the mother.

'That'll be handy then,' I smiled. 'Having a

156

beautician in the family.'

Even as I said it, I knew it was a mistake. She retreated back into her many chins and regarded me blankly. 'I mean,' I stumbled on, 'for leg waxes and things.'

'Mum doesn't really go in for that sort of fing,' said Dawn.

My own mother was trying to catch my eye, and I just knew she was trying to direct my gaze to the luxuriant growth sprouting beneath Purple Coat's fifty deniers. Luckily Dad came back with the crisps.

'That's what I like to see,' he said, tossing them on the table and rubbing his hands together as he sat down, 'all my family around the same table together—marvellous. Cheers! God bless us all.' He raised his pint and beamed around, and actually, you couldn't help but smile back.

'Cheers, Dad.'

Yes, as dysfunctional families go, I thought as I sipped my lager, ours didn't do badly. All thanks to Mum, of course, who kept us steadfastly together, and actually, who could blame her her occasional digs at Dawn when she managed to put her feelings aside to ensure her family always spent the odd weekend and Christmas and Easter together? But then, as Hannah had once remarked, it was precisely *because* she had no feelings for Dad that she was able to do it. She'd moved on, she didn't love him any more, and although I sometimes wished there could be someone in her life, she didn't appear to need anyone. In fact, when I'd tentatively raised the subject, she'd shuddered.

'What, go back to running around after a man again? All that cooking and socialising and wondering if we owe the Fergusons—no, thank you. I'm much too selfish, darling.'

She wasn't, actually; was generous to a fault, but she'd learned how to look after number one. Life was on her terms now, and she was comfortable with it.

'Have you seen Dad's shoes?' Hannah murmured in my ear.

I nodded. The white Gucci loafers with elaborate tassels hadn't escaped me.

'And the black leather jacket,' I muttered back.

'Well, what do you expect from a middle-aged man with a twenty-six-year-old girlfriend?'

'Twenty-six!'

'Apparently. One of the mothers at school told me. She knew Dawn when she was . . . oh God, he's not.'

'Not what?'

Hannah swung round. I followed her eyes. Dad and Dawn had got up from the table, and Dawn, her arm linked through Dad's, was leading him away conspiratorially, up the garden path.

'They have karaoke hour at lunch time sometimes in this pub, and I've got an awful feeling that's why they wanted to—'

'Oi, listen, you lot.' Dawn turned back importantly. 'Martin's gonna sing "Love Me Tender" in the saloon bar if you wanna watch, and I'm doin' "Stand by Your Man"!'

Mum's face was a picture. 'Wouldn't miss it for the world,' she breathed, stubbing out her cigarette and getting hastily to her feet. Dad and Dawn were already halfway up the garden now, Dad's head thrown right back, his hand trailing behind his tight-bottomed jeans as he minced away in a rather

158

camp fashion.

'Mum,' Hannah shot out a restraining hand and grabbed her arm. 'He makes a complete tit of himself,' she hissed. 'Our neighbour was in here the other day and saw him do it, and Dawn's tone deaf.'

'*Is* she?' Mum's eyes widened. 'Oh, what heaven. Come on, Rufus, quick, before we miss it.'

'Mum, d'you really think Rufus should—' But he'd scampered off before I could even finish, without giving me a backward look.

'Consider it part of his education,' said Hannah, drily. 'The first time he saw his grandfather on stage. A defining moment.' She got up.

'You're not going too?' I said, appalled.

'No, I'm all through with being defined by Dad. More prosaically, I need a pee.'

She squeezed with difficulty between the bench and the table and made her way heavily up the garden path. Eddie and I watched her go.

'Eddie . . .'

'Yes, I know,' he said quickly. 'She's put on weight.'

'*Lots* of weight, Eddie,' I turned to face him. 'Why?'

He shrugged miserably. 'I don't know. She just doesn't seem to be able to stop eating, and when I ask her if she's unhappy, she snaps—no, just hungry. She's touchy about it, Imogen. I can't talk to her any more.'

'What—about anything?'

He hesitated. 'This weight thing *is* everything, as far as she's concerned. And I know she's eating for a reason, but . . .' he trailed off miserably.

'But the two of you are fine? I mean, as a

159

couple?'

'Oh, yes, couldn't be happier. It's just,' he hesitated. 'Well, I know she feels there's something missing.'

'Eddie . . .' I licked my lips. 'Have you thought of adopting?'

He looked at me. 'We went down that route a year ago.'

'Did you?' I was astonished.

'Yes, didn't she tell you?'

'No. She didn't.' I felt hurt.

He shrugged. 'She didn't want to tell anyone at the time in case people got their hopes up for us. And then—well, then when we got turned down, she didn't really want to talk about it.'

I swallowed. 'Why did they . . . ?'

'Turn us down? Oh, you know. Our combined ages, the state of the house, Hannah apparently being medically obese, that kind of thing. It was all there in a charming letter sent back from the authorities.' He sighed. 'No. Evidently only young, slim, tidy couples can adopt babies, no matter how much love you've got inside to give. It's the outside that counts.'

I was silent. She'd gone down that route and been rejected. I couldn't even begin to imagine how that must hurt.

Eddie shifted in his seat, a regrouping gesture. 'But as I say, that was a year ago. She's over the disappointment now, and we've accepted it. It was our last hope, and now that it's gone we've got some sort of closure. The baby business is over as far as we're concerned. We'll never have them. Or she'll never have them. And that's the problem, Imo. As a man, I can sort of accept it. But I know

160

she feels unfulfilled.'

'But having children isn't everything. I mean— she has such a full life! She's a wonderful teacher, all her kids adore her, and all that Sea Scouts and Brownies and youth club and everything—she never stops. And at home, always baking and cooking and—'

'But that's just it. She never stops. Never stops to pause for thought. It's almost as if she daren't, because the sadness would overwhelm her. She's got to be busy.'

I swallowed. 'She's grieving, Eddie. It's a phase, but she has to go through it. It'll pass.'

'I know.' He nodded sadly. We were silent for a moment. Then he straightened up beside me on the bench. 'I thought we might get a cat.'

'Oh!'

'You don't think that's a good idea?' He looked at me anxiously.

'No, it might be. It's just the way you said it. Like—instead of.'

He shrugged. 'Well, in a way it would be. And I'd prefer a dog, but what with both of us working . . . I thought Rufus would like a kitten too.'

I smiled. It was typical of Eddie to think of Rufus. 'He'd love it,' I said warmly.

He nodded, pleased.

'Come on,' I said, before his mood could dampen again. I got to my feet and pulled him up with me. 'We're missing the cabaret.'

\*         \*         \*

Inside, the pub was heaving. Even in the garden we could hear the music from *Grease* being belted out

161

of a sound system with a throbbing base, and as I walked down the passage towards the saloon bar I recognised my father's tones booming out 'You're the One that I Want!' at full volume. It was still something of a shock, however, when I pushed through the smoky glass door.

Up on a makeshift stage at the far end of the room, my father, a.k.a. John Travolta, was on his knees and leaning back, the collar of his leather jacket turned up, as Dawn, a.k.a. Olivia Newton-John, stood astride him, hands on hips as she ooh, ooh, ooh, honeyed, down. The room was full of people urging them on with my mother and Rufus at the front, convulsed with laughter. Hannah appeared at my elbow from the Ladies, looking horrified.

'This is practically my local,' she yelled in my ear. 'What is he *thinking* of?'

'Well, it's my local too now, so let's get him off after this.'

The song ended on a rousing note and Dawn leaped into Dad's arms with a flourish as they took their applause. Dawn was helped off the stage by admiring hands, but as Dad was about to step down too, the opening chords of 'Brown Sugar' struck up. His face registered a flash of recognition and in another moment, he'd resisted Eddie's outstretched hand of help and scrambled back on stage. Suddenly his leather jacket was shrugged halfway down his back, his pert bottom thrust out, lips pursed like a gorilla—and he'd morphed into Mick Jagger, strutting about and punching the air aggressively.

Hannah moaned low. 'Tell me it's a bad dream.'

'I wish.'

'Someone pull the plug!' she wailed.

But Dad was unstoppable. The crowd loved him and wouldn't let him go, clapping along, joining in the chorus, and breaking into raucous applause at the end, yelling, 'More—*more!*'—Mum and Rufus the most vocal. Mum even put two fingers in her mouth and executed a wolf whistle. By now, Dad was on a roll, but as the opening chords of 'Satisfaction' struck up and he strutted about complaining he couldn't get no—*no no no!* Hannah and I looked at each another determinedly. As one, we hustled to the front, elbowing our way forwards. We saw 'Satisfaction' through to the bitter end, but before the mournful opening chords of 'Angie' had even struck up—we seemed to be stuck in something of a Rolling Stones medley here—we'd formed a pincer movement, and like a couple of bouncers, had bustled on to the stage and hustled him bodily off the other side, Hannah taking his microphone away as if he were a naughty child.

'But I was going to do "Don't Go Breaking My Heart" next,' Dad complained.

'You'd have broken mine if you had,' Hannah said crisply as we marched him out.

'We do that as a duet,' Dawn informed us, tottering after us in her high heels. 'Goes down a storm.'

'I think let the others have a chance, hmm?' I cajoled with a sweet smile, wondering exactly who the parent was here as Dad sulked all the way back to the table in the garden, slumping down on the bench with crossed arms.

Mum and Rufus followed us, Mum sinking weakly into her chair, mascara streaked down her face where she'd cried with laughter, Rufus still giggling uncontrollably.

'Did you enjoy that, lad?' Dad ruffled his hair, perking up a bit.

'You were awesome, Grandpa,' Rufus assured him, hiccuping.

Dad beamed. 'It's all in the timing, lad, you see. All in the timing. Now, another drink? Do the honours, Eddie, there's a good chap.' He put an arm round Dawn's waist and pulled her towards him on the bench crooning 'Don't Go Breaking My Heart' into her ear whilst taking little pecks at her shoulder.

'No, thanks, Dad,' said Hannah firmly as she and I gathered up coats and bags and put the glasses back on the tray. 'I think we'll get off home. I've got some cakes in the oven.' We glanced around, keen to go, but there was no sign of Dawn's mother.

'Perhaps she went back inside and we missed her? I'll go in and take a look,' suggested Mum, and I blessed her for that. Whatever she might think of Dad's domestic arrangements, she was too well-mannered just to slip away and tell Dad to say goodbye for us. When she reappeared two minutes later, her eyes were like dinner plates.

'Come and look at this!' she urged from the pub doorway.

We dutifully hastened back, and when she'd ushered us excitedly down the passage and back into the smoky saloon bar, our jaws dropped. There, on stage, in a red spangly dress that had clearly been under the coat the whole time, was Dawn's mum, standing under a spotlight, singing Barbra Streisand's 'Evergreen'. Our jaws

164

slackened even further as we listened, spellbound, to the tones of pure gold that rang out. The whole bar stood in awe-struck silence, and when she'd finished and the final wistful note drifted beautifully away over our heads, there was a moment's silence—then everyone broke into spontaneous and enthusiastic applause. Dawn beamed and clapped the hardest.

'She used to be an opera singer,' she shouted over the din, 'but she gave it all up after she had me. Good, i'nt she?'

We all agreed that she certainly was, and as I said to Rufus on the way home later that afternoon, it just went to show, that you should never judge a book by its cover.

'Or even,' he added sagely, 'by its purple coat.'

## CHAPTER TEN

When Rufus and I got back to the cottage there was a reception committee waiting for us. The chickens, seeing our car draw up, left whatever they'd been pecking in the yard, and rushed up in an enthusiastic gang. Rufus and I peered from the car windows in alarm.

'Why do they do that?' Rufus whispered.

'They're just . . . terribly tame, darling. They've come to greet us.'

'Oh. I don't really like it when they chase me, though, Mum. Can I have a piggyback?'

I swallowed, looking at the squawking, clucking squad that had surrounded the car with their fierce, beady eyes. I'd quite like a piggyback myself.

'Right. Climb on my back then.' He clambered across the front seat and put his arms round my neck as I opened the driver's door. Gingerly I put one foot out. 'Off we . . . go!'

With Rufus bouncing around on my back I sprinted across the yard and up the front path as fast as I could. Chickens can run jolly fast, though, and as I ferreted feverishly in my bag for my key, they swarmed around my legs, pushing and shoving. Hadn't they got a coop to go to, I thought in panic as feathers and—ugh—*beaks*—brushed my legs. I was all for free range, but they'd be in the house soon if— 'Oi!' One large mother-clucker put her head down and steamed through the gap before I could stop her.

'No! Out!' I grabbed a cushion from a chair and shooed her out as Rufus hid behind the door. When she'd gone, we clutched each other.

'I don't like that, Mummy. I don't like that they're so tame they want to come in.'

'No, I'm not wild about it either,' I admitted. 'They'll be sitting up in bed with us soon.' I dropped the cushion and gazed around. 'Oh, but, Rufus, look at *this*!'

'Cool,' he agreed.

Vera and her team had worked wonders. The wooden floorboards shone like a ship's deck, and bright, jewel-coloured rugs had been put down to cover the knotty bits. The windows gleamed, and through them, the fields, green and pleasant, shone back. The few sticks of furniture we'd originally been allocated had been replaced with basic, but much more comfortable sofas and chairs in a cheerful floral pattern. Pretty green checked

166

curtains hung at the windows, and upstairs, all our linen had been unpacked, the beds made, and our clothes hung up in wardrobes.

'Golly,' I spun around in wonder as I came back down. 'Mary Poppins has been in.'

Rufus's eyes were huge. '*Has* she?'

I laughed. 'No, but you'd think so, wouldn't you? And look at this.' A huge bunch of flowers sat in a blue and white striped jug on the kitchen table, and next to it, a bowl of fruit with a note. I picked it up.

Dear Imogen,

There's milk and eggs in the fridge and a pile of logs outside should you need a fire. The chimney's been swept so it *should* work! Hope everything is OK. *So* sorry you saw it in such a state yesterday.

Love, Eleanor

'How kind,' I murmured. 'She must have brought the fruit and flowers down herself.'

'It does look amazing, doesn't it, Mummy?' said Rufus anxiously, jumping on a sofa and bouncing. I could tell he wanted me to be pleased, not the complaining, carping mother of yesterday. 'It's very kind of Eleanor and Piers, isn't it?'

'Very,' I smiled. 'And it looks fantastic. And actually, Rufus, I think we're going to have a lovely time here.'

'But where will you paint?' His brow puckered up as he stopped bouncing. 'You haven't got a room like you had at home.'

'Well, I can paint in here.' I sat down at the little table under the window. 'Not oils—too smelly and messy—but I can do watercolours. You know, try

167

some book illustrations, like I've always meant to do. I'll get a sketch pad.'

'Yes, and draw the lambs and stuff! Look, you can see them from the window.'

I smiled. So I could. And I liked the sheep. They dotted the green hillside attractively, like bits of cotton wool; all sort of pastoral and calming. They kept their distance too. If only the cows could be encouraged to do the same, but the cows were lining up even now in a rather alarming manner at the gate, mooing horribly. Were they supposed to do that? All day? They'd been doing it when we'd left this morning—surely they'd need to do some grazing now and again, stop shouting at me? They didn't seem to have grasped the concept of personal space.

I moved around the cottage, familiarising myself with it, opening cupboards, marvelling at all our china stacked neatly on shelves, all the cutlery in drawers. They'd even put our crystal glasses in a hanging corner cupboard in the sitting room. I was touched. And all under Eleanor's instruction, no doubt. I wondered, rather guiltily, if I'd got it all wrong. If she really did just want to help, and for us to be happy? I remembered her worried face and twisting hands this morning—'I would so love us to be friends'—and how I'd snubbed her. I went upstairs. From the landing window I could see that the grass around the cottage had been mown, and that the manure heap in the yard had miraculously re-located to a corner of a far field. In Rufus's room, all his soldiers were lined up on shelves in his bedroom, his slippers under his bed. Part of me wondered if I'd have liked to have done that, but most of me was jolly grateful. On an impulse, I went back down and picked up the phone. Eleanor had thoughtfully put a list of numbers by it—her own private line, the doctor, farmer, vet—and I dialled her number.

'Hello?'

'Eleanor, it's Imogen. Listen, thank you so much. We've just got back here and I can't tell you how pretty the cottage looks. Vera and her girls have done a brilliant job.'

'You like it?' I could almost feel her flush with pleasure at the other end. 'Oh, Imogen, I'm *so* pleased. I was a bit worried you'd think they'd gone too far, unpacking all your stuff, but otherwise you'd have come in to piles of suitcases and—'

'It's perfect,' I said, cutting her short. 'Honestly, Eleanor, you've saved me a backbreaking day tomorrow. The whole place looks fab, and wonderful views now that you can see them!'

She laughed. 'Apparently they had to hose the windows down, they were so filthy. Oh, good, I'm so glad you're pleased. I took the liberty of choosing the sofas for you from Piers's mother's barn—it was much the best stuff—and if you want to light a fire—'

'The logs are out the back. I saw your note. And thank you for the fruit and flowers.'

'My pleasure,' she said happily. 'I was wondering if you'd like a kitchen supper with us tonight? Only yesterday was a bit like Piccadilly Circus here; we hardly got to speak to you.'

I hesitated. I quite wanted a quiet supper down here on our first night, but didn't want to appear rude.

'That's really kind. Tell you what, can I ask Alex

169

when he comes in? I'm not sure how bushed he'll be after the commute. I'll give you a ring later, if I may?'

'Oh, but he's here now. I'll ask him, shall I?'

I paused. 'Sorry?'

'Yes, he's around somewhere, hang on—ALEX!' she called.

My heart began to pound. He'd gone straight to her house on returning from work? Hadn't even bothered to come to the cottage first? Was this to be a pattern? He came on the line.

'Hello, darling, had a good day?'

'Alex, what are you doing there?'

'What d'you mean, what am I doing here?'

'Well, why didn't you come back here from work?'

'Oh, I haven't been to work, darling.'

'What?'

'No, I didn't go in the end, because by the time Piers and I got back from walking around the farm, it was nearly midday. Simply wasn't worth it. Piers had a meeting to go to, but Eleanor and I went to a really nice bistro in town. Apparently you were invited.'

I couldn't speak I was so angry.

'Why didn't you come and have lunch with Hannah and Eddie?' I hissed eventually. 'With us!'

'I tried,' he said patiently, 'but there was no answer from their house, and your phone was switched off.'

'You could have tried the pub! You might have known we were in the pub!'

'I did, actually. Eleanor and I stopped at that pretty whitewashed one with the hanging baskets, but there was no sign. I'm sorry, darling. I did my

170

best.'

I had to sit down I was so furious. I massaged my brow feverishly with my fingertips. Shut my eyes tight. 'Right,' I said quietly. 'Right. OK. Fine. You're coming home now, I take it?'

'Well, Eleanor's asked us for kitchen supps. They've got a brace of pheasants from the freezer so—'

'COME HOME NOW AND FUCK THE PHEASANT!'

There was a long silence.

'Right,' he said eventually. 'I won't do the latter, if it's all the same to you, but I'll be back shortly.'

The line went dead. I sank back in the kitchen chair, arms hanging limply, the phone dangling in my hand. I'd behaved like a crazy woman. A mad, unhinged, deranged woman. And I imagined the scene unfolding now, in the Latimers' kitchen: Eleanor, wide-eyed, whilst Alex, replacing the receiver carefully, explained that I was a bit . . . overwrought. A bit tired, perhaps, from the move. It had been a trying time, and—and maybe we'd have a quiet night in. Eleanor would be nodding, pretending to understand, making sympathetic noises about how she'd feel just the same, about how stressful moving was, or—or maybe, I thought suddenly, they'd just smile secretly at each other. Shrug, as in, oh, well, at least she's getting the message, before falling into each other's arms and kissing the life out of each other, his hand shooting up her skirt. My hands flew to my mouth. My lips felt very dry. Was I going mad? Were they deliberately sending me mad, were they having a steaming, torrid affair, or was it all in my mind? Was this an Othello-Desdemona-type thing, this

171

jealousy of mine, all of my making? I tried to remember the play from school. There hadn't been anything in it in the end, had there? And didn't he end up killing her, or something? Oh God. I moaned and lowered my forehead slowly to the table. Had I overreacted, as usual? I eyeballed the pine. Yes, of course I had. I'd behaved appallingly. She was an old family friend, who was simply trying to help us through a financial hiccup, and here I was, behaving like a . . . like a . . .

I was aware of a rustle behind me. I turned. A little white face was watching me through the banisters.

'Are you all right, Mummy?'

'Yes, love. I'm fine.'

'Is . . . Daddy coming home?'

'Yes. Yes, he is. Very soon.'

Rufus nodded and crept back upstairs.

I rubbed my forehead again, ferociously, with my fingertips. This was not good. Not good for Rufus. Not good at all. I got up and walked to the window, arms wrapped tightly around me.

And anyway, I thought staring out, aware that I was trembling slightly, what if I did ask him if there was anything going on and he said—yes? Yes, there is. I am. What then? Would I leave him? Would I walk out? My breathing became shallower. In my darkest moments I'd asked myself that question before, and the awful truth was, I knew I wouldn't. Knew that deep in the craven depths of my soul, the answer was no. I loved him too much. I'd never leave him. I stared into the empty fire grate.

Ten minutes later the front door slammed. Alex strode in, his face suffused with barely controlled rage. A muscle was going in his cheek.

172

'This is how you repay them.' He swept his hand around the room, his voice trembling. 'For all this. This cottage, this hospitality, this—this *kind*ness, which they don't have to do, but have done, out of the goodness of their hearts—this, this rudeness! This jealousy! *This* is how you thank them!'

I hung my head. 'I'm sorry,' I whispered.

'I had to make something up. Tell them you were ill, that the move had been too traumatic for you, that you missed your friends—anything. They both heard you screaming on the other end of the phone—thought you were barking!'

'Piers was there too?'

'Yes, of course he was, jointing the bloody pheasants!'

Right. So he hadn't been exchanging secret smiles with Eleanor and gathering her into his arms when he'd put the phone down.

'I'll apologise,' I promised. 'Tomorrow. I'll go and see them, tell them I was overtired.'

'Yes, well, don't make a meal of it,' he snapped, raking his hands through his hair as he went to the window. 'Forget it now. But just . . . get a grip, Imo, OK?' He swung round, looked at me pleadingly. Desperately, almost.

'OK.' I nodded, knowing I was about to cry.

I gazed dumbly at him, not trusting myself to speak, and after a moment, his face changed. His anger seemed to dissipate and he just looked tired. Defeated. His shoulders sagged. I took a step, uncertainly. He opened his arms and I walked into them. Clung on.

'I love you, Imo, you know that, don't you?' he whispered.

I nodded, tears streaming down my face as I

gazed into his blue jumper. 'I love you too.'

*     *     *

The following morning, when Alex had gone to work, I rang Kate.

'Oh, hello, stranger!'

I laughed. 'Don't be ridiculous, I've only been gone a day. Anyway, I rang you yesterday and you weren't there.'

'Out at a rehearsal, probably. Busying myself, you see, trying not to notice my mate across the road has gone and that some strange people are moving into her house.'

'Already? Golly, how weird.'

I didn't want to think about it. Didn't want to imagine them in my house, moving round my blue and white kitchen, touching the slate work surfaces, admiring the pretty, Provençal tiles, realising the cutlery drawer stuck and the blind over the sink didn't work. But actually, how much worse for Kate, who was watching it all. At least I couldn't see them and had other distractions.

'So how's it going?' she asked.

'Oh, Kate, it's great,' I enthused, determined to be upbeat; to support Alex in this decision, as, lying in each other's arms last night, we'd agreed was so important.

'I know it's difficult, Imo,' he'd said stroking my hair, 'but we must put on a good show. God knows, no one wants to downscale, no one wants to be helped out by friends, but let's at least put a brave face on it, eh?'

I'd felt so ashamed. But I'd glowed inside too. For the second time in two days we'd made love.

174

That was unheard of in London. Perhaps getting away from it all was making a difference. Well, if this was the result, I was all for it.

'Really? You're enjoying it?' said Kate in surprise. 'I thought it was all cowpats and yokels.'

'Well, obviously there *are* cowpats, and some of the yokels do take a bit of laughing off, but the countryside is glorious. Even as a fully paid-up, card-carrying urbanite I can appreciate that. Right now, for instance, just from my kitchen window I can see—'

'No, no, don't describe it,' she moaned. 'I beg you. What—baby lambs gambolling in clover, their mothers grazing peacefully beside them as the first swallow sweeps overhead and roosts in your gables? Go on then, make me puke.'

'Something like that,' I admitted, 'although I have to say, it's a lot noisier than I imagined. The lambs bleat all night—and the cows! They bellow, Kate, really bellow. Not to mention the racket the chickens make.'

'Probably hungry,' she observed. 'Animals tend to make themselves heard if they want something. And what about wicked Queen Eleanor in her castle on the hill? Still casting spells from her ivory tower?'

'Actually she's been terribly kind,' I said loyally. 'She's provided us with a heavenly cottage, and yesterday, had it cleaned from top to bottom and left flowers and a basket of fruit for us.'

'Nice rosy apples?'

'Yes, why?'

'Don't touch them, Imogen. Think of poor Sleeping Beauty. She ended up flat on her back for a hundred years. You need to keep your eyes wide open down there.'

I laughed. 'I've decided I've got that all out of proportion. I've allowed Eleanor to become some sort of monster in my mind—ridiculous. How's the play going, incidentally?' I deliberately changed the subject. 'Don't the Chelsea Players usually do a Shakespeare thingy at this time of year?'

She groaned. 'They do. And the answer is— slowly. The director has got some idiotic notion that we should play it in modern dress. *As You Like It* has an awful lot of thigh slapping in it, and it isn't quite the same when you're slapping your jeans instead of your doublet and hose. I think I'm pretty dire too,' she said gloomily. 'Still,' she brightened, 'it's only am-dram. I don't suppose *Time Out* will be in the front row.'

'I'm sure you'll be terrific.'

'I doubt it. How's Rufus?'

'Fine.' I lowered my voice. 'Well, no, a bit nervous actually, Kate. He starts school tomorrow and he's a bit—you know—worried. We went to look at it yesterday.'

A major mistake, on my part, as it turned out. We'd cruised past it on the way back from Hannah's, and in a fit of enthusiasm, I'd stopped the car.

'Isn't it pretty?' I'd gushed as we'd drawn up outside a little brick and flint school house with a clock tower. 'Look, it's got dear little leaded lights at the windows.'

'I don't think that's the school, Mummy. All the children are coming out of that building over there.'

He'd pointed to some modern Portakabins beyond, where, sure enough, hordes of noisy

176

children in red and grey uniform were running into a playground. We'd obviously hit break time.

'Oh. Right. Well, let's wander over there, shall we?'

'No, Mum.'

'Come on. Just for a moment.'

'It'll look weird.'

'Nonsense.'

We got out and I walked breezily up to the railings, Rufus trailing behind. I reached back and took his hand, pulling him with me. We watched as various games of skipping and football unfurled.

'Lovely!' I smiled.

Rufus dropped my hand as the football came towards us and bounced over the low railings. As a shaven-headed boy ran to get it, I picked it up and smiled.

'Oi! Gimmie that!'

I threw it back over. 'I was about to!' I said chummily. 'Catch!'

He caught it and glared at me. 'Tosser.'

He ran back to his game.

'What's a tosser?' asked Rufus, when he was out of earshot.

'It's someone who . . . tosses the ball back,' I said faintly. 'In a ball game.'

'Oh.'

We walked back to the car and got in silently. My hands felt rather clammy as I fumbled for the ignition and I wondered, nervously, if all the boys were like that. They all seemed to have skinhead-style haircuts; looked rather rough. Well, maybe the girls then. I glanced back at the playground and swallowed. Right. So what if they had pierced ears and were all chewing gum? I really mustn't be

177

such a snob. It was fine, he'd love it. It was just a bit more . . . rough and tumble than he was used to, that's all. Terribly good for him, actually. Less precious.

'Mummy, what's that sign there for?'

'Well, what does it say?' I muttered, irritated now. I was trying to pull out, and as I looked in my rear-view mirror for traffic, I could see that boy again, showing off in the playground, bouncing the ball on his head and not letting the others get it.

'No shagging on the grass.'

My head spun round a hundred and eighty degrees.

'Playing,' I breathed. 'No playing on the grass. Someone's crossed out playing and graffitied over it.'

'Oh.'

We drove on in silence.

'Is shagging like playing, then?'

I licked my lips. 'Um, a bit. In a . . . more grown-up sort of way.'

'And did he like it?' demanded Kate down the phone, now.

'Quite,' I said cagily. 'It—you know—gave him a flavour, anyway.'

'Well, let me know how it goes. Orlando's going to start fencing next term, isn't that adorable? Apparently Peregrine's daddy's a bit of a star and he's going to give them lessons.'

'Lovely,' I said faintly, thinking that the only fencing Rufus would be doing at that school would be buying and selling stolen goods. I put the phone down and rang Hannah in a panic.

'No, no, it's a lovely school,' she chided. 'You've obviously just got a bad glimpse of it. It does very well in the league tables and I hear the children are delightful.'

'You hear? You mean you don't know any of them?'

'Well, one or two are in my Scout group, but not a lot because they mostly come from the private school in Highmore . . .'

'Right.'

'And yes, OK, they are quite noisy and boisterous, but they're little boys, Imo. They're hardly going to be sitting in huddles doing tapestry, are they?' She laughed and I tinkled along merrily; felt sick inside.

'And the headmaster's a real honey.'

'Is he?' I said eagerly, grasping at this like a drowning man to a float.

'Yes, the children love him. Quite strict, apparently, but very approachable. You always see them hanging round his legs. The mothers too.'

'Oh!'

'Well, he is rather gorgeous. I'm surprised you haven't heard. Quite the local heart-throb, and unattached too, so quite a lot of panting one way and another.'

'Well, I don't think Eleanor's endeared herself. When I spoke to him on the phone he was complaining about her dogs defecating in his playground.'

'Yes, well, I wouldn't imagine the Latimers are quite his type. He doesn't think much of the local nobs throwing their weight around, and Piers and Eleanor are inclined to do that. They recently asked if the School could take its lunch break inside for a few days because Piers was putting some pheasants down in a nearby field. Said the noise was disturbing them.'

'Good grief. How did that go down?'

'Like a cup of cold sick. Apparently the children were told to play a boisterous game of British Bulldog on that particular day, organised by the head himself. Daniel Hunter is not one to tug his forelock to local landowners with delusions of grandeur. Anyway, you'll meet him tomorrow. Apparently he always makes a point of greeting the new children. Has a little chat.'

'Right.'

Well, that sounded promising, anyway. Hannah was clearly rather taken with Mr Hunter; he'd obviously made her bleeding heart beat a little faster, and my sister was not easily charmed. Maybe he'd turn out to be Rufus's defender and champion, and all would be well. Maybe he'd recognise Rufus's leadership qualities and make him—I don't know—form captain, or something. And maybe all the other boys would look up to him. Time would tell, I thought gazing out of the window and watching Rufus run after a butterfly with a fishing net. I reached into the fruit bowl for an apple and took a bite out of it. It was sourer than one would have hoped.

## CHAPTER ELEVEN

The following day when I tried to take Rufus to school, we could scarcely get out of the house.

'Oh, this is ridiculous,' I spluttered as we opened the door to twenty, tight-beaked, beady-eyed hens, all jostling for position like very determined

Jehovah's Witnesses. 'Come on, darling, let's make a run for it.'

We legged it to the car, slammed the doors and roared off, scattering feathers, no doubt, in our wake.

'But where do they live, Mum?' asked Rufus, twisting in his seat and gazing out of the back window. 'I mean, where do they go at night?'

'Well, most chickens live in a pen but these are free range, so—God knows. Up in the trees, I expect.'

'Oh. Can they fly?'

'Of course they can fly. They've got wings, haven't they?'

I glanced at the clock. Christ, we were going to be late. First day, and we were going to be late. Alex had left early and forgotten to reset the alarm for us, so I'd woken, literally about twenty minutes ago, to the sound of birdsong and pale yellow light streaming through the thin, muslin curtains. We'd scrambled into our clothes and I'd poured some cereal into Rufus, but he was still swallowing his toast and Marmite beside me now in the car.

'So do they migrate?' he asked, wiping butter off his mouth.

'What?'

'You know, fly south in the winter like other birds?'

'Not sure,' I said absently, flicking on the radio for a time check. Come on Terry, less of the Irish charm. Half-past eight by my watch. Or was I fast? I was, sometimes.

'What, all the way to Africa?'

'What? No, of course they don't migrate. They stick around, stay on farms and things.'

'Like the robin.'

'Yes, I suppose.' I glanced in my mirror and raked a hand through my hair. 'Pass me my scent, Rufus. It's in my bag at your feet.'

'Oh, look, another lamb's been born!' Rufus dumped my bag on my lap and leaned out of his window as, sure enough, just as we'd witnessed yesterday, a tiny long-legged lamb was suckling its mother, its tail whisking the air.

'Just two minutes, Mummy—please! I want to see!'

I stopped, nervously chewing the inside of my cheek, one eye on my watch, one ear on Terry, as the ewe tenderly turned to nuzzle her baby, which was palpably only hours old but already standing squarely, albeit on wobbly legs. Alex, Rufus and I had seen the first lambs yesterday as we'd enjoyed an evening walk in the meadow and been amazed at their precociousness. Right now, though, we didn't have two minutes to be amazed.

'You'll see it this afternoon, Rufus,' I said shifting into first and accelerating brutally up the track. 'When you get home.'

'But I won't know which one it is!' He swung back.

'I'll remember,' I promised. 'The mother had a black face.'

'They've all got black faces,' he pointed out sulkily, twisting forward in his seat. 'We spotted that last night.'

Yes, last night, when Alex had finally returned from work after a bloody commute—'Two hours door to door,' he'd announced bitterly as he'd slung his briefcase on a chair. 'So much for an hour and ten minutes!'—we'd gone out into the fields,

182

the three of us, to try to remember what the hell we were doing here. We'd walked in silence for a bit, and I'd felt him seething quietly beside me; but the crab apple blossom was heavy on the boughs over our heads, and beneath it, the new lambs skipped around bleating in the lush spring grass. It would have taken a heart of stone not to succumb.

'Worth it?' I'd hazarded at length, looking up at my husband's profile beside me.

'Worth it,' he agreed, his face relaxing as he squeezed my hand. 'Sorry I was in such a foul mood earlier.'

We stopped to lean on a low, mossy stone wall and gazed into the misty blue yonder. Alex narrowed his eyes to the vista; a couple of fields away in the dip of the valley, a stream, clear and glistening, rushed on its way fringed by nodding buttercups, and beyond that, the hills rose up in a comforting swell, green and wholesome. He nodded. 'This is exactly what I wanted for us, Imo. What I envisaged. Just you, me and Rufus, far from the madding crowd. What could be better?' He'd bent his head to kiss me.

Something tight and clenched had unfurled within me, like a fern releasing its fronds and stretching out into the light.

'I honestly think that in time we might buy somewhere of our own down here, don't you?' he went on, hugging my shoulders. 'The cottage is fine for a bit, but in six months' time—well, who knows? It'll be so much cheaper than London.'

'Who knows,' I agreed blithely as he kissed me again. Oh, yes, I thought, hanging on to the wall for dear life, anything was possible if Alex was as loving as this. Anything.

Rufus had turned at that moment and wolf-whistled, and we'd laughed and strolled on, but the look of pleasure on my son's face hadn't escaped me. It couldn't be much fun, as a solitary nine-year-old, to have your parents yelling and screaming at each other as we'd done the night before. As Alex hoisted Rufus up on his shoulders and took my hand and we'd walked, the three of us, back to the cottage, I'd felt like we were a family in a cereal commercial, strolling in slow motion through a daisy-strewn meadow, shiny hair bouncing. That was yesterday, though, and right now, my hair lacked bounce and we had to get down to the village school pronto.

The children were all pouring in through the gates as we parked by the Spar—not too close—and made our way across the road, assisted by a smiling lollipop lady. Encouraging, I felt, as we exchanged a cheery good morning. Even though I'd been short of time I'd made a bit of an effort for Rufus's first day, throwing a little Armani jacket over my jeans and cowboy boots: a mistake, I now realised, as most of the other mothers looked like they'd just crawled out of bed. The bare legs, trainers and anorak look I'd spotted earlier abounded, and I felt horribly self-conscious in my London yummy-mummy kit. Had I overdone the scent? It had all been rather de rigueur in Putney, particularly on the first day—Kate always looked like she'd just stepped out of *Vogue*—but here, an overcoat over pyjamas seemed more the norm. One mother appeared to be giving her children—all five of them—bowls of cereal in the back of a rusty Honda, before bundling them out and giving them a swift clip round the ear for not

184

being quick enough. Secretly appalled but desperate to ingratiate myself I gave her a sympathetic smile as I passed. She glared back. I was also uncomfortably aware that Rufus appeared to be the only one wearing a blazer. Was uniform optional, I wondered.

To achieve the school gates we had to negotiate a clutch of mothers who'd clearly already dropped their children and gathered for a gossip. They stared at me with hostile eyes as I approached, jaws rotating as they masticated gum, looking rather like the cattle I'd just left behind. They made no effort to move.

'Excuse me, please,' I said pleasantly.

An overweight, pasty-faced girl nudged her companion and they parted for me grudgingly, ostentatiously moving buggies and kicking toddlers. 'Go on, move it, Darren.' They all had identical stripy blonde hair with black roots and were pierced liberally. They looked about eighteen. Rufus and I muttered our thanks, but we were both blushing and I could feel their eyes in our backs as we went through. Too much scent. Definitely too much scent.

'Do I go straight to my class?' asked Rufus nervously as we pushed through a swing door to a noisy corridor, thronging with children.

'No, we go and see the headmaster first. He's down the end on the right, apparently, but that must be your class,' I said, as we passed a glass door marked Year Five. 'Doesn't it look nice?'

It didn't, in fact. All hell was breaking loose as two boys at the back of the room stood on desks and lobbed books at some other boys below, who were flicking rubbers back efficiently with their rulers and goading them on. Elsewhere children were banging desk lids shut and shouting across the room at each other. There wasn't a teacher in sight.

Rufus went pale. I swallowed and hurried him down the corridor to the office at the bottom.

'Mr Hunter: Headmaster' it read in reassuring gold letters on the door. Well, that was something, surely? Someone was at the helm.

I knocked, and a clipped voice barked back, 'Yep?'

I pushed on through.

Mr Hunter's head was buried in some papers, but he raised it when he saw us. Smiled.

'Mrs Cameron?'

I nearly fainted with relief. At least someone was expecting us. 'That's it.'

'And you must be Rufus.' He came around the side of his desk, proffered his hand, and Rufus shook it. I relaxed. Good. This was more like it.

'It's lovely to have you here with us,' he told Rufus, bending down to his level. 'You're going to be in Year Five and I hope you'll be very happy at St John's.'

'Thank you,' whispered Rufus shyly.

'We, um, passed his classroom, actually.' I pointed tentatively back over my shoulder as Mr Hunter straightened up. 'But there didn't appear to be anyone . . . ?'

'Ah, no, Mrs Harding's on her way. She got struck in traffic, just called in. Sit down, sit down.' He waved us into seats as he went back and resumed his. We perched on chairs on the other side of his desk.

'No doubt you saw it in uproar then,' he grinned.

'But don't worry, in no time at all you won't hear a pin drop. Ah, look, here she is now.'

He swivelled around in his chair to face the window and I glanced out of it behind him. I half expected to see a grey-haired battleaxe emerge from her battered Escort, but instead, a red Mini performed an emergency stop under the window and a ravishing blonde in a short skirt and long black boots got out. She grinned up at the window.

'Mrs Harding doesn't take any nonsense,' he said as she slammed her car door.

I swallowed. I bet she doesn't.

'Neither does Mr Harding. He runs the PE department,' he went on as a tall, thick-set blond man got out of the passenger side and gave us a theatrical stagger, hand to brow, presumably referring to the traffic.

Mr Hunter turned back to me. 'Did you think I was running more of a zoo than a school, Mrs Cameron?'

'Oh, no,' I said, embarrassed. 'It's just—'

'It's not quite what you and Rufus are used to?'

'Sort of.'

He nodded. 'I understand. I used to teach at a very similar school to Rufus's. Not far from you actually, The Falcon, in Barnes.'

'Oh!' I was surprised. The Falcon was a very sweet school. 'So . . . how come—'

'I ended up head of a rural state school when I could still be in the cushy private sector?'

I blushed. Hannah was quite right. This man was devastatingly good-looking and had a very direct, engaging manner. Despite the slightly old-fogey corduroy jacket and the horn-rimmed spectacles, he had a head of springy tawny curls and a pair of

187

bright blue eyes, which were fixing me intently.

'I needed a change,' he said simply, swinging his feet up on the desk suddenly. 'Teaching well-behaved boys like Rufus,' he nodded at him sitting quietly in his chair, 'was a delightful pastime, but not terribly testing. It got to the stage when I could do it standing on my head. Running a school where discipline was a dirty word and the children pretty much ruled the roost was a little more challenging. It's been an uphill struggle and I've had to bring in some new blood to replace the tired old guard—a bit traumatic, as you can imagine—but it's worked. You'll be pleased to hear you're not joining us in the eye of the storm. The battle's been won. Ofsted have recommended us for commendation, this year.'

I smiled. 'I'm impressed.'

He grinned and scratched his head sheepishly. 'Sorry. Blowing my own trumpet. But it's the kids I'm proud of, not me. Having said that, I warn you, they're no angels. We've still got a few reprobates, and there's no controlling what they do *out* of school.'

'Yes, we, er, saw the sign. On the grass outside the Spar?'

'Ah.' He grinned. Swung his feet down. 'Yes, the lad concerned will be setting to with some elbow grease and a bottle of white spirit this afternoon.' He sighed. 'Unfortunately the staff in the shop don't exactly endear themselves to the children, don't encourage much *entente cordiale*. Anyway,' he straightened up, 'enough of village politics. Let's show Rufus to his class. If we don't hurry up it'll be playtime.'

He came round his desk to swing the door wide

for us, ushering us out, then overtaking in the corridor to lead the way. Rufus and I hurried after him. Sure enough, the room we'd passed earlier was now in silence. Through the glass door we saw all the children working away quietly at their desks, while Mrs Harding, her back to them, wrote sums on the board.

I glanced at Rufus. 'All right?'

He nodded, still very pale.

'Good luck, darling,' I whispered, feeling sick.

Daniel Hunter guided Rufus through the door with one hand on his shoulder. For a moment there I nearly scuttled in after them, but a surprised look from the headmaster just stopped me. I waited in the corridor.

'This is Rufus Cameron,' I heard him say. 'He's just moved to the village and he's starting here today. I want you all to be kind to him and help him find his feet. Er . . . yes. Damien Phillips, you'll be in charge of looking after Rufus for the rest of the week, showing him the ropes et cetera. Thank you, Mrs Harding.'

He nodded to the teacher and came out, closing the door behind him, and made to move off down the corridor. I was still rooted to the spot though, watching Rufus nervously take his place at an empty desk over by the window, all eyes on him.

'He's allergic to tomatoes,' I whispered, as Rufus took his pencil case out.

Daniel Hunter came back. 'Well, he can help himself at lunch time, so I'm sure he can avoid them. Shall we . . . ?' He attempted to usher me down the corridor.

'And if there's any cross-country running, could he not participate? Only the one time he did it, he was sick. Terribly sick.'

'I assure you, we don't make them go cross-country running aged nine.'

'Oh, and if they're using glue and he gets it on his fingers, could he be sure to wash it off properly? Only he has a habit of rubbing his eyes and—'

'Mrs Cameron,' there appeared to be a firm hand on my left elbow, 'I promise you, Rufus will be fine. Shall we leave him to it?'

He didn't exactly escort me from the building, but there was something very authoritative about the way he ushered me down that corridor and out of the double swing doors to the playground.

'Three fifteen?' I asked, anxiously.

'Three fifteen,' he agreed with a ravishing smile, almost as if he were agreeing to a date, I thought with a jolt. 'Give him a couple of days and he'll be right in the thick of it.'

'Yes. Absolutely.'

I nodded and hurried away, knowing full well that he wouldn't. If Rufus wasn't in the thick of it at Carrington House, what chance did he stand here?

I drove back through the lanes, one hand on the wheel, the other at my throat as I itched my neck nervously. But then again, perhaps a completely different environment was the answer? Maybe Rufus would thrive in a more robust atmosphere? And, of course, co-ed was so marvellous. Girls had such a softening influence. I put my hand back on the wheel but noticed, in the rear-view mirror, the tell-tale signs of eczema at the base of my throat.

As I arrived back at the cottage, the usual bestial reception was waiting for me. I ran the chicken gauntlet to the front door, then slammed it shut behind me, irritated. God, this was going to be a pain on a daily basis. What if I was laden with shopping? Or picking my way carefully down the cobbled path in witty little heels—as I fully intended to do occasionally—on my way out to some charming little bijou restaurant with my husband? I didn't want filthy feathers sticking to my tights. Suddenly a thought occurred. What was it Kate had said about them being hungry? I wondered when Piers wanted us to take over the feeding from his farm manager. Was he going to pop down and see me, this morning perhaps, knowing I'd got Rufus off to school? I glanced at the list Eleanor had left by the telephone and rang him, rather efficiently I felt, on his mobile.

'Is there a problem?' Piers barked immediately.

'Er, no. No problem.'

'Right. Sorry, Imogen, it's just that if I get tenants on the phone they're usually bellyaching about something. A blocked washing machine is the norm, and I generally suggest something as prosaic as a plumber.'

That put me in my place, didn't it? A tenant.

'No, nothing's wrong. I just wondered when you wanted me to start feeding the animals,' I said pleasantly.

There was a silence. 'I assumed you started two days ago when you moved in. I ran you through it at dinner the other night, remember? Please don't tell me you expected me to walk you through it too?'

Out of the window, a posse of tight-beaked hens, and behind them, a row of wide-eyed, reproachful cows, waited with bated breath for my response.

'No, no, of course not,' I croaked. 'I meant . . . feeding them—you know—vitamins. Extra nutrients, that type of thing.'

'Oh, I don't hold with any of that nonsense,' he said impatiently. 'Supplements are a big con on the part of the manufacturers. The cows get enough nutrients from the hay, and there's everything but the kitchen sink in the chicken feed. I don't mollycoddle my animals.'

'Right,' I whispered. 'Just checking. I'll . . . pass, on the vitamins.'

As I put down the phone it seemed to me the whole window filled up with emaciated, Biafran-like animals: the cows, bellies shrunken, ribs like toast racks, eyes like sad lakes gazed at me, whilst the chickens' eyes were no longer cross and beady, but dull with hunger, their heads drooping. My hand flew to my mouth. Oh God. I was starving them. Oh, how *awful*!

I tore outside—the chickens hot on my heels—and ran to the large covered barn. Right, now think, Imogen, think. I spun around wildly, looking at the various bins and sacks. What was it he'd said? Hay for the cows, and corn for the chickens? Or was it the other way round? I opened a dustbin full of yellow popcorn stuff. The chickens gathered eagerly, goading me on. Ah yes, this must be it— with a handy scoop too. I dug deep, took the brimming scoop out to the yard, threw it up into the air and, as the grain rained to the ground, the hens fell on it, famished.

'Sorry, sorry,' I whispered, as they pecked away furiously. 'I'm so sorry, my chick-a-dees. I'll make it up to you, I promise!'

One huge brown hen waddled out from under a bush with a row of yellow chicks behind her. My eyes popped. Chicks! I didn't even know they existed! Oh, how divine! And to think I'd nearly killed them. Oh—and water? They must have water! Happily, I discovered that the water in the water butt seemed automatically to run into a shallow basin. Well, thank God for that. At least I hadn't parched them to death. I scattered a bit more corn—too much, probably, but I was Lady Bountiful now—and turned my attention to the cows. Their heads were over the yard gate and they were bellowing balefully as usual, up to their knees in mud. Not much grass in that field.

'I'm coming, my darlings, I'm coming—oh, you poor things!'

I tore back to the barn. Hay, that was what I needed. Four bales, apparently. Oh, so *stupid*, Imogen, to listen to your husband. What was it he'd said the other night? Don't wade in until you've been told? Well, I *had* been told, at dinner, but as usual, hadn't had the courage of my convictions. Not in the face of Alex, who seemingly knew better. Never mind, never mind, you're doing it now, Imo. Just grab one of these bales. Attagirl. I seized one from the top of a stack by its binder twine, but—Jesus. I buckled under its weight. Literally, collapsed in a heap. I boggled at it, huge and yellow in my lap. It was nearly as heavy as me. Nearly as *big* as me. There was no way I could carry this. I wriggled free and, covered in hay, dragged it backwards out of the barn, across the yard to the gate, panting with exertion as the cows bellowed louder, pushing and jostling excitedly at the sight of it.

193

'Just a minute,' I muttered through gritted teeth, 'it's coming.'

Somehow, I managed to open the gate, drag the bale through, and shut it just in time behind me. The cows were on top of me now, snatching at the hay with their teeth, and frankly, I was bloody terrified, but I wasn't going to give up; wasn't going to just leave it in the mud to be trampled underfoot. Oh, no, I was jolly well going to put it in one of those jolly old roundel things like Piers had told me; would do it if it killed me. Except—no. I tottered precariously as they jostled me. I didn't want to be killed. And these were big beasts.

'Steady, Homer . . . easy now, Bart . . .' Rufus had had a hand in the naming, 'that's my foot . . . don't push, don't—oh!'

The next minute, Santa's Little Helper had given me an enthusiastic head butt in the backside and I nose-dived into the mud. And not just mud, mind, but . . . oh . . . Lordy. I picked myself up, wiping my poo-streaked face on my sleeve and admiring the Armani jacket I'd neglected to take off. I had, by measuring my length, though, made it to the roundel, and keen to complete the task—but knowing I didn't stand a chance of tossing the bale over as Piers had teasingly suggested—I began laboriously to work the hay free of its binder twine and chuck it over in handfuls. I tore at it and tossed it up in the air, but the wind was against me, and as I tossed, it blew straight back in my face, sticking to my moisturiser, my lipstick, my cow shit. Marvellous. And only three bales to go.

Each bale, I worked out over a soothing cup of coffee some time later, would take precisely fifteen minutes to get out of the barn, drag to the field, break into sections, and throw over into the roundels. Ergo, each day, it would take me precisely one hour to feed the cows. Well, that was fine, I reflected as I sipped my coffee in my dressing gown, my clothes gurgling away in the washing machine behind me, jacket in a bag to take to the cleaners. After all, I had nothing else to do, did I?

I gazed over the rim of my mug to the fields beyond. Nothing else to do. My heart lurched with fear. It was quiet now that the animals had been fed, very quiet. I pulled my dressing gown around me. What I'd generally do now, of course, I thought, running my finger round the rim of my mug, was pop upstairs to my studio. I narrowed my eyes out of the window. I should go and buy that sketch pad. Go into town right now, get some watercolours too. Despite my show of enthusiasm for Rufus, though, my heart wasn't in it. I gripped my mug, feeling panic rising. Well, I didn't *always* paint in London, did I? Sometimes I'd force myself to have an admin day. And then pop over the road for a coffee with Kate, I thought with another rush of panic. Well, I couldn't do that. Couldn't pop and see anyone; didn't *know* anyone. A lump rose in my throat. Apart from Eleanor, of course, I thought quickly, and I knew she'd be keen to introduce me to her friends, but . . . I sort of knew what they'd be like. Hannah had already scathingly suggested they'd be riding to hounds with one hand and juggling charity committees with the other. Hannah's friends, then? No, equally scary. Terribly worthy and right-on. I'd probably have to save the rainforests whilst simultaneously singing 'Ging Gang Goolie'. Neither group exactly appealed, but hey, there were other girls round here, weren't there? What about the mothers at school? I took a quick gulp of scalding coffee as my eyes bulged with terror. Right. Looked like I was going to be friendless. I licked my singed lips. As well as occupationless. But . . . wait a minute . . . I narrowed my eyes out of the window. It was a beautiful day and the sun was dappling the grass in the orchard, throwing the distant hills into hazy relief and making it look like a film set. I sat, watching as the shadows from the waving trees played in the long grass, the wind rustled the leaves above, seeming almost to beckon me on. Yes, of course. Of *course*.

In a trice I'd abandoned my coffee and nipped upstairs, discarding my dressing gown on the landing and flinging on jeans and a jumper in my bedroom. Then I ran back down again and opened the cupboard under the stairs. I'd carefully, and rather ruefully, stashed my easel and paints in here, thinking that without a studio they'd be there for some time. But why? Why should they stay in here when I could paint outside? I dragged them out. Why not set my easel up in the garden—or even the field? My heart raced with excitement. Also in the cupboard were about a dozen of my paintings—the rest I'd put in storage—brought on the pretext that I might want to fiddle with them, touch them up, but actually, I thought, flicking quickly through them now, I knew they were perfect. No, what I'd really wondered was whether some little country restaurant might like to hang them on their walls with a price tag on them. I hadn't had the nerve to attempt such a thing in London, but one of these days—I dragged my easel down the hall—one of these days, I'd summon up the courage to pop them in the back of the Volvo and have a go. Today, though . . . I kicked open the front door and the sun poured through like liquid gold; oh, no, today was definitely a creative day.

I set up my easel in the orchard, deliberating for ages on the best view, moving it back and forth, but all the time, glancing furtively about. I felt guilty about painting at the best of times since it didn't constitute gainful employment, but here, out in the open, I felt even more vulnerable. Anyone could wander up, peer over my shoulder and say incredulously, 'What on earth is that? Call that art? My *six*-year-old could do better than that.'

Happily, though, apart from a few inquisitive lambs nudging my duffel bag full of paints, there wasn't a soul in sight. I threw my old smock over my head, seized my palette, and squeezed out Prussian Blue and Cameron Yellow in thick swirls, savouring the heady smell I'd missed. I felt almost faint with relief. Then I raised my eyes to the view—and blanched in surprise. God, those colours! Look at the way the sun was glancing off that field of rape in the distance, and the grass— much more vivid than I'd imagined. I needed more yellow. I squirted it out excitedly. Much more yellow—and white. Now. I raised my brush again. I never sketched before painting, finding it too restrictive, too controlling, but as a result, my first brush strokes were often tentative. Today, though, emboldened by the landscape and also, by a sense of urgency—a feeling that I had to catch this perfect light before it disappeared—I set off with a flourish.

I worked fast, my brush moving swiftly as it darted from palette to board, palette to board, following my eyes, my mind becoming less and less engaged as my senses took over. Colours were rapidly filling the white space as I layered the paint on thickly, using broad, confident strokes. I didn't notice the passage of time, only that the sun, as it moved slowly overhead, began to cast different shadows: sharper, shorter ones. But far from it being a problem, this shifting subject matter became more interesting. It was working . . . it was really working, I thought feverishly, trying to control my excitement. The sun went behind a cloud, throwing a ploughed field on the horizon into relief, and I was about to capture it in its more subdued, less garish state, squeezing great coils of paint out impatiently, when I became aware of a familiar noise behind me.

'Mooooooo . . . Mooooooo.'

I ignored it and painted on.

'Mooooooo . . . MOOOOOOOOOO!!' More insistent, this time. More demanding.

I turned, exasperated. The cows were in a row again, staring at me with huge brown eyes, their heads over the fence.

'What?' I snapped. 'You've been fed, now jolly well shut up.'

They stared balefully back. I resumed my contemplation of the ploughed field. There was silence for a moment, then it started again. Loudly. I turned. They stopped. I turned back to paint— they started. It was a bit like playing Grandmother's footsteps. Every time I swung round to face them, they shut up, but the minute my back was turned, they bellowed again. Finally I flung my brush down with an angry flourish and stalked across.

'What?' I demanded shrilly in their faces. 'What is it?'

They gazed mournfully back. The hay, I noticed, hadn't been touched. Most of it was still in the roundel, but some had been pulled out and trampled underfoot.

'What's wrong? Why aren't you eating it?'

I reached through the fence rails, picked up a handful and offered it—rather bravely, I thought—to Marge. She turned her head away. I frowned, tried to tempt another one, Santa's Little Helper, but she coughed, hoarsely, in my face. Coughed? Did cows cough? Were they ill? What was wrong with them, for God's sake. Why weren't they eating? Suddenly I realised there was one missing. Where was the fifth cow? The little brown one called—don't ask—Princess Consuela Banana Hammock?

I ran up the fence line a bit, but the cows didn't even attempt to follow me. I hopped over nervously, keeping an eye on them, but they just stood still, heads hanging, eyeballing the ground with dull, listless eyes. I picked my way fearfully through the mud until I got to grass, then ran towards the copse of trees. I had the most awful feeling. The most *awful* feeling. The fifth cow—where was she? Was she in the copse? I ran fast, glancing wildly round the field as I went, until I got to the clump of beech trees where I'd noticed they sometimes sheltered from the rain. Inside the copse was a clearing. I pushed my way through to it, protecting my face from the brambles with my arm; and there, in the middle of it, in a shallow ditch, lay Princess Consuela Banana Hammock. She was stretched out on her side, eyes shut, mouth gaping, surrounded by flies. My heart leaped in my throat. I stole across and gazed down. Not a flicker. Not a raising of an eyelid, not even a hint of a heaving side to suggest a struggle for life. Oh God—she was dead!

## CHAPTER TWELVE

I backed away from her, but as I did, I saw a great glob of green slime flood from the corner of her mouth. It was all over the earth beside her mouth, puddles of it, and there were bubbles in it. Foam. She was foaming. My eyes shot to her feet. They were stiff, and her cloven hoofs were sticking out straight, peculiar in their rigidity. I crept forward and bent down for a closer look. On the bottom of her hoofs were white lumps. Like giant clumps of acne. My eyes went back to her mouth, then to her feet again; from foot . . . to mouth . . . foot . . . to mouth . . . And then I turned and fled. I raced across the field, splashed through the mud, over the fence, across the orchard and, wrestling with the little iron gate, my heart pounding, flew up the garden path and into the cottage, not bothering to shut the door behind me. I raced to the kitchen and with trembling hands, rifled through a pile of papers on the table by the phone. Where was it? Oh, where was it, that handy list of numbers Eleanor had so thoughtfully—ah, there.

I pounced on it, the paper shaking in my hands, and punched out the vet's number. The knacker's yard was actually what I wanted, I thought desperately as it rang and rang, but presumably someone had to come and look at the corpse first; verify it.

'Marshbank Veterinary Practice,' purred the receptionist.

'Um, yes, hello.' I could barely speak. My breath was coming in short shallow bursts and my voice wasn't working. I tried to get some air into my lungs. Tried to get a grip.

'One of my cows has died and I think it might be foot-and-mouth,' I said in a rush.

There was a silence.

'Where are you?'

'My name's Imogen Cameron,' I rattled on, 'and I'm just looking after the cows, they're not actually mine, but her feet look extraordinary and there's this like, green foamy stuff coming out of her—oh!'

She'd cut me off. A blast of classical music filled my eardrum for a brief moment, then a curt male voice cut in.

'Where exactly is this cow?'

'Are you the vet?'

'Yes, I'm the vet. Where's the cow?'

'She's at Shepherd's Cottage. It's a little house on the Latimers' estate. You go past their main gates and—'

'We'll be there directly. Stay where you are and don't go near any other stock.'

'No, I won't, but I was just saying to your receptionist, the cows aren't actually mine and— oh!' Now *he'd* cut me off. I was left holding a buzzing receiver. Rude man. Didn't he want a bit more info? Directions to the cottage? Although I supposed everyone round here knew the Latimers.

201

Should I ring Piers, I wondered feverishly, pacing up and down the tiny kitchen. Tell him one of his beloved exotics had died? I quaked at the thought and decided better of it. No, let the vet do that. It would be better coming from him; better he told Piers there was nothing I could have done and that I'd—you know—nursed it to the end. Done all I could. Yes, leave it to the professionals.

I stood in the open front doorway, my arms tightly crossed and looked at the four remaining cows standing mournfully at the fence. Did they know? Yes, of course they knew. Animals could sense it, couldn't they? And did any of them have it, I wondered. Were they all going to die? I trembled. Oh, thank God Rufus hadn't been here. He'd have been so upset. Would still be upset, I thought with a pang. The little brown one was his favourite, the most friendly. I hoped it could be dealt with . . . efficiently. Taken away before he got back. But what did one do with a dead cow? Bury it? You'd need a bloody big hole. No, incinerate it, probably. I shuddered.

Don't go near the other stock, he'd said, but I had, I thought with a jolt. Just before I'd gone to find the little brown one, I'd tried to give them some hay. Had they licked my hands? Yes—one of them had. I remembered her big pink tongue. Although, now I came to think of it, it was yellow in the middle. I looked at my fingers in horror. Ran to the loo and washed them thoroughly. But what if I'd bitten my nails, could I still catch something? I thrust them under my armpits, clamping my arms down tight.

Minutes later, as I stood at the front gate, my eyes avidly scanning the horizon behind the cottage, a dark blue Land Rover sped along behind the hedge and down the zigzag track towards me, followed by a white van. The Land Rover screeched to a halt in a cloud of dust, and out leaped a man in a white plastic boiler suit and a space mask. Two similarly dressed men jumped out of the van behind. They ran round the back to open the double doors, and seemed to be dragging some sort of tarpaulin tent out between them. It looked like something I'd seen on the news, ages ago, some kind of isolation unit. I went a bit hot; made to go towards them.

'*No, stay there!*' One of them swung round and shouted thickly through his mask. I stopped obediently in my tracks.

'*This way?*' shouted another, spacemanlike figure from behind his mask, pointing towards the cows' field.

'Um, yes. But—listen, when I said I thought it was foot and mouth, I wasn't entirely—'

'IS SHE SEPARATED FROM THE REST OF THE HERD?'

This was boomed at me from a loudspeaker, making me leap in the air. One of the masked men was crouched down on the opposite side of the van and was directing his foghorn at me from across the bonnet. The other man seemed to be spraying stuff all over the wheels, all over the track, and all over my car too, from a long thin hose. Good Lord.

'Yes, she's in that copse over there,' I yelled back. 'But look, I'm not *entirely* sure she's even—'

'STAY . . . IN . . . THE HOUSE!!'

This was blasted at a million decibels. The echo from the megaphone hung portentously in the air and I froze, paralysed in its reverberation. When

203

I'd come to, they were off, the three of them, at the double: gripping their equipment and their plastic tent, running as fast as their space suits would allow, across the field towards the copse, looking for all the world like some sort of anti-terrorist squad. Like something out of the SAS, I thought nervously. Heavens. Was this really necessary? I watched them disappear into the trees. Well, I assumed they knew what they were doing, but it seemed a bit over the top to me. I chewed my thumbnail, remembered the yellow tongue and shoved my hand hastily under my arm. Actually, no. Best to be on the safe side. And anyway, I was pretty sure any farm animal death had to be attended to fairly rigorously these days, what with all those bossy EU restrictions from Brussels. The Common Agricultural Policy, or whatever it was called. No, you couldn't just go burying a cow in a field. It might be diseased, might infect the land. Yes, I'd definitely done the right thing, I thought, going more buoyantly now to the kitchen to put the kettle on. Acted very promptly.

I bustled around the kitchen getting out proper leaf tea, not bags, and a plate of biscuits. I had an idea vets were rather like vicars, and you had to offer them the works. James Herriot always seemed to be swigging it in farmhouse kitchens— obviously a perk of the job.

A few minutes later the front door burst open. I jumped in surprise. Well, I suppose I had left it on the latch.

'In here!' I sang, pouring boiling water in the pot.

A white-suited man strode through, still in his mask. He took up most of the kitchen. I could just

204

see his eyes and mouth, through the mesh.

'Do you mean the Murray Grey?' he demanded thickly.

'Sorry?' He had a rather unfortunate manner, this chap. For a vet. Not exactly bedside.

'Are we talking about the same cow? The Murray Grey?'

'Well, it's the little dark brown one, without the horns,' I said patiently. Golly, there were only five of them and only one was flat on her back with her legs in the air. Perhaps he was newly qualified? I went to the window. 'The others are all paler, see? With horns.' I pointed at them lined up at the fence. 'She's more—oh!'

'That one?' He jabbed his finger on the pane of glass. My hand shot to my mouth. Princess Consuela Banana Hammock had mysteriously joined her friends, and was lined up alongside them, gazing over the fence at me.

'Oh. My. God.' I clutched the windowsill. 'That's *amazing*!' I turned to him. 'How did you do that?'

'I'm Jesus Christ in disguise.'

I gaped.

'I nudged her with my foot, Mrs Cameron. That cow has a dust cough. She does not have foot-and-mouth.'

I stared at him some more. 'Oh!' I clutched my heart. 'But . . . the green slime—'

'Grass. Cud, to be more precise, regurgitated from her stomach as she slept.'

'Cud! Really? And she was just asleep? But— what about all that white stuff on her feet?'

'Chalk. Which adheres to hoofs in clumps in the wet.'

'Gracious. Oh, well, that's a relief, isn't it? I did

say before you went rushing out there in such a tearing hurry that I wasn't entirely—oh, *what* a relief.' I clasped my hands, beaming delightedly at him. 'Rufus will be *so* pleased—that's my son— he's only nine. I was dreading telling him Princess Consuela Banana Hammock had bitten the dust. She's his favourite. Cup of tea?'

He didn't respond. The eyes behind the mesh stared fixedly at me. His voice, when it eventually came, was dangerously low. 'Have you *no* concept, at all, of the mayhem, you've caused? The chaos?'

I paused as I tipped the pot to pour. Righted it. 'Sorry?'

'On the way over here I put a restriction order on all neighbouring farms within a twenty-mile radius, stating that no livestock, absolutely nothing, should be moved. On farms within a five-mile radius, I placed an order instructing that all cattle should be prepared for slaughter and incinerated.'

I put the teapot down. 'Killed?'

'And burned. The lot of them.'

I stared at him. A vision of mountains of burning cows swam horrifically before my eyes. Carcasses and bones dripping with acrid flesh; the fumes, the stench . . . My mouth dried. I sat down slowly on a stool.

'You mean . . . all Piers's stock? You've ordered them to be . . . ?'

'Such is the highly contagious and virulent nature of foot-and-mouth, I had no option.'

'Oh Christ.' My hand flew to cover my mouth.

'Happily I was able to reverse the order on my mobile just now.'

'Oh, thank God!' I jumped up and clutched his

plastic hand. Nearly kissed it.

He snatched it away. 'And thankfully, no lives have been needlessly lost. But, Mrs Cameron, your reckless and alarmist behaviour would most certainly have spelled the end for this local farming community, and probably for the whole of the South of England. The ripple effect would have sent shock waves throughout the entire country, and because of the last outbreak, I'm not sure English farming would ever have recovered. The beef industry certainly wouldn't, maybe not even the government.'

The government? I'd almost brought down the government? I sat down again, rather abruptly this time. The stool rattled.

'I'm . . . so sorry,' I whispered. 'I had no idea. I—I just knew cattle got that disease. It was the only one I'd heard of, and—and, well, I looked at her mouth and then at her feet, and I—'

'You applied the same impulsive, cavalier attitude that you do to your underwear?'

I frowned. 'What?'

He took off his white hat and mask. I stared. Oh my God. It was the gypsy with the curls. Heathcliff. My dinner companion from the other night, the one I'd sat next to at the Latimers', with the twinkly eyes, only his eyes weren't nearly so twinkly now.

'Clearly whipping your pants off and causing a national disaster are all in a day's work to you, Mrs Cameron. I'm not suggesting, incidentally, that the one could in any way lead to the other.'

'Oh!' I stood up, furious. 'How dare you? How dare you come here and—and hoodwink me like that!'

'I dare,' he said in level tones, taking a step towards me, 'because you dared to breeze in from London and apply a ridiculous warped logic to what you saw as a simple rural situation. In one blasé knee-jerk reaction you almost brought down an entire community. You made no attempt to consider the repercussions your alarmist telephone call would cause, or the devastation your amateur diagnosis would create. And then you attempted to brush it off brazenly, and offer me a cup of tea.'

I swallowed, caught in the barely controlled fury of his flinty dark eyes. 'I—I'm sorry,' I muttered. 'You're right, I didn't think. It was stupid of me.' His eyes continued to bore into me. Then his hand went to the zipper at his neck. He unzipped his entire boiler suit, right down to his crutch as I quickly averted my eyes. I had an awful feeling he was naked underneath.

'It's all right,' he said, stepping out in jeans and a T-shirt. He bundled the suit under his arm and made for the door. 'You're quite safe.'

I watched him go, rooted to the spot for a moment. Then I ran after him. He went down the path and stashed his suit away in the open boot of the Land Rover. The white van had disappeared.

'Where have the others gone?' I spun around.

'Back to the lab to report a false alarm to the Ministry of Agriculture. As fast as possible, I hope. We don't want DEFRA sniffing around. We'll never get rid of them.'

'I'm truly sorry,' I said humbly, twisting my hands agitatedly. 'And will Princess Cons—the Murray Grey recover? I mean, from her cough?'

'She will if you stop giving her straw to eat and give her hay instead. The straw's full of dust. It's getting in her throat.'

'Oh Lord, you mean—'

'Don't you know the difference?' he said irritably, throwing his space shoes in the boot, sitting on the back bumper and getting out some Wellingtons. He thrust his feet into them. 'Come with me.'

In another moment he was striding off towards the barn and I was mincing after him, picking my way through the mud in my beige suede boots.

'This is straw,' he said, plucking a handful of the stuff I'd been giving them, 'and this, is hay.' He snatched an identical handful from another bale.

I blinked. 'Er . . .'

'Feel it,' he said impatiently. 'It's much finer. It's dried grass, as opposed to dried stubble.'

'Yes it is, isn't it?' I marvelled as I fondled it. 'Gosh, how awful. I've been giving them the wrong stuff!'

'They'll live,' he said crisply. 'Cows eat straw *in extremis*. It's used as bedding in the winter, but if they're not getting hay they're not getting essential minerals so they're more prone to magnesium deficiency. Then you really will get them keeling over with their feet in the air, frothing at the mouth.'

'Heavens.'

He turned and gave me a probing look. 'How about a lick?'

I bristled. 'I *beg* your pardon?'

'A cow lick,' he said impatiently. 'Have you got one?'

'Oh!'

'Provides them with essential vitamins until the grass comes through properly.' He strode off towards the feed bins, picking up lids and peering in.

'Here.' He reached in and brought out what looked like a gigantic soap on a rope, then went across the yard to the cows and tied it on their fence. The cows clustered instantly, licking avidly.

'Oh, look!' I said delighted. 'They love it.'

'Course they do.'

We watched as they slurped away.

'But why do they need licks and hay in the first place? Why can't they just go in that lovely green field over there, behind the orchard?' I pointed. 'They keep looking at it longingly. I nearly let them in the other day.'

'It's too rich, got too much clover, and clover's got a hollow stem, full of air. If they eat too much they blow up like barrage balloons.' He looked at me. 'Cows can't burp. Didn't you know that?'

'No, I didn't.' *Why would I?* 'So . . . what happens?'

'They explode.'

I stared. 'Don't be ridiculous.'

He shrugged and made off towards his car. 'OK, give it a whirl. Put them in the clover field. I'd stand well back though, if I were you.'

I gazed after him. I wasn't at all sure I liked this man's attitude: half hectoring and half, I felt, poking fun at me. All the same, I wasn't entirely sure I wanted to return from the school run and find bits of exploding cow all over the place.

'No—no, I'll give them hay,' I said decisively, scuttling after him again. God, this man could shift. 'And I'll take the straw out of the roundels.'

'You'll have a job. Most of it's been trampled into the mud. Piers won't be too thrilled at having his fields wrecked like that.'

I turned back to see that the cows had indeed pulled it out and flattened it comprehensively into the mud. One of them was even lying on it.

'Don't tell him!' I breathed cravenly.

'What, that his cows were on death row, or that you've been feeding them bedding?'

'Either,' I trembled. 'I've only been here a few days. He'll think I'm incompetent, probably kick us out. And Alex will kill me,' I added in a low voice.

He gave the first hint of a smile I'd seen since he'd arrived. 'Your secret's safe with me. Luckily for you, we weren't able to contact Piers this afternoon. And anyway, the straw will rot in time.' He sat in the open boot of his Land Rover and took his boots off. He shot me a quizzical look. 'Alex is your husband, I take it?'

'Yes.'

'The one sitting next to Eleanor at the far end of the table the other night?'

'That's it.'

He gave me an odd look.

'What?'

He shook his head. 'Nothing.'

'No, what?'

He shrugged. 'I thought I'd seen him here before, that's all.'

'Yes, you probably have. He often pops down here. Piers and Eleanor are very old friends of his.'

'Ah,' he said shortly.

He stashed his Wellingtons away, and changed into deck shoes.

'And why isn't he feeding the cows for you?' His dark eyes flashed up to meet mine. 'That's hard work, heaving those bales into roundels.'

211

'Oh, because he's not here during the day. He works in London. And actually,' I lied, 'he gets terrible hay fever.'

'Does he now.'

It was said in a slightly mocking way that made me bristle. And all in that lilting Irish accent. Why hadn't I recognised it in the first place? But his mask had muffled it. I felt stupid. He'd made a fool of me.

'Right. Well, if that'll be all . . .' I said crisply, drawing myself up to my full five foot three.

He stood up slowly and regarded me a moment. 'Yes. That'll be all. Although I saw from my records on the way over here that these cows are due a booster soon. They'll need it if you want to take them anywhere.'

'Oh, they're not going anywhere,' I said impatiently. What—off on their holidays? With their suitcases and sunglasses? 'They don't need that.'

'This isn't an optional flu jab,' he snapped, 'it's mandatory. If you're moving them to different pastures, which, I happen to know Piers does in the winter, they'll need it.' He slammed the boot shut. 'I'll be up in due course to administer it. Good day, Mrs Cameron.'

'Good day,' I snapped back as he got in the car and shut the door. He started the engine with a flourish and roared off in zigzags up the track, the dust hovering in his wake.

Rude man, I thought as I watched him go. Thoroughly, rude man. There was no call to speak to people like that. Particularly to clients. I squared my shoulders. I mean, OK, I'd rattled his cage with the foot-and-mouth scare and I could see

212

how that might be annoying, but actually, what he'd really been worried about was an outbreak occurring on his patch; in his own back yard, so to speak. I stalked into the house and shut the door. Yes, he'd been more concerned about saving his own professional skin than about saving the cows.

At three o'clock, I went to get Rufus. I'd dressed down a bit this time: I couldn't quite bring myself to do the whole bare legs and trainers bit, but I looked suitably casual, I thought, in old jeans, a white T-shirt and sunglasses. Perfect. I got there deliberately early, hoping for a bit of car park chat, but in the first place there wasn't a car park, and in the second place, the only mothers that were there collecting their offspring—most children appeared to walk or cycle home—steadfastly refused to look at me. I flashed encouraging little smiles hither and thither, but to no avail. They stood in impenetrable circles, their backs to me, buggies in the middle like wagons at Custer's last stand, armed with toddlers and Tesco carrier bags.

'Hello!' I said brightly to one young mum, standing on her own having a solitary fag. Her mouth fell open and she dropped her cigarette in her pram.

At last the bell rang, the doors opened and the children spilled out. Not in an organised crocodile as they had from Carrington House, but at the double, spewing from all orifices like a bean bag that's burst its seams, with an awful lot of noise and dragging of coats and bags. I glanced around anxiously, trying to spot Rufus in the scrum. Finally I saw him, right at the back on his own, socks around his ankles, head down, dragging his blazer, looking pale and tired. My heart lurched.

'Hello, darling!' I couldn't help it. My hand shot up in the air too. Quite a lot of incredulous heads swivelled. I later learned that a grunted 'Orright?' was the more familiar, maternal greeting.

'Hi,' he muttered as I took his bags.

'Oh, Rufus, your face! What happened?' He had a nasty cut above his right eye.

'I fell over.' He walked past me towards the car.

'Did you? Oh, darling, poor you. What, playing footie or something?' I hastened after him.

'It's not footie, it's football. And no.'

As we reached the car, a group of children, obviously intent on raising Linda's stress levels and muscling into the Spar *en masse*, turned and nudged one another.

'Woof!' one of them said to Rufus.

'Woof woof!' another agreed, and giggled.

I smiled, thinking perhaps they were new chums, but they guffawed and turned away.

'They looked nice,' I said brightly as we drove off.

'They're not,' he said bitterly. 'No one is.'

I swallowed. Felt my throat tighten. 'Did you have a good day?'

'No.' He stared out of the window.

I licked my lips. 'Oh, well. First day is always tricky. Takes time to settle in.'

He didn't reply and stayed with his head resolutely turned away from me. When we got home he went straight up to his bedroom and shut the door. I made to follow, then thought—no, food, that's what he needs. And anyway, he wouldn't talk to me yet. I knew Rufus. He'd want to be alone. With trembling hands I peeled potatoes and made sausage and mash, then called

214

from the bottom of the stairs. For a moment I didn't think he was coming, but finally, the door opened and he came down slowly. I could tell he'd been crying. I wanted to fly to him, wrap him in my arms, but Rufus wasn't always amenable to that sort of behaviour and might well just stand there like a statue. He ate his tea slowly and I washed up the pans behind him, prattling away about the cows, about my stupidity, hoping to make him laugh. He didn't. As I put the milk back in the fridge I snuck a look at him, watching anxiously for signs of blood sugar levels returning, trying not to wonder at the cut over his eye.

'Why did you give me a dog's name, Mummy?' he asked eventually.

I turned. 'I . . . didn't, darling. I gave you a lovely name.'

'Everyone says it's a dog's name. And, by the way, I can't have violin lessons—they don't do them. And no one wears garters in their socks.'

'Right,' I said faintly.

'I'm going to see the lambs.' He slid off his chair and out the back door before I could suggest accompanying him.

It was quite obvious, though, I thought as I moved to the open back doorway, clutching my tea towel to my breast, that he didn't want company. The tilt of his head said it all: leave me alone, you're the cause of my unhappiness, you're why I'm here, I hate you. I gripped the door frame. My heart burned for him.

It was always tough, though, a new school, I reasoned. Some were tougher than others, admittedly, but he'd get there. He'd settle in. And lovely to have all this to come back to, I thought as

215

I watched him sitting cross-legged in the orchard, pulling at the grass, surrounded by lambs, who, naturally inquisitive, came to sniff him and take grass from his hand. Thank God he didn't have a dead cow to come back to, too.

That night, as I put him to bed, though, he broke down.

'It's too different,' he sobbed into my neck, clinging to me as he sat up in his Harry Potter pyjamas. 'It's all too different, and I don't feel right. I'm *not* right!'

'Nonsense,' I said, my heart pounding as I held him tight. 'Of course you're right. Who says you're not?'

'There's this boy,' he hiccuped, drawing back from me, face drenched in tears, 'called Carl. He started the woofing and everything, and then everyone joined in and started saying "walkies", and then I got pushed over by him on the way out of lunch. Accidentally, I think,' he said, seeing my horrified face.

'Right.'

'Mum, you won't say anything, will you?' he pleaded.

'Of course not, darling. Of course not.' I swallowed. 'Shall we read a bit more of *The Hobbit*?'

He nodded mutely and lay down, his face pale, turned away from me to the wall. I read to the end of the chapter, my voice faltering in places, but it seemed to soothe him as he listened to the rhythm of the words. I kissed him when I'd finished, and turned out the bedside light.

'Go to sleep.'

'Mum, promise you won't say anything?' He

turned his face back to me.

'I promise.'

When I got downstairs, Alex was at the kitchen table eating a pork pie, which I'd earmarked for his supper with some salad, straight from the wrapper. He'd clearly just walked through the door.

'He's being bullied,' I said, my voice catching as I said it.

Alex swallowed the last mouthful and looked up. 'Is he?'

'Yes, by a boy called Carl in the year below.' I pulled out the chair opposite and sat down. 'He pushed him over on his way out from lunch.'

'Well, tell him to push him back if he's in the year below. He needs to stand up for himself a bit more. You wrap him up in cotton wool.'

'He doesn't want me to say anything,' I said abstractedly, scrunching the pork pie wrapper fiercely in my hand, my nails digging into my palm. I gazed bleakly over his shoulder.

'Good. Well, don't.' Alex picked his teeth with his finger. 'What's for supper?'

'And they're making fun of his name.'

'Kids will, Imo. They'll get bored, though. Don't fret.'

'I know, but I do.'

He sighed. 'Good day at the office, darling? No, lousy, thank you. And good journey home? Well, if you can call two hours in a steel box full of human lasagne good, then yes, it was delightful.'

I got up from the table and put the wrapper in the bin. Turned and noticed him properly for the first time.

'How was your day?'

'Oh, for God's sake!'

217

And then, for the second time that evening, another member of my family mysteriously flounced from my presence and stomped upstairs.

## CHAPTER THIRTEEN

The next day, when I'd dropped Rufus off at the school gates, I went back to the car. I got in, but didn't drive away; instead, I shrank down behind the wheel outside the Spar. Linda peered at me suspiciously through the window as she stacked her Andrex, but I pretended I was on my mobile. Five minutes later, when the playground had cleared and I reckoned they'd all be safely in registration putting their spring flowers on the nature table, I nipped back across the road, through the school gates and, eschewing the main entrance, quietly entered the building via a side door. Keeping my head low and wishing I had a headscarf on, I hurried furtively down the corridor to Daniel Hunter's office. I knocked and got no answer, so knocked again, more urgently this time, then stuck my head round.

He was on the telephone and looked momentarily annoyed, then he recognised me and smiled. He waved me in while he was still talking and I tiptoed in theatrically, sitting across the desk from him, trying to look as if I wasn't listening to his conversation and was more interested in the décor. There was nothing really to look at, though: shelves of books and files lined two walls and there were a couple of Monet prints on the others, but no photographs on the desk, I noticed. No wife and kids. But no, that's right. Hannah had said he wasn't married.

' . . . all right, Mrs Carter . . . Yes, I understand if Craig is still ill, but these headaches are getting rather recurrent . . . Well, if you could just make sure he gets here tomorrow . . . Thank you so much. Goodbye.'

He put the phone down. 'Truancy,' he informed me, snapping a register shut. 'Aided and abetted by the parent.'

'Really? Good heavens. I thought most mothers were keen to get the little darlings out of the house.'

'Not if the little darling gets breakfast while Mum sleeps off a hangover and then does the shopping and takes Dad's betting slip to the bookies and changes the baby's nappy and generally becomes indispensable.'

'Oh.' I was shocked. 'Poor little scrap.'

'Exactly,' he sighed. Scratched his head. 'We do our best to give the blighters an education but sometimes it's an uphill struggle. The parents are often harder work than the pupils. Now, what can I do for you?'

It was said pleasantly enough, but I could tell this was a man who had a school to run and needed to get on.

I straightened up. 'I'm afraid Rufus is being bullied.'

He frowned. Pushed the register aside. 'I'm sorry to hear that,' he said. 'Anyone in particular?'

'Yes, he's called Carl, he's in the year below him. He got everyone to bark at him yesterday, and then he pushed him over in the lunch queue. Rufus has got a cut over his eye.'

'Right.' He looked thoughtful. Picked up a pen and doodled, lips pursed. Then put the pen down, laced his fingers together and leaned towards me on his elbows. 'Mrs Cameron, it is only day one, and you know, after a bit, things do have a habit of shaking down. I could wade in now and have a word with Carl but sometimes that exacerbates the problem. Since he's not in his class and Rufus won't come across him that much, my advice would be to let things be. Carl Greenway has a short attention span and he'll probably get bored with baiting Rufus—who, I suspect, he gets zilch reaction from—and go back to sniping with Mark Overton, who gives as good as he gets.'

I stared, horrified. 'You mean . . . you're not going to get him in here? Suspend him?'

He suppressed a smile. 'Not immediately. I'll certainly have a quiet word with Mrs Harding and ask her to keep an eye on the situation, but I don't recommend hauling Carl over the coals just yet. If, in a couple of days, things haven't improved, I certainly will, but I think you'll find this is best. These things generally have a way of sorting themselves out.'

'Well, I hope you're right, because obviously if things don't sort themselves out, I'll have to make other arrangements.' My voice was a bit shrill.

He frowned. 'I'm sorry?'

'Well, obviously if this school isn't right for Rufus, I'll have to take him elsewhere. Back to London, if needs be. I'd live in a bedsit if it meant Rufus could go to the right school and be happy.'

I wasn't sure he'd got the picture. See how things shake out? Keep an eye? This was my baby. My precious Rufus.

'I'm sure that won't be necessary,' he soothed.

'And what if he comes home tonight with another cut? Over the other eye? Or even *in* his eye? Or—or worse still, a deep psychological scar? One that stays with him for ever, one that will never heal!'

At this point, to my horror, my voice cracked. My eyes filled up and I raised them to the ceiling, but to no avail, it was all too close to the surface and—oh God. The next thing I knew, Mr Hunter was pushing a box of tissues across his desk towards me, and in another minute, he'd left his seat and pulled up a chair beside me.

'Blow,' he ordered, handing me a fistful of tissues, as if I was one of his pupils. I obeyed, forcibly, and actually, felt a lot better.

'I'm so sorry,' I muttered, appalled as I blew again and wiped my nose. 'I don't know what came over me.'

He grinned. 'Fierce maternal protection, I'd hazard. Crying mothers are not unusual in this office, Mrs Cameron, I assure you.'

'I thought you were pretty quick on the draw with the tissue box,' I gulped, dabbing my eyes.

'Years of practice. And I don't blame you for being upset. It's very hard to see your child unhappy, but nine-year-olds do scrap a bit, and being a new boy is always difficult. Children of that age are intrinsically kind, though, which is why I like teaching them so much, before they've hardened off a bit at secondary school.'

'Isn't that what the Jesuits say?' I sniffed, scrunching the tissue into a soggy ball and blinking hard. 'Give me a boy until he's seven and I'll show you the man?'

'Exactly. They're generally very biddable. Very suggestible to correct behaviour.'

I nodded. This was a sensitive, intelligent man. I was aware that his right knee was about two inches from mine and suddenly, I wished I'd made a bit more of an effort this morning. I really hadn't. No make-up, an old denim skirt, and yes—bare legs. I'd be dropping my fag in my pram, next.

'Mrs Cameron, may I suggest something?'

'Imogen,' I muttered, keeping my eyes low and pulling my skirt down a bit. 'And yes, please do.'

'Imogen. Sometimes, in my experience, it's best not to meet these situations head on. Sometimes it's better to go round the houses, take a different tack.'

'What d'you mean?' I glanced up. His face was quite close to mine now. God, he was handsome. His eyes were blue, but flecked with gold, like a tiger's, and his tawny hair was attractively rumpled in a just-got-out-of-bed sort of way. He didn't look like a headmaster at all, more like something out of a Richard Curtis film.

'Well, maybe have a go at charming Carl. Make a friend of him.'

I gazed at him. 'Oh!' A light bulb went on in my head. 'Oh—you mean like—invite him for tea or something? A sleepover!'

'Well, I wouldn't necessarily go that far but—'

'Oh, yes, that's a marvellous idea—yes, you're quite right! I remember now, Kate—my great friend from Carrington House—she had a similar problem with Orlando when Torquil kept pinching his Rubik Cube, and she did exactly that. Torquil's mother came too and it was a great success. She did a fondue!'

222

'Ye . . . ss.' Mr Hunter licked his lips doubtfully. 'Although I'm not convinced you'd have to go to those lengths to—'

'Oh, you're a genius, Mr Hunter, a genius. Thank you so much!' I stood up, eyes shining. He stood up too and our eyes met and d'you know, I damn nearly kissed him. Just managed to stop myself.

'Daniel,' he smiled.

'Daniel,' I breathed.

Golly. For a moment there we really *were* in a Richard Curtis film. Any minute now the camera would pan out, the music would swell in a crescendo, snowflakes would whirl and—

'Er, right.' He glanced away, shuffling some papers on his desk, breaking the moment. 'And now I really must get on.'

'Yes. Yes, I must too,' I agreed, coming to. I hastened to the door. Before I exited, though, I turned, clutching my handbag to my chest, beaming widely. 'And thank you so, *so* much.'

He smiled. Shrugged. 'Hope it works. Good luck.'

And with those words ringing in my ears I hastened away, heart pounding.

\*     \*     \*

The rest of the day couldn't pass quickly enough. First I fed the cows. I was an expert now, taking out a bale at a time in a wheelbarrow in my wellies, remembering a knife in my pocket to cut the binder twine, standing on an upturned milk crate to hurl the hay over in sections, my back to the wind—oh, I could do it in my sleep. Then off to the chickens to give them some grain; feeding the baby chicks and the proud mother, skipping out of the way of the cockerel, who could be a bit aggressive when he felt like it, before zooming off to Waitrose for provisions, my heart soaring. I had a plan, you see, a project, and armed with that, I could go from despair to elation in nought to sixty. And I could see it all now: Rufus and Carl would be playing footie—football—in the orchard, passing to each other—'Oi! Rufus, over here!' 'Nice one, Carl!'—scoring goals and flying into each other's arms to celebrate. Perhaps I should put a couple of makeshift goals up. I roared into Waitrose car park. Some flowerpots, maybe? Or even bales of hay! When I got back, I loaded some into the wheelbarrow, trundled them out, and positioned them at either end. Perfect. Then I paced around the fields a bit, too keyed up to paint, and at three o'clock exactly, raced off to the school.

Outside the gates, as I assiduously chewed my gum—oh, yes, and I'd even found a suitably dismal grey hoody in Primark—I scanned the mothers a little more carefully. Which one was Carl's? Or did Carl walk home? Yes, if he was a bit of a lad, he probably did. Oh, well, if need be we could follow him. Ask his mum when we got to his house. I did hope that wasn't his mother, I thought, nervously eyeing a woman I'd spotted yesterday. She was an unbelievably scary-looking specimen, massively overweight with huge rolls of fat encased in a hoody similar to my own but about ten sizes bigger, greasy jet-black hair and rings in every orifice. Hordes of small children—well, five at least—were grouped around a fully occupied double buggy, and a muddy Alsatian strained from the handle on

224

a string. Even the other mothers seemed in awe of her as she yelled and cuffed her brood and tugged at the dog. She glared at me and I glanced hurriedly away. Now that one, I thought, eyeing up a thin, washed-out-looking girl with straggly hair carrying a baby, that one I could cope with. Feed her up a bit, make some strong, sweet tea; give her a Hobnob.

A bell went, and as it was still ringing, children began to pour out of the doors. As usual, Rufus was well at the back, but I was relieved to see that he didn't look quite as despondent as yesterday.

'Good day, darling?' I took his bag.

He shrugged. 'All right.'

'Rufus, which one's Carl?'

'What?'

'Carl. Which one is he?'

He glanced around. 'Over there.' He pointed to a tall, tough-looking boy with a shaved head.

'Right. Come on, we're going to ask him to tea.'

'What?' Rufus looked horrified.

'We're going to ask him to tea today.' I bent down to whisper in his ear. 'Clever tactics, you see, Rufus. Reverse psychology.'

'But, Mum, he left me alone today. I didn't really see him.'

'Nevertheless, it'll stand us in good stead for the future. You've got a hundred and twenty five more days until the end of term, I worked it out last night. We need to put in some ground work.'

I marched towards him. 'Hello, Carl,' I smiled chummily. 'I'm Rufus's mummy.'

The boy broke off from his mates to turn and stare at me, open-mouthed.

'Rufus and I wondered if you'd like to come to

225

tea today.'

A silence fell amongst the bunch of lads.

'Wha'?' He screwed his freckled face up to me.

'Yes, we thought you might like to come and play, with your mummy, perhaps. Is she here?'

'Nah, she's inside.'

'Is she? Well, perhaps we could ring her.' I whipped out my mobile.

'Nah, I mean she's in prison.'

I swallowed. Put my phone away. 'Right. Well, um, maybe—maybe whoever looks after you, can come?'

'Me nan looks after me, but I don't wanna come to tea.'

I had a fairly captive audience by now: every mother and child at the school gates was listening to this exchange, agog. Rufus tugged at my arm, puce with shame.

'Come on, Mum.'

'Oh, well, that's a pity. I've got some lovely Vienetta ice cream and I've set the badminton up.'

'Nah, you're orright.' The boy looked embarrassed and turned away.

'And Rufus has got a PlayStation,' I wheedled desperately. I began to feel hot. 'I've just bought him a new game today actually. *Invaders of the Lost Stratosphere.*'

'I'll come,' said a voice behind me. I glanced around to see a skinny little girl with pigtails and a pinched face.

I laughed nervously. 'Well, I'm not sure—'

'No, I will. I'll come.'

'Right,' I breathed. 'And you are?'

'Tanya. I'm in 'is class, ent I?' She turned to Rufus defiantly. My son nodded miserably.

226

'And this is my mum.' She turned to the enormous black-haired woman with the zillions of children, the rolls of flesh, and the straining Alsatian.

'Yeah, we'll come,' the mother agreed.

A profound silence fell. All eyes were on the new mum, Mrs Cameron; with the bright white legs, the posh voice, the grey hoody, and the incongruous Mulberry handbag.

'Right,' I gulped. 'Okey-doke.' I cranked up a smile. 'Marvellous.' *We'll* come—Christ, there were about twenty of them now that she'd collected what looked like half the school. Yes, absolutely marvellous, I thought, my palms sweaty now as Rufus and I walked wretchedly to our car, Little Harrington's answer to the Von Trapp family trooping along behind us, a million amused eyes boring into our backs. I couldn't look at Rufus. Just couldn't.

'D'you want to follow me?' I asked brightly as I opened the driver's door.

'Oh, we ain't got a car,' said the mother, as she stood, looking at ours.

I licked my lips. No car. Right. 'Well, I'm not sure I've got enough seat belts to—'

'Nah, we don't want seat belts. They'll just pile in the back. Jason! Paula! Get the baby, and Darren and Jasmine, you get in the boot wiv' the little uns. Tanya, get the twins out of that buggy. Come on, look lively.'

And they did just that. Piled in. All twelve of them—I counted—squashed in any old how, on laps, in the boot, faces squashed against windows, looking like a family of illegal immigrants trying to make it across the border.

'Well, I hope we don't meet a policeman,' I twittered nervously, a muscle going in my face. 'Because I have a feeling it's against the law. And I haven't a clue where you're going to sit because Rufus absolutely *has* to have a—'

' 'Ere, come on, little 'un. On my lap.'

She'd plonked herself down in the front seat and scooped a startled Rufus effortlessly with her arm, into her vast lap. His nose was about six inches from the windscreen.

'Perhaps if you put the belt around both of you,' I squeaked.

'Won't reach,' she assured me without even trying, although admittedly she was probably right. I wasn't convinced it would encircle her *without* Rufus on her lap. 'Anyway, our Ron's the local bobby. He'll turn a blind eye. Come on you, get in.'

Thinking she was talking to me I hastily obeyed, but she was addressing the Alsatian, hauling him in on his string, somehow getting him past her well-upholstered legs to lodge him between us. He stood with his front paws on my handbrake, panting heavily into my face, jaws wide, tongue lolling, saliva dripping.

'Good boy,' I breathed, shrinking back.

'She's a bitch,' growled my new best friend.

'Oh, I'm sure she's n— Oh. I see.'

Nervously, I burrowed around amongst the furry feet, found the handbrake, and let it out. Without the brake for support, though, the dog lurched forward on to my knees. As I crawled down the road, the best part of an enormous hairy dog lying in my lap, a wet nose in my crutch, I prayed. Please God, let us get there in one piece. Please don't let tomorrow's headline's read, 'Mother's Vitals

228

Mauled by Alsatian as She Drove Car of Fifteen.'

I drove at a snail's pace, my eyes glued to the road, only leaving it occasionally to monitor the progress of my son's nose, which periodically jerked alarmingly towards the windscreen as she swung around to clout her recalcitrant brood.

'Shauna! Pack it in!' Or: 'Ryan! Shut it!'

Finally we reached the cottage and they all piled out, in an eclectic jumble, on to the grass. As they picked themselves up and gazed around, getting their bearings and taking in the unfamiliar surroundings, I went on to the cottage and opened the door. After only a moment's hesitation, the ones that were mobile ran through the front door and on up the stairs to check out Rufus's bedroom. Happily, he did have a PlayStation, and a football table, I thought, pressing myself against the wall as they thundered past me, plus a lovely wooden fort with proper lead soldiers whose lives I feared for, but no matter.

I ran around getting the tea as my new friend— Sheila, she informed me—proceeded to change a brace of filthy nappies on the kitchen floor. She dealt with them in seconds flat, making me wonder why on earth changing mats had ever been invented, pausing only to suck a dummy that had fallen on the floor and got dusty and replace it in a baby's mouth, whilst with the other hand, extracting a toddler from inside a cupboard where it was rearranging my china, and all the time punctuating proceedings with, 'Leave it, Darren,' or, 'Touch that and I'll knock your block off, Lorraine!' She was like the old woman who lived in the shoe, except that the shoe was my house.

As I arranged the tea things on the table, she sat

up on her haunches and looked up at it doubtfully. 'Wha's this then?'

'It's a hot cheese sauce,' I said brightly. 'You dip bits of carrot and celery and bread in. Rufus loves it.'

She got to her feet and picked up a bit of cauliflower in wonder. 'They won't eat this. Got any chips?'

I had, as it happened, in a bag in the freezer, which I produced nervously. 'Yes, but I'm not convinced these will go with the—'

'Give it here.'

She took it from me, waddled across to the oven, found a tray, then shook the entire bag, literally hundreds of chips, on to it, and shut the door.

'Right,' I gulped. 'Good idea.'

All hell appeared to be breaking loose upstairs judging by the noise, and it occurred to me to wonder if Rufus was still alive. Had they chucked him out of the window? Was he being dangled out, even now, by his shiny Start-rites? I didn't know, and what's more, I didn't know what I was more afraid of: that, or the look on his face if I went up and found him sitting mutely in the midst of his chaotic bedroom, watching the anarchy. With shaking hands, I lit the fondue.

'Tea time!' I warbled up the stairs, and moments later, a stampede engulfed me.

When I'd peeled myself off the stairwell wall, I tottered to the kitchen to find that, somehow, they'd all got around my tiny table: on stools, on counters, two to a chair, on an upturned milk crate, or just plain standing. They fell on their chips greedily, then gazed in wonder as Rufus solemnly dunked cherry tomatoes and chunks of bread into the bubbling sauce.

For a while they just chomped away in silence, but in time it became hard to resist, and the oldest boy, Ryan, a disreputably handsome lad of about twelve, plonked a chip in with a giggle. The others watched in awestruck silence as he chewed. Eventually, he pronounced a verdict.

' 'S orright,' he declared grudgingly.

There was no stopping them then. Chips were dunked in by the fistful as I steadied a precarious bowl of bubbling cheese, then Ryan picked up a bit of celery.

'Wha's this then?'

'Celery.' I eyed him. 'I dare you.'

'Yeah? What ya gonna give me?'

'50p.'

'A pound.'

'Done.'

He looked taken aback, but gamely dunked his celery in.

'Yeah, 's orright too.' He crunched away. 'Where's my pound?'

I reached in my bag and handed it over.

'Can I still have some more, though?' he asked warily, picking up another piece of celery.

'Course you can.'

'Can I?' asked Tanya.

'Of course.' Feeling rather flushed and elated, I cut up some more for the others, who naturally also wanted to try.

'You won't like that,' Ryan advised them all. 'It's too s'phisticated. You might like the carrot, though.'

Well, of course they all wanted to be

231

sophisticated, and after that, tea disappeared in a flash. Out of the corner of my eye I caught Sheila, giving a baby a bottle on a stool in the corner, looking impressed. She sat the baby up on her knee and rubbed her back, burping her efficiently, then jerked her head outside.

'Who looks after the stock, then?'

'The stock? Oh, you mean the cows. I do.'

'Yeah?' She went to the open back door, jiggling the baby across her arm. 'And all them Jacobs. They're 'is majesty's, are they?' She nodded.

Jacobs. This girl knew her stuff. 'Yes, that's right,' I said, picking up an already assembled tray of tea and biscuits. She moved aside as I went through the door and set it on the little table in the garden. 'They belong to Piers.' I sat down to pour. 'D'you know the Latimers then?'

She followed me out, sat down heavily opposite me and made a face. 'Everyone round here knows the Latimers. They own half the village. Me mum cleans for them, don't she?'

'Vera?'

'Yeah.'

'Oh, so you're *Vera's* daughter. Oh, Vera and I are like that!' I beamed and held up two crossed fingers, hoping to ingratiate myself.

She gave me a sharp look, and it occurred to me that she might know if her mother and I were joined at the hip.

'Does she enjoy working for them?' I rushed on, handing her a mug of tea.

She looked suspicious, and I realised that job satisfaction might not be high on Vera's priorities. The job was there, she needed it, she got on with it. ' 'S all right, I s'pose. She's bin there twenty years

232

so what's the difference? Mum says *she's* all right, but he's a funny one.'

'Piers?'

'Yeah, Piers. I wouldn't want to be married to him for all 'is money. Can't say I blame her neither, though there are some round 'ere say she should know better.'

'Who, Eleanor?'

'Yeah.'

'Blame her for what? Know better than—'

But Sheila's tantalising observations on the Latimer ménage were cut short as she got to her feet, pink with fury and pointed her finger accusingly at the bushes.

'CINDY! GET THAT COCK OUT OF YOUR MOUTH—NOW!'

My eyes bulged in horror, my tea-cup rattled. Lordy. What on earth was going on? Who was Cindy in the bushes with? *Where was Rufus?*

Sheila bustled away at the double and it was with some relief that I saw her emerge moments later from the undergrowth, wrestling the Black Rock cockerel from the jaws of the Alsatian. The cockerel gave an angry squawk and bustled away indignantly, minus a few feathers and some pride, but otherwise intact. Sheila, though, was distraught. She whipped a piece of binder twine from her pocket, put it round the dog's neck, and dragged her back to the chair to tie her up.

'She ain't used to chickens,' she panted, her face pink, 'not free range like that, at any rate.'

'Don't worry,' I soothed, 'he'll live. So, um, Eleanor. I mean, Mrs Latimer. She can't be blamed for—'

'She's more than likely never seen 'em runnin'

233

wild before. Specially not a great big cock like that.'

'No. No, it is a big one. But, um, the Latimers—'

'An' she's used to chasing birds, see. Never catches 'em, like, not quick enough, like the cat, but these great big chickens, well, that's different. It's like pheasants, innit? *Bad* girl, Cindy!' She admonished her, tugging hard on the string.

'Honestly, it couldn't matter less,' I assured her

'Yeah, but it's best we go,' she said nervously, draining her tea and getting to her feet. 'Before we do any more damage. Don't want Mr Latimer counting his chickens. I'll be shot. I'll get the kids rounded up.'

'Honestly, there's no need—'

But she was already marching around the garden, yelling like a sergeant major, calling the children to heel, and I realised it was going to be neither decently nor indecently possible to steer the conversation back to Eleanor again. I got to my feet with a resigned sigh and followed her. Most of the children were in the orchard with the lambs, where Rufus was proudly showing Tanya how to pick one up, explaining how a little orphaned one would drink from a bottle with a bit of persuasion. I had to admit, it was a something of a sylvan scene and I leaned on the fence, looking on proudly.

'Me granddad had all this,' said Sheila, joining me at the fence and nodding around as we watched. Ryan was getting involved too now, taking the lamb from Rufus's arms. 'Tenant farmer, like. Up Pasterton way. Never 'ad 'is own land, but we grew up there. An' it's good for them, isn't it? The kiddies?'

'It certainly is,' I agreed as we watched one of

234

the toddlers stagger across the orchard, an enormous nappy between his knees, and squat down to turn his face up inquisitively to a tiny lamb.

'You've got yer 'ands full,' she observed, glancing round at all the animals.

'Not as full as yours,' I jerked my head at her brood.

She laughed. 'Yeah, but only five are mine. We foster the rest.'

'Foster? Really?'

'Yeah, an' we don't do it for the money, neiver.' She looked at me sharply. 'We get sweet FA from Social.'

'I wouldn't dream of suggesting you did.'

'Well, there's some round here would, and they want to try cutting a hundred fingernails at bath time an' getting all them teeth brushed. They'd soon realise a few measly quid ain't worth it.'

'I quite agree,' I said with feeling. 'I find it hard enough coping with just one.'

'And they're good kids, anyhow,' she reflected. 'Just 'aven't much of a chance, you know? Up to now.'

I nodded. Yes, I did know. And she was giving them one. Twelve children in all, and all in a tiny house, no doubt full to the brim with baskets of washing and ironing and pants and socks drying on every radiator, Sheila working her butt off. I felt humbled as she gathered them all together now with what I realised was a lot of good-natured shouting, which the children took in their stride. And God, I'd yell if I had all those, I thought. Shriek, more like. I watched her herd them together, getting as many as possible to come up

235

and say goodbye and thank you. Sheila declined a lift back to the village, saying she only lived across the valley and hadn't realised where we were otherwise they'd have walked. Then, with two in the double buggy, another two riding pillion on the back and Ryan pushing all four, she scooped two little ones up in her arms and herded the rest across the meadow, down into the valley, and up the other side. The two boys on the back of the buggy jumped off and helped Ryan push it uphill, and Rufus and I shaded our eyes into the setting sun and watched them go. When they got to the top of the hill, Sheila got them all to turn round and wave. We waved back frantically.

After a moment, I lowered my hand and folded my arms. 'Sorry, darling,' I murmured, as we watched them disappear over the horizon.

'For what?'

'For being such an embarrassing mother. For asking half the school over and getting it wrong as usual.'

'You didn't, actually,' he said slowly. 'I like Tanya.'

And flashing me a quick grin, he ran off to see the chickens.

I watched him go; his shoes kicking up the dust in the yard. Then I went back through the buttercups to retrieve the tray of cups and saucers in the garden. I couldn't keep the smile off my face. Well, that was something, I thought, picking up the tray and heading back to the kitchen with a spring in my step. For once, then, I hadn't got it entirely wrong.

# CHAPTER FOURTEEN

The following day Rufus came running out of school beaming from ear to ear.

'How was it?' I hazarded nervously.

'Cool. Tanya and I played on the apparatus both breaks and I sat next to her at lunch. She showed me her goodie spot.'

'Her *what*?'

'Her goodie spot. It's a camp in the bushes where her and her gang hang out.'

'Oh! Well, that's a relief. And Carl?'

He shrugged. 'Didn't see him. He doesn't hang out with us. He's with the losers, mostly.'

'Oh! Right!'

'He tried to join in, but Damien told him to piss off. Damien's ten.'

I blessed Damien from the bottom of my heart and wished all power to his bad language. But could it go on, I wondered. I slightly held my breath, but all the following week it was a similar story.

'I've cracked it,' I told Hannah proudly when she popped round for a sandwich one day a few weeks later in her lunch hour. 'It's quite extraordinary. Rufus has got more friends than he ever had in London and he's in with the real dudes. Not comparing stamp collections or practising the oboe with the geeks, but really in the thick of it with the footballers and the conker boys.'

'The drug dealers of tomorrow, you mean,' she said, helping herself to salad at my little kitchen table. 'So how did you manage that?'

237

I told her about Sheila.

Hannah put the salad tongs down, astounded. 'Sheila Banks? Wife of Frankie "Fingers" Banks? Blimey, Imogen, you've tapped right into the local mafia. She and her old man rule the roost round here. No one farts without consulting Sheila and Frankie first. No wonder Rufus has found his feet. He'll be laundering money in the spare room next, and when he grows up to be the next godfather, you, as his mother, will live a life of sybaritic luxury in Capri.'

'Bring it on,' I purred. 'They're not too dodgy, though, are they, Hannah? I rather liked her.'

'Not *too* dodgy, but they do sail fairly close to the wind. They run the local pawnbrokers in Rushbrough, and rule it with a rod of iron. Put it this way: in ten years' time you wouldn't want Rufus getting Tanya up the spout and leaving her in the lurch. You might wake up to find a horse's head in your bed.'

'Thanks. I'll bear that in mind,' I said nervously, thinking that actually, I was rather hoping he might be at university by then, mixing with a slightly different crowd to Little Harrington's answer to the Corleone brothers.

Hannah eyed me over the coronation chicken. 'What? Had him more in black tie at Cambridge, taking Lucinda Many-Acres to the May Ball?'

'Certainly not,' I bristled. 'I'd be very happy whoever Rufus chooses to—you know—consort with.'

She grinned. 'Well, I'm sure the Bankses would see him all right. Probably give him a nice little caravan for Tanya's dowry. This is delicious, by the way. Any more?'

238

'There is,' I said doubtfully, getting up to reach for the bowl of coronation chicken on the side but privately thinking my sister had had enough. She'd eaten most of it already. And half a loaf of bread, and a bowl of salad. Where did she put it all? Under that vast blue dress, presumably, I thought looking at the latest Monsoon number. How did she find clothes to fit? Would this be a good moment to mention it? I hesitated. It was never a good moment with Hannah.

'Speaking of Lady Many-Acres,' she said, through a mouthful of chicken and mayonnaise, 'what's occurring up there? D'you see much of her?'

'Surprisingly little. Not since dinner that first night, which pleases me, actually. I wasn't sure whether we'd be living in each other's pockets, but in fact this cottage is a good half a mile away. I had a horrid feeling I'd be drawing my curtains every evening and catching her eye as she closed hers. Having to give a cheery little wave and an embarrassed smile.'

'I'm pretty sure Eleanor Latimer doesn't draw her own curtains,' Hannah said sourly.

I giggled. 'Well, she certainly doesn't feel compelled to "pop in", either, which is a blessing. Although she did come past with her dogs the other day and admired the painting I was doing in the orchard. She didn't stop, though.'

'Yes, I saw your easel out there as I came in. Rather idyllic, isn't it? Sitting out there amongst the buttercups? Must be more inspiring than an attic in Putney?'

I shrugged. I didn't want to be disloyal to my lovely London studio, but I was loath to admit,

239

these last few days, I'd felt something profoundly moving as I'd painted out there in the long grass; the ox-eye daisies brushing my knees, the sun warming my back, a soft light on the hills. A heady rush, an inner glow, and also a deep concentration that surprised me, and that I hadn't felt in London.

'Yeah, it's OK. I mean, obviously, it's not ideal not having a studio, but—oh, Hannah, you *can't* want more, surely!'

She glanced up at me, spoon frozen above the bowl of coronation chicken as she went to help herself.

'Why not?'

'Well, no, quite. Why not?' I said flustered. I got up to get a bottle of Evian from the fridge and to hide my flushed face in its cool depths. Jesus, she'd need two kaftans soon. Two seats on the bus. Be like one of those women you read about in the *Daily Mail*—'Why I can't fly on an aeroplane any more.' What the hell was wrong with her?

'Imogen, is there something you want to say?' she said icily.

I quaked as I put the water bottle on the table. This was serious Siberia from my sister. I dug deep and found some steel.

'No, absolutely nothing, Hannah. If you want to eat for England and end up with heart disease and respiratory problems and possibly diabetes, who am I to stop you? You go right ahead.' I sat down again, whipping my napkin out over my lap with a flourish. 'It's your body.'

She regarded me stonily but I held her eye, and my nerve. She reached defiantly for the spoon again and was about to dig in, when she put the spoon back in the dish. Her face crumpled, and for

240

an awful moment, I thought she was going to cry.

'I'm sorry,' I said quickly. 'I didn't mean that.'

She struggled for composure. Took a deep, shaky breath and swallowed hard. 'No, you're right. And it's about time someone had the guts to tell me. Eddie certainly hasn't.'

'Because he's too scared to,' I said, hastening round and pulling my chair up beside hers. 'Hannah, what's wrong, for heaven's sake? You're so strict about everything else in you life, so disciplined—why not this?'

She sighed. 'You wouldn't understand, Imo. You're thin. How would you know?'

'I'm not thin,' I retorted. 'I've got a big backside and my tummy's like jelly—I'm like most women of our age. But I'm not . . . well, I don't . . .'

'Stuff yourself with food at every opportunity, sneak down for bowls of cereal in the night, keep biscuits in your car. Your life doesn't revolve around it. I know.'

'So why?'

She shrugged miserably. 'I can't help myself. It feels nice, and so much of my life doesn't feel nice. It's sort of, the only bit I look forward to. And I feel hungry too, I really do. I really feel I need it, although obviously I *can't* need it, because look at me. I'll be a fairground attraction soon, next to the woman with the beard. But I just can't stop putting stuff in my mouth, and I hate myself afterwards.'

'Do you?' I pounced. This was a start. I thought perhaps she didn't care, had just let herself go and was sticking up two fingers to the world.

'Oh, yes,' she said, surprised. 'Loathe myself. So much so that the other day I thought I'd make myself sick, to get rid of it.'

241

'You didn't!'

'No, I didn't. But it made me realise I had to do something about it. I've joined Weight Watchers, for a start. I'm going tomorrow.'

'*Are* you?' I clasped my hands delightedly.

'Anyone would think I've just told you I've won the lottery. Yes, and I'm going to see a counsellor. Correction, have *been* to see a counsellor.'

'Oh!' I was stunned into silence. This was ground-breaking, for Hannah to admit she needed help.

'Who rather predictably told me I'm eating for comfort, to feel better about myself, and that it's all borne of insecurity, yawn yawn, but she also said comfort eating is very common in women of my age. Apparently a lot of peri-menopausal women—'

'Peri-menopausal? Don't be ridiculous, you're only thirty-eight, Hannah!'

'And Mum got hers at forty.'

'Did she?' I was staggered.

'She did. And it's hereditary, you know. Oh, I'm definitely going through the change.'

'Blimey. I had no idea. I thought fifty, fifty-one . . .'

She shrugged. 'Is the average, but you're always going to get variants on either side.'

Golly. Alex and I had better get a wiggle on, I thought. If we wanted to . . . you know. And I certainly did. Although it seemed indelicate to mention it right now. Hannah sensed as much and smoothly changed the subject.

'So. Tomorrow I stand up in front of a roomful of lardy women and say, "Hi, I'm Hannah, and I weigh fourteen stone," before some stick insect

242

hands me a diet sheet that wouldn't satisfy a rabbit. But right now . . .' She slumped back in her seat and rolled her eyes lasciviously, 'what's for pudding?'

I laughed. 'Seeing as it's your last day of freedom, a cup of coffee and a piece of chocolate cake. Good for you, Hannah. I'm proud of you.' I put an arm round her shoulders and gave her a squeeze before I got to my feet. I could see she was moved by this; did a fair amount of blinking and swallowing as I moved tactfully around the kitchen with my back to her. We weren't demonstrative as sisters, never had been, mostly because she'd always shied away from it, but I wanted her to know I was on her side.

'How's Alex?' she asked brightly, changing the subject as I came back with the coffee, and only just giving herself away by the little tremor in her voice.

'Fine,' I said, putting a mug down in front of her. 'Although . . .'

'What?' Hannah pounced, sensing my hesitation and also keen to get off the back foot and into her more usual, dominant role.

'Well, he loathes the commute. It's much worse than he was led to believe. He has to get up at six and doesn't get back till gone nine.'

'I thought it was supposed to be an hour and a bit door to door?'

'That's the fiction, and if you work in the West End it's probably true, but it's another half-hour to the City. He's thinking of getting a flat or something, actually.'

'What?' Hannah's jaw dropped theatrically.

'Well, not a flat, exactly,' I said quickly, although

my reaction had been much the same as hers last night, when he'd told me. 'Not on his own. Maybe share a place with a friend. There's a mate of his who's got a two-bedroom flat in Chiswick he says he can share with. Terribly cheaply, actually.'

'Who?'

I bit my thumbnail miserably. 'Charlie Cotterall.'

'Charlie Cotterall! That old dog, the one who left his wife because he was having an affair with his secretary whilst still maintaining his mistress and finding three women just a *little* too much to handle?'

'He's a reformed character now,' I said staunchly. 'Alex said. He's broken up with the secretary—that was just a fling—and he's mad about Trisha. That's his, um, long-standing girlfriend. They're going to get married as soon as his divorce comes through.'

She snorted. 'And then he'll cheat on her again, no doubt. A leopard doesn't change his spots just like that, you know, Imo.'

I ignored her. Stirred my coffee.

'And you're happy about Alex spending the week with him?' she persisted.

'Of course I am,' I snapped, although I hadn't been quite so happy last night. No, last night, after Alex had come home at nine thirty yet again, slumped down on the sofa and declared himself too tired to sit at the table and eat and could he just have it here, in front of the telly with a bottle of wine, I'd been horrified when he'd suggested it. In fact the chilli con carne had almost slipped off the plate on to the Conran rug as I'd put the tray in front of him.

'What—spend the whole week in London?'

'Only four nights, Imo. Only half the week, really. It's just that, to be honest, by the time I get to work I'm so knackered I can hardly think straight some days. It took me two hours to get in this morning because of points failure or something inept, and I didn't even have time for a cup of coffee before I was plunged into a presentation, having to think on my feet, juggle figures—it's too much.'

I perched on the arm of a chair opposite beside the telly, watching as he scooped up the chilli hungrily with his fork. I licked my lips.

'But Charlie Cotterall. I mean, he's quite a lad, isn't he?'

'Not any more,' he said with his mouth full, one eye on the football. 'He and Trisha are blissfully happy, although word has it she's keen to have children.' He grinned. 'I'm not sure how old Charlie feels about that. He's already got two from his first marriage, and when I had lunch with him today, he was talking about having the snip without telling her.'

I stared. 'That's an awful thing to do. If he's planning on marrying her.'

'It's only a joke, Imo,' he said, glancing away from the match. 'Old Charlie wouldn't do a thing like that. No, he was just, you know, bemoaning the fact that however hard you try, you always end up with the trouble and strife and 2.4 into the bargain.'

'Like you, you mean. Two kids the first time round, and now Rufus, and golly, who knows, maybe another one. Yes, how dreadful.'

He put down his fork. Looked at me, surprised.

'How much more entertaining would it be if you and Charlie could just—just shag around to your hearts' content, with as many women as you liked and have absolutely no ties or responsibilities at the end of it.'

'Imo—'

'Wouldn't *that* be bloody marvellous!'

And with that, predictably, I threw down the tea towel I'd been clutching, burst into tears, and rushed upstairs.

A bit later, as I sobbed piteously, face down in my pillow, Alex came up and sat beside me. He stroked my back. Rubbed between my shoulder blades.

'I won't take it, Imo. Won't take the flat.'

'No!' I sobbed, flipping over, my face wet. 'Of course you must. It's hopeless going on like this. You're exhausted. Of course you must take it. It's just, I wish—'

'That I didn't have to. I know.' He sighed. A great weary sigh that seemed to come from the very depths of his soul. 'Imo, I don't want to share a flat with Charlie Cotterall. Don't want to live with an overgrown schoolboy who still grades his farts for potency and picks his toenails and leaves the trimmings on the carpet. I don't want to be in some ghastly dive in Chiswick where the washing-up piles up in the sink and there's never anything in the fridge except beer and the only nourishment arrives on the back of a motorbike. I don't want to sleep in a tiny single attic room, listening to Charlie and Trisha humping away below. Believe it or not, it was not part of my plan at this particular stage of my life.'

His voice broke slightly at this. I had a sudden

246

mental image of Alex ten years ago; leaving his elegant Chelsea town house in the morning for his job in the City; kissing the beautiful Tilly goodbye on the doorstep, dropping his two little girls in blazers and boaters at their private school in Eton Square. I wondered, not for the first time, if he regretted the break-up of the old order? Missed his old life? Even if he didn't, I could see that sharing a flat in Chiswick was not something he'd envisaged for his later years.

'But needs must,' he went on firmly, looking steadfastly at the carpet, 'and frankly, at the moment, darling, I can't afford to look this gift horse in the mouth. Charlie doesn't want any rent, and—'

'I know,' I said quickly, sitting up and interrupting him, 'you must. Of course you must take it.' God, this was humiliating enough for him; I mustn't emasculate him further by making him spell it out to me. 'I'm just being selfish, Alex. It's terribly kind of Charlie and I'm just being . . . well . . .'

Insecure, was the word I couldn't say. I couldn't say I was scared: I mustn't let him think I was a clinging wife who couldn't let her husband out of her sight for fear of him chatting up a pretty girl. And let's face it, that's all Alex would do, chat. He did flirt, yes—God, who didn't—but he was absolutely all gong and no dinner. I mustn't lose sight of that. I must be confident and secure about this.

I reached for a box of tissues by the bed and blew my nose. Smiled at him.

'Of course you must take it, darling. And I'll tell you what. I'll pop up occasionally, shall I? Leave

Rufus with Hannah, and maybe spend one night a week in the flat. Give Charlie and Trisha something to talk about.'

He hugged me delightedly. This was absolutely how he liked me to be: funny, positive, spirited— like Eleanor, I thought with a pang. And it was how I was going to be in future, I determined. Classy. Confident. Not needy and cringing.

'In fact, why wait for Charlie and Trisha?' he'd murmured in my ear. 'Why not give the cows something to talk about now?'

And with that we'd slipped under the covers. He'd kissed my tear-stained face and then my lips, and then we'd made love: seamlessly, beautifully, wonderfully.

As I was running myself a bath afterwards, though, still smiling foolishly, I did wish that one day I could make love to my husband without congratulating myself. Did other wives monitor their love lives so closely, I wondered, dipping my toe in the water? Perhaps they did. Or, perhaps second wives did.

I turned to Hannah now as I put the milk away in the fridge, remembering my new, positive frame of mind: my half-full glass.

'Oh, yes, I persuaded him to take it, actually. Told him it was madness to pass up such a terrific offer. He'd be suffering from exhaustion, otherwise. I don't want him laid up in the Priory.'

'Yes, but a flat in town,' she said doubtfully. 'With Alex's track record. Slippery slope, surely?'

I rounded on her, slamming the fridge door shut.

'Hannah, do I make snide references about Eddie's lack of control? Do I raise my eyebrows at him teaching at an all-girls' school, suggest he might be touching up some sixth former when he shows her how to scan iambic pentameters on a trip to see *King Lear*? Do I imply he might be bonking the science mistress in an empty staffroom when he's late home at night?'

'No, no, you're quite right,' she said hastily. 'I said that without thinking. Just—a figure of speech.'

'We don't *have* a choice, I'm afraid. We don't *want* to have flatmates at our time of life, believe me,' I said, shamelessly parodying Alex. 'We don't want to live a—a beer-and-biryani lifestyle, any more than we want to live in a crappy little grace-and-favour cottage in the sodding countryside, thanks to Lady fucking Muck!'

Hannah stared at me, frozen. Her grey eyes were huge with meaning and her head jerked slightly to the left. Towards the back door, behind me. I swung round and nearly swallowed my tonsils. Eleanor was hovering, embarrassed, on the back step.

'Sorry, only I would have knocked, but the door was wide open so I—'

'Oh God, yes, come in, come in!' I said getting up, flustered, and knocking my chair over backwards. I picked it up, horrified. Golly, had she heard? She must have. How *awful*. 'How lovely to see you. You know my sister, don't you?' I was aware that my face was burning.

'Yes, we have met, haven't we?' smiled Eleanor, stretching her hand across the table. 'It's Hannah, isn't it?'

'That's it,' said Hannah, getting to her feet to clasp her hand, clearly surprised she knew her name. She pulled down her skirt and flicked her hair back as she sat down again.

Despite my confusion, I couldn't help noticing the startling disparity between Hannah, huge and lumpen in her ethnic dress, and Eleanor, glowing with good health, copper curls shining, slim figure encased in skin-tight jodhpurs and a red shirt.

'Been riding?' I hazarded stupidly.

'Well, it's such a glorious day I thought I'd take Cracker for a gallop. I've tied him to your fence outside. Hope you don't mind!'

'No! Not at all. I mean it's . . . your fence,' I said awkwardly.

There was a silence as we all digested this. My face, by now, was the colour of her shirt.

'Cup of coffee?' I rushed on, brightly. 'We were just finishing lunch, but there's some cake, so do—'

'Oh, no, I won't stay, you're very kind. No, I just came to see if you were around this weekend. Only the weather's supposed to be wonderful on Sunday and we thought we'd have a barbecue. Do say you'll come.'

Well, if she had heard me, she'd obviously forgiven me pretty swiftly.

'That's very kind, but actually, Hannah and Eddie are coming for lunch here on Sunday. They're bringing Mum with them.'

'But that's marvellous—come too!' She turned to Hannah. 'Do, it would be great to see you both. I don't feel I've really got to know you and Eddie, and you only live in the next village. I've heard so much about you from friends. You're a potter, aren't you?'

'Oh, well,' Hannah demurred, 'that's putting it a bit strongly. I dabble.'

250

'More than dabble. I know people who've bought your pots and I've seen them too—they're beautiful. I'd love to come and have a look one day.'

'How kind,' Hannah murmured pinkly, flicking her hair again, clearly deeply charmed. 'Yes, you must come. I don't have many at home because there isn't room, but I've got a wheel at school. And we'd love to come to lunch, only as Imogen says, we have got Mum . . .'

'Oh, but I adore your mother! And she can give me advice on my hideous formal garden with her marvellous plastic flowers.' She giggled. 'I do think that's inspired, don't you?'

'Mum is . . . full of inspiration,' Hannah agreed.

'Good, well, that's decided then. We'll see you all on Sunday. About one o'clock? Dead casual.'

'As long as Alex hasn't got too much work,' I said firmly. 'He's so busy at the moment, he's working weekends. I'll have to check.'

'Oh, don't worry, I've already spoken to him. I couldn't get hold of you so I rang, and he said he'd get everything done on Saturday and leave Sunday free.'

I stared. 'Right.'

'And isn't it marvellous about the flat?'

'The . . . flat?'

'Well, it'll ease the commute, won't it? Honestly, I don't know how these men do it. I get completely exhausted whenever I pop up to London.'

'Are you there a lot?' asked Hannah in a pally-wally way, resting her elbows on the table and cupping her face prettily in her hand. I shot her a look that went beyond loathing.

'*Far* too much at the moment,' groaned Eleanor.

251

'We're working on the winter collection, you see. I don't know if you know, but I've got this shirt business. We only do white shirts, but in lots of different styles. I started it with a friend.'

'Yes, I'd heard,' said Hannah eagerly. 'It's The White One, isn't it? Haven't you had some publicity recently in the *Guardian*?'

'We *have*! How clever of you to know that.'

They glowed at each other. *Puke.* I seized a knife to cut the cake, holding it like a dagger and wondering which breast to plunge it into. Would it take more than one stab, I wondered, to kill? And would it make a terrible mess? Blood-splattered windowpanes?

'And at the moment, we're frantic. Completely rushed off our feet. So much so that I've decided to stay in London for a bit. I really can't be doing with all that to-ing and fro-ing.'

'Oh, right. Have you got a place there, then?'

'Piers's mother has a flat in South Ken.'

'Oh, perfect. No, thanks, Imo.'

'No cake?'

'No.' She gave a prim little shake of her head as if she never touched the stuff and turned back to Eleanor. 'Sorry, you were saying?'

'Yes, it's just sitting there, and she never uses it, just down the road from the Natural History Museum. And actually, I quite fancy getting away from all the mud for a bit. I sometimes long for a cappuccino on a pavement, long to get a bit of good old carbon monoxide into my lungs!'

'Oh, I know the feeling,' groaned my sister. 'Yes, it would be nice to take the straw out of one's mouth occasionally. Imogen even found a piece of straw in her knickers the other day, didn't you,

Imo?'

'No,' I said icily.

There was a silence.

'Right, well, I must go,' determined Eleanor, slapping her whip against her leather boot. 'Cracker will be getting impatient. It was lovely to meet you properly.' She shot Hannah a special smile. My sister looked captivated. 'Toodle-oo. See you on Sunday. I'm *so* pleased you're all coming.'

And with that she gave us a cheery wave and the benefit of her pert little backside as she sashayed off across the grass, back to her mount. I watched her untie a huge bay gelding and spring effortlessly into the saddle, and then she spun him round on the spot, pointed his nose up the hill, and galloped off over the horizon in a cloud of dust.

## CHAPTER FIFTEEN

When she'd disappeared from sight, I swung round to face my sister. 'Why didn't you snog her?'

'What?'

'Well, you were flirting with her, chatting her up—why didn't you go the whole hog, wrestle her to the floor and stick your tongue down her throat?'

'Oh, don't be ridiculous,' she scoffed.

I was so furious I could hardly speak. I slammed around the kitchen, throwing plates in the dishwasher, chucking the salad bowl in the sink.

'I can't believe you said yes to lunch,' I fumed, my voice shaking with emotion. 'I thought you didn't like her, couldn't bear her and Piers and

253

their stuck-up ways!'

'Actually, I thought she was charming,' she mused, cutting herself a slice of cake and picking the chocolate icing off the top with her nails. 'Sweet of her to comment on my pots.'

'Flattery,' I spat, snatching the cake from under her. 'And you're not having that.'

'Why not?' She looked up, astonished.

'Because you said you didn't want it!' My eyes blazed at her as I threw the cake in a tin, jamming the lid on and tossing it in the cupboard. 'God, you were the one who told me to watch out for her, said she was after my husband!'

'Yes, but I think I was wrong about that. I mean, after all, it was years ago, wasn't it? And I very much doubt she'd have you down here if she was after Alex. Too obvious. No, I've revised that theory.'

'Oh, have you?' I snarled. 'When it suits you!'

'Be interesting to see the house, though.' She narrowed her eyes speculatively and leaned back in her chair, folding her arms against her large bosom. 'I've never been up there before.'

'And that's what she's banking on,' I spat. 'That your nosy-parker instincts will get the better of any *real* instincts you might have about her!' I scraped the remains of the coronation chicken noisily into the bin with a fork.

'Don't you want that? I could have taken that home for Eddie's supper.'

'Tough.' I threw the bowl in the sink. Swung around to face her. 'And how dare she have spoken to Alex already?' I was trembling with rage. 'Christ, I only knew about the flat last night, and there she is telling *me* about it. What is she—

phoning him every day?'

'I think she said she rang him to ask about lunch when she couldn't get hold of you, remember?'

'Couldn't get hold of me? I'm here the whole frigging time! I'm welded to the place, never go anywhere except to feed her bloody cows!'

'Do calm down, Imogen. You're sounding like a jealous schoolgirl. And anyway, if she *was* after him, she'd hardly be mentioning the fact that she'd rung him, would she? She'd be keeping that very quiet.'

'That's where you're wrong,' I hissed, a little too manically perhaps, waving a dirty fork in her face. 'That's where she's so clever! It was the same with Tilly, the same pally friendship, the same holidays abroad and then—*wham!*—in she goes, under the wire. It's a smokescreen, you see, a cover—what, me and Alex?' I opened my eyes innocently, aping Eleanor. 'Lord, no, we're just good friends, always have been. Oh, she is *so* smart, Hannah, *so* smart, you have no idea. She manipulates people, draws them into her web. It's her forte. I mean, Christ, look at you! A couple of days ago you thought she was scheming and untrustworthy. Remember the gymkhana lady, Sue, who had a team Eleanor wanted Theo in, and—and the one she got to make curtains right before Christmas and then snubbed at church? Blimey, didn't take you long to forget them, did it? Didn't take long to get round *you*!'

'She didn't get round me, she simply asked me and Eddie to lunch and I accepted. Now grow up.'

'And now she's going to be staying in London at the exact same time as Alex,' I seethed.

'Oh, for heaven's sake.'

'And wasn't she quick to tell me that, hmm? *Very*

255

quick off the mark to get that out into the open so I can't turn round and say—I didn't know! Didn't know I'd be the one parked down here, stuck in the frigging mud while they're both up in town. It's her modus operandi, Hannah, can't you see that? She *doesn't* sneak around, *ever*, she's *so* much bolder than that. She's, she's brazen!' I fixed her with feverish eyes.

She shot me a pitying look as she got to her feet, plucking her handbag from the back of her chair. She swung it over her shoulder.

'Imogen, she's staying in London because she's got a business to run, she told you. A winter collection to get out. Honestly, you're starting to sound a bit unhinged. I'm beginning to wonder who needs the counselling around here.' And so saying, she gave me an arch look then swept past me out of the cottage, stalking off through the mud in her heels to her car.

When she'd gone, I stood at the window, staring blankly at the wet fields encased with little drystone walls, arms crossed, my hands clutching the tops of my arms tightly. I was trembling slightly. Suddenly, on an impulse, I went to the kitchen drawer. I pulled out a pad and a pencil and sat down at the table. I chewed the end of the pencil feverishly for a bit, then I wrote a list of all the reasons I *should* worry about Eleanor, and all the reasons I shouldn't. When I'd finished, I stared at it. Under *'Should Worry'* I'd written:

1) Still beautiful.
2) He loved her once so could fall for her again.
3) More likely to now he's in such close proximity.

4) Light years ahead of you socially (charm, *savoir faire*, confidence, etc.).

Under 'Shouldn't Worry' I'd written:

1) All over years ago.
2) People don't go backwards.
3) No one shits on their own doorstep.
4) He's your *husband*, for crying out loud!

I stared at the second list. At number four. Yes. Of course. Hannah was right. I was being ridiculous. Quite, ridiculous. Suddenly I felt stupid for making such a scene in front of her. Well, thank God it was only Hannah, I thought, tearing the paper off the pad and scrunching it up. Only my sister. Thank God I hadn't got it all off my chest while Eleanor was still here, before she'd swung a leg over Cracker. I imagined her astonished face as I let rip, saw her hazel eyes widen. Then I imagined her telling Piers about it later over supper—'You know, darling, I'm really rather worried about her.' I got up quickly from the table and threw the ball of paper in the bin. Then I took it out, tore it into shreds, and threw it back again. I stared at the bits of paper lying there on the lettuce, the act of someone who had something to hide. Hurriedly, I fished the bits out, scrunched them into a tiny ball and glanced around the kitchen for a match. No matches. On an impulse, I put the ball in my mouth. And then, through the open doorway, I caught sight of myself in the hall mirror, trying to swallow. Slowly, I took the ball of paper from my mouth and dropped it in the bin. I bowed my head and stood for a moment, in silent

257

contemplation.

After a few moments, I made myself walk calmly to the cupboard under the stairs. As I crouched down and drew out my comfort blanket, I noticed my hand was shaking. I stared at it. Made a fist. What was happening to me? Why was I behaving like this? And what about that leaf I was going to turn over, the one that would make me all confident and classy, all shiny and new? As I straightened up, my duffel bag of paints over my shoulder, I couldn't help feeling it was offering some fairly weighty resistance.

*     *     *

Later, as I stood at my easel in the orchard, knowing I had barely an hour before I collected Rufus, which wasn't nearly long enough, but knowing too that this was the only way to clear my head and banish the demons, I calmed down a bit. It wasn't hard, actually. Although I was loath to admit it, there really was something about this place; something about capturing the movement of nature—those beech trees, for example, their delicate lime-green leaves casting lacy patterns on the grass, or the chestnuts with their heavy swirling skirts and secret depths—about responding immediately to light and colour that was so exhilarating, so exciting, it almost took my breath away. It left no space in my head for gnawing doubts.

I worked quickly, my brush moving in swift, confident strokes across the board, until I reached the point—and it came quicker outdoors—when my strokes were less measured, more impulsive, and I entered that heavenly phase where I almost lost consciousness and painted from instinct, the paint seeming to fly by itself on to the canvas, giving depth to clouds, trees, hillsides, in a way that later, as I came up for air and blinked at what I'd done, made me giddy with pleasure.

Occasionally, during one of these moments of oblivion, the inevitable happened: a splash would fall on my nose, then another, then finally one on my canvas, and by the time I'd come to my senses and unscrewed the board from the easel, hurrying across the meadow with it face down, desperate to get it back to the cottage, the skies were opening.

Today, it was the wind that was against me. I hunched my back against a strong north-westerly and impatiently brushed hair from my eyes as it whipped around my face. Occasionally a leaf stuck to the canvas, sometimes even a feather. A feather? I picked it off and carried on, but then another one landed on my palette, and another. I frowned as I removed them with my nails from the swirl of Prussian Blue, and surfaced sufficiently from my creative reverie to wonder where they were coming from. I glanced around. Stared. A horrific scene met my eyes. A large hen—Cynthia, one of my precious Silkies—lay about twenty feet away, decapitated.

I froze, paintbrush poised, transfixed. Then, hastily chucking my palette on the grass, I fled across, both hands clutching my mouth. Omigod, Omigod! I glanced around in terror. I wondered if there were more. Had he killed them all—for he, I was sure, was the fox—and had he left them all in the same sorry state as my lovely lady Cynthia? Heart pounding, I tore round to the compost heap where I knew they liked to hang out, gossiping and jostling, and saw, to my intense relief, that a fair-sized squad was perched on top, pecking at the grubs and worms as usual. Most of them were there, surely? I counted feverishly. Ten, eleven, twelve . . . no. There should be fourteen. Cynthia was one, but another was missing. The big brown hen, Mother Theresa, and—oh sweet Jesus—the chicks!

I rushed to the barn where Theresa often retreated, preferring its dark cavernous shade and shelter for her babies, and as I adjusted my eyes to the gloom I saw her, at the foot of the hay bales, keeping watch over a dead chick, all the others missing. Oh Christ, had they all been . . . ? I looked at her. Her dark, button eyes communed silently with mine. Oh dear God, they'd all been taken, eaten, except this one little scrap, this chick, which . . . yes. I crouched. It was still moving. It was still alive! To the hen's consternation, I picked it up, took one last tortured look around—no, all gone, all of them—and ran, with it cupped in my hands, to the house. What would Rufus say? Oh, what would he say? I had to save one. I had to!

Theresa followed anxiously, legs planted wide apart as she put her head down and charged, feathery skirts billowing around her, hot on my heels as I barged through the back door and lunged across the table for the phone.

'Marshbank Veterinary Practice?' said a familiar voice as Theresa skidded round the table after me on the lino floor.

'I need the vet,' I whispered. 'Fast.'

'He's on a call at the moment. Can I give him a message?'

'Yes, tell him it's an emergency. Tell him to get over to Shepherd's Cottage on the Latimer estate right away, please.'

I put down the phone. The chick was getting weaker, I could tell, its little yellow body going limp in my hand, eyes half shut. It needed warmth and it needed it quickly. With Mother Theresa still at my feet, nervously shadowing my every move, I hastened to the old solid-fuel Rayburn. I'd cursed it when we'd first arrived, wondering who on earth, in this day and age, was prepared to shovel coke into their cooker, but now I blessed it for its constant heat. I opened the oven door and tentatively put my hands in, cupping my precious bundle. Too hot? Roast chick? I glanced at the mother. Yes, perhaps it was too hot. Maybe I should have left it in the stable where she'd been keeping an eye on it? It had certainly had more movement then.

'Sorry—sorry,' I whispered, scuttling back outside again.

Across the yard we hastened, Theresa and I, and into the barn where I lay the chick down on the same patch of hay. Maybe she would sit on it; cover it with her feathery warmth. She didn't seem inclined to, and after nudging it with her beak in a desultory manner, wandered off to peck in the dirt. I watched her go in horror. No! No, come back! She was sauntering towards the door. Towards the others on the dung heap. Screwing up all my nerve and holding my breath, I lunged—and picked her up. A nasty bundle of brittle bones and feathers squirmed and flapped horribly in my hands, but I held on tight and, at arm's length, deposited her on her offspring. She gave an indignant squawk and

261

bustled straight off again. I watched her go, impotently.

'You've got to keep it warm,' I begged, brokenly. 'It'll die!'

She shot me a sharp look and went back to her mates.

Desperate now, I kneeled over the chick in the hay. I breathed hard on its little yellow body, as if I were misting up a windowpane. I couldn't actually bring myself to give it the kiss of life, couldn't—you know, go beak to beak—and it smelled ghastly, like a bad chicken nugget, but I was convinced I was getting somewhere. I was just getting into a rhythm, bending forward on my knees as if at some religious devotion, breathing out with a loud 'HUH', ruffling the feathers, when I became aware of footsteps behind me.

Pat Flaherty, backlit dramatically by a shaft of sunlight, was marching through the open barn door, a tall silhouette in faded jeans and a white T-shirt, carrying his leather bag.

'What is it? What's happened?'

'Oh, thank God!' I swung round and nearly squashed the chick with my knee. 'Ooops—Christ . . .' I hastily rearranged it in the hay. 'Thank goodness you've come!'

'What's happened?'

I stumbled to my feet and pointed a quivering finger at the body in the straw.

'The chick!'

He stared. 'What?'

'It's dying, you must save it!'

He stooped, picked the chick up, gave it a cursory glance and tossed it in the straw. 'It's dead. What's the emergency?'

262

'Dead?'

'It's stone cold, for God's sake. What's been going on here?'

'Oh!' I crouched down and picked it up tenderly. 'Then we must bury it. Rufus will want to. Oh, how ghastly!' I sank down on my knees and started to cry.

'Mrs Cameron, what exactly did you call me out for?'

'The chicks,' I sobbed, 'they're all dead. And Cynthia.'

'Cynthia?'

'The Silkie. That bloody fox, he's killed the lot of them!'

'Well, that's bad luck,' he said impatiently, 'but what d'you want me to do about it?'

I turned my wet face up. 'Well, I thought you could save this one! That's what you do, isn't it? Save lives?'

He looked at me aghast. 'You called me out for a chick? I was told something terrible had happened here; assumed, at the very least, a rabid dog had got amongst the sheep and was tearing them limb from limb!'

'What'll I tell Rufus?' I trembled.

'That it's country life!' he snapped. 'Mrs Cameron, when I got your urgent message I was delivering breeched calf twins, one of which has still yet to be born, but hopefully *will* be born, no thanks to you!'

'Oh, so my chickens aren't as important as someone else's cow, is that it?' I flared.

'Of course they're bloody not!'

'Why, because they're not as big?'

He leaned over me, his dark eyes blazing into

mine. 'Yes, as it happens. In this instance, size matters.'

'Well I—'

'And value, Mrs Cameron. Ted Parker's prize heifers are worth a damn sight more than your Easter chicks, I can assure you. This is the second time you've called me out on a wild-goose chase. Don't let it happen again. Good day to you.' He turned on his heel.

I got up and hastened after him. 'Aren't you even going to look at Cynthia? She's been decapitated, for God's sake!'

'Well then, there's not much I can do for her, is there? Now instead of running around like a headless chicken yourself, I suggest you shut them up a little earlier. The fox is around at about five o'clock these days.'

'Shut them up?'

'Yes, when you put them in for the night.' He threw his bag in the back of his open-topped Land Rover.

'Oh!' I stopped.

He turned. 'What?'

'N-no. Nothing.'

He fixed me with a steely gaze. Took a step towards me. 'You don't shut them up?'

'Well, I . . .' I licked my lips, 'I sort of assumed they put themselves to bed.'

He gazed at me in wonder. 'Where?'

'Well, I don't know.' I looked around desperately. 'In the trees?'

'In the trees?' he echoed. 'What, like robins and blackbirds? In cosy little nests, perhaps?'

'Well, I don't know. I—'

'Have you ever seen chickens flying around your

264

garden, Mrs Cameron? Soaring up into the stratosphere in close formation? Doing loop the loop?'

'No, but—'

'Oh, perhaps they *climb* into the trees, hmm? To get to their nests? Haul themselves up the branches with their spindly little legs?'

'Well, I've seen them roost!' I spluttered. 'In the barn, on a high pole!'

'Yes, *in extremis*, they will flutter up to roost, but their wings have been clipped so they certainly don't fly into trees. Where's your chicken house?'

I stared at him. 'I . . . don't know.'

'You don't know? Well, where do they lay their eggs?'

I rubbed my forehead with my fingertips. Eggs. Yes, I had wondered about that. I cleared my throat. 'I had noticed they didn't lay, actually, but I assumed it was—well—wrong time of the month, or something.'

'Wrong time of the month?' He boggled. *'Wrong time of the month?* These are laying pullets, Mrs Cameron, not a load of whingeing females with headaches!'

And with that he turned sharply on his heel and made off round the back of the cottage. I hurried after him. He was heading off down the little dirt track, past the gorse bushes and the muddy paddock, along the long cinder path that led to the Wendy . . . oh.

'What the hell d'you think this is?' he said, lifting the little wooden door.

I swallowed. 'Yes, well, I can see now that it is probably a . . . It's just that Rufus and I . . .'

No. No, don't tell him what you thought. That

265

they'd stupidly made the door too small for even children to get in, and that we'd even tried to shove Rufus through one afternoon. 'It's for Lilliputians, like in *Gulliver's Travels*!' he'd declared as we'd collapsed, giggling on the grass.

'Jesus wept.' Pat lifted a flap at the back of the house. A little flap I hadn't noticed. In a row of small, straw-lined boxes, dozens, literally dozens, of eggs twinkled up at us.

'Oh Lord.' I crept across and stared. 'Will they all be stale?'

'They'll be a darn sight fresher than any you'd buy at the supermarket. Just make sure they don't float.'

'Float?'

'Yes,' he said impatiently. 'Put them in a pan of water. Any stale ones will float to the surface, the rest you can eat.' He lifted another lid. 'Ah yes, I thought as much. You've got a broody one here. She's sitting, so if you don't disturb her, these eggs could hatch.'

'Oh! You mean, more chicks?'

'That tends to be the usual pattern,' he said drily. 'The cycle of life.'

'Oh, and this is the hen that went missing ages ago. And she looks just like Cynthia, identical! I could tell Rufus it *was* her, he'd never know!'

'Could do,' he eyed me. 'Or you could tell him the truth.' He let the lid go with a bang and started off back up the cinder path. I seemed to be forever running after this man.

'And what time should I put them to bed?'

He stopped in his tracks, a few feet short of his Land Rover. Turned. I saw his mouth twitch.

'What time? Well, the moment they've had their

266

cocoa and you've read them a story, of course.'

I flushed. 'No, I just meant—'

'Jesus, when it gets dark. But if you're worried about the fox, a bit earlier for the next couple of days, OK?'

I nodded. He got in his Land Rover, leaping over the door. I screwed up my eyes and my nerve.

'One more question,' I breathed.

He shook his head wearily as he started the engine. 'Don't tell me. No, please, let me guess. How do I get them to have an early night? When I can't turn off the telly and shoo them upstairs?'

I nodded mutely, eyes still shut.

'You *herd* them in, for God's sake, with a stick, like wild animals, which brings me to another tiny point.' He twisted round in his seat to face me, crooking a brown forearm over the door, engine still running. 'If you anthropomorphise your animals and give them all names, it's very hard when they die. Particularly for children. If it's just "the brown one", or "the white one", and not—I don't know,' he waved a despairing hand at a solitary cockerel strolling past—'Cocky Locky?' he hazarded.

'Nobby,' I muttered.

'Nobby?'

'Always on his own. No mates.'

'Right,' he said faintly. 'Well, hopefully that's one funeral I won't be called out for. Presumably no one will mind when *he* bites the dust. All I'm saying is there's a great temptation to sentimentalise farm animals and it makes it that much harder when they snuff it.'

'Thank you,' I nodded stiffly. His dark eyes on mine were softer than they were wont to be. 'I'll

267

bear that in mind.'

'Do.' He revved the engine hard and reversed a smart circle in the yard. 'And now if you'll excuse me I'll get back to Ted Parker's place and attend to another hormonal female. Stick my hand up that cow's arse.'

And with that he sped off up the zigzag track, a cloud of dust shimmering in his wake.

He had to go and ruin it, didn't he? I thought, watching him go. Had to—hurl an insult, paint a picture. For a moment there, as he'd been telling me how to make death more bearable for Rufus, I'd almost detected a glimmer of compassion, but then he'd reverted to his usual warts-and-all style of vetting. He should learn, I thought, going back into the cottage and slamming the door behind me, that he was in a service industry, and patients came first. If he wanted to get on in his private practice he should cultivate a few manners!

## CHAPTER SIXTEEN

The following day, I rang Kate and told her the whole sorry tale.

'Oh dear, poor you. But you know, he's right, I'm afraid,' she said to my surprise. 'You don't call a vet out for chickens, certainly not baby chicks. My father used to just wring their necks if they were looking a bit dodgy.'

'No!'

'They're not pets, Imogen. You can't get too attached to farm animals. Where d'you think your M&S Chicken Kiev comes from?'

'I suppose,' I agreed humbly.

I couldn't help thinking she sounded a bit sharp today. It occurred to me that I'd forgotten to return a call she'd left on my answer machine last week and I wondered, guiltily, if she was feeling peeved. 'When you've got a moment,' the message had said mournfully, and the awful thing was, I hadn't. Recently, I'd either been painting furiously or running round after the animals. I just hadn't had time.

'Rufus must have been upset, though,' she went on in a gentler tone, perhaps regretting her no-nonsense approach.

'Yes, he was, but actually he was more furious than anything else. He spent the whole of last night setting traps for the fox.'

Nevertheless, when he'd come home from school, his face had gone white.

'What, all of them? He killed them all, and Cynthia too?'

'I'm afraid so, darling,' I'd said anxiously, twisting my hands. 'But the vet says it was all terribly quick, they wouldn't have known anything about it.'

I didn't go into the last, dying moments of one particular chick, whose life had been needlessly protracted by a crazy woman shoving it in hot ovens and suffocating it with halitosis.

'Bastard,' he'd said, changing colour again.

'Rufus!'

'Well, he is. I want to kill him.' And taking his frog in a jam jar, he'd stormed out of the kitchen, tears stinging his eyes, to see the rest of the hens.

Luckily I'd had the presence of mind—and the courage, I felt—to dispose of Cynthia's headless body. With the protection of a pair of Marigold gloves I'd put her first in a dustbin, then, panicking that she'd honk and the fox would come back, had plucked her from the potato peelings and taken her, arms outstretched, appalled face screwed up and averted, to the cow's field, where, much to the interest of the cows who clustered round, I'd dug a hole, panting and sweating and wielding a pickaxe, the ground was so hard (and this a woman who was more used to wielding a handbag as she sauntered down Putney High Street), thereby disposing of the evidence. Thus it was that now, when Rufus went out to the yard, he found the remaining chickens pecking away quite happily, callously unconcerned that their numbers were reduced.

He was gone for about half an hour, I think for a cry, and then ran back inside to use the phone. Ten minutes later, I looked out of the kitchen window to see Tanya, in a yellow T-shirt and blue leggings, running down the hill and leaping across the stream in the pit of the valley, with what looked like a length of rope in her hands. When I popped out a bit later, I found the pair of them in the barn, right on top of the huge haystack: Tanya was on Rufus's shoulders, swaying precariously as she slung one end of the rope over a rafter, the other end tied in a noose, which draped on the floor. Through this, apparently, the fox would put his head in order to get to one very dead, maggoty magpie that one of Tanya's brothers had caught and which was lying in state in a shoe box, whereupon the noose would tighten, and the fox strangle. I had my doubts and wondered nervously what Health and Safety would have to say about it all, but Tanya claimed huge success with the contraption, as I now told Kate.

'Sounds like Rufus has really landed on his feet,' she observed. 'Found a new best friend already.'

'Oh, no, he really misses Orlando,' I said quickly. 'He said so the other day. It's just that, well, you know, a new boy on the block is always a novelty. Tanya will probably go back to her old friends next week.'

'And he's in all the teams?' Kate probed. 'At school?'

'They don't exactly have teams, Kate. Dan— Mr Hunter thinks nine is terribly young to have organised cricket and football. He thinks ten is a much better age, and favours balls skills at this stage, which Rufus loves because he's not always last, or left out, and actually he's getting much better. He plays football all the time now, whereas before he didn't because he thought he was hopeless at it. Mr Hunter thinks there's plenty of time for competitive sport.'

'Mr Hunter will be sprouting wings and a halo soon. You haven't got a thing about him, have you?'

'Certainly not!' I blushed furiously, fervently wishing I hadn't rung Kate at what was clearly a prickly moment. 'He's Rufus's headmaster, for heaven's sake.'

'Didn't stop Ursula Moncrief, did it?' she retorted. 'Remember poor Mr Pritchard at the school ball?'

I giggled, recalling Ursula Moncrief at the Carrington House school ball, pissed as a fart in an off-the-shoulder dress that was more like off-the-elbow, nuzzling into Mr Pritchard's neck and taking little nips at it as he manoeuvred her

271

nervously round the floor to 'Lady in Red', his eyes huge with fear.

'Yes, well, there's no danger of that. A ball is the last thing this little backwater of a school is likely to hold.'

'Damn. That's the doorbell. Can you hang on?'

''Course,' I agreed, relieved she'd been deflected, particularly since she had, rather annoyingly, scored a bit of a bull's-eye. I was aware that I did have a very tiny crush on Mr Hunter, and that in my duller moments, while I was cleaning my brushes, or rubbing down my palette, had found my mind turning to him. Not in any nasty lustful way, of course, more—well, more in a maternal way, if anything. I was pretty sure he was younger than me and he had such gentle eyes and soft springy hair, and that tatty old corduroy jacket that even I, who didn't have a domestic bone in my body, was itching to patch at the elbows. A couple of those leather ones would suit him, I thought; give him an academic air. They sold them in the local department store in town, and the other day, I'd found myself lingering in haberdashery, fondling them. It was only because he'd been so kind to Rufus I'd reasoned as I'd left the shop—happily minus the elbow patches—given us such marvellous advice about the bullying, for which I was so grateful. So grateful that I did, actually, make what I regarded to be an entirely legitimate gesture—albeit an impulsive one—and gathered a huge bunch of bluebells from the woods behind the cottage, dropping them off at school one morning when I knew everyone was in assembly, on his desk, with a note of thanks. Unfortunately, he'd forgotten his assembly notes and popped back in the room just as I was going.

'Oh!' I coloured up. 'I was—just leaving these. To say thank you.'

His eyes widened as he looked beyond me and saw the flowers. 'For what?'

'Well, you know, for your advice. About not tackling the bullying head on. It worked a treat. Rufus is really happy now.'

'Oh, well, good. I'm delighted. But you really shouldn't . . .' he gestured, embarrassed, at the flowers.

'It's nothing, only a few bits from the garden,' I said quickly, making an even more embarrassed gesture as I flicked back my hair. We were surely too old to be going quite so pink? The two of us?

'Have you got a vase?' I ventured.

'A . . . vase? Er, no,' he stuttered, 'I—'

'Never mind, I brought one,' I said, shamelessly whipping an old jug from a Tesco bag, horribly aware that through the glass partition, Mrs Harris, the school secretary, had eyes like saucers as she tapped away at her computer.

'Well, I must be getting on,' he'd said, coming to and reaching past me for the sheaf of papers on his desk. 'Er, thank you, Mrs Cameron.'

'Imogen,' I reminded him.

'Imogen,' he'd agreed, and for a moment there, our eyes did meet, briefly. Then we'd both made a convulsive movement to the door, and there'd been a nasty after-*you* moment as we'd exchanged overbright smiles on the threshold.

Yes, a school ball *would* be lovely, I mused, cradling the receiver under my chin as I waited for Kate, gazing out of the window at the cows chewing rhythmically in the meadow. Give me a

273

chance to—you know—dress up. Look my best, in a pretty floral number, something a bit Sarah Jessica Parker—I was fairly sure this didn't call for anything Londony and vampy—with Alex beside me, of course, elegant in black tie. Or perhaps it would be lounge suits, round here? I couldn't quite see Sheila Banks's husband in a dinner jacket.

I'd met him at the school gates the other day, Frankie Banks. Frightened the life out of me as he'd come up behind me, put a large paw on my shoulder and growled, 'You Rufus's mum?' 'Y-yes,' I'd stuttered, swinging round to boggle at his shaven head, bulging muscles and tattooed arms. 'Nice lad,' he'd said gruffly, and I'd gulped my thanks. Yes, it would be good to see him in a more social setting. Daniel Hunter, not Frankie Banks. Maybe he'd like to come to supper one night? Meet Alex properly? Very relaxed, just a lasagne or something. Although, of course, as from Monday, Alex was away all week. My heart lurched at the thought. Away at that flat in town.

'Imo? Are you still there?'

'What? Oh, yes, still here. Who was at the door?'

'Caroline Harvey, popping round with a leaflet about some ghastly chamber concert she's in. God, I can just see Sebastian's face; he'd pay *not* to go to that. Anyway, happily we're in Venice that weekend. Listen, I'd better go, I've slightly lost track of time and I've got to get to the shops. I'll ring you later.'

'Um, Kate, before you go, I've got a bit of a favour to ask. Quite a big one, actually.'

'Fire away,' she said cautiously.

'Well, you've got to promise that if it's really

274

cheeky of me, you'll say no immediately, OK?'

'What is it?'

'It's quite an imposition, so—so think about it and—'

'Imo, what?'

I licked my lips. 'It's just . . . well, you know Alex is going to stay in town during the week now?'

'Is he?' she said, surprised. 'No, I didn't know that.'

'Oh God, didn't I tell you? I must have told Hannah. Yes, he is, because the travelling's getting him down, so he's going to spend a few nights a week in London.'

'Oh, right. Where?'

'Well, that's the thing, Kate. He's been offered a room by this friend of his, Charlie Cotterall, but Charlie's left his wife and he's a real rogue. You know, always out on the piss, chatting up girls, and the thing is, I was just wondering—well, it's a huge imposition—but now that Sandra's gone and you've got the nanny flat downstairs, I was thinking—well, if you haven't already rented it out—if you'd think about renting it to Alex for the time being?'

I shut my eyes. Held my breath. There. I'd said it. Ever since Kate had let slip that she was sick of having a nanny about the place now that most of her children were at boarding school and had been dithering over whether to keep the flat for guests or rent it out, I'd wondered if I'd dare suggest it. There was a pause on the other end as she digested this. Suddenly I went hot. How stupid. I shouldn't have asked; it was rude and crass of me to put her in such an invidious position.

'Kate, I'm sorry, I—'

'You mean, for a few days, or to actually move in?'

I flushed. 'Well, I suppose I meant to move in, but, Kate, forget it. I—I should never have asked,' I stammered. 'It's just, I've been so worried recently, and I don't know why because I'm quite sure he *wouldn't* be led astray by Charlie—I mean, apart from anything else Charlie's got a steady girlfriend—but you know what these boys are like together, egging each other on, and I just thought—well, I don't know what I thought,' I finished lamely. 'Pathetic. I shouldn't even be worried. And I'm not, in all honestly, I'm really not, but . . . forget it, Kate.'

'I won't forget it,' she said slowly. 'I'll think about it.'

I held my breath. 'Will you?'

'I'll have to ask Sebastian, of course.'

'Of course, of *course* you'll have to ask him,' I said, clutching this straw. Golly, if she was at least going to *ask* . . .

'And naturally we'd pay the going rate,' I rushed on.

'Imo, I wasn't going to rent it out, so there won't be a going rate.'

I bowed my head, feeling hot. Yes, that was my shame. That I'd known Kate had more or less decided to keep it for guests; had decided against renting, so that although I'd offered to pay, I was pretty secure in the knowledge that she wouldn't take anything from us. My face burned. Suddenly I wished I didn't have a husband who required me to manipulate my friends.

'We'll see,' she said briskly, 'OK? I'll talk to Sebastian and let you know.'

276

'Yes, and thank you, Kate, for even considering it. I feel awful asking . . .'

But would feel even more awful, I thought, putting the phone down, if I hadn't asked. Would have worried myself senseless, for weeks. Particularly now I knew Eleanor was going to be up there. I licked my lips, which were very dry. Narrowed my eyes out of the window. In my next life, I decided, straightening up in my chair, as well as being supremely confident, I was also going to be extremely rich. It might not buy happiness, but it sure as hell eased the way.

I sat there a moment, a mixture of guilt and relief making me feel a bit heady, and watched as a red van filled the window. Paul, the postman, drove through the gate and parked in my yard. I waved and went out to meet him, wrapping my cardigan around me against the chill wind, pleased to have a distraction. In London I hadn't even known what my postman looked like, let alone his name, but here, things were different. Much more friendly. When I'd mentioned this to Mum, she'd looked at me in surprise.

'But of course, darling. Rural life is much more civilised. In France, the postman even stops for a tincture. When I first moved to Provence I went out and greeted him with, "*Bonjour, monsieur. Un petit calvados?*" To which he'd replied, "*Oui, mais pourquoi petit?*"'

I'd laughed, but had drawn the line at offering Paul whisky at ten o'clock. Tongues might wag if I was known, not only to be saying it with flowers to the headmaster, but getting the postman pissed too.

'Morning, Paul, what have you got for me?' I

277

said cheerily, buoyant now that I'd done the deed with Kate: ready to face the day.

'Just a brown one and some junk mail, I'm afraid.'

'Shame. Nothing exciting?'

'Not unless you count a garden hose catalogue.'

'I might,' I grinned. 'Got to take your thrills where you can these days!'

As soon as I'd said it, I wished I hadn't. Paul looked startled, then reddened and hopped back smartly in his van. As he roared off up the chalky track, I scurried inside, smarting.

There's cheerful banter and there's idiotic rambling, Imogen, I said to myself as I shut the door. Try not to come across as too much of a frustrated housewife, hmm?

As I went to the kitchen to chuck the junk mail in the bin, simultaneously opening the brown envelope, I frowned. Sat down. A hundred and fifty pounds? For what? My eyes shot to the headed paper, Marshbank Veterinary Practice, and then, itemised:

April 5 . . . Home visit and consultancy £75
May 18 . . . Home visit and consultancy £75

My eyes bulged in disbelief. A hundred and fifty pounds? For a couple of visits? Oh, for heaven's sake. I reached for the phone and punched out a number.

'Marshbank Veterinary Practice?' purred my friend on the other end.

'Can I speak to Pat Flaherty, please?'

'Mr Flaherty is on a call at the moment,' she said icily, perhaps recognising my demanding tones.

278

'Is he. Well it's Imogen Cameron here. Perhaps you can ask him from me why I've been charged a hundred and fifty pounds for absolutely nothing! All he did was prod a cow with his foot and show me where my chicken house is. Is that what he went to veterinary college for?'

'We have a basic call-out charge, Mrs Cameron. A home visit is more expensive.'

'Well, I could hardly bring the cow into the surgery, could I! Although I might just, next time.'

'You do that, Mrs Cameron. It might be worth watching.'

And with that, she put the phone down. I stared into the buzzing receiver, outraged. Ooh . . . I seethed. *Bloody* woman. Well, it would be the last time I'd be calling on Marshbank's services. There must be other vets in the neighbourhood; I'd patronise them next time. Take my animals elsewhere. Meanwhile, though, there was the vexing little problem of this bill to pay. I got up from the table, biting my thumbnail savagely. Alex had gone ballistic the other day because he'd seen a new carrier bag—what was he going to say about this?

'New shoes, Imogen!' he'd yelped, taking them out of the bag where I'd hidden them at the bottom of the wardrobe. 'What the hell are you up to? You know we're on a shoestring at the moment.'

'They're flip-flops, for God's sake,' I'd said, snatching them from him. 'Hardly handmade Italian mules, and I can't live in sweaty trainers all summer!'

I couldn't, but a totally unnecessary vet's bill would justifiably send him into orbit. No, I had to sort this one out myself.

Money again, I thought, sitting down and raking despairing hands through my hair, a sick feeling in the pit of my stomach. If only I could make some of the filthy stuff. If only I wasn't so hopeless. If only I could *do* something . . .

Half an hour later saw me driving very fast down the country lanes into town. Fast, because if I slowed down and thought about what I was doing, I might stop, turn round and go home. My hands felt sweaty on the wheel and my heart was full of fluttering and trepidation, and not only that, I had a very full car too. Packed to the gunwales. And no doubt I'd come straight back with my full car, with my tail firmly between my legs, but as Dad said, if you didn't stick your head above the parapet, how the hell did you know if it was going to be knocked off? Although as a caveat, he'd always add, 'But never agree to play Macbeth in drag,' something he'd done to his cost. Well, I wasn't about to do that. No, no, something much more terrifying.

I parked squarely outside the wine bar that Sheila had assured me the other day was just the place—'Just opened, luv, and right poncy it looks too'—and regarded it nervously. It did look poncy. With its smart, bottle-green livery and 'Moulin Rouge' written in loopy gold scroll above the two bow-fronted windows, it looked chic, smart, and expensive; just exactly how I didn't feel right now.

It was a full five minutes before I steeled myself to get out of the car and walk through the door. Inside it was dark and dimly lit, and I had to adjust my eyes to the cavernous depths. The walls were painted a dark matt red, and bentwood chairs were grouped around polished wooden tables dotted about the room. A long mahogany bar ran the entire length of the left-hand side, and behind it a pretty girl with a shiny dark bob and a cupid's-bow mouth was polishing glasses. Aside from that, the place was empty. She smiled.

'Can I help?'

'Yes, I . . . is the manager in, please?'

'I am the manager.'

'Oh.'

'Yes, I know, I should be drinking café cognac in my little back room reading *Paris Match* while someone else does this, but due to sluggish business I'm also the washer-upper, glass polisher and general dogsbody.' She grinned.

I grinned back, relaxing slightly. 'I know the feeling. I mean, the dogsbody one. My name's Imogen Cameron, by the way. I'm an artist.'

It was an old trick, but she looked suitably impressed as she offered me her hand.

'Hi, I'm Molly. Should I have . . . ?'

'No, no,' I said humbly, instantly regretting my bravado, 'you won't have heard of me. But I was just wondering—well, someone said you occasionally have local artists' work hanging in here, and I wondered if you'd consider taking mine?'

There. It was out.

'Oh, right. Who said that?'

'Sheila Banks.'

She threw back her head and laughed. 'Sheila Banks! Well, you've been misinformed. I've never had art here—haven't been open long enough— but if Sheila sent you, I'd better take a look. Don't want my legs chopped off, do I?' She balled her cloth and tossed it down on the bar. 'What are

281

they, watercolours?'

'No, oils actually. Rather large ones. They're in the car, I'll—'

'Oh.' She stopped, looked disappointed. 'Might not be our sort of thing then. Watercolours tend to go best, apparently. Cheaper, I suppose, and I think people find them more accessible.' She must have seen my face fall. 'Tell you what, let's take a look. 'She came out from behind the bar, slim and elegant in a white shirt and black jeans, a long white apron tied over them. 'You go and get them, and we'll spread them out on this big table here.'

Of course, by the time I'd made various trips to the car and struggled back with them, puffing and panting whilst she'd looked on wide-eyed, they wouldn't all fit on the table, so we ended up putting them on the floor around the room, propping them against the dark red walls. There was another, smaller room through a low archway at the back and Molly took a few in there, which I thought was encouraging. I then waited an agonising few minutes, what felt like the longest few minutes of my life, as she walked around them all, biting her thumbnail; really looking at them properly, head on one side, squatting down to get a better look, peering closely, then moving back to get the perspective. Finally she straightened up, turned and smiled.

'I'll take them,' she said. 'What the hell, they're huge, but they look great. And even if the customers don't go for them, I like them. They certainly go a long way to brightening up my bar.'

What I wanted to do was leap up and punch the air and shout *'Yesssss!'* before jumping, footballer style, into her arms, but I managed to restrain myself and gasp 'Thank you!' instead.

'What shall we say—sixty forty on the price tag if they sell? To you, of course.'

I gaped. I hadn't got as far as that. 'Perfect,' I said dazed. God, I'd have given her ninety per cent; would have agreed to anything if she did but know it. We then spent the next ten minutes writing prices on sticky labels—rather high ones, I felt, but who was I to argue?—and putting them on the frames, and then Molly went upstairs to borrow a hammer and a fistful of nails from her builders who were working in her flat above the bar. When she came back down, we set about hanging the pictures there and then. As I passed nails up to her, I felt as if I was walking on air.

'No time like the present,' she'd declared, halfway up a ladder and banging one in, taking a painting from me and hanging it carefully above the low archway. 'And it's not as if I've got any bloody customers!'

We hung eleven in all, and one, my largest and favourite, a Parisian street scene, we put right behind the bar under a convenient picture light. As I stood back and surveyed it, nestling there amongst the bottles of Martini and vermouth, then turned slowly round and took in the rest of my work, above tables, over the archway, a couple in the back room, all cheaply framed but at least on walls, and not in an easel or stacked away in a wardrobe, I felt such a rush of pleasure I was nearly sick.

'They look great,' said Molly in surprise, turning about. 'Really—you know—professional. And they transform the place. Looks like a proper French café now.'

It did. What had been a dark, gloomy bar with north-facing bow windows, now looked cheerful and atmospheric, like a nineteenth-century Impressionists' retreat. One could almost imagine them in here, in fact, in their smocks and berets, smoking their Gauloise, knocking back their pastis, bitching about Toulouse-Lautrec, before bustling back to their easels in their garrets.

'You need some of those ashtrays,' I said suddenly. 'The yellow ones, triangular, with something written—'

'Pernod! Got some—I just haven't put them out.' She dashed behind the bar and tore open a box. Polystyrene bobbles spilled everywhere, and we then had a very jolly time dealing out the ashtrays, one to each table. She hesitated.

'What I really want is candles. You know, in bottles, with the wax dripping down the sides, but it's so tacky and seventies, I just wonder . . .'

'Why not?' I said staunchly. 'This is a retro French café, isn't it? You're being intentionally kitsch.' She looked at me a moment, and then, in another, she'd whipped a whole load of waxy bottles from a cupboard behind the bar where she'd clearly stashed them, uncertain as to what they said about the proprietress.

'Let's light them,' I said decisively, taking a few from her and popping them round the room, adrenalin making me bossy.

'What, at lunch time?'

'Well, it's a gloomy old day, and people will see them flickering invitingly through the windows. Might lure them in.'

We lit the whole lot in the end, and even put a few on the bar, and then, with the place glowing

284

soft and sumptuous in the candlelight, my paintings shimmering magically in the flickering flames, Molly went to the fridge and took out a bottle. She popped the cork expertly.

'Come on, we need a drink. Even if no one else in this sodding town does.'

I laughed and we moved to perch on stools at the bar. Molly poured us each a large glass of Chablis, and as we sipped companionably she told me about her hopes for this place; about her dream of bringing a little bit of Paris where she'd worked for some years to this small market town; about her sleepless nights as she'd borrowed more and more money to open it, about her bank manager's misgivings, and about her despair as the clientele walked resolutely by to the Dog and Duck. To console her I told her about my own gnawing guilt that I wasn't a real artist at all, just a dilettante fake—unwise perhaps, since she'd just taken eleven of my pictures—but she seemed to take it in her stride, and we were on the point of going beyond work to our more personal lives—which, in my case, fired by two glasses of wine on an empty stomach would probably have gushed forth torrentially—when we were saved by the bell. A tinkly one over the door that Rufus would have liked. A young couple stuck their heads round. The man looked apologetic.

'Oh. We didn't know if you were open yet, or—'

'Yes! Oh, yes, we are.' Molly nearly fell off her stool, just managing to save herself, as she slipped, with a ravishing smile, behind the bar. 'What can I get you?'

I drained my glass, shooting her a wink, then, gathering up the solitary landscape we hadn't been

285

able to find space for and attempting to leave some money on the bar which Molly refused with a firm 'On the house', I went out into the street.

The air was still and calm, and a soft rain was falling, so light it was almost a mist. I stood there for a moment, relishing it, letting it cool my cheeks, flushed with wine and success. I'd found a home for my pictures. I'd found a new friend—who, if I was honest would probably turn out to be more of a soul mate than Sheila. I'd had a good day. Not the first since I'd been here, but the best for a while. Still smiling foolishly and with my warm glow threatening to reach furnace proportions, I tossed the solitary picture in the back of my car, and headed off out of town.

Thank you, Mr Pat Flaherty, I thought, gripping the wheel tightly and raising my chin as I swept off down the narrow lanes, cow parsley brushing the sides of my car. Thank you very much indeed. If you did but know it, you've given me the very kick up the backside I needed.


# CHAPTER SEVENTEEN

The barbecue at the Latimers' started badly. I was getting ready upstairs, dithering between a long floaty skirt or some smart linen trousers—I'd been caught out last summer when Eleanor had asked us to an informal barbecue and there'd been two hundred people there, complete with marquee, caterers and hog roast—and was just wondering if what I actually needed was a tiara, when the phone rang.

'Hello?'

'Damn. I was hoping to get the answer machine.'

'Hannah? Why, what's up?'

'Er, well. You're not going to be awfully thrilled.'

'You're not coming?'

My heart gave a quick, guilty flip. Not being responsible for my family might help enormously today.

'Oh, no, we're coming. But Dad's coming too.'

'Dad!' I sat down abruptly on the side of the bed.

'Yes. Now don't go ballistic, Imogen. I couldn't help it. He rang, you see, reminding me it was his birthday—'

'Oh, *shit.*'

'Exactly, and had I remembered that we might meet for a drink, which of course I hadn't, so I said, oh, Dad, I'm awfully sorry, we're going out to lunch. And then of course I put the phone down and felt awful, so I rang Eleanor to say, actually, so sorry, we won't be coming, I've forgotten Dad's birthday, and she said, bring him along, the more the merrier.'

'To which you replied, oh no I couldn't possibly,' I growled dangerously.

'Well, of course I did, but she wasn't having any of it. She said he must come, and bring his girlfriend too, and that she'd got enough food to feed a battalion and—well, what could I do?'

'You could have insisted, that's what!' I yelped. 'God—Mum, Dad, Dawn—please don't tell me Purple Coat, too?'

'Well, I don't imagine he'll leave her behind, do you?'

I shut my eyes. 'No, I don't imagine he will. Well done, Hannah.'

'There's no need to be like that,' she said testily. 'It wasn't my fault and, if you must know, I'm feeling pretty lousy myself today and would rather stay at home.'

'Sorry,' I said meekly. 'What's wrong?'

'Chronic constipation and stomach ache, since you ask. I'll see you later. And don't forget a card for Dad.' And with that she put the phone down.

Marvellous, I thought as I pulled on the floaty skirt and quickly slicked on some lipstick. My sister was honing her sanctimoniousness under the aegis of my father's birthday, when the simple truth was that Dad never celebrated. For reasons best known to his vanity, he never wanted to be reminded of the passing of the years, was almost offended if you rang and offered birthday greetings or presents, yet this year, had chosen to come out of denial and celebrate at the Latimers'. Perfect.

'Aren't you ready yet?' Alex yelled up the stairs.

'Coming!'

I grabbed my bag and pashmina and went down. Alex, fresh from the shower, looked like he'd stepped out of the *Sunday Times Style* magazine: pink shirt, pale cotton trousers, blue cashmere sweater slung casually around his neck, his blond hair swept back from his forehead. A Man in his Prime, the caption read.

'Come on, darling,' he said impatiently. 'We were due there twenty minutes ago.'

'I know, but no one's ever on time for these things. I've just got to find a card for Dad.' I rifled around in the kitchen drawer—a futile gesture—found a piece of plain white paper, folded it in half and pressured Rufus into making one. As he wielded his felt pens at the table, the phone rang again. Alex rolled his eyes to heaven and left the room.

'Hello?' I snapped, anticipating another family member.

'Yeah, it's Sheila here, luv. Have you got Tanya's snake?'

'Her what?'

'Her snake, only she's lost it, an' Rufus was at our place Friday, wasn't he? It crawls in people's bags an' that.'

'Oh! Er, hang on. Rufus, have you got Tanya's snake?' I hissed.

'No, but check my book bag.'

'*You* check your book bag!' I said, appalled.

'What the hell is going on?' thundered Alex, coming back into the kitchen, jingling coins in his pocket in irritation. 'Rufus, haven't you finished that card yet? Who's on the phone?'

'Hannah,' I lied.

Alex hadn't quite warmed to Sheila yet. The one and only time he'd met her, he'd come home from work unexpectedly to find her and her brood filling the entire cottage and eating us out of fishfingers. 'I am *not* running a mini welfare state!' he'd seethed to me afterwards.

'She er, left something here the other day. Wants to wear it. I'm just going to look.'

'Can't it wait?' he roared as I took the stairs two at a time.

I nipped into Rufus's room. Book bag, book bag—ah. I snatched it from the bed and, holding it at arm's length, peered in cautiously. Just the usual exercise books and pencils. Oh, hang on—

289

swimming bag. I picked it up off the floor and gingerly teased out his wet towel and trunks, then realised, with horror, that there was something slimy lodged in the bottom. Lip trembling I ran to the bathroom, tipped the bag upside down in the bath and shut my eyes as . . . out it dropped.

'AARGHH!'

I was still shaking when Alex came in. 'Swimming goggles,' he said, hooking them out. 'Are these what Hannah wanted?'

'Yes,' I breathed, opening my eyes.

'To wear today?'

'Er . . .'

'Like Biggles?'

'N-no. Tomorrow. A fancy-dress party.'

'Thank Christ for that. Your sister's dress sense is eccentric at the best of times. Can we go now, please?'

By the time we'd all tumbled out of the cottage—deciding to walk, on the grounds that we could both have a drink which I badly needed—we were indeed late. Actually, I was secretly pleased. If Eleanor had loads of people coming, I reasoned, raking a brush through my hair as we hurried along up the track, we could just creep up on the fringes and mingle discreetly, and hopefully Dad and his entourage would do the same. I lunged at Rufus's curls with the brush, but he dodged and I put it back in my bag, taking a deep breath to steady the nerves. As we strolled up the hill, the unseasonably hot sun shimmering on the buttercups, Rufus scampering ahead, I thought, that to an impartial observer, we must look like the perfect little family. A terribly handsome man with his not altogether ghastly wife—rather losing it round the hips but still with youth on her side—their russet-haired son blowing dandelion clocks as they went. And we were the perfect little family, I thought, sneaking a sideways glance at Alex.

He gave me a quick smile, making an effort to forget his irritation. 'All right?' he said gruffly.

'Yes, fine. And you?'

'Of course.'

My heart began to beat fast. Too formal. Far too formal for the perfect couple. Where was the reconciliatory arm around my shoulder? The nuzzling in for a quick make-up kiss? Oh, everything has to be perfect for you, Imogen, doesn't it? Well, only because I'm nervous, I reasoned, although I shouldn't be, because actually, I'd decided in the bath last night, I was being completely neurotic about Eleanor Latimer. I'd had a bit of a Damascene moment as I lay there in the bubbles, and in fact it was my own little crush on Daniel Hunter that had done the trick. Married people *did* have crushes, you see, but it didn't mean anything. Not a thing. And it wasn't the first one I'd had, either. No, there'd been that French chap who sold olives in the market at Turnham Green; the one with the silky blond curls and the blowtorch smile; lovely hands. God, I'd bought olives from him for *weeks*, practically lived on them, and one night, I'd even dreamed about him. About his hands. Had woken up in a muck sweat imagining them gliding up my jumper, cupping my bare breasts— 'Oh!'

'What?' Alex had woken up blurrily beside me.

'Bad dream!' I'd gasped guiltily, clutching the duvet under my chin as his arms encircled me.

'No monsters in this bed,' he'd said sleepily,

nuzzling into my damp neck, my pulse racing. 'Go back to sleep.'

But I'd lain awake thinking—how *awful*! An erotic *dream*! I'm *married*! But . . . was it so awful? Or was it, in fact, perfectly normal? And was it just the same for Alex? A bit of harmless fantasising? A perfectly natural crush that the two of them had on each other? And would it help, I thought, now, as we waded through the buttercups together, if I joked about it? Said things like, 'So, lunch at your girlfriend's today, Alex—can't wait!' To which he'd laugh, scratch his head sheepishly and reply, 'Yeah, I suppose I've always had a soft spot for her.' And I could joke around with Piers too, say, 'Crikey, Piers, the heat from those two—phew!' (Fan myself.) 'We ought to join forces, you and I.' (Link his arm.) 'We'd make a good team!' And he'd throw back his head and bray delightedly. Yes, that was the way forward, that would defuse the situation, and good heavens, if the roles were reversed it was exactly what Eleanor would do, wasn't it?

As we rounded the side of the house and approached the back lawn through the rose gardens, it occurred to me that it all was rather quiet: no hum of voices I'd expected, no shouts of laughter, no clinking of champagne glasses. Odd. As the terrace came into view, I saw Piers, sitting up ramrod straight on a bench with Dawn beside him. Hannah was slumped lumpenly in a wicker sofa in the manner of one who's reached her journey's end, and Mum was beside her: Eddie was assiduously turning sausages on the barbecue, talking to my father, whilst Eleanor, stunning in a salmon-pink T-shirt and denim shorts, buzzed around barefoot with a jug of Pimm's.

Alex glanced at me, horrified. 'Your entire family's here!'

'Yes, I . . . forgot to tell you. I thought it was a big bash. Had no idea it was just us. And Eleanor invited them,' I added quickly. God, and here I was in a long dress more suitable for Ascot. I tried to hitch it up. Could hardly tuck it in my knickers, though.

'Christ Alive,' Alex muttered. 'Piers will freak.' It occurred to me that he already had. 'Who's the girl with no clothes on?'

'That's Dawn,' I muttered. 'Dad's girlfriend.' I'd forgotten Alex hadn't had the pleasure.

'Sweet Jesus, she looks like a hooker!'

Dawn had obviously expected quite a gathering too, and had dressed up—or down, depending on how you looked at it—in a lot of heavy make-up, a pink crop top, and a skirt, if you counted the white thing around her waist.

'Imogen, Alex, how lovely!' Eleanor did look genuinely delighted as she tripped lightly across, and although I tried not to notice how she kissed Alex, I decided it was just a nice, friendly kiss. Not lingering, but not too carefully social either.

'And I don't need to introduce you to anyone, because of course you know them all!' she laughed. 'Isn't this jolly?'

'Very,' remarked Alex drily, stepping forward to shake hands with Dad, who came across, beaming with pleasure and looking like the cat who'd got the cream. He was wearing tight white trousers and a Hawaiian-print shirt of such dazzling hue I almost had to shade my eyes.

'Happy Birthday, Dad,' I smiled, kissing him and

293

handing him the card. 'Sorry I forgot.'

'Oh, don't worry, when you get to my age you stop counting. I say, quite a pad your mates have got here, haven't they?' His eyes roamed admiringly over the balustrade to the landscaped acres beyond, shimmering in the heat. 'You've landed on your feet getting a toe in here, haven't you? I gather Ellie here is an old girlfriend of yours, Alex.' He nudged me. 'Better watch that, love. They'll be rekindling old flames!'

Eleanor laughed and filled up his glass. 'Don't be ridiculous, Martin. He's far too besotted by your daughter!'

'Oh, I don't know,' I said boldly, in my new vein. 'Alex can always slip in another one.'

A surprised silence fell. I hadn't quite meant it to come out like that.

'Well, he's a better man than I am, then,' quipped Dad, saving my blushes. 'I was just saying what a fine place your friends have got here, Alex. No wonder you took the cottage.'

Alex agreed and I moved away to greet Mum. I hadn't quite got the hang of the jolly banter yet. Might have to work on it. As I bent to kiss my mother, I relaxed slightly. At least I could count on her not to let the side down. She was looking effortlessly elegant in a cream linen dress and a floppy straw hat, her eyes, bright with amusement as she puffed away on her cigarette.

'Isn't this marvellous?' she chuckled quietly as I sat down beside her. 'Look at that man. He's about to pass out with shock!'

Piers, it was true, was a picture: veins standing up in his forehead, eyes bulging, as Dawn, tapping his arm for emphasis with a long black fingernail, explained, in carrying tones, about her friend Malcolm who had a big house—almost as big as this—in Peckham.

'He keeps llamas, right,' she was saying, 'and ostriches. It's new-wave farming, see?'

Piers blinked. 'Good Lord. In Peckham?'

'Yeah, it's a great little business. You should try ostriches, Piers, wiv all your fields an' that.'

'Well, it's a thought,' agreed Piers vaguely.

'You sell the meat, see, to the local farm shops, *and* you sell the feavers.' She tapped his arm. 'So it's all economically—whatsit?'

'Viable?'

'That's it.'

'But who on earth buys the feathers?'

'Christ knows. But I've got an ostrich pompom G-string, 'aven't I? So someone must! They probably use it to stuff pillows an' that.'

'And . . . where does it go?'

'Pillows go on beds, Piers.'

'No, the pompom.'

'Oh, on the front. Blimey, not round the back. You'd look like the frigging Easter Bunny!' She roared and elbowed him in the ribs. He looked genuinely delighted and roared back.

'Where did he meet her?' Alex bent to hiss in my ear.

'Who?'

'Your father! Where on earth did he meet someone like that?'

I looked up into his furious blue eyes. 'At the opera house, of course,' I said smoothly, getting up to find a drink. I wasn't in the mood to be my father's apologist. I moved on to speak to Hannah.

'Isn't this just the best fun?' she drawled as I

295

sank down beside her on the wicker sofa. 'Dawn hasn't drawn breath since we arrived.'

'I think it's a case of beam me up, Scottie. How are you feeling?'

'Ghastly. I haven't been to the loo for days and my stomach feels like reinforced concrete.'

She looked terrible, admittedly: pale and slightly damp at the edges as she held her breath, wincing.

'Well, go and see the doctor tomorrow. They'll give you a suppository or something.'

'Charming, then I'll have the trots for days. No, I'm banking on getting food poisoning here and then letting it do its worst. Eddie's convinced the sausages are passed their sell-by date so he's frazzling them to a crisp.'

'I wondered why he'd taken charge of the barbecue. But is it really just us, Hannah?'

'Piers's mother is knocking around somewhere.' She glanced around vaguely. 'She went inside, I think, claiming it was too hot, but you could see she was pained by the company.'

'Oh God,' I giggled. 'Lady Latimer and *Dawn*!'

'Oh, yes, you missed that floor show. Dawn asked her if she was really a lady, to which the great woman replied, "So my gynaecologist tells me."'

I snorted. 'But no Purple Coat?'

'No, she's got a gig, apparently. Singing at that hotel in town, the one with the piano bar.'

'The Regal? Blimey, good for her.'

'Isn't it? Oh, and there is someone else here actually, some local chap who lives on the estate, but other than that it's just us. Honestly, you might have warned me, Imogen. I've come dressed for a sodding garden party.' She pulled at her long dress and shifted uncomfortably in her seat.

'Well, you were there when she asked us—how was I to know?' I smiled up as Eddie blew me a kiss through the barbecue smoke. 'I'm going to kiss my brother-in-law,' I said, getting up.

'Do. It'll be the biggest thrill he's had all week.'

Eddie paused in his manic sausage turning to greet me. 'Salmonella type C and full-blown dysentery is what we're getting here today,' he informed me sotto voce. 'Don't go *near* the pork chops, and give the burgers a very wide berth until I've truly incinerated them. Warn Rufus.'

'I'll bear it in mind,' I assured him. 'What's up with Hannah? Dodgy prawn?'

'Not in my house,' he bristled. 'No, I think she's just been overdoing it. She's started this Weight Watchers thing, you know, and she's exercising as well. Frankly I'm worried she's not fit enough to go to the gym yet. I reckon she's pulled something.'

'Hannah's at the gym?' I boggled.

'Only late at night, Imo, when most people are safely tucked up in bed. And no, she doesn't wear a leotard.'

'Ah,' I said humbly.

'Isn't he doing a marvellous job?' Eleanor, her hazel eyes bright, was suddenly at my shoulder.

'He is,' I agreed. 'Eddie's a very good chef.'

'Well, he's a godsend today. Piers really can't be bothered and I always end up doing it and getting hot and bothered. So much for men being macho with tongs. Imogen, you haven't met Piers's mother yet, have you?' She shot me a warning look and I turned to see, in the shadows, just inside the French windows, an older, female version of Piers, complete with large, beaky nose and watery blue

297

eyes, giving me a very fishy stare. She was ostensibly talking to someone whose back was to me, but clearly wondering why this newcomer hadn't come to say hello. Hadn't presented herself. I hastened across the terrace with Eleanor.

'Louisa, this is Imogen Cameron, Alex's wife,' Eleanor said in a loud voice. 'Remember I told you? She and Alex have taken a cottage.'

'What?' Lady Latimer frowned and cupped her ear.

'Remember I told you they've taken a cottage!' Eleanor shouted, as at that moment, I realised who her mother-in-law was talking to. I caught my breath.

'And Pat you know, of course. You sat next to him at supper,' Eleanor reminded me.

I took the dry, papery hand the old lady had extended. 'I remember,' I said coldly. 'How do you do, Lady Latimer?'

Pat Flaherty looked about to greet me cordially, then registered my frosty features and dropped the smile.

'He's a vet,' Lady Latimer informed me in sepulchral tones. 'Rather a good one.'

'I know. I mean, that he's a vet,' I added, thereby clarifying, for his benefit, which part of her sentence I agreed with. I turned to him.

'Thank you so much for your letter, which arrived promptly on Friday. I shall, of course, be responding forthwith.'

Pat looked taken aback and Eleanor bemused. Good. That would teach him to send exorbitant fees by return of post. He didn't like being shamed in front of these people, did he?

'Mr Flaherty's fees,' I explained for the benefit

298

of the audience. 'For services rendered.'

'Oh. Right.' He squared up to me. 'Well, that tends to be the form, doesn't it? Something for something else?'

'Oh, absolutely,' I replied sweetly, and was about to continue sarcastically, that's the quid pro quo, but I'd never said it before, so what I actually said was 'That's the pwid crow po.'

For a moment I thought no one had noticed, then:

'What?' Lady Latimer's hand cupped her ear. 'Crow what?'

'Po,' Pat informed her solemnly.

She frowned, none the wiser. Then turned to me. 'Got marvellous hands,' she said loudly. 'Looks after my fanny.'

'That's Fanny the Yorkshire Terrier,' breathed Eleanor quickly.

'She got a nasty infection in her bladder last Christmas, but I think you caught it just in time, young man.' She tapped his arm with a liver-spotted hand. 'You've got very good instincts!'

'Oh, I don't know about that.' Pat looked uncomfortable.

Yes, he might well look awkward. This was clearly the sort of vet he was; the sort that charmed old ladies out of their savings and administered to their pampered pooches. Although, this was one old lady, I decided, looking at her crumpled silk dress caught together hastily at the neck with gigantic diamonds, who could probably spare a bob or two. And he certainly looked the part with his ready smile and easy manner: a twinkly-eyed charmer in a sapphire-blue shirt and jeans. I felt awkward in my flowery dress and high mules.

'Eleanor, would you get Piers to turn that dreadful racket down?' asked her mother-in-law, holding a hand to her ear again. Gentle reggae was filtering through the drawing-room speakers. 'I can't bear that sort of music. It makes me feel I'm about to be robbed.'

'Of course.' Eleanor's mouth twitched as she made to go.

'And who are those dreadful people on the terrace?' hissed her mother-in-law, catching her sleeve. 'I had to pretend it was the heat driving me inside, but they really are beyond the pale.'

'Oh, er—'

'I'm afraid that's my family,' I said smoothly, noticing her nose was very pink at the tip. She looked like a drinker, and I could smell her gin from here. 'Actually, they're perfectly pleasant when you get to know them. Ah, look, the sausages are ready, I must go and feed Rufus.'

I sailed outside, my heart pounding, and went down the slope of the lawn to find Rufus. He was playing with the youngest Latimer on the swings.

'Come on, boys. Lunch time,' I muttered.

Rufus caught my tone and followed meekly. 'What's wrong?'

'Nothing.' We climbed the terrace steps, hand in hand, Theo following. 'Here, have a seat on this bench next to Eddie. There doesn't seem to be a seating plan. I'll get you each a hot dog.'

Eleanor came rushing up as I collected the food from Eddie. 'I'm so sorry, Imogen. She's a terrible old snob. I mean—' She broke off, awkwardly.

I grinned, suddenly rather liking her. At least I wasn't the only one whose brain didn't engage before speaking.

'It's OK, I know what you mean. And actually, one or two of them do take a bit of laughing off.' Out of the corner of my eye I caught Dad doing his Kenneth Williams impersonation for Piers's benefit, hand on hip, head thrown back, nostrils flared, mincing round the terrace. Happily, Piers thought it was even funnier than Dawn's pompom.

'By the way, how come Pat Flaherty's here?' I asked casually as I split Rufus's bun. 'He seems to be a permanent fixture in your house.'

'Oh, he's got the lodge house at the moment, so he pops up quite a lot. He's renting it while the builders do up his place, an old rectory in the next village. He's good fun, isn't he?'

I ignored her eager question, pretending to be intent on getting the ketchup from a nearby table. By the time I'd got back with it, she'd gone.

'We call it Crumpet Cottage,' remarked Piers, lining up behind me at the barbecue, his plate clamped to his chest, like a small boy at prep school.

'Sorry?'

'Pat's place. He seems to entertain a never-ending stream of women down there. Lucky dog.' He chuckled. 'A pork chop and a burger, please, dear boy.'

Did he indeed, I thought, going to sit beside Rufus with my hot dog. So he really was the local stud as well as the charming vet, eh? Pretending to listen to Rufus and Theo's prattle, I watched as Pat collected his burger from Eddie with a joke and an easy smile, then went to sit next to Hannah on the sofa. Well, that was one female he wouldn't be able to get round, I thought as I bit into my bun. One bird he couldn't work his magic on. I saw him lean

301

in to talk to her as she sat—or lay, almost—prostrate beside him. If she wasn't feeling so grim she'd give an obvious charmer like that very short shrift. She'd never had any truck with playboys, and had only really warmed to Alex because I'd married him. Had Alex been a playboy, I thought with a jolt? I looked across at him by the barbecue, and as I did, something terrible happened. I intercepted a glance between him and Eleanor. It was a secret, raised-eyebrow look across a crowded terrace and she gave a quick shrug and a half-smile back. I looked away, horrified. Then I went hot. Really hot and panicky. I lunged for my Pimm's and knocked it back too vigorously, half of it missing my mouth. I reached for a napkin to mop myself. Get a grip, Imogen, for heaven's sake. It probably wasn't that sort of look at all, probably perfectly innocent. Probably—d'you want a sausage? No! Not a sausage. A—a burger? To which she'd replied, with a shrug, 'Yes, I might.' Yes, that was it.

I watched feverishly under lowered lashes as Eleanor sat everyone down; not formally round a table, just scattered about the terrace, balancing plates on laps, then offered knives and forks wrapped in napkins. As I reached for my drink again, I noticed my hand was shaking. Perhaps Hannah was right. Perhaps I should have counselling. Yes, perhaps I should go and sit in a room with a complete stranger and say, I've got this irrational fear; this fixation that my husband's having an affair with his ex-girlfriend. Or perhaps, I thought, tightening my grip on my glass, I should confront her—Eleanor. Go up to her when I was totally plastered—which wouldn't take long—in the dying moments of this party, when she was saying goodbye to the last of her guests, push my way through and shout drunkenly, 'Get your hands off my husband, you bitch!' Watch her face fall and my entire family go quiet as everyone turned to stare. Or perhaps I'd do neither, I thought miserably, as I stabbed viciously at some salad. Perhaps I'd just carry on as usual, wondering and worrying, fretting myself to a stupor. Yes, probably. I took a deep breath. Let it out shakily.

Luncheon continued. Not feeling up to adult chat, I stuck with the boys and pushed food around my plate. Behind me, Pat's mobile rang and he went inside to take it. I tried not to notice his rather perfect bottom in his jeans as he went through the French windows. Then I decided that if I could notice other men's bottoms, even unspeakably arrogant ones, it was surely a good sign? I couldn't be too suicidal.

'You're not eating?' I said in surprise to Hannah as she waved away Eddie's offer of a burger. This was a first.

'No, thanks. In fact,' she staggered to her feet, 'I think I'm going to go to the loo.'

'Good luck,' I grinned up at her, then saw that she really did look very pale. 'Are you going to be all right?' I made to get up, concerned.

'Fine, fine,' she waved me away impatiently as she moved heavily across the terrace, making painful progress.

'She looks terrible,' I hissed to Mum, who'd sat down beside me with her plate.

'I know, and personally I agree with Eddie. I think she's pulled something at the gym. It's the same one Dawn goes to, you know, and Dawn says

303

they really make you work out. What Hannah's doing there I simply can't imagine.'

I regarded my mother beside me. 'You get on well with Dawn, don't you?'

'Yes, I do, but not for much longer. She's moving to Newcastle next week, leaving your father in the lurch.'

'I didn't know that.'

'Apparently that's where the best beauticians' course is, and she applied and got in. I think even your father's mid-life crisis doesn't extend to living in student digs complete with bean bags and cheese plants, so he's staying put.'

'Well, that'll be the end of that relationship, then. He's also far too lazy to go up for weekends, and she'll probably get distracted by the local talent.'

'Shame,' mused Mum.

'Let's see who he comes up with next,' I grinned.

She grimaced. 'That dreadful Tessa Stanley asked him to dinner at the Hurlingham last week. I do hope he doesn't take up with her.'

I shot her a sideways look. It was odd. Mum was positively gleeful about the likes of Dawn, yet didn't want him consorting with any of their old friends in London. That was her territory. Her stamping ground. It seemed she was happy for him to make a fool of himself in the country where no one knew him, but not amongst old muckers.

'Who's that terribly attractive Irishman in the blue shirt who was here a moment ago?' she asked in a low voice.

'That's the supremely arrogant Pat Flaherty. He's a hugely expensive vet—don't let him anywhere near Samba.'

'Well, you know Samba: she's the most unfriendly cat imaginable. Totally arrogant herself, so she probably wouldn't let him anywhere near *her*. Why, only the other day I tried to take her for an injection and . . . darling, what's wrong?'

I was on my feet. Pink with shock and fury. For there, through the open French windows, in a dark corner of the drawing room, reflected in the mirror above the fireplace, my worst nightmare was unfolding before my eyes. I've heard that when faced with trauma, the human psyche deals with it by shattering the evidence; fragmenting it, there being only so much shock it can take in one go. And shatter this image did; it fairly spun too. But even in its disjointed, kaleidoscopic state, a few immutable facts remained. The look on my husband's face as, presuming himself to be hidden from view behind the door and exquisitely alone, he took Eleanor in his arms; the longing in Eleanor's eyes as he gathered her towards him; the way their bodies melded seamlessly together. The bald, simple truth.

# CHAPTER EIGHTEEN

My hand gave an involuntary jerk and my glass let loose a stream of Pimm's, which flew through the air, splashing into Mum's lap.

'Oh!' She leaped to her feet, shaking her dress.

I stared at the large dark stain as if I'd never seen anything like it, then back to the drawing room. I couldn't speak.

'Don't worry, darling, it washes beautifully,'

Mum was saying as she seized a napkin and began mopping frantically. 'I spilled some balsamic vinegar on it the other day and thought—oh well, that's the end of that, but—oh . . .'

I was vaguely aware of her pausing in her mopping to stare, as I hurried away without even an apology, across the terrace to the French windows. I flew into the room and spun around. No canoodling couple sprang apart at my dramatic entrance; no one gasped in horror, no eyes grew wide with fear, no hands flew to mouths. Eleanor was sitting in an armchair talking animatedly on the telephone, and Alex was on the opposite side of the room on his hands and knees, his head in a cupboard full of glasses.

'Yes, that's fine,' Eleanor was saying, 'and if you could deliver on Tuesday that would be even better.'

'Can't find them anywhere,' Alex muttered into the cupboard's depths. He drew his head out and glanced round. 'Oh, hello, love. Eleanor's tasked me off to find some water tumblers before everyone gets too pissed. Apparently the party needs diluting.' He rested back on his haunches. Frowned up at me. 'Are you all right?'

I stared down at him, flummoxed.

'Good.' Eleanor put the phone down with a decisive click. 'That was the silk flower company, they're coming with some samples on Tuesday.' She grinned at me. 'Your mother's really enthused me, Imogen. I've got the bit between my teeth about having a pastiche garden. Can't you just see Louisa's face when she fingers a lily and gets the shock of her life!' She laughed. Then her face clouded over. 'Are you OK? You look a bit pale.'

'Yes . . . no. I'm . . . fine.'

'D'you mean these?' Alex took some tall tumblers from the cupboard.

'Perfect. Grab a few of those, would you, and make sure Louisa gets one. She's flying already. I've put a few bottles of Perrier on the table.' She got to her feet. 'Are you sure you're OK, Imogen?'

'Yes, I—I'm fine,' I stammered. I tried to regulate my breathing. It was coming in sharp, heavy bursts.

'It is terribly hot,' Eleanor peered at me, worried.

'Yes. I—I think I'll have a glass of water too.'

'Do. Help yourself. Oh, and if you wouldn't mind taking a few glasses out, that'd be great.'

I picked up some glasses and went back outside in a daze. I felt a bit faint. I went over to the drinks table. Held on to the edge. Then I poured myself some water. Suddenly I glanced sharply back over my shoulder at Alex. He'd followed me outside, dropped off the glasses, and was talking to Eddie now, over by the terrace steps; hands in his pockets, leaning back and roaring with laughter at something Eddie said. Eleanor was crouched down in front of Rufus and Theo with a tub of ice cream, letting them scoop it out inexpertly themselves into cones. No furtive looks were being exchanged, neither of them looked unsettled, rattled. I put the water to my lips and realised my hand was shaking. I put the glass down and raised a hand to my forehead. It was damp. I was going mad. I was actually going mad, seeing things that weren't there, that weren't really happening. Not just imagining the worst, but seeing the worst. Going insane.

I walked shakily back to Mum and sat down mutely beside her. She was dipping her napkin in water now, still dabbing at her lap. She glanced up as I sat down.

'Are you all right, darling? You look as if you've seen a ghost.'

'I'm fine,' I muttered. 'Sorry about your dress.'

'Couldn't matter less. I told you, it'll come out in the wash.'

I picked up my plate of food wordlessly from the York stone, but couldn't touch it. I was aware of someone watching me. Pat, over by the drinks table, was ostensibly talking to my father and Piers, but looking at me. Had he seen me stand up, spill my drink and dash inside like a lunatic? Well, I'd embarrassed myself in front of that man so many times, one more wasn't going to make any difference, I thought bitterly. And I'd been so sure, I thought, staring blankly back into the drawing room. So sure I'd seen them there together, but— well, that was classic, wasn't it? Classic jealous imaginings, the mind playing tricks, the green-eyed monster feeding on whom it preys. Of course. Truth or illusion. Illusion or truth. In this case, very much illusion. And it was very hot. Too hot, for May. I glanced around at Dad, fanning himself with his napkin; Mum, beside me, reaching for her straw hat. Yes, that must be it. The sun had got to me. And the Pimm's.

Behind me, Piers was bellowing with laughter as he teased Pat.

'. . . don't give me that, Pat. Your place is a complete totty magnet! You've got no end of fillies trotting in and out of there. I saw one myself going in only the other day!'

'Nonsense,' drawled Pat, 'that was my Great-aunt Phyllis.'

'What, with long blond hair, dark glasses and pink jeans?'

'Ah, you must mean Cousin Dorothy.'

'Don't believe you for one moment, old boy. My money's on that being some poor, unsuspecting bastard's wife!'

Everyone's at it, I thought feverishly, scrunching my napkin tight in my fist. This man for starters. And God knows who else, at every conceivable opportunity. You only had to look over the balustrade into the fields beyond to see squirrels chasing each other into thickets, bunnies fornicating in bushes, sparrows doing it in mid-air. Was my husband at it too?

'I'm worried about Hannah,' Mum muttered in my ear. 'She's been gone an awfully long time.'

'I'll go and look,' I said, getting up again, glad of the excuse to go inside; to get out of the sun, splash my face with water. My head was throbbing now.

'Oh, would you? Thank you, my sweet.'

I went, with careful, measured steps, back across the terrace, and in through the French windows to the drawing room. As I crossed the threshold I stood for a moment, my eyes darting around; taking in the mirror that had so recently played tricks on me, presenting me with a false image, and which even now was shocking me again with my own reflection. I raised a hand to my cheek, astonished by my pallor. How pale I looked; how huge and troubled my eyes. I hurried away, and was about to leave the room when my eyes fell on the telephone. It was an integral part of a fax machine, on a table near the chair Eleanor had been sitting in. Glancing quickly over my shoulder to check I wasn't being observed, I lifted the receiver and quickly pressed redial. After a couple of rings, a clear, fluty voice rang out.

'Good afternoon, Marlborough College?'

Marlborough College. Where Eleanor's elder children were at boarding school. Not the silk flower company she was ordering her pastiche garden from.

'Hello?' the voice said impatiently.

'I—I'm sorry. Wrong number.'

I put the phone down, my heart pounding. Well—perhaps they'd rung her, the flower company, to say they could deliver on Tuesday. I punched out 1471 then pressed 3, but it was the local butcher in Little Harrington, not a silk florist. I swallowed. My mouth was very dry. I barely had any saliva. I could hear my heart hammering in my throat. Was I . . . not going mad, but being sent mad? By the pair of them? I paused for a moment, steadying myself on the arm of the chair. No, I thought suddenly. No, you're wrong, Imogen, because of course, she'd been using a mobile, hadn't she. Had she? I racked my brains feverishly, tried to think back, but my memory was confused. I could visualise her sitting in this chair, talking animatedly, pushing back her brown curls . . . Had she been on her mobile? Yes, I decided slowly. Yes, I think she had. Was fairly sure, anyway. Because apart from anything else, this phone was attached by a cord to the apparatus. It wasn't a hands-free, so . . . would it even stretch? To the chair? I lifted the receiver and tried to sit down with it. Only just. I held it to my ear. And not comfortably. The coiled cord was taut—wouldn't I have noticed

310

that? If the cord had been—

'Press nine for an outside line, Imogen.' Piers had stuck his head through the open French windows. 'That one doesn't have a direct line.'

'Oh!' I threw the receiver down, but missed the apparatus. On the carpet, the receiver thrashed about, like a snake. I flushed as I retrieved it. 'N-no, it's OK.'

'No, go ahead, it's just you need to press nine.'

'I will. Later. It was engaged, you see.'

'Yes, but you would have dialled the wrong number,' he said coming through the doors. 'If you didn't press nine you—look, try again but this time—'

'I will. In a minute,' I said through clenched teeth, wanting to bite him. He stopped, astonished. I flashed him a nervous smile, and left the room.

So stupid, Imogen, I thought as I hastened away, to be caught sniffing around suspiciously, re-enacting the scene of the crime, when there wasn't even a crime. You saw for yourself how entirely innocent it all was—Eleanor on the phone, husband in a cupboard—your eyes had been deceiving you. Yes, my eyes *had* been deceiving me, I thought with a jolt. That was a well-known expression, wasn't it? A cliché. And cliché's wouldn't exist if they hadn't been borne out hundreds of times, if countless pairs of eyes hadn't been deceived over the years, would they?

After the bright buzz of the terrace, the big empty house seemed cool and still. Its heavy dark boards and oak-panelled passages soothed me as I padded down them. This wasn't my world, or even the real one, but it was a much more comfortable one than the one outside, with its searching

311

flashlights; its many pairs of eyes, the sun. I made my way to the main hall with its wide, heavily carved staircase, the gallery above running around three sides of it, and for a moment, couldn't remember what I was doing there. I stopped. Put a hand to my forehead. Oh, yes, Hannah. I went on quickly and tried the loo by the front door. It was more like a study than a lavatory, with its framed prints, humorous cartoons and bookcase stuffed full of paperbacks, an ancient cistern in the corner—but no Hannah.

Back across the hall I went, turning into a corridor, and pushing through the green baize door to the back passage. This was a different world again, and my footsteps clattered noisily as I swapped soft oak boards and Persian rugs for shiny terracotta tiles. It smelled of dogs and steam irons: a radio played loudly. As I passed the open kitchen door I saw Vera with her back to me, humming away as she washed up at the sink. There was another loo down here, the one I'd tried to use during the dinner party, but that too was empty. I popped back to the kitchen and stuck my head around.

'Vera.' My voice didn't sound like my own. Too husky. I cleared my throat as she turned. 'Vera, you haven't seen my sister, Hannah, anywhere, have you?'

'Would that be the rather large—I mean . . .' she stopped, embarrassed.

'That's it, in a blue dress.'

'She went upstairs, luv. Someone was in the downstairs one, so I sent her up there.'

'Thanks.'

I retraced my steps and mounted the main

staircase, my hand brushing the oak rail as I went. Piers's ancestors gazed sourly down at me through layers of blackened varnish, all with that same cold, disdainful look of his mother. Not for the first time I decided I didn't envy Eleanor the bed she'd made for herself. My heart gave a sudden lurch. But that doesn't mean she envies yours, I told myself quickly. What, swap all this for Shepherd's Cottage, with its tiny mildewed rooms and a view of the muckheap at the back? Don't be soft.

Upstairs was vast, creamy and sprawling, and the first few rooms I encountered looked distinctly pristine and spare. No Hannah. I began to get rather irritated. How far into the bowels of this house had she gone? Exactly how nosy was she being, here? I pressed on further down the corridor and reached another staircase where the rooms were more colourful: a couple had rock stars and models on their walls, another had ponies, and all three were clearly awaiting their occupants back from school. Only Theo's room had the look of full residency, with soldiers and cars all over the floor and a splodge of red paint on the carpet. And Theo was off next year, I remembered, shutting his door again, so this room would be empty too. I wondered if I could ever send Rufus away, and knew immediately, with thumping great certainty, that I couldn't. God, I wasn't even sure I'd let him go to university. Everyone said when they were six foot two and lay horizontal on your sofa all day with their size ten trainers, I'd feel differently, but Rufus I knew, would never be like that. He'd always be nine years old, with dimpled cheeks and russet-red curls.

As I passed the landing window, I spotted him

down in the garden, on the swings with Theo. I paused to look fondly as he soared high into the air, laughing into the wind. Immediately below me, on the terrace, Dad was talking to Mum. I saw her finger his Hawaiian shirt, roll her eyes expressively and then do a quick hula-hula movement with her hands. Dad laughed, taking it in good heart, as Dawn did too, and then Dawn really *did* do a hula-hula dance, whilst Eddie grabbed the barbecue tongs and pretended to bang bongo drums. Dad then felt compelled to do a spot of limbo dancing, and Mum threw back her head and roared. I smiled. Whatever anyone thought, they were really rather jolly, my family. And anyway, who cared what anyone thought? I did, I thought nervously, craning my neck to see if Piers had spotted the cabaret, but he seemed oblivious, and was helping himself, rather furtively, I felt, to a gin and tonic from the drinks table. Eleanor was talking to Lady Latimer and Alex was there too, looking bored and picking his nose. I jolted with relief. Would he look bored and pick his nose if he were in love with her? Of course he bloody wouldn't! You are a fool, Imogen Cameron, I decided, moving on. A silly, neurotic fool.

The next landing looked very plush and private, and I guessed I was entering Piers and Eleanor's own quarters, judging by the family photos dotted around the walls. I was just wondering which of the four white-panelled doors around me would yield a bathroom and my shameless sister, when I heard a shout of pain coming from one of them.

'Hannah?' I tried the handle. It was locked. I rattled it. 'Are you in there?'

'Yes!' she gasped back.

314

I went cold.

'Hannah, are you OK?'

'No, I'm bloody not! Hang on.'

I heard movement within, and then she unlocked the door, hanging heavily on to the handle, before collapsing in a heap on the cream carpet. I flew to her side.

'Oh my God—Hannah, are you all right?'

She was breathing heavily, holding her side. 'Appendix,' she gasped. 'At least I think that's what it is. It's too bloody painful to be constipation!'

'Appendix! Christ, are you sure?'

'Well, I had something similar about three months ago,' she panted, 'and the doctor said it could be rumbling appendicitis—apparently they can rumble on and on for ever. But it's turned into Mount Vesuvius now and—ouch!' She gave a shriek as the pain hit her.

'I'll call an ambulance.' I got up hastily.

'No, not an ambulance, just drive me there, Imo, and get Eddie to help me downstairs. I don't want to make a scene, not here, not— AARRGHHH!!' Her eyes bulged as she shrieked.

'Oh God, I am *so* ringing an ambulance, Hannah! I'll get Eddie up here, but if it's your appendix, you need to get to hospital fast.'

I turned to dash away but she held my arm.

'Painkillers,' she hissed, white-faced, 'in the cupboard up there. I've seen them, but couldn't stand up long enough to grab them. Give me a handful.'

With shaking hands I found the packet, punched out a few, got her a glass of water and held it to her lips.

'Thanks,' she muttered swallowing them down.

315

'Not that it'll do much good when it's up against this sort of eruption.'

'Well, it's better than nothing. Now stay there and don't move. I'll be back.'

'I *can't* bloody move.'

'And—here—put this behind your head.' I seized a lacy cushion from a Lloyd Loom chair and shoved it behind her, manoeuvring her so she was propped up against the bath. She looked a bit more comfortable.

'Better?' I said anxiously.

'A bit. I might even be able to make it to that chair.'

'Don't,' I said dangerously. 'Just stay there, I'll be back. Oh joy, a phone.'

My eyes had spotted it through an open door into what was clearly the master bedroom—huge, with a four-poster bed and a chaise longue, and all a riot of blue toile de Jouy—on the bedside table. I flew to it. As I punched out 999 I realised I'd never done this before, and was taken aback by the bored tones of the girl who asked me if I wanted fire, police or ambulance. I supposed it might get repetitive if one did it every day.

'Ambulance!' I barked. 'And make it snappy. My sister's got a burst appendix!'

God, had it burst? In horror I beetled back down the stairs to get Eddie, because if it had—well, that was bloody serious, actually: blood poisoning, peritonitis . . .

I ran through the hall and down the passage, pausing a moment to get my bearings. If only this house wasn't so flaming big. Yes, this was the way to the terrace. I flew outside at racing speed, but only Mum and Lady Latimer were there, chatting quietly under a huge parasol. They looked up in surprise as I burst out.

'Where's Eddie?' I gasped, trying to keep the panic from my voice.

Mum took off her sunglasses and frowned at me. 'Piers took everyone off to look at his aviary, darling. Rufus wanted to see the lovebirds. Why, what's wrong?'

'I think Hannah may have appendicitis,' I said, as calmly as I could.

'Oh God.' She stood up quickly.

'I've called an ambulance, but, Mum, I need you to get Eddie.'

'I'll show you.' Lady Latimer, suddenly galvanised, was on her feet.

'You know where it is?'

'Well, it used to be *my* aviary, young lady, so I should do!' she said with some force. She strode off with Mum hurrying along beside her, in the direction of the stables.

I ran back inside and made for the staircase again, taking the stairs two at a time. Down the long corridor I flew, past the spare rooms, the children's rooms, on to the next landing, and into the bathroom. I spun around. Empty. No Hannah. No gasping sister slumped on the floor holding her side, berating me for not getting back quickly enough, for taking my time; just acres of cream carpet.

'Hannah!' I yelped, spinning about.

No answer. Shit. Had she tried to stagger somewhere more comfortable? A bedroom perhaps? I'd *told* her not to move!

At that moment a piercing shriek rang out. It was a primeval sound, full of pain, full of fear, and it went right through me, anchoring me to the spot.

*'Arghhhhhh!'*

I flew in its general direction. It was coming from the master bedroom, the door to which was now shut. I burst through—and a horrific sight met my eyes. My sister was flat on her back on the four-poster bed, dress rucked up, knees bare and bent, legs wide apart—being forced apart—by Pat Flaherty, who loomed over her, pinning her to the bed, his dark eyes glittering as he ripped off her knickers.

# CHAPTER NINETEEN

'What the hell do you think you're doing!' I thundered from the doorway, fists balled.

'I'm delivering a baby, what does it look like?' he snapped, his back still to me as he threw Hannah's pants on the floor.

'A *baby*!' I nearly fainted with horror. My hands shot out and gripped the doorframe, crucifix style.

'Your sister's in labour. I was in the downstairs loo and heard her shouts from down there—came running upstairs to find her practically giving birth on the bathroom floor. Somehow I managed to get her in here, which was no mean feat, I can tell you.' He paused a moment to step back and assess the situation, sleeves rolled up to his elbows.

I stood there, mute with horror. Then: 'Oh my God—*Hannah*!'

But Hannah couldn't speak, had neither breath nor vocabulary to draw on, could only stare at me with a mixture of terror and pain, panting hard.

Suddenly she threw back her head and howled like a dog. I flew to her side.

'I've called an ambulance,' I gasped, my mind whirring, struggling to comprehend. A *baby*!

'Too late for that,' Pat informed me. 'She's fully dilated. Look, she's pushing already.'

'Oh my *God*, she thought she was constipated! Hannah, you're *preg*nant, didn't you know?'

'Of course I didn't bloody— AARGH!!' she shrieked as another contraction gripped her. 'I want to push!'

'Well, push, next time that happens,' Pat ordered, his hands—well, his hands somewhere really terribly intimate and personal.

'Do you know what you're doing?' I shrieked, springing from Hannah's side to hover behind him anxiously, wringing my hands. 'Have you done this before?'

'I have, as it happens, for complicated reasons, along with countless animal deliveries, but feel free if you think you'd do a better job.' He took his head from between my sister's legs and turned to glare at me, black eyes flashing.

'No!' I shrank away. 'No, God, I haven't a clue, but shouldn't we wait? Shouldn't she—you know— cross her legs or something, until the ambulance gets here?'

'What, and cut off the oxygen supply and damage the baby? That's about the most dangerous thing you can do. No, if this baby's coming, it's coming, and there isn't a damn thing you can do about it. Look,' he stood back a moment to let me see, 'she's fully dilated and the head's engaged. You can see it crowning.'

I conquered my qualms and crouched down to

319

where . . . oh . . . my . . . *God*! I clapped both hands over my mouth. A dark head *was* crowning—I could see hair! Black hair!

'Oh, Hannah!' I gave an involuntary sob and rushed round to seize her hand. She was blowing hard now, her face livid, eyes popping. 'I can see it, it's a baby, a real baby!'

'Well, I certainly hope it's a baby,' said Pat, wiping his mouth on his sleeve and crouching down to take up his position again. 'I'd hate to think what else she could have up there. What about getting me some water?'

'Oh! God, yes, water! Hot?'

'Yep, and some towels.'

'Towels!' I yelped, running into the bathroom, glad of something to do. I knew I was on the verge of panicking. 'Towels, towels,' I muttered, pulling them from the rail with shaking hands. 'Keep calm, keep calm.'

'No, from the cupboard,' he snapped, as I ran in with them trailing on the floor. 'They've got to be absolutely clean.'

'Clean towels, clean towels,' I agreed, fleeing back, spinning around the bathroom, then flinging a cupboard door wide. Oh, deep joy—a pile of sage-green towels was stacked neatly on a shelf.

'Hot water from the tap?' I yelled.

'That'll do, in a bowl.'

All I could find was a child's potty. 'Best I could do,' I muttered, coming back with it sloshing everywhere.

'Don't be ridiculous, I can't use that. Just get back here and hold her hand.'

'Hold hand, hold hand.'

'AARRAGGGH!' Hannah shrieked as I ran to

her side. She gripped my fingers so tight I thought my knuckles would break, and her head was right off the pillow now, eyes squeezed tight with pain and effort, as at that moment, Eddie came in.

He stood there in the doorway, mouth open, blinking behind his spectacles.

'What the . . . ?'

'She's having a baby!' I screamed. 'She's giving birth!'

Befuddled and mystified beyond belief, Eddie staggered in a few more steps. He took in his wife's condition, looking her up and down in naked disbelief.

'She can't be,' he whispered.

'I bloody am!' hollered Hannah, her face bright red and contorted with pain. 'Look at me! I'm not doing this for attention!'

'Oh my God. Oh . . . my . . . *God*!' Eddie's face went through a myriad of emotions in the space of seconds: horror, disbelief, incredulity were all etched up there—then he settled on wonder. He came in unsteadily and sank down beside her, seizing her hand.

'Oh, darling. Oh, my darling. But . . . but how?' His eyes were wide, uncomprehending. 'How did it happen?'

'Well, I'm pretty sure you had something to do with it!' she shrieked.

'Oh, my precious. My angel!' He put her hand to his lips and kissed her fingers fiercely. 'Does it hurt?'

'Does it—' She attempted to treat this enquiry with the contempt it deserved but was thwarted by another contraction. 'AARGH! SHIT! CHRIST!'

'Push,' instructed Pat, crouching down at the

sharp end again. 'Go on, go with it this time.'

'Yes, and breathe,' enjoined Eddie eagerly, bending over her and urging her on. 'You must breathe, I've read that, and you must relax, not tense up, and—'

'AND YOU CAN FUCK OFF!' she screeched, lashing out in fury with her fist, and catching Eddie, with her sizeable diamond engagement ring, squarely on the temple. His eyes bulged for a moment, pale and blue, his face lost all of its colour. Then, as blood spurted from his head, he staggered backwards, lost consciousness, and collapsed on the floor.

'Christ! Eddie!' I leaped back in panic. 'Pat, she's knocked him out!'

'Bugger.'

Pat hesitated, torn between the two of them, then hastened round to put Eddie in the recovery position.

'Nice timing, mate,' he muttered, throwing Eddie's arm over his chest and slapping his face. 'Nasty cut you've got there. Oi, Nurse, put a towel on it.' He threw one at me. 'Staunch the flow.'

'Oh God—is he still breathing?' I crouched over him, putting my ear to his heart. 'I can't hear him breathing! Is he dead?'

'Of course he's not dead. His chest is moving. Just keep the towel there.'

'WHAT . . . ABOUT . . . ME?' roared my sister murderously, rising massively on her elbows from the bed, like a sea monster from the depths, as, at that moment, the door flew open. Piers and his mother stood there in the doorway, bug-eyed with amazement as they took in the scene.

'What the . . . ?' began Piers, inadequately.

'Hannah's having a baby and she's knocked her husband out for being oversolicitous,' Pat explained patiently, hastening away from Eddie to resume his position between Hannah's knees. 'Now unless you're going to make yourselves useful, I suggest you disappear. She doesn't want an audience, and if there are any unhelpful comments, she'll probably knock you out as well. Yes, that's *it*,' he encouraged suddenly. 'Good girl, it's coming!'

'Good grief!' Piers yelped, as at that moment, like something out of a French farce, another door opened, this one in the far corner of the room, which appeared to lead to a dark green dressing room. Alex and Eleanor stood there, gaping with amazement.

Alex's jaw dropped as he regarded his sister-in-law on the bed. 'Bleeding Ada!' he gasped. In times of real crisis my husband reverted right back to prep school. 'She's having a baby!' He gaped in astonishment, then turned on me, horrified. 'Imogen!'

'Well, it wasn't my fault!' I squeaked. 'I didn't impregnate her. Blame Eddie! Actually, don't, Hannah's already done that. Oh, Hannah, it's coming, it's coming!' I sobbed, fists clenched, torn between seeing it come out and holding her hand.

'But shouldn't she be in hospital?' blabbered Piers. 'The bedcover . . . this is the Tudor Room!'

'Oh, for God's sake, Piers, it's too late for that. Can't you see it's coming?' snapped Eleanor, hastening to Hannah's other side.

It was. As Hannah bore down with one final, mighty, primeval moan that seemed to come from a long way away, from way back in time, and gave a

323

last, vein-busting push, suddenly the whole head appeared, bright red and covered in black hair, swiftly followed by a slippery little body, slimy like a seal, covered in mucus.

'Oh!' we all gasped as Pat caught it expertly in his hands. There was a moment of complete silence, then:

'It's a boy,' he said, gazing down at it in wonder.

In the gasps of shock and amazement that followed, Pat somehow managed to cut the cord, clean the baby up a bit, wrap him in a towel, move around the bed, and hand him carefully, tenderly, to his mother.

Hannah, her hair soaking wet and plastered to her head, struggled to raise herself on to her elbows, to sit up and take the baby in her arms. As I flew to help her, propping her up with pillows, she gazed down in disbelief.

'A boy,' she breathed. 'I've got a baby boy.'

Tears fled down my cheeks as I looked into her astonished face.

'Oh, Hannah!' I gasped.

In another moment, we heard footsteps pounding up the stairs.

My mother's voice rang out, 'Up here—she's up here somewhere. Quick!'

At the double, the ambulance crew arrived, bursting into the room in their plastic yellow jackets, complete with stretcher and equipment, followed by my mother. They stopped, stood stock-still for a moment as they took in the scene: the mother and baby on the bed like a modern-day nativity scene; the unconscious man beside her, bleeding into a towel like the passion of Christ; the assembled multitude. The first ambulance man

324

gaped around the room bemused. He took off his cap and scratched his head.

'Which one's got the burst appendix, then?'

*      *      *

Later, much later, as I said to Mum that evening, in the hospital cafeteria, it was ironic that in the end it was Eddie who needed the stretcher to the ambulance. Hannah was one the one who had walked down the stairs—slightly hypnotically perhaps—with her baby in her arms, past Dad and Dawn standing wide-eyed and bereft of speech in the hall, past Rufus and Theo, who paused in their game of marbles on the front steps, past Vera raking leaves in the drive, across the gravel sweep and into the waiting ambulance. Eddie told me later that as they'd driven off and were en route to the hospital, he'd come round, and was deemed well enough by the ambulance crew to sit up and hold the baby. Thus, this brand-new family trundled off to Milton Keynes General with stars in their eyes and wonder in their hearts, Mum and I following on behind in the car.

'But why didn't she know?' Mum insisted as she drank the second strong black coffee I'd ordered for her to bring her out of her shock. 'I can't believe she didn't *know* she was pregnant.'

'But, Mum, she'd been told she couldn't *have* babies; told it was almost a physical impossibility, given her sticky tubes and Eddie's dodgy sperm. It wouldn't have occurred to her that she was.'

'Yes, but she'd have missed a period!' she squeaked. I glanced nervously round the room as a few people looked across. Mum's cup rattled

325

forcefully in its saucer as she put it down. 'Several!' she hissed.

I leaned forward. 'Mum, Hannah thought she was getting the menopause.'

She sat back. Regarded me in horror. 'Did she?'

'Yes, because apparently you got yours early, so when her periods stopped, she just thought, oh well, this is it then. Early menopause, on top of everything else—terrific. And of course she was getting mood swings—'

'All those pregnancy hormones—'

'Exactly, and feeling tired and flushed—'

'Or blooming, I suppose—'

'Well, quite. And I suppose . . .' I hesitated, feeling disloyal, 'well, if you've always been as big as she was . . .'

'What's a bit more on the tummy? And let's face it, she was getting huge, but—oh God, it just didn't *occur* to me.' She looked distressed. 'I blame myself.'

'Don't,' I said, putting my hand over hers.

'It could have been so dangerous. She could have been on a bus or something . . .'

'Hannah doesn't go on buses, and the point is, Mum, she was fine. *Is* fine. She's had a baby, which is what she's always wanted. It's a dream come true for her and Eddie.'

'Yes.' Her face softened as she looked at me. 'Yes, it is, isn't it? And thank God for that marvellous man. What was his name?'

'Pat,' I said shortly, sinking into my coffee.

'Pat. He was so capable, so level-headed. More help than those ambulance men, who seemed to want to bundle her off immediately and not clean her up. Did you see how he dealt with everything?'

326

'Yes, well, he's a vet, Mum. It sort of goes with the territory.'

'Hardly,' she snorted. 'He's used to sheep and cows. No, I thought he was absolutely fantastic. And as for Piers—did you see his face? I thought he was going to pass out! Thought we'd have him carted away on a stretcher too!'

'Yes, well, I don't suppose we'll be invited back next Saturday for a barbie,' I said wryly. 'Can you imagine—oh, Piers, we'd love to come, but would you mind if another member of my family gave birth between the main course and pudding? Be surprised if he lets us stay on at the cottage,' I said gloomily.

'Nonsense. Eleanor was sweet about it. Said there weren't many people who could claim a baby born impromptu in the master bedroom; said she'd dine out on it for weeks.'

Yes, she had been sweet. Had run around finding a clean nightdress and a toothbrush for Hannah to take to hospital and had shoed all the gawping men out of the room and given me a big hug: said how exciting it was. Terribly sweet.

I cleared my throat. 'Mum, you know when you went to get Eddie from the aviary?'

'Yes?'

'Was Alex there too?'

'No, he and Eleanor went inside when the rest of them headed off there. She wanted to show him something upstairs. She'd redecorated one of the bedrooms, I think. In the west wing.'

'Ah.'

So that explained why they'd appeared through the dressing-room door. They'd obviously heard the shrieks and Eleanor had led them there via a different route. Yes, that was it. I swallowed.

'And are you all right, my love?' Mum leaned across the table. She reached up and took my hand away from my throat. 'Don't do that. You're scratching your neck to bits.'

I put my hand back in my lap. She looked at me, concerned.

'I know this has taken it out of everyone, but you've been unsettled all day. Is everything all right?'

I smiled at her. Nodded my head. 'Everything's fine. Couldn't be better. Come on, let's go and see Hannah.'

*     *     *

The doctor was just leaving Hannah's bedside and swishing back the curtain when we got there, assuring Eddie that she was in very good shape. Eddie stammered his thanks, relieved, and hurried to resume his position by her pillow. He took his wife's hand, seeming almost to swoon with love as he sat down and leaned over her, beaming broadly. Hannah looked tired.

'Where's the baby?' I asked as I sat down beside Eddie.

'He's got a bit of jaundice, so he's under a light in the nursery,' she explained.

'Ah.'

'That's quite normal,' said Mum quickly, sitting down too. 'You were a bit jaundiced, Imogen.'

'So was Rufus, actually. Oh, Hannah, how wonderful, a baby!' My eyes filled up again. I couldn't help it.

She smiled weakly; looked all in.

328

'And the proud father.' Mum patted his arm. 'How does it feel?'

Eddie's chest, which was skinny and bony—pigeon, even—seemed to swell to gargantuan proportions. 'I can honestly say,' he began portentously, his glasses steaming up, 'that aside from the day when Hannah agreed to marry me, this is the happiest, proudest day of my life. I feel—well, I feel I could do anything. Take on the world, slay dragons, scale mountains—with my beautiful wife and my newborn son beside me.'

'Oh, Eddie!' It was no good, my eyes were brimming over now. 'And have you got a name yet?'

'Not yet. I've got millions—Eureka's top of my list—but Hannah's still thinking about it, aren't you, darling?'

Hannah gave a weak smile. She didn't answer.

'Would you like to see him?' Eddie asked eagerly.

'Oh, *please*!' Mum and I groaned ecstatically.

We stood up as one, and went to follow Eddie out of the room, when I glanced back at Hannah. Her head had rolled to one side, away from us. She was staring blankly out of the window.

'I'll catch you up,' I said quickly, as Mum and Eddie went on down the corridor. I hastened back to the bed and took her hand.

'What's wrong?' I said, sitting down again.

'Nothing.'

I regarded her anxiously. Her face was inscrutable. 'Hannah, this is marvellous, isn't it? The most fantastic thing that ever happened to you, surely?'

'Of course.' Flatly.

329

'And—and it doesn't matter—'

'What?' she interrupted sharply, her head coming back from the window. 'Doesn't matter that I was walking around for nine months with a baby inside me without the faintest idea?'

'Of course not! God, it happens all the time, Hannah, much more than you think!'

'Yes, to teenagers on sink estates, maybe, but not to someone like me. Not a middle-aged woman, a parish councillor, a teacher, a pillar of the community—albeit a fat one. I feel such a fool!'

Tears sprang from her eyes and slid sideways down her face on to her pillow. I was shocked.

'Hannah, so what?' I shook her limp hand. Tried to shake some life into it. 'So what? Surely it's the outcome that matters, a healthy baby, a *miracle* baby, what you've always wanted! Just think of that: how you'll be a proper family now, how it'll change your life!'

'But that's just it,' she blurted out suddenly. 'It will change my life, and I'm not sure I want that. Not sure I can cope!'

I was stunned. My bossy, larger-than-life sister; domineering, slightly scary, always judgemental, who juggled Sea Scouts with teaching and cake-making for fêtes, and parish council committees—couldn't cope?

'He's so tiny,' she whispered in a voice I didn't recognise, 'so fragile—I—I'm scared to touch him! Oh, Imo, I'm not sure I can do it!'

I saw the fear in her eyes.

'And Eddie,' she tumbled on, 'Eddie's brilliant. He's just a natural, just picks him up and cuddles him—you should have seen him in the ambulance.

It's all so quick, so unexpected, and everyone expects me to be so thrilled and just adapt, but I'm not sure I can!'

'Of course you can,' I said staunchly, horribly worried. 'Have you fed him yet?'

'No.' She turned her head away, back to the window. 'He has to be under the light, you see. I've told the nurses to give him a bottle.'

I nodded. 'Right.' I swallowed. 'Hannah—I—I'm sure this will all be fine. This is all hormones, you see, racing round your body, and—and the shock. You'll be a brilliant mother, simply brilliant!'

'Will I?' she said bitterly. 'I'm not so sure.' She turned her head back from the window. Her eyes were dead. 'I'm not sure I want him at all.'

I stared at her, dumbfounded. I didn't know what to say. At length, I took a deep breath.

'Hannah, I'll be back, OK? I'm just going to find Mum and Eddie, but I'll be back.'

She nodded wordlessly, disinterested, detached.

I scuttled away, my heart pounding. I found Mum and Eddie in the day nursery, leaning over a cot and cooing over the tiny naked baby, one of three in a row under a bright, ultraviolet light.

'You can pick him up,' a nurse was advising Eddie. 'He doesn't have to be under there all day, just for a few hours at a time.'

'Right.' Eddie looked nervous, but none the less picked him up, wrapped him in a blanket the nurse gave him, and cradled him adoringly in his arms, his eyes shining.

'Hello, son,' he whispered. 'Welcome to planet earth.'

He cooed over him, gently kissing his nose, and

after a minute, handed him proudly to Mum for a turn. The baby gave a little whimper and she rocked him expertly, holding his head in her hand as she walked him round the room.

'Eddie.' I took his arm and drew him into the corner as Mum walked across to the window, crooning and soothing. 'Eddie, I'm a bit worried about Hannah.'

'Why?' He looked startled. 'The doctor said she was fine, didn't even need stitches or anything. Said he slipped out a treat.'

'No, it's not that. It's just . . . well, she should be in here, with him.'

He looked doubtful. 'Is she allowed?'

'Yes, look.'

The mothers of the other two babies were in their dressing gowns, leaning over the cots, watching their babies under the lamps. One was stroking her baby's toes.

'She's only just given birth, Imogen. Maybe tomorrow?'

I nodded. 'And—and see if you can persuade her to feed. It does make a difference, builds up their immunities, that sort of thing.'

'But it doesn't matter, does it? I mean—a bottle's fine?'

'Oh, yes, a bottle's fine,' I said quickly. 'It's just that—well, I think it would help her. Help Hannah.'

He frowned. 'Help Hannah what? I mean . . . surely that's her department, Imo. I can't tell her what to do.' He looked worried. 'And I certainly can't tell her to feed if she wants to give a bottle.'

'I know, I agree, but you could—you know—encourage her, Eddie. Take a deep breath and maybe . . . give a lead. Tell her you've heard it's a good idea. She won't know. She wasn't expecting a baby, hasn't read up on it.'

'A lead?' He looked at me in astonishment. This was uncharted territory for my brother-in-law.

'Yes, you know, be a bit authoritative. She's had a terrible shock, Eddie. Her body's in turmoil. She needs you to help her.'

Eddie looked anxious. I turned to the nurse. 'Um, excuse me, can we take the baby to the ward for a bit?'

'Sure you can,' she said in a soft Irish lilt as she mixed formula for a bottle feed. 'Just bring him back in an hour or so. The mum can come too.'

'You see?' I whispered.

Eddie hesitated. 'I'll try.'

I grinned. 'Good man.'

This was all very new for them, I thought. Very new. I didn't want to push it. He went to go to Mum by the window, to relieve her of the baby and take him to Hannah, when suddenly, he turned. Came back to me. He looked anguished.

'Imo,' he said in a low voice, taking me to one side, 'just one more question. A terrible question, actually.' He swallowed avoiding my eyes. 'This jaundice the baby's got . . .'

I looked into his fearful eyes. Smiled. Then patted his arm reassuringly. 'No, Eddie, relax. It's not catching.'

# CHAPTER TWENTY

When Mum dropped me back at the cottage later that evening, I pushed through the front door and saw Alex coming down the stairs towards me. He put a finger to his lips, letting me know he'd just put Rufus to bed: that he'd call out for me if he heard my voice. I was too tired to go up so I nodded and followed him mutely into the sitting room, shutting the door behind us.

'How is she?' he asked.

'She's fine.' I peeled my coat off wearily.

'And the baby?'

'The baby's fine too. Healthy, if a bit small. The doctors reckon he was a few weeks premature, so he's only six pounds.'

'But not in intensive care, or anything?'

'Oh God, no, nothing like that.'

'Good.'

I threw my coat on a chair. My shoulders sagged as I looked at him. 'I'm sorry, Alex.'

'For what?'

I raised my hands from my sides; let them fall in a helpless gesture. 'For my sister giving birth, I suppose. For it all being so awful and embarrassing, in Piers's house. In the frigging Tudor Room.'

'Don't be silly.' He came across and held my shoulders. 'As long as Hannah and the baby are fine, that's all that matters, isn't it?'

'Oh, darling,' I flooded with relief and rested my head on his chest as he took me in his arms. 'Thank you. Thank you for that.'

334

'What?' He stepped back, his eyes searching my face. 'You think I don't know that? That that's all that matters? Everyone knows that. Everyone was—well, euphoric, almost, after you'd gone. Eleanor rushed off to get some champagne from the fridge and we all wet the baby's head, toasting him. It was very jolly.'

'Really?' I brightened. Yes, I could imagine Eleanor doing that; taking the lead, saying, 'Isn't this exciting? A baby born in the house, a first, maybe! Let's celebrate.' Good for her.

'And Piers?'

Alex's mouth twitched. 'Piers's rapture was slightly more modified, it has to be said.'

I snorted. 'I bet it was!'

'He got Vera stripping that bed pretty damn quickly, but Eleanor forced him to have a drink when he came down from his room inspection. Your father was flying, of course. Did a little impromptu waltz with Dawn on the terrace.'

I groaned and sank down weakly into an armchair. 'Will I ever grow out of being embarrassed by my parents?' I massaged my forehead with my fingertips.

'Doubt it,' he said cheerfully, going out to the kitchen where I could smell Bolognese sauce bubbling away on the hob. 'Certainly not your father, anyway. Eleanor thinks they're both terrific incidentally, particularly your mother.'

Oh, so that was all right then. If Eleanor thought so, she must be. I rested my head back on the chair and watched through the open kitchen door as he buzzed around getting supper, draining spaghetti at the sink in a cloud of steam.

'And I have to admit,' he was back a few

moments later, bearing a tray, 'she does have some amusing ideas.'

I made a space on the coffee table and unloaded the plates of pasta as he went to switch the television on.

'I thought you always said Mum was whimsical and wacky? On a different planet?'

'Oh, yes, she's all of those,' he poured me a glass of wine, 'but she's still rather fun.'

Eleanor talking again. Oh, *stop* it, Imogen. God, he's made supper, put Rufus to bed, what more do you want?

Alex settled down in the armchair opposite and turned his attention to some celebrity reality show. I picked up my fork and toyed limply with my pasta.

'She thought she might pop in and see the baby tomorrow, if that's OK,' he said, twirling spaghetti on to his fork, his eyes glued to a page three girl about to eat maggots in the jungle, her artificially enhanced breasts jiggling in a black bikini. 'Christ, that's enough to put you off your pasta.' He popped in a mouthful and chewed hard. 'You know, take a present or something. Some flowers.'

'Great,' I nodded. 'Hannah would like that.'

He glanced down at his plate. Made a face. 'Too much wine in this.'

'No, it's good.'

'Should have boiled it off a bit more. Oh, and Kate rang, incidentally, while you were out.'

'Oh?' I looked up.

'Apparently I'm moving into their basement flat next week.'

I flushed to my roots. Put my fork down.

'Oh, Alex, I'm sorry. I meant to tell you. I asked

336

Kate last week because—well, I thought you'd be so uncomfortable in Charlie's poky attic room. And Kate and Sebastian have that lovely flat just sitting there, and I know I should have consulted you first, but Kate was going to talk to Sebastian so I thought—well, I'll wait till she gets back to me before—'

'It's fine,' he interrupted, laughing. 'Stop worrying. You were quite right. It'll be much nicer to have a flat of my own, much more grown up. It was just a bit of a surprise, that's all. Kate said to pay whatever I was going to give Charlie.'

'Did she?' I glowed with pleasure. Of course, I should have known she'd say that. They didn't need the money and were doing it purely as a favour, but they'd been sensible enough to charge a nominal rent so as not to embarrass Alex.

'Oh, darling, I'm so pleased, aren't you?' I glowed.

'Of course. The lap of luxury as opposed to a grotty old flat in Chiswick, but—why are you so pleased?' He eyed me beadily.

'I . . . don't know.' I reached for the bottle of wine on the coffee table, topped up my glass. It was quite full already though, so a bit spilled over.

'I suppose—well, I suppose it means when I come and meet you in town, I get to see Kate too,' I said brightly.

'True,' he nodded. 'And meanwhile I can keep an eye on those pesky tenants of ours across the street. Make sure they're not trashing the place.'

'Exactly!' I agreed jovially. My smile was very ready now, my heart lighter. Oh, thank you, Kate. Thank you.

'I told her about Hannah. I hope that's all right.'

'Oh. Yes, fine.' I realised I was momentarily disappointed that such a momentous piece of news had been dispatched to my best friend via my husband, but then Alex could hardly have avoided it.

'Sorry.' He made a face. 'I had to say where you were.'

'Of course you did. And I can ring her later, give her all the gory details.'

'Gory's the word,' he shuddered.

'Was she staggered?'

'Totally! God, everyone will be, Imo. You do realise that?'

'I know,' I said, putting my fork down. 'And Hannah's really worried about that.'

'I mean, why the hell didn't she know?' He boggled at me. 'I know she was fat, so what's a few more pounds—blimey, six, a mere bagatelle in the scheme of things; she must weigh about thirteen stone anyway—but surely a woman knows her own body a bit better than that?'

'For complicated reasons, Alex, she didn't,' I said shortly, scratching my neck. 'And yes, she is feeling extremely foolish. She's worried everyone's going to think she's a complete idiot. As you clearly do.'

'She could always pretend she knew but wasn't saying anything,' he suggested. 'Pretend she and Eddie wanted to keep it to themselves?'

'What—lie?' I looked at him.

'Well, only a little white one. Just say she wanted to surprise everyone and it came a bit early, that's all.'

'Lie,' I said again. 'Be economical with the truth. That's what you'd do, is it, Alex?'

He laughed. 'Well, if it meant getting myself out of a corner, yes, anything to save face. Eleanor and I were both saying that's what we'd do, just say— *Shit!*'

A plate of spaghetti narrowly missed his ear as it flew past him and smashed on the wall behind him. I was on my feet.

'Is it!' I trembled. 'Is that what you'd do?'

He stared at me, open-mouthed. Behind him, broken china, spaghetti and Bolognese sauce slid slowly down the magnolia paintwork.

'Jesus, Imo,' he breathed. 'What's with you?'

I stared at his bewildered face. His wide astonished eyes. My fists were still clenched, and my whole body felt as though it were about to go up in flames. About to spontaneously combust. With a strangled sob, I turned and fled upstairs.

\*       \*       \*

About an hour later, when he came upstairs, I was lying way over on my side of the bed, facing the wall, curled up in the foetal position. I'd heard him downstairs cleaning up: wiping down the wall, sweeping bits of china into a dustpan, chucking it in the bin, then going into the kitchen to wash up. No dishwasher in this tiny cottage. I heard him go out and shut the chickens up—my job—then lock the door and come upstairs. Slowly. Heavily. I listened to the sounds he made as he shuffled prosaically around, brushing his teeth, blowing his nose, using the loo: the sounds of a husband. Then he came into the bedroom and got undressed in the dark. He shut the curtains carefully at the top where I'd pulled them hastily together and where a

339

carrot of moonlight still shone through, and got into bed beside me. We lay there in silence. I could hear an owl screeching far away in the woods. At length I spoke.

'I'm sorry,' I whispered.

He slid across and put his arms around me from behind, resting his chin on top of my head. We lay there like spoons, facing the darkened window. It was very quiet.

'It's OK,' he said softly.

I gripped his hands around my waist. Held on tight. Ask him, I told myself fiercely. Ask him now. Outright. I took a deep breath. Nothing came out. Just a shuddery gust of air.

'You're tired,' he said, listening to my erratic breathing. 'It's been a long day and you're emotionally strung out. It's not every day your sister gives birth unexpectedly.' He squeezed me affectionately.

'Yes,' I whispered, acknowledging this was true. Even so. Ask him. Stop this aching inside of you. This terrible, visceral gnawing. Ask him to tell you the truth.

'I'm fairly shattered myself,' he yawned. 'Could quite happily throw some pasta.' He sighed and hugged me again. 'Night, darling.'

My mouth opened impotently in the dark and my eyes widened to the wall. *Ask him,* my head screamed. *Ask him now, you coward!*

'Up at six thirty,' he groaned. 'No peace for the wicked. Still, could be worse. Could be moving into an attic room in Chiswick tomorrow—how gloomy would that be?' He nuzzled into the back of my neck.

Still my voice wouldn't come. Fear was

strangling my vocal chords. I wanted to know, but didn't want to know. I wanted to talk, but didn't want to talk. Instead, in desperation, I twisted round. My hands reached for him in the dark. I held his face in my hands like a precious vessel, and my lips found his. I kissed him, tenderly, precisely. And again. I ran my tongue over his lips, slid it in his mouth. We never slept in anything, Alex and I, and I ran my hands down his bare back, over his bottom; pulled it towards me.

'And you, my little one,' he murmured in my ear, patting my bottom, 'have had a very stressful day. You need to get some sleep. And you need to get some cream for your neck too, incidentally. Your eczema's come back.' He turned over and reached for the alarm clock. Sighed. 'Better set it for six fifteen, I'm afraid.'

I stared, wide-eyed and mute, into the darkness as he set the clock and replaced it on the bedside table. Pulling the duvet over his shoulder, he turned away from me.

'Night, darling.'

I gazed at his hunched form in the gloom, at his back. Eventually I heard his breathing, heavy and rhythmic; saw his body gently gather momentum as it rose and fell. I felt tears gather in the back of my throat and fall silently across my face on to the pillow, trickling slowly into my ear. My nose filled up and I wiped my face with the duvet, trying not to sniff, trying not to let him know I was crying. Clutching the duvet like a child with a comforter, I held on tight as though everything I had was about to slip from my hands. The last thing I expected was to fall asleep, but often, when the system's taken a battering, it's the body's only defence. It

341

was for me, that night.

The following day I found I was almost relieved when he left for London.

'See you on Friday,' he whispered in my ear, leaning over the bed, his tie tickling my face.

As I opened my eyes, I remembered. Felt sick. Heavy. But then, the weight dropped off me. Yes, go, I thought. So long as he was away from her, I reasoned, it was fine. I was fine. And Mum had let slip yesterday, on the way back from the hospital, that he would be. Away from her. That he and Eleanor, geographically at least, would be miles apart.

'Louisa Latimer's going to be in London next week,' she'd said casually as she'd turned the car down my track. 'Going up for the Chelsea Flower Show. We thought we might meet up.'

'But . . . Eleanor's using that flat next week,' I'd said, turning to her. 'She's working in London.'

'Yes, but it's only got one bedroom, you see. And Louisa wants it. So that's rather that. Eleanor's going to have to work from home. From Stockley.'

'But she isn't going to the Flower Show every day, is she?' I'd said, my mind racing.

There was a pause. 'I think Louisa thought she might go up all week,' Mum said lightly. 'Do some shopping. Anyway, we thought we'd have a spot of lunch. She's a nice woman.'

I'd got out of the car, marvelling at Mum's capacity to get on with anyone from Dawn to Lady Latimer, and in my exhausted state hadn't really thought any more about it, but as I got out of bed now, I blessed Lady Latimer from the bottom of my heart for inadvertently scuppering Eleanor's

342

plans. Yes, I thought, pulling on my dressing gown; knowing they were miles apart meant I could breathe again. Take a break from my demons. Take a break from losing touch with reality.

Later that morning, when I'd taken Rufus to school and hung out the washing—humming even, I was surprised to note, as I pegged away—I made a coffee and rang Kate, thanking her profusely.

'Oh, it's not a problem. The flat's just sitting there empty. Might as well be used by someone,' she said, brushing away my effusive thanks. 'But your *sis*ter, Imo—good heavens! Tell me all!'

So I did, sparing her nothing.

'Good grief,' she said faintly, when I'd finished. 'And they thought they couldn't have children. They must be delighted. Is she completely over the moon?'

'I think she will be,' I said cautiously. 'I'm not sure it's sunk in yet. It was such a shock, and Hannah's a bit of a control freak. Her life is planned with military precision. She doesn't like surprises.'

'Well, they don't come any bigger than this,' Kate snorted. 'Still, it's a dream come true for both of them, surely?'

'Of course, and I think she's thrilled. She's just very tired at the moment.'

'God, I bet. Well, you can tell her from me that that bit doesn't get any better. I reckon I'm still suffering post-natal exhaustion and Orlando's nearly nine. I'm still on my knees.'

I laughed. 'Come and see me, Kate. Get away from it all. You haven't been down here yet. Take a break from the London treadmill.'

'I know, I must, and I will. But you know what

343

it's like.' She sighed.

I did. It was bad enough with one child, but with three and a large house to run and a frantic social life, Kate was chasing her tail on a permanent basis. I, on the other hand, I thought, walking slowly out to my easel in the meadow, carrying the new picture I was working on, was going to have plenty of time on my hands now. Yes, my life was about to get considerably easier, I thought as I screwed the painting in. I stood back and narrowed my eyes speculatively at it. With a weekly boarder for a husband, I could really let things slide. No pork chops to grill, just a few eggs from the chicken house for me and Rufus; no bed to make properly, just crawl in under the duvet. Heaven, I thought guiltily. Odd, wasn't it? I picked up my paintbrush. I wanted him so badly, but if I knew he was away from her, from my nemesis, I was also quite happy for him not to be here. Happy without him. The thought brought me up short. But—it was only that I had more time to paint now, I thought quickly. Something which, for once, *wasn't* making me feel guilty. I smiled as I mixed my colours on my palette. No, for once, something had happened to ensure I didn't even feel a twinge.

After I'd dropped Rufus at school that morning, feeling the need to drive around—anywhere really, just not straight home to that stain on the wall, that glaring reminder of my metamorphosis yesterday into a spaghetti-throwing loony—I'd cruised back through the town, and seeing the wine bar already open, drawn up outside. Molly was washing the front door step like a true Parisian café owner, on her hands and knees, in a long white apron, with a bucket. She looked up when she saw me; sat back

344

on her haunches.

'Sold one!' she announced with a grin.

I stared at her through my open car window. My mouth fell open. 'You *haven't?*'

'Yep, this weekend.' She got to her feet. Laughed at my disbelieving face.

'Which one?'

'The one of the cows in the water meadow that hung over the archway. You'd better get painting. I need another one for there now.'

'No!' I was still staggered. 'How much for?'

'Well, the asking price, obviously.' She picked up her bucket and went inside.

'But . . .' I got out of the car and hastened after her, 'we put four hundred pounds on that, I thought it would be a laugh!'

'So who's laughing now? You get about three hundred and I get the rest—marvellous.'

'Blimey . . .' My mind was still spinning. 'Who bought it?'

She shrugged. 'No idea. I wasn't here yesterday, and Pierre, my new Sunday chap, didn't know. He paid cash, whoever he was.'

'Oh!' I sat down heavily on a handy bar stool. It rocked a bit.

She grinned. 'What's the matter, didn't you expect them to sell?'

I looked up at her. 'In all honesty, no. Not in a million years.'

She laughed. 'That's how I felt when someone first came in here and ordered a drink. "You want to drink it here? In my bar?" When someone ordered a meal, I nearly passed out. We've got to start believing in ourselves, Imogen. If other people do, and put their money where their mouths are, why the hell shouldn't we?'

'You're right,' I said, looking at her with new eyes.

'We can do anything,' she said. 'Anything. We've just got to believe it.'

Nine thirty in the morning seemed a little early to toast my success with anything alcoholic, so we'd settled for a cappuccino and a croissant each on her sunny pavement. I'd come away in high spirits.

Yes, I thought now, raising my brush and narrowing my eyes into the vista beyond the shimmering beech trees; yes, I *would* believe it. This was my career now, my occupation: not a time-consuming hobby to feel shifty and apologetic about, but a money-making venture. All ironing and bed-making could legitimately be ignored. I had work to do.

Rufus, though, I thought with a jolt some time later, couldn't be ignored, and if I wanted to visit Hannah before I picked him up—I glanced at my watch, one o'clock. *One o'clock Christ!*—I had to fly. I hastily threw my brush in some turps and hurried inside with my wet painting. I had been known to leave it in the easel for the birds to wonder at, but a sudden downpour the other day had made me think twice.

Hannah was sitting up in bed in a pretty nightdress, suckling the baby when I pushed through the ward door, and my heart soared with relief. Eddie was washing the floor beside her with a mop and a bucket, which didn't surprise me in the slightest. There were five other new mothers in the ward and it was warm and cosy, smelling of cotton wool, milk, newborn babies and, thanks to Eddie, disinfectant. He paused in his mopping to look on proudly as I sat down beside my sister and pecked her cheek. She looked up briefly to flash me a smile, then gazed down adoringly at her bundle again. I caught Eddie's eye. He winked.

'I saw that wink,' murmured Hannah, keeping her eyes on her suckling child, 'and I know exactly what it means.' She looked up at Eddie and his eyes widened innocently. 'It means you two have been in cahoots, and you,' she cut me a look, 'persuaded him to have a go at me.'

'Nonsense,' I said firmly.

'Told him to tell me to stop wallowing in self-pity and squirming with embarrassment, wondering what the world would say, and start focusing instead on the most precious thing there is.' She gazed at her baby's downy head. Her eyes softened. 'And you were right. Of course you were right. Who cares? Who cares what anyone thinks when I've got him?' She looked up at me, her eyes damp and slightly appalled. 'How could I ever have thought public opinion mattered, compared to this?'

'Hormones,' I smiled. 'They do funny things to us women. They should be banned.'

'Do funny things to blokes too,' chipped in Eddie.

'Rubbish, you wouldn't know a hormone if it hit you in the face,' chided his wife. 'You men have no idea.'

'Got a few other things in perfect working order, though, eh?' Eddie's eyes glinted behind his spectacles as he swaggered across to his bucket. 'Got at least one strong swimmer who made it up the old elementary canal, eh?' He waggled his eyebrows at us as he squeezed his mop out.

Hannah gazed at him in disbelief. She turned to me. 'Unbelievable. Un . . . believable. He stirs the paint then thinks he's done the decorating. Thinks he's had the blinking baby!'

I smiled, pleased to see them joshing and sparring again, the balance of power firmly restored to the distaff side, Eddie, happy in his more familiar role as sidekick, a.k.a. the Rock of Gibraltar.

'What are you going to call him, have you decided?'

'Well, Eddie likes Seymour, but we're not having that.'

'Why not? I like it.'

She raised her eyebrows at me. 'With our surname? Sidebottom? See more side bottom?'

I gave a snort of laughter. 'At least it's not front bottom!'

She gave me a withering look. 'I think you can safely assume that had there been any prospect of me being called Mrs Frontbottom, I'd have changed my name by deed poll. Either that or not married him.' She shifted position in the bed. 'And he also likes Cyril, but we're not having that, either.'

I groaned. 'Oh, no, Eddie. Not Cyril!'

'Why not?' objected Eddie. 'It's a good old-fashioned name.' He stood to attention with his mop. 'Sir Cyril Sidebottom. Major General Sir Cyril Sidebottom. Brigadier Sir Cyril Sidebottom . . .' And off he went, marching down the ward, mop clamped firmly to his shoulder, pulling more and more rank.

'Isn't it funny?' murmured Hannah in my ear. 'Eddie's the woolliest liberal on the planet, but put

348

a son in his arms and suddenly he's conquering the Balkans. Oh, hello, talking of the cavalry . . .'

I followed her eyes as, behind me, the door swung open and my parents bustled in, laden with flowers. Dad was beaming from ear to ear, his pink face clashing violently with his orange shirt.

'Where is he then?' he boomed in his strongest Welsh accent, causing several babies in the ward to throw out their arms in reflex and unlatch from their lactating mothers. 'Where is my little grandson, eh?'

All six babies wailed mightily.

'Shh, Dad,' I hissed.

'Sorry, ladies,' he whispered contritely, nodding his apologies as he tiptoed theatrically in. 'Sorry. Ooh, look, there he is!' His eyes lit up. 'There's my little lad. Let's be 'aving him, then—div*ine*!' He stooped to scoop the baby from his daughter's arms, pausing only to plant a kiss on her cheek. 'Well *done*, pet.'

Happily his grandson was replete and didn't object to the change of venue. Mum and I smiled at each other as Dad cradled him in his arms. Dad had a bit of a thing about babies. Apparently, when we were tiny, he'd been the one to get up in the night, warming bottles and jiggling us on his knee as he watched reruns of Kojak at five a.m. Even now he peered into prams in the supermarket, making goo-goo faces.

'Where's Dawn?' I asked as he rocked and crooned away, his face wreathed in smiles.

'Outside in the car,' he whispered hoarsely over his grandson's head. 'Hospitals make her feel a bit woozy. Yes! Yes they *do*, don't they?' he crooned as the baby frowned up at him, trying to focus. 'Ooh, he's got his grandpa's eyes! Look at that—blue, like mine!'

'All babies have blue eyes, Martin,' said my mother.

'Not as blue as this. Bit yellow, though, isn't he?' Dad frowned at the baby, then at Eddie. 'Got a bit of Chinkie in you, have you, Eddie, lad? Not that I mind, like, but you might have mentioned it.'

'It's jaundice,' said Mum. 'Remember Imogen had it? And don't jiggle him so much. She's just fed him; he'll be sick. Here, let me.'

She went to take him, but Dad swept him swiftly out of her reach. 'Ooh no you don't. If she's fed him, he needs to get his wind up, don't you, laddie?' He put him gently over his shoulder, holding his tiny head as he rubbed his back, walking him round the room.

' "Hush, little baby, don't say a word, Mumma's gonna buy you—" Seen my grandson?' He broke off, beaming delightedly to ask the mother in the next bed. 'Handsome lad, isn't he?'

She smiled, agreeing that he was.

'Perhaps it's as well Dawn didn't come,' said Hannah as Dad went from bed to bed, encouraging complete strangers, who'd come to visit their own grandchildren, to drool over his and admire his tiny toes. 'Don't want her getting broody.'

'God, that really would finish me off,' Mum said darkly, rolling her eyes.

Would it? I thought in surprise. One never quite knew with Mum: never knew what would be hysterically funny because Martin was making a fool of himself, and what wouldn't be so droll. His girlfriend of twenty-six giving birth clearly wouldn't.

'You're feeding, my love,' she observed to Hannah. 'That's nice.'

'Well, I wasn't, but my sister bullied me into it.'

'Oh, Hannah, I hope I—'

'I'm joking,' she laughed. 'Thank God you did. I just needed a push, lacked confidence, you see. Didn't think I could do it.'

God, it was all coming out today, wasn't it? Something I'd found as natural as falling off a log, my sister had been scared to attempt. This baby business was certainly revealing. I got to my feet.

'Well, I must go. I've got to go and get Rufus, but I'll pop in tomorrow, Hannah, if you think you'll still be here.'

'Oh, no, I won't. I'm going home in a minute, just waiting for the doctor to sign me off. But come and see me at home. I'd like that. There's so much I don't know, Imo. So much I want to ask you.'

I tried to keep my astonishment to myself but it was hard, and Mum and I exchanged incredulous glances. Jeepers.

'I need the loo before I go.' I glanced around.

'That way.' Hannah pointed through the swing doors. 'But you have to come back through the ward.'

'I'll leave my bag then.'

I kissed them all goodbye and nipped to the Ladies. As I found a cubicle and whipped up my skirt, I wondered if I still had any of Rufus's baby clothes. I was pretty sure I had. All those Babygros and nightgowns, they'd be in a suitcase somewhere, I'd dig them out when I got back. Ooh, and my Penelope Leach book, that had been my bible for the first couple of years, and Hannah was a great one for doing things by the book. I'd bring it in

351

tomorrow, she'd love that. I came out, racking my brains as to what else I could do for her, thrilled to be in such an important, advisory capacity for a change and marvelling at the sudden shift in filial hierarchy. But as I went to go back through the double doors to the ward to get my bag, the door was opened for me. I glanced up in surprise, for there, standing back to let me pass under his arm as he propped the door, looking disreputably handsome in a faded pink shirt, his dark hair tousled, and bearing a big easy smile and a bunch of primroses, was Pat Flaherty.


## CHAPTER TWENTY-ONE

'What the hell are you doing here?' my mouth said before my brain could stop it.

He looked taken aback. 'Well, it's not every day you deliver a baby, so I thought . . .' he trailed off, embarrassed.

'Oh God, yes, sorry,' I flustered, flushing. 'I— wasn't thinking. Of course you'd want to come and see how—'

'Well, helloa, look ye 'ere!' A voice, similar to that of a town crier, boomed out, and my stammering apologies were cut short by my father, who couldn't cross the room quickly enough; couldn't deposit the baby en route in Hannah's arms in sufficient haste, in order to embrace Pat, taking him firmly by the shoulders, his eyes shining.

'This is the man!' he roared at full volume, giving Pat's shoulders a vigorous shake. 'This is the man who delivered my grandson, saved my daughter's life—and the baby's too, I'll warrant—marvellous *marvellous* man!' he announced to the astonished ward, clasping Pat to his bosom and slapping him heartily—spine-shatteringly—on the back, only briefly releasing him so that Eddie, pink with delight, could come up and shake his hand too, stuttering his thanks.

'I'm so very grateful,' said Eddie earnestly, blinking behind his spectacles. 'Really grateful. I don't know where we'd have been without you.'

'In the shit, laddie!' roared Dad. 'Reelly reelly deeply in the shit, that's where, the mon's a genius!'

'Oh, I don't think so,' began Pat nervously.

'Ooh, I doo, I doo,' bellowed my father, deep in the Valleys now. 'Good God, mon, just imagine if you hadn't been there! Noa, noa, don't think about it, it's too 'orrible to contemplate. Thank you—thank you soa much!' he beamed, pumping Pat's hand furiously.

Pat smiled. 'You're very welcome. But I honestly didn't come here to lap up the gratitude. I just popped in to see how the little chap was doing.'

'He's fine,' smiled Hannah from the bed, holding him up so Pat could see. 'Look, *so* lovely, and all thanks to you.'

'Well, he certainly looks in good shape. Oh, I, um, picked these for you, stopped on the way.'

Mum took the primroses from him, smiling broadly. 'You're a dear, sweet man and we don't know how we can thank you enough.'

'I knowa how I can,' thundered Dad. 'I can take him oot for a pint or ten, that's what. Come on, laddie, let's goa and find a watering hole, leave

353

these women to their mothers' meetin', like. Come on, Eddie lad, you come too.'

Pat laughed. 'I'd love to, but I've got to stay sober, I'm afraid. I'm operating in an hour.'

'Nonsense! You'll have a pint!'

'No, really.'

'Well, you'll take a pull on this then.' Dad produced a hip flask from his pocket, knocked back a slug, and handed it to Pat, who politely took a sip and handed it back.

'Imogen?' Dad passed it to me.

'I won't, thanks, Dad.' It was the first time I'd spoken since I'd rudely enquired what the hell he was doing here—Pat Flaherty, that is—and for some inexplicable reason I found I couldn't look at him. 'I've got to drive,' I mumbled. 'Got to get Rufus.' Head down I made for the door.

'And I won't linger,' Pat said quickly. 'I just popped in to—'

'Noa, noa, linger away!' roared Dad, pulling up a chair for him. 'Sit down, boyo, sit. We want to hear more, don't we? Imogen said you'd done it once before, like, delivered another babe. Is that right?'

'Yes I . . . well. It was my wife, actually. She gave birth in the back of a taxi in Dublin as we were on our way to hospital.'

I'd got as far as the ward door. Stopped. His wife. Right. That was the ex, then. The one he'd left. And the child.

'No!' Mum was exclaiming. 'How dreadful! But you managed?'

'Had to, really. With the taxi driver's help.'

'God, worse than me,' Hannah said. 'At least I had a bed. But you got her to the hospital all

354

right?'

I pretended I'd paused at the door to search for my car keys in my bag.

'Yes, we got there.'

'And what did she have? I mean, what have you got?'

'A girl,' said Pat shortly.

'Lovely! How old?'

'She's twenty-two months.'

'Oh, *such* a sweet age.'

'Yes, look, I must go,' he said awkwardly. 'I just wanted to make sure you were OK.'

'Fine,' beamed Hannah.

'All thanks to you!' said Dad, taking Pat's hand in both of his and shaking it vigorously.

A moment later I realised Pat was coming up behind me. I snatched up my keys and moved on through the door.

'Bye!' my family shouted cheerily to his departing back, and it was at this point, that I was about to turn to him, really I was. About to smile, thank him, make polite conversation as we headed off down the corridor together, but when I turned, a bright smile at the ready, I realised—he'd gone. In the opposite direction, heading off, presumably to another exit, down the other end of the corridor. Too late, I was going the other way.

I got to the car park, glancing about for him to no avail. I drove off to the school, feeling cross and confused. Why had I found it so hard to look at him? To talk to him? I hadn't even thanked him like the rest of my family, but he had rather shot off, hadn't he? I'd meant to walk out with him, though, thank him then, not with all my family all standing around, which, for some reason, I'd found embarrassing; all eyes on me, as it were—although . . . why should they be on me? And why should I feel like that? But he'd obviously felt uncomfortable too, to disappear so quickly. *I'd made him uncomfortable by being so unfriendly.*

I shifted in my seat, irritated, as I raced down the narrow country lanes towards the village, my wing mirrors whipping the cow parsley heads. Oh, well, what did I care? I pushed a hand through my hair. I didn't even like the man. I frowned into the rear-view mirror as I pulled into a bank to let another car go past. But, then again, he had brought my new nephew into the world, hadn't he? Had possibly saved his life by delivering him safely. I licked my lips. I wished I'd at least said thank you. Wished I'd managed that.

Rufus ran across the village green to meet me as I drew up, an alligator made out of egg boxes in one hand, Tanya in the other. I smiled, despite my irritation. This was what I liked about this school: the fact that the kids didn't consider egg box alligators too immature, or holding hands too uncool.

'Mum, can Tanya come back for tea with us? We want to see if we've got any rabbits.'

Disappointed, but not undaunted by the conspicuous lack of foxes in their Heath Robinson trap, Rufus and Tanya had turned their attention, less ambitiously perhaps, to rabbits, and created a contraption that was essentially a salad bar with a trap door. My lettuces and carrots were disappearing apace, but thus far, the rabbits were still skipping merrily around the fields.

'Is that OK with Mummy, Tanya?'

'Yeah, she says it's fine.'

356

I glanced over her blond head and saw Sheila at the school gates collecting her zillions. She saw me and smiled, nodding that she knew.

'I'll whiz her back later, Sheila,' I called.

'Do not. She can walk,' she yelled.

I grinned and, as we drove off, listened to the children's chatter in the back. Any homework they had could be polished off in minutes before racing out to play in the fields, unlike in London where sometimes it took up an entire evening, and for what? Just to bolster the league tables? Just to shin another inch up the greasy juvenile pole? My mind wasn't really on homework or league tables, though, or even the children; my mind was still, ridiculously, on Pat Flaherty. I'd offended him by ignoring him, and now I was ashamed.

'Come on!'

As I parked in the yard, Tanya and Rufus were even now leaping out of the car and legging it through the gate, running in the direction of the meadow and their trap.

I wandered inside to get their tea, pausing en route to scatter some grain for the chickens. Damn, I thought miserably. Now I'd be back to giving him tight little smiles as we passed in the lanes in our cars, muttering good morning with my head down if I spotted him in the high street. Well, so what, I thought with a jolt as I threw some more corn. Why on earth should that matter? How on earth does offending the local vet impinge on your life, Imogen, hmm? I banged the lid down on the grain bin with a clatter. Not one iota, actually. Not one little jot.

'Mummy!'

I turned to see Rufus running back towards me.

357

'Mum, come quick,' he panted, his face pink with excitement. 'We've got one! We've got a rabbit!'

'Oh, Rufus, you haven't.'

'We have!'

'Well, you'll have to let it go, you know.'

'I know, we will, but come and see first!'

I hurried after him across the yard; down the cinder path, through the gate to the large paddock next to the cows' field, the one full of clover. Tanya was in the middle of it, squatting down on her haunches over a large wooden box.

'He's huge!' she squeaked. 'Look!'

I bent down beside her to see. Through the mesh trap door, an enormous grey rabbit with round, scared eyes, his ears flattened to his back, stared back at me.

'He certainly is. And he's lovely, guys, but he's a bit frightened. I should set him free.'

'I know, we will, but we just want to keep him for a little bit. For observation,' pleaded Rufus.

'It's research,' Tanya informed me grandly. 'For a school project. Very ejucational. We've got to keep him for at least an hour. And anyway, we may have to look after him longer, 'cos I think he's limping.'

'Is he?' Rufus bent to see, unused to such ploys to get his own way.

'Tanya,' I made a face, 'he is not limping.'

'He is a bit,' she insisted. 'Maybe we should take him to see the vet?'

I laughed, straightening up. 'We are not taking this rabbit to see the—' I broke off. Stared at her a moment. Settled back down on my haunches beside her.

'Limping, you say?' I enquired softly.

'Yeah, look!' she said, thrilled to bits that her little ruse had been so easily bought. 'I think it's his back leg!'

'Where?' demanded Rufus, peering in.

'Oh dear. Yes. Poor thing,' I murmured. 'Well, maybe we should.'

Rufus's eyes nearly popped out of his head in astonishment, unused to his mother being such a pushover. 'Really, Mum? Can we?'

'Why not?' I straightened up. 'Just to—you know—check him over. See that he's OK before we set him free. Wouldn't want him hoping round on a dodgy leg, would we?'

'Ye-esss!' The children leaped up and punched the air in delight, thrilled to be taken seriously for once, although I could see Tanya looking at me with something approaching derision. Never in a million years would she have got that past her mother, but then, never in a million years would Sheila need, so very urgently, to see a man about a rabbit.

Without giving myself a moment to question my motives and with the car keys still in my hand, we retraced our steps across the meadow and piled as one into the car, the rabbit cowering in submission in a corner of his box in the boot. As we drove up the chalky zigzag track, though, my mind was whirring.

'Um, listen, guys,' I called over my shoulder to the back seat, 'I'm not convinced the vet treats wild animals, so we might have to say that the rabbit's— you know—ours.'

'OK,' said Tanya quickly.

'Really?' Rufus's eyes were huge in my rear-view

359

mirror. This was a whole new side to his mother, one he'd never seen before. Not only a pushover, but a fibber too. A very exciting side. He beamed and bounced delightedly in his seat.

'Yes, we can say we bought him last week,' he said warming quickly to the duplicity. 'For my birthday or something.'

'It wasn't your birthday last week, Rufus.'

'I know, but he won't know that, will he?' he said, justifiably miffed that I'd found holes in his fabrications when he'd accepted mine wholesale. Marvellous moral code you're expounding here, Imogen, I thought, licking my lips nervously as we belted along the lanes. Marvellous. The boy will grow up with a terrific sense of integrity.

We were on the outskirts of town now, pulling up in a tree-lined road outside the rather smart Victorian house with the brass plaque, which bore the legend 'Marshbank Veterinary Practice'. I'd always rather cringed as I'd driven past, head well down behind the wheel, but now, as the children jumped out with alacrity and ran round to the boot to get the box, I got out confidently. Yes, I thought as I followed them up the path to the green front door; and when he saw that the rabbit was OK— Pat, I mean—I could just—you know—have a dizzy blonde moment. Say—oh gosh, is it? How silly of me, I could have sworn he was limping, the children were convinced—or something like that. And he'd laugh delightedly at my charming fluffiness and say—don't worry, it happens all the time, and then the children would wander off to look at all the other poor, sick animals, and he'd say—why didn't I have a coffee while I was here? And we'd settle down for a cosy chat, and that

360

would be that. What would be what, Imogen? I wondered fleetingly, as we pushed through the green front door. But only fleetingly. I mean, dammit, we were here now.

I took a deep breath and approached the desk in the waiting room. I deliberately hadn't rung for an appointment, knowing there was little chance of getting one at the last minute. No, we'd come as an emergency, and when he heard who was here, I was sure he'd see me.

The pretty blonde receptionist looked up and smiled: a mummy with two small children and a bunny in a box.

'Can I help?'

'Yes, I'm awfully sorry, we don't have an appointment, but we've got a rather sick rabbit here and we wondered if the vet could see him.'

'Oh dear, poor thing.' She leaned over her desk to peer into the box, then down at her diary. 'Let me see what I can do for you. I might be able to squeeze you in. Name, please?'

'Mrs Cameron.'

Her eyes shot up from her book. Her face changed dramatically. It was no longer so friendly and smiley. Quite wintery, in fact.

'We are rather busy, actually,' she said shortly, closing the diary.

'Oh, but you did say you might be able to squeeze us in,' I said, shamelessly, particularly since I recognised her icy tones. 'The children would be so grateful.'

The china-blue eyes were cool. She regarded me a long moment. 'Just a minute.' She got up with a flick of her blonde hair over her shoulder and slipped her pert little bottom out from behind her desk. Then she exited stage left and went down the corridor.

'Is he going to look at him?' hissed Rufus.

'I don't know, darling. We'll see.'

There was only one other man sitting in the waiting room: a huge chap with a bulbous red nose and a bull terrier on a heavy chain. I turned and gave him an apologetic smile, but he glared at me, none too pleased at being shunted down the queue, no doubt. The bull terrier gave a low growl as it lay with its head between its paws at its master's feet. I dropped the smile and quickly turned back.

In another moment, the receptionist had returned. She gave a tight little smile. 'Yes, OK, the vet will see you. But he's operating in five minutes, so you'll have to be quick.'

'Thank you so much,' I gushed disingenuously.

'No problem,' she muttered, sitting down again. 'Now. Name?'

'Mrs Cam—'

'The rabbit's,' she snapped.

'Ah.'

Rufus, Tanya and I looked at each other wildly. Then we all spoke at once.

'Bunny.'

'Thumper.'

'Cuddles.'

The receptionist raised her eyebrows.

'Um, yes. That's his . . . full name,' I murmured. 'Bunny Thumper Cuddles.'

'I see.' She filled in the form, her face inscrutable. 'And how old is Bunny Thumper Cuddles?'

More wild looks. I willed the children into

silence with my eyes. 'He's . . . twenty-two months,' I breathed, for some reason, thinking of Pat's daughter.

'Twenty-two months,' she repeated slowly, writing it down. 'Very precise,' she observed drily.

I swallowed.

'And sex?'

'Good heavens, no, he's only a baby!'

'What sex is the rabbit, Mrs Cameron?'

'Oh! Right. He's . . . a—a male. A man rabbit.'

She scribbled some more, then glanced up. 'Right. Well, if you'd like to take this form,' she said sweetly, 'together with your "man rabbit", down the corridor to the first door on the right, the vet will see you now.'

'Thank you,' I muttered, almost snatching the form from her, ignoring her heavy sarcasm.

We scurried away down the corridor, glad to be out of the scrutiny of her glacial gaze. As I turned the handle of the door on the right, I instinctively sucked in my tummy and straightened up, summoning up a gracious smile, a pair of twinkling eyes, as we swept in. He was over on the far side of the room by the sink, in a white coat, his back to us; but even before he turned, I felt a pang of dismay.

'Mrs Cameron?' A vinegar-faced man with a Scottish accent, his hair, intellectually withdrawn from his temples, peered at me over half-moon glasses.

'Oh! I was expecting . . . Mr Flaherty. Is he . . . ?'

'Operating, I'm afraid. I'm Mr McAlpine, the senior partner. Will I do?' he enquired scathingly, a quizzical gleam in his eye.

I flushed. 'Yes, of course.'

'Now.' He crossed the room. 'Samantha tells me we have a very sick rabbit here. So sick I must delay operating on a Border collie with a malignant tumour. Is that right?'

My heart gave a palsied lurch. 'Well, I—'

He took the form briskly from my hands. 'Bunny Thumper Cuddles aged twenty-two months.' He glanced up. 'What seems to be the trouble?'

I attempted to back towards the door with the box, pulling Rufus with me by his sleeve.

'Oh, I—I think . . .' I smiled foolishly, 'well, he had a slight limp. But actually, I didn't notice it in the waiting room just now. And you're so busy, we'll come back another—'

'Nonsense, you're here now and I've broken off my pre-med to look at him. Come on, let's be having him.'

He took the box from my hand and put it on the table in the middle of the room. 'Now, laddie,' he turned to Rufus, 'would you like to get your bunny out for me?'

Rufus turned terrified eyes to me. He shook his head mutely. I glanced at Tanya, but she shook hers fiercely too and took a step backwards.

I licked my lips. 'Um, the thing is, he hasn't been handled that much, so maybe,' I attempted a fluffy laugh. 'Well, I'm fairly hopeless with animals and you're the professional . . .' My dizzy moment fell on stony ground as he regarded me scathingly.

'I see. Who mucks him out, then?'

'Who mucks him . . . oh! Well, yes, of course I do. But—not very often.'

He raised his eyebrows enquiringly.

'I—I mean—because he's frightfully clean. Hardly any ponky-poos at all!'

364

'Really. Constipated as well as limping. Well, let's have a look.'

He flicked back the clasp, opened the lid and peered in, at which point, the rabbit spun round and, like a Kung Fu boxer, delivered a powerful kick with both hind legs straight to the vet's face. He caught Mr McAlpine squarely in the right eye, and sent his glasses flying to the ground. Then he leaped high into the air and sank his teeth into his finger.

'Jesus Christ!' the vet yelped with pain, shaking his hand vigorously, as the rabbit clung on, then, seeing his chance, leaped away. He jumped down to the floor and fled to a corner of the room, ears flattened back with terror.

Blood pouring from his finger, the vet looked at me aghast. 'That's not a tame rabbit, Mrs Cameron,' he roared. 'That's a wild hare!'

'Oh!' I gasped. 'Is it?'

'I thought it was big,' volunteered Tanya, in awe.

'What the hell are you doing bringing it in here? It could be diseased, could have anything!' He shrieked, his face contorted with rage.

'I—I'm sorry,' I stammered. 'I thought—I mean—we all thought, it was limping a bit, and we felt sorry for it so—'

'Limping?' he bellowed, as the hare, desperate to escape, jumped up on the counter, across the sink, and on top of a cupboard, for all the world like a Russian gymnast, knocking over bottles, sending test tubes flying and crashing to the ground, and generally creating mayhem. 'That hare is no more limping than I'm Olga Korbut! He's got springs in his back legs that would grace a suspension bridge!'

The hare was, indeed, extremely well-sprung, and looking horribly agile now as he careered around the room, sending specimen jars full of vile-looking liquid smashing to the ground. We watched in horror.

'Get him out of here!' he yelled.

'Right-oh,' I croaked.

With the children cowering behind me I dithered ineffectually around the room, flapping my arms, waving my handbag, bleating, 'Here, Bunny' as I attempted to corner him, but knowing in my heart it was futile. What if I did? I couldn't *touch* him, for God's sake, let alone pick him up.

'Oh, for heaven's sake!' Mr McAlpine, exasperated beyond belief, advanced on the hare, who, crouched in a corner in terror, was evacuating copiously out of his rear end. I sincerely hoped I wouldn't follow suit, for terror was surely gripping me too. The vet lunged and caught the animal by the haunches, but the hare wriggled free, and as the vet made a valiant attempt to hang on, he skidded in a mixture of broken bottles, faeces and urine, and landed, with a resounding 'Oomph!' face down on his academic forehead. The children and I gasped in horror, but Mr McAlpine got to his feet, his poo-splattered face set and determined, and advanced again, whereupon the hare, sensing another attack, leaped up and bit him hard on the nose, drawing a spurt of blood.

'Oh!' shrieked Tanya, her horror betraying a hint of ecstasy.

The vet swore darkly and made another lunge. There was a palpitating moment when he nearly caught the hare by the ears, but the animal dodged nimbly, causing Mr McAlpine to bang his head squarely on a cupboard door, just as the hare, spotting the open window above the sink, sprang out.

'Oh, no!' the children gasped in alarm.

'Best place for him,' panted the vet, holding his head and staggering to slam the window shut behind him. 'Back to the field, where he belongs. *Jesus* Christ!' He put a hand to his bleeding nose.

'But he won't know where he is!' said Rufus, running to the window. 'Won't know the territory!'

'So he'll make new friends,' snapped the vet, 'charm a few locals, a very advisable thing to do when you're new to an area!' He flashed me a look then turned back to glare at my son. 'And anyway, sonny, you should have thought about that before you set about trapping the poor wee animal, shouldn't you?'

Rufus hung his head with shame and his eyes filled up. My blood briefly boiled.

'There's no need to take it out on a small child!' I snapped. 'If you're going to yell at anyone, yell at me. I'm the one who suggested bringing him here!'

'Aye, well, you'll think it through a bit more thoroughly next time, won't you? Now if you'll excuse me, I'm a busy man and I've got a surgery to clean up!'

He snatched a tissue from a box and held it to his nose, his gaze sweeping around his decimated surgery. My eyes followed his in dismay.

'Oh God, I'm awfully sorry,' I mumbled, suddenly contrite. 'Here, let me . . .' I crouched down, attempting to pick up bits of broken test tube from the floor, but my handbag swung off my shoulder and got mixed up in all the wee and glass.

'Och, away with you,' he shooed us, exasperated,

swinging the surgery door wide. 'I'd rather do it myself. Go on, be off!'

Needing no further prompting and mumbling yet more effusive apologies, I grabbed the box and backed out, bowing low like Uriah Heep, ushering the children ahead of me from the room. We passed like spirits down the corridor, through the waiting room, and were halfway to the front door and freedom when a voice behind me brought me up short.

'Would you like to settle up now, Mrs Cameron?'

I stopped. Spun round.

'Only, we always ask emergency calls to settle up on the spot,' the receptionist informed me, tapping her pencil on her pad, lip gloss and blue eyes gleaming. 'Since we're taken by surprise in the first place, we think it's only fair, d'you see?'

'Um, yes. I see,' I muttered, shuffling meekly back. She leaned over her desk and peered into the empty box.

'Ah. No Bunny Thumper Cuddles, I see?'

'No,' I cleared my throat. 'He, er . . .'

'He's staying here for a bit,' Tanya informed her coolly. 'With the vet.'

I glanced down at her admiringly. Nice one. And true, after a fashion.

'Really,' said the receptionist drily, handing me a bill for £30. 'That's our standard charge, Mrs Cameron, but perhaps you'd like to settle your whole account while you're here?'

My whole account. Damn. I looked into her mocking blue eyes and wished I'd thought to cash my cheque for the paintings; put some money in the bank.

'Er, no, just the thirty pounds, for now,' I mumbled, getting my cheque book out. I scribbled away.

'So . . .' she murmured silkily, resting her elbows on the desk, lacing her fingers together and resting her chin on them as she watched me write. 'Flowers for the headmaster, flirting with the postman, and now wild rabbits for the vet. Whatever will you pull out of the hat next, Mrs Cameron?' I glanced up in horror. A little smile played on her lips. 'Something for the farrier, perhaps?'

She caught the eye of the ruddy-faced man behind me, with the bull terrier. He snorted with laughter.

'Fine by me, luv. Just don't tell the missus, though, eh?' He winked. 'Keep it shtoom!'

I went pale. Rufus glanced up at me anxiously.

'Word gets about in a small place like this, you know,' the receptionist said softly as she took my cheque, whipping it from my hand with her long red fingernails. Her eyes were hard and knowing. 'You want to be careful, Mrs Cameron. Very careful indeed.'


# CHAPTER TWENTY-TWO

A few minutes later found me sitting very still in the driving seat of my car, the children clambering into the back. I gazed blankly out of the windscreen, my eyes wide and staring. She'd been trying to tell me something in there. No, correction: she *had* been telling me something in

369

there, very forcibly in fact: telling me in no uncertain terms that I was making a fool of myself. My eyes cut back through the plate-glass window and I saw her side on at her desk in reception. I watched as she flicked back her long blond hair and leaned forward in her pink jeans to reach a sheaf of papers . . . long blond hair and pink jeans . . . oh God. Piers's remark came winging back to me. Of course. She was one of the girls he'd seen coming out of Crumpet Cottage, one of Pat's girls. How many were there, I wondered. And what was I doing swelling the ranks? I went hot. Looked down at my hands in my lap. They were tightly clenched.

'Are you all right, Mummy?' Rufus's face in the rear-view mirror was anxious.

'Yes. Yes, fine.'

I gave a bright smile and turned the ignition. Then I let out the handbrake and we drove away.

We passed out of town and into the lanes. The hedgerows flashed by in a riot of late spring colour: red campions and yellow cowslips nodded and tossed their dazzling heads in the breeze, but I hardly saw them. My mind was racing. I knew what this was all about. This wasn't about me throwing myself at headmasters, or vets, or any other local hunk you care to mention. This fiasco with the rabbit, this excuse to see Pat, was symptomatic of something much more worrying, something much more visceral. It was about a deeper insecurity, to do with being scared, and lonely, and reaching out and clutching—well, at whatever was there, frankly: at whatever alternative came my way and could fill a gap. A gap in a marriage. This wasn't about me finding other men attractive. This had nothing to do with Pat Flaherty. This was about me counting the number of times my husband made love to me, about living with someone but not being able to reach them, about a vacuum in a marriage. It was a cry for help. And actually, what Pink Jeans had done was point this out very succinctly. This wasn't really *me* behaving in a desperate manner, this was me reacting to a desperate situation. A situation I couldn't control—had no control over—and was too scared to confront, for fear of what I might find out.

My breathing became shallow as I raced down the lanes, gripping the wheel. I hadn't wanted to face this, had done my best to sit on my hands and deny it, but now, here it was, served up on a plate in front of me. And I'd denied it many, many times before. Oh, yes.

I remembered once in London, when I'd known Eleanor was in town, Alex coming back late from work, very late. I'd crept out of bed, and from my window, had seen him get out of a taxi, seen the spring in his step, the confident swagger: not the gait of an exhausted man who'd been ploughing through a workload at the office—no, the step of an elated man. And as he'd turned and bounded up the path, I'd seen the look in his eyes and known too that this was a man brimming over, a man who wanted, finally, to unburden himself, to come clean. I'd nipped back to bed, and when he'd come into the room, I'd pretended to be asleep. I'd heard him breathing, could feel him standing over me, could smell the fresh air on his suit as he watched me. Then he'd said my name.

'Imo? Imo, are you asleep?'

I'd kept my eyes tightly shut, digging my nails

into my hand, staying still, but remembering too, to breathe. I'd sensed him hovering there a moment longer. Eventually, though, he went to the bathroom. When he got into bed beside me, he let out a sigh that had ripped through me: a sigh full of sadness and regret; full of longing.

By morning, of course, his confessional moment had passed and he was sober and rational: no longer full of the need to communicate, no longer so keen to share the news with me that he was in love with another woman. And the moment passed for me too: I made it pass. I put it from my mind to such an extent that I managed, not to pretend it had never happened, because after all I still had the nail marks in my hand, but to pretend I'd been mistaken. Pretend that, in fact, all he'd wanted to do as he'd stood there in the moonlight calling my name, bursting with information, was tell me his plans for the summer. Our plans. To take a villa in Spain with some old friends, the Frowbishers—'too expensive but let's do it anyway, darling, let's take a break'—and later that year, we had. Yes, that had been it. But in my heart, I knew I'd ducked the moment.

When love is withdrawn from a marriage, its absence is not felt immediately. After all, the fabric of the union is still there: the house, the mortgage, the child, the sofa that needs cleaning, that fact that you still owe the Hamiltons—but slowly, and I mean drip drip slowly, over time, you realise the jewel has gone, and you miss its sparkle. Everything goes just a little bit darker, like God fiddling with the dimmer switch. But you stumble on in the gloom, taking care not to trip over the evidence, until one day, quite unexpectedly, you're sent sprawling by a crassly stuck-out leg—almost a cartoon leg—and in my case, with pink jeans on. Me, who'd nimbly sidestepped some much firmer evidence, who was adept at ignoring The Signs.

In London, The Signs had tended to start at the weekend: Alex, sitting in the drawing room in Putney, the *Sunday Times* in his hands, not reading, just gazing ruefully over the top into space. When I'd inadvertently catch his eye, he'd give me a quick, overbright smile before returning hastily to the Business section. He'd drink quite a lot too, sitting up alone, late into the evening, creeping to bed when I'd gone to sleep.

Then would come the spurious errands: the nipping to the shops for extra milk when we already had plenty, the trips to check the tyres at the garage, always with his mobile, and then—a less pensive, less reflective Alex: an Alex with a spring in his step, an excited light in his eyes, a man with a plan. Finally would come the late night at the office. Never a whole night—he was never that careless—but it would be midnight before he was back, and then, for a day or two afterwards, the excited light would dim to a more contented glow. He'd be very sweet to me, and to Rufus, and very good about the house. Washing up would be done, clothes would be tidied away, flowers would appear, and there'd be trips to the park too, which ordinarily had to be prised out of him: Alex pushing Rufus higher and higher on the swings, a fun daddy, a cool daddy, and then walking home together, Alex insisting we hold hands, the three of us, like a family in a soft-focus photograph. But always the three of us, never the two of us in a quiet restaurant for supper with a baby-sitter for

Rufus—no, Rufus had to come too. And this, a man who was impatient with children; who sometimes treated his son like an irritating friend of mine who'd come to stay—why can't he just go to bed? Why is he crying? Why won't he eat his food? But on these occasions, Rufus was crucial. He was his shield.

And of course, Rufus wasn't going to question this mercurial good humour. He loved having a daddy who played football, a daddy who took us all to Starbucks on a Saturday morning, but always, I noticed, a daddy who watched his diet. Who, as Rufus and I tucked into hot chocolate and muffins, would sip his black espresso in clothes that a cynic might suggest were slightly too young for him. Never ridiculously so: the leather jacket was brown, not black; the jeans never too low slung or tight, but still . . . And the hair, always recently washed—possibly blown dry—swept back continually with his hand. Once, when he'd got a spot on his chin, I could see he'd covered it with my concealer. I didn't mention it.

But these carefree days wouldn't last and soon he'd be back to the sad, wistful Alex, gazing over the top of the *Sunday Times*, snapping at Rufus if he suggested a card game or a bicycle ride, and then there'd be impromptu trips to the garage, and then the overexcited husband, then the late night—and so the cycle of our lives would go on. He was like a junkie who needed a fix, and the fix wasn't me.

It is to my eternal shame that I never investigated his mobile or went through his pockets. I'm not proud of that. There were no depths to which I would not sink to protect my family, to remain uninformed, to be innocent of all charges of knowingly living in a faithless marriage. I was ruthless in my denial. But now this. A well-aimed catty remark from a woman who was intent on protecting her own domestic interests, but in a much pluckier way than I was: a combative blonde who fought for her man—'Hands off!' with a flash of her red nails—whilst I shrank from the evidence: condoned it by my silence.

I took a deep breath, the deepest I'd taken for some time—most of my breathing tending towards the shallow these days—and let it out shakily. Right. This was it, then. A final demarcation line. A line that I'd stumbled upon quite by accident, but a line there was surely no mistaking.

Driving too fast, but actually quite skilfully, I swung the car left down a narrow lane and drove off towards the next village. After a while, Rufus broke off from playing Scissors Stone Paper in the back with Tanya, and glanced around at the unfamiliar scenery.

'This isn't the way home, is it, Mummy?'

'No, but it's the way to my home,' remarked Tanya, twisting round in surprise as I bumped down the track towards the trailer park. 'Scissors!'

'Oh, I wasn't ready!'

I drove slowly through the grid of caravans and mobile homes, venturing where the local police daren't, and drew up outside the largest one, surrounded by pansies planted in piles of old tyres. There were net curtains at the windows, and by the open front door, Cindy the Alsatian dozed on a chain. An assortment of old baths, prams and bicycles were piled in a heap round the back, like an avant-garde climbing frame, and three or four

375

children were using it as just that. A couple of old men sat smoking in ancient deck chairs, watching them, as Shelia hung rows and rows of grey school knickers out on a washing line.

'Shelia?' I called out of the window. 'Would you do me a favour?'

She turned. 'Oh, hello, luv.'

'Would you have Rufus for me for an hour or so? There's something I need to do.'

She came towards me, round the side of the trailer, taking pegs out of her mouth and regarding me quizzically. My voice was rather shrill, perhaps.

'Course, luv.' She bent and peered in at the window. 'You all right?'

'I'm fine,' I assured her brightly as the children clambered out, Rufus making gleefully for the hideously dangerous-looking climbing frame. 'I haven't fed them yet, I'm afraid. We've been at the vet's.'

'You're all right. I was just about to feed this lot. They can have fish paste sandwiches with 'em. Sure you're OK? You look a bit peaky.'

'Fine.' I plastered on a smile. 'Really fine. Thanks, Sheila.'

She opened her mouth again, but whatever kindly concern she had for me was lost as, with a screech of tyres that had the lad next door polishing his Harley Davidson glancing up admiringly, I was off.

I headed towards Little Harrington and the Latimers' with a remarkably clear head, and for once, something approaching steel in my heart. Yes. Yes, I flaming well would. As I swept up the front drive, past the little lodge house—Pat's house, otherwise known as Crumpet Cottage, I

376

thought grimly—the steel didn't waver. Nor did it waver as I got out of the car in the vast gravel drive and sprinted across to the looming manor house, nor when I mounted the steps to the heavy front door guarded by a matching pair of stone griffins. Oh yes, the front door was very definitely where I wanted to be right now, not cringing apologetically round the back at the tradesmen's entrance, not creeping and crawling, and who cared if the dogs barked? I gave the door a mighty rap with its brass knocker, all nerve endings tingling, face set and determined, but no fear. Oh no, no fear, and no second thoughts, either.

As the huge house resounded to the outraged howls of various Labradors and lurchers, footsteps came across the marble hall; soft but hurrying. Who on earth could it be, banging like that, they seemed to say. The door opened cautiously and Vera peered around, frowning. Her face cleared as she saw me, and she blinked in surprise.

'Oh. Hello, pet.'

'Is Eleanor in?' I blurted out, feeling, I realised, as Alex must have felt when he came home late that night in the taxi, brimming over with the need to unburden himself, to spill his load, only my load was all the more heavy for being so overdue.

'She's not, I'm afraid, she's—'

'In London?' I cut in accusingly, not recognising my harsh tone.

Vera looked taken aback. 'No, not in London, although she has been up there, but no, she got back this afternoon. She's gone out to see a girlfriend.'

'Oh.' I was deflated for a moment. Damn.

'Will she be long? Can I wait?'

'Well, she's out for the evening, like, but she's going to be ever so cross because she's forgotten her handbag.' She jerked her head across to a quilted Chanel bag, sitting on the hall table. 'Must have gone out in a rush with just her car keys, but it's got her purse an' that in it, and her door keys, and Piers goes to bed early so I suppose Muggins here will have to wait up to let her in.'

I looked at the bag on the table.

'D'you know who the friend is? Where she lives?'

''Aven't a clue, luv, but she's renting in the village, I'm told. Not been 'ere long—friend from London, I think. Milly? Mandy? Something like that.'

'Well, it's not a big village. She shouldn't be difficult to find.'

She snorted derisively. 'That's as maybe, but if you think I'm crawling round looking for her with her ladyship's handbag, you've got another think coming. I don't know the number or nothing. Any road, I don't suppose she'll be that late. I'll tell her you called, luv.' She went to shut the door.

'I'll take it,' I said, not quite jamming my foot in the door, but near as damn it. I reached deftly across to the table and my hand closed on the bag's chain strap.

'Oh, well, I don't know . . .' she faltered, confused.

'Honestly, it's not a problem, Vera,' I said smoothly. 'I'm going that way anyway. And I know Eleanor's car. It's bound to be parked outside.'

'Well, I suppose . . .' she looked anxious. 'But I'm not sure I like handing her bag over, just like that.'

I laughed. 'You're only handing it to me, Vera. And don't worry, if I don't find her, I'll pop it back, OK?' I flashed her a smile.

'OK,' she said slowly, looking as if she might say more, and was about to, but by then I'd turned my back on her and was halfway down the steps—halfway across the gravel, putting distance between us, already with my seat belt on in the car, glancing back at her, a diminutive figure standing uncertainly in her housecoat on the top step, looking rather temporary, as if she might come down.

Without giving her a chance to, I sped away in a spray of dust and gravel, hurtling down the front drive, my precious booty beside me.

Oh, no, Vera, I thought—watching her in my rear-view mirror as she shaded her eyes on the steps, watching me go—you shouldn't be handing over your employer's precious possessions. That's a foolish thing to do, very foolish indeed.

The village, in truth, was not that tiny. It sprawled down back streets and up cul-de-sacs, diving off into strips of new development that seemed to go on for ever, and I knew I hadn't given myself nearly as simple a task as I'd pretended to Vera. I drove around for a bit without spotting so much as a hint of Eleanor's dark green Range Rover. Damn. Just when my blood was up, just when I knew I was in the mood to finally confront her, to tell her to take her thieving hands off my husband, to tell her I knew exactly what she'd been doing in London, and with whom, and now she was no flaming where to be found.

And then I saw it. Turning down a lane I'd originally dismissed as being so unmade up it was

379

surely just a farm track, I saw there was a row of cottages at the end, and outside one of them, Eleanor's four-wheel drive.

Which cottage was it outside, though, I thought wildly as I rattled down the track and parked at the end of a line of cars? I got out. This one—I ran lightly across to the most obvious cottage, number nine—or the one next door? Or was she, in fact, installed at one much further along, but had had to park on the end, like me, because there wasn't a space? There were quite a few houses here; was I going to knock on every single door, like Wee Willie Winkie, until I found her? And if I did find her, was I going to drag her out by the hair and confront her on the doorstep, in front of lots of prying eyes? My courage momentarily deserted me, then—yes, I decided. I would. I'd come this far, I was damn well going to see it through.

Blood storming through my veins, I marched up to number nine and leaned on the bell. A huge, barrel-chested man in a skimpy white T-shirt, his arms covered in faded army tattoos, swung back the door in irritation. He loomed over me as a football match blared from the television behind him.

'Yeah?'

'Oh, er, I'm sorry. I'm looking for a friend of mine, Eleanor Latimer. She's visiting someone who lives in one of these cottages, but she clearly isn't—'

'Never 'eard of her,' he growled, slamming the door in my face and going back to his game.

The lady at number ten was slightly more helpful. She listened, plump arms tightly folded in her yellow dressing gown, occasionally scratching a heavily veined leg. Then she rubbed her cheek thoughtfully.

'Well now, that could be number twelve, two doors away,' she said at length. 'It certainly wouldn't be number eleven 'cos old Mrs Greenway lives there, but . . . yeah, try number twelve.'

I thanked her profusely and hurried away.

Number twelve, in fact, looked far more promising. It was a sweet, whitewashed number with roses round the door and pots on the step: something of a feminine effort had been made. I rang the bell but there was no answer. I rang again—still no response. And yet . . . I stood on tiptoes and peered through the small pane of glass in the front door. If I wasn't very much mistaken, that was Eleanor's Puffa jacket thrown casually on that chair. I recognised the distinctive tartan lining. She wasn't coming to the door, though, was she? And neither was her friend. I rang again. No, because presumably, I thought with a jolt, they'd already spotted me from the front-room window: spotted me ringing all the bells in the street, and maybe Eleanor had seen my determined stance, recognised the cut of my jib, as it were, and said nervously, 'Don't answer it, Milly. I have a feeling I know what this is about.' And then they'd both slipped down the hallway into the kitchen, taking their bottle of Sancerre with them, where they were hiding even now, fighting their giggles, spluttering into their hands. Oh, *were* they, I thought, incensed. I squatted down and pushed open the letter box. James Blunt drifted through from the hi-fi.

'*Eleanor!*' I screamed. '*Eleanor Latimer, I know you're in there! Open the door this instant!*'

381

I put my ear to the letter box. Heard voices. Muffled voices, and then a giggle. My eyes bulged. My blood boiled. I put my mouth to the vent again.

'ELEANOR LATIMER! COME OUT, YOU TWO-TIMING HUSBAND-SNATCHING HUSSY! YOU SLACK-MORALLED JEZEBEL, YOU— *oh!*'

I shrieked as the door flew open. Shot forwards on to my knees. To save myself from sprawling flat on the doormat, I threw out both hands—and clutched at a pair of feet. Large, bare, hairy feet, which I gripped hard. As flesh met flesh I screamed again and let go. As I rocked back on my haunches, a dark green dressing gown flapped in my face. My eyes travelled up it . . . and I found myself looking into the unmistakable features of— Daniel Hunter, Rufus's headmaster.

## CHAPTER TWENTY-THREE

'Oh—Omi*god!*'

'Mrs Cameron!' He stared down at me on his doormat, astonished.

'Imogen,' I mumbled stupidly, through force of habit, blushing madly and pulling myself up hand over hand by the doorframe. Behind him I saw Eleanor, at the top of the stairs, glance over the banisters, also in a dressing gown.

'Shit!' She shot back into the shadows as our eyes met, and in that instant, as I looked back at Daniel Hunter's face, I understood everything. My mouth fell open.

'Good grief . . . you mean . . . ?'

382

My eyes flitted up again as Eleanor reappeared on the landing. She'd whipped the dressing gown off and was pulling on some jeans, simultaneously tugging a jumper over her head.

'Wait there!' she ordered fiercely.

'Er, yes. You'd better come in.' Daniel scratched his head sheepishly and stood back to let me pass.

'Oh—no, no!' I shook my head wildly, the palms of my hands up. 'I—I'm terribly sorry, I've made a mistake. I didn't realise . . .' I backed away rapidly, hands outstretched. 'You—you carry on as you were. I mean—as it were . . .'

'Imogen, wait!' Eleanor came hurtling down the stairs as I backed frantically down the path, horribly aware that quite a few neighbours had not only come to their windows, but were now in their front gardens, ostensibly watering bedding plants—Yellow Dressing Gown—or putting notes out for the milkman—Tattooed Man—but actually watching wide-eyed, and waiting on tenterhooks for the 'two-timing husband-stealing hussy, the slack-moralled Jezebel' to appear.

Eleanor didn't disappoint them.

'Don't go,' Daniel implored her, reaching out to catch her arm as she made to dash past him down the path. As he held on to her sleeve and swung her round to face him, I saw the naked entreaty in his eyes. So did Yellow Dressing Gown. She dropped her plastic watering can. Tattooed man's fag was hanging from his lower lip. As street theatre went, it had a lot going for it.

'I'll be back,' Eleanor promised in a low voice, and I saw the tenderness in her eyes as she removed his hand from her arm. 'But I need to explain, Daniel. I need to talk to Imogen. I must!'

'You don't need to explain!' I squeaked, embarrassed beyond belief now, squirming for England, crouching low as I backed through the gate, but also—also stupendously joyous. Not my husband. Not Alex. Daniel Hunter—oh, deep *deep* joy. 'Honestly, it couldn't matter less!'

'It does, because listen,' Eleanor hastened after me. 'He *was* married, you're quite right, but it was all over years ago and he's divorced—or practically divorced—I promise!' Her hazel eyes pleaded with me as she took my arm and hustled me towards the cars. 'Come on, we'll go for a drink. I'll explain.'

'Oh!' I stopped in my tracks. 'You mean—what I yelled through the letterbox!' God, I must have sounded like a marriage watchdog unit, checking up on all adulterers: Come out, you filthy philanderers, we know you're in there! All I needed was a foghorn. 'Oh, no, I don't mind if *he's* married, couldn't give a monkey's, just so long as he's not married to me!'

'What?' She gaped, and now it was her turn to stop still in the street. I was aware of Yellow Dressing Gown and Tattooed Man walking hypnotically to their front gates to listen, keen not to miss a word, all inhibitions gone now. I hurried to my car, flinging the passenger door open for her as I ran round.

'Come on, we'll take mine. No, I'm just so happy it's not *my* husband, not Alex!'

I couldn't stop the joyous smile that was spreading over my face as I flopped into the driving seat and turned the ignition. Oh, thank you, God. Thank you! I shut my eyes tight and clenched my fists. *Yes!*

'You mean . . .' she got in slowly beside me, 'you

thought me and Alex . . . ?'

'Yes, and now you're not, and—oh, Eleanor, for heaven's sake, go back and have a lovely time! I'm really sorry I've spoiled your evening, please go back and—and do whatever you were going to do—bonk for Britain, cover yourselves in golden syrup, lick it all off, hang sticky and naked from the chandeliers—have one on me!'

'Me and *Alex*!' she gasped, hanging on to the upholstery as we shot off down the road, away from the delighted eyes of the neighbours, who were still, no doubt, digesting the golden syrup scenario.

'Yes, but you and Daniel *Hunter*—oh, Eleanor, that's *so* different. Honestly, I couldn't give two hoots, and I feel dreadful about dragging you away!'

'And I feel dreadful about Piers,' she said firmly. 'And obviously I need to explain.'

'Oh no, you—'

'Oh yes, I do!'

We drove in silence for a minute, my mind racing, but my heart so light.

'We'll go here,' she said eventually, pointing her finger as we approached the edge of the village, with Molly's wine bar on the corner. She plucked her handbag from the floor where I'd stowed it.

'Yes, well, obviously there's Piers to consider,' I said as soberly as I could as I parked outside, 'and—and that's terribly difficult, obviously, but honestly, none of my business, Eleanor.' It was no good, I was euphoric, and I couldn't care less who she was cuckolding, particularly Piers, actually. Stuck up git, serve him jolly well right. 'But I dare say he'll get over it,' I said cheerily as I got out and slammed the door.

She shot me a startled look as we hastened into the wine bar.

'He doesn't know. No one knows!'

She sat down heavily at a table just inside the door by the window, almost as if her legs wouldn't take her any further. I slid in opposite her.

'And listen, Imogen, it's really important he doesn't find out, OK?' She leaned across the table. 'At least, not from anyone but me. Can I count on you?'

Her face was pale in the gloom, and she looked at me beseechingly, her fists clenched. I thought how ghastly she looked, so drawn, haunted almost.

'Of course you can!' I assured her, waving jauntily at a waiter. Molly didn't seem to be around. 'Golly, you can always count on me, I'm the soul of discretion. What shall we have—a bottle?' I felt like celebrating.

'Just a Perrier for me, but, Imogen, please say you won't breathe a word.'

'I won't,' I assured her, beaming.

I ordered the drinks, feeling sorry for her as she sat back, slumped and defeated in her chair. She looked all in. I watched as she nervously twisted a beer mat in her hands, just managing myself to resist doing a little jig under the table. Eleanor and Daniel. Who would have thought?

'God, I didn't even think you liked each other,' I blurted out when the waiter had gone. 'In fact, when I rang him from London about Rufus coming to his school and mentioned your name, he was positively rude about you. Said your dogs were a menace!'

'I know,' she gave a twisted smile. 'We . . .

386

slightly planned that. I told him to be off hand about me. Didn't want you smelling a rat when you came down here. We have to be so careful.' She glanced about furtively as if someone might be listening, spies everywhere, lurking behind newspapers in raincoats.

'Has it been going on long?' I asked. It seemed as if she wanted to talk about it.

She nodded. 'Three years.'

'Three years!' That brought me up short. I was shocked. And quite impressed too. That was a pretty long extra-marital relationship to have managed to have kept from the rest of the world.

'But—what about the neighbours in his road? Surely they see you going in and out?' Well, they would now, I thought guiltily, now I'd spread it loud and clear throughout the village.

'Oh, that's not his house. It belongs to a friend of mine in London, Milly Tempest. She uses it at weekends but she's in Spain at the moment so she asked if I'd keep on eye on things, although she probably has no idea what I'm actually doing there.' She blushed. 'No, that was a rather daring first, for us, to be so close to home. We usually meet at the flat in London, but obviously, with the school to run, that's tricky for Daniel. Sometimes we go to his house but it's all a bit risky, being close by, so it's really just snatched, occasional moments. Precious moments.' She looked up from her beer mat. 'I love him,' she said simply, and her eyes filled.

I nodded. 'Yes. I can see that.'

We were silent a moment as the waiter arrived with our drinks. I wondered about the mechanics of it all; how it had started. How she and Daniel,

387

people with very different lives, let's face it, had come across one another. He wasn't exactly in her social milieu . . .

'I met him when he first took over the primary school,' she said when the waiter had departed, reading my thoughts. 'I wanted Theo to go there, thought he'd thrive in a cosy village school. I also thought it would integrate us into the community a bit more, make it a bit less Us and Them. Piers wouldn't hear of it, of course. He wanted Theo to go to Shelgrove like the others, but I went to see it, anyway. Daniel showed me round. After I'd spent an hour or so with him, strolling round the playground, peering into fish tanks, I went home and found I couldn't stop thinking about him. He had such soft kind eyes . . .'

I nodded. Yes, I remembered feeling much the same. Those eyes were a killer. I blushed as I remembered the flowers. Hoped he hadn't mentioned it to her.

'Anyway, I made some pathetic excuse about wanting to go back for a second look and he showed me round again, but . . . looking back, I think we both knew it was strange to be wanting to see the science block again, fondling Bunsen burners for the second time . . .' She smiled. 'Anyway, he walked me back to my car, and by some lucky chance one of the tyres was flat. He changed it for me and I passed him the tools in the sunshine and we chatted, and by then, it was well into the lunch hour and he suggested a sandwich in the pub. I'm afraid I leaped at it.' She looked sideways out of the window. 'I felt . . . very isolated, at the time.' She glanced back at me. 'Marriage can be like that, you know.'

388

I nodded, remembering that I'd thought that too. But not now. Oh God, no, not now.

'He is . . . very different to Piers,' I ventured.

She smiled sadly. 'Yes. And I know what you're thinking. How can I have fallen for two such different people? How come I was ever with Piers in the first place?' She dredged up a sigh that seemed to come right from the soles of her expensive loafers.

'Where shall I begin, with Piers? By citing mitigating circumstances, and saying I'd just broken up with a serious boyfriend when I met him? That I was feeling raw and unloved and very definitely on the rebound? That I bumped into someone I thought was strong and protective but turned out to be dull and arrogant? Or shall I tell you that when he drove me out from London in his convertible Aston Martin and we cruised up the long drive to Stockley I fell for his beautiful house, the rolling acres, the whole lady of the manor bit?'

She met my eye. 'Partly true. I don't believe Jane Austen's heroines are so very different to us, actually. And if I'm honest, I think it was a little of both. Added to which, all my friends were getting married, I was twenty-eight years old, and suddenly, had gone from being quite a catch—a girl lots of men would like to be seen with—to being horribly available. Suddenly, all those men were with younger girls.' She took a slug of her drink. 'I met and married Piers within three months.'

I nodded, eyes narrowed. 'And was one of those men Alex?'

She sighed. 'Yes, Alex had been a boyfriend. He asked me to marry him once, actually, but I said no.' She shrugged. 'Anyway, he married Tilly.'

I caught my breath. Right. I hadn't known that. That he'd asked her to marry him.

'So . . . when did you realise you'd made a mistake?'

'With Piers? Oh, very early on. But I was too proud to admit it. Too proud to do anything about it.' She struggled with the truth. 'There's nothing terribly wrong with Piers, Imogen. He's just . . . a bit dull, that's all.' She made a despairing gesture with her hands. 'Naïvely, I thought children would help—who doesn't in an unhappy marriage? So I had four. Safety in numbers, I thought.' She smiled ruefully. 'After Theo was born I realised there was no point having five. It wasn't diluting my husband.' She looked up. 'That's when I had an affair with Alex.'

I nodded, wondering when she'd get to that. 'Tilly's husband,' I said firmly.

'Yes.' She sighed. 'And I'm not proud of it. Not proud at all. And I know it doesn't redeem me to tell you that he was unhappy too, and that we just sort of fell into it, two old friends with problems who got together in his lunch hour to chat, in bars, in restaurants . . . which led to hotels . . .' She trailed off. 'It was pain relief for me, and,' she puckered her brow, in an effort to remember, 'sort of an exorcism for him, I think. Getting me out of his system. The one who'd turned him down. But the moment he knew of your feelings for him, it dwindled between the two of us. You were too much for me. Far too much competition.'

I caught my breath at this. And I'd always thought that of her. That she was too much. My mind scuttled back to the days when I'd sat behind a desk outside his office in the City and she, Eleanor, had swept in to take him out to lunch, in jewels, scent, cashmere; older than me, but terribly glamorous, and I'd felt like orphan Annie. Had she been thinking, I can't compete with her youth, her freshness?

'He was captivated by you,' she said softly. 'Talked about you all the time—Imogen this, Imogen that—real mentionitis. But I think he never believed he stood a chance.'

'But he was in love with you,' I said firmly. I wasn't having that, entirely. I remembered Alex's distress when she refused to leave Piers. He'd even cried in the office. I'd comforted him.

She nodded. 'He was, but more so, I think, because he couldn't have me. I'd finished with him before we were both married, remember, so there was a bit of pride involved. And when I decided to make a go of it with Piers, he fell so head over heels in love with you that . . . well. I'd never seen him like that. Ever. And I've seen Alex with many girls.'

She eyed me sharply. Yes. No doubt she had.

'That was no rebound, Imo. He adored you. Still does. You *must* know that. I can't believe you don't know that!'

She looked at me incredulously and I saw that her eyes were both honest and astonished. How awful. I hadn't always known it.

'I . . . suppose I have, sometimes, doubted it,' I twisted a napkin in my lap. 'Often felt insecure . . .'

'You mustn't!' She insisted, leaning forwards across the table. 'It's only ever been you, Imo, for years now, believe me, and I would know,' she said with feeling.

391

Yes. Yes, she would. I screwed the paper napkin on my lap into a ball. My heart began to pound. I felt as though it were swelling, might burst even, with joy and relief.

'I . . . don't really know why I've doubted him,' I whispered, almost not daring to speak I felt so happy. 'He—he has these moods, though, you see, Eleanor, these real ups and downs. One minute he's a proper family man, loving towards me, adorable with Rufus, and the next—well the next he's distant, irritable, late coming home, and I thought—'

'It's his job,' she said, putting her hand over mine. 'Don't you know that? Don't you know he's terrified of losing his job, of being a failure?'

'But I wouldn't think he was a failure—'

'*He* would, though. And he'd feel it for you too. Stress does funny things to men, Imo, in the bedroom, at home, it's all about being the alpha male, and he was *such* a big shot in the City, and now . . . well, now there are younger, brighter men coming up behind him and he feels threatened.'

I looked at her directly. 'Does he tell you this?' I felt a pang of jealousy. A familiar twinge.

'Yes, because he's too proud to tell you, and also because . . .' she struggled. Looked away.

'What?'

'Well, he says you say it doesn't matter.'

'It doesn't!' I cried. 'I couldn't care less if he lost his job, couldn't care if he was a bloody dustman!'

'It matters to him,' she said fiercely. 'Maybe you should talk to him about it,' she urged, 'not just say, "Who cares?" Say, "I care." Maybe he'd like that.'

I flushed as it dawned. I sat back. Rocked back,

392

in fact, in my chair. I hadn't been a very good wife. Hadn't listened to him, hadn't sympathised, hadn't let him talk about it. I'd forced him to bottle it up because I'd thought he was bottling something else up and I'd been afraid of uncorking that, of spilling the beans, the Eleanor beans. And all the time . . . his *job* was the beans.

'I've been so stupid,' I whispered. 'So blind.'

She stretched across and squeezed my hand. 'No, you've just been barking up the wrong tree. It happens. He loves you very much, Imo. Take it from an old mate who knows. His world would fall apart without you.'

I looked at her across the little wooden table, and, for the first time, saw her for what she really was. A good friend; an old friend who, by dint of longevity, was bound to be privy to more information about Alex than I was. But not privy to the beat of his heart, which was mine, all mine. And that was all that mattered. I felt as if a film were sliding off me; a murky slick of grime that had clung to me for years, but which now I was shedding like dead skin, as I emerged from it, all gleaming and shiny and new. I reached for my wine glass and took a gulp. I'd make it up to him, I determined. I'd be a better wife. A good wife, not a jealous, resentful suspicious wife, but an understanding supportive one. And—and maybe I'd encourage him to do something else, if work was making him so miserable? I gazed out of the window, at the traffic flashing by. Maybe we could—I don't know—salmon farm in Scotland or something, I thought wildly. Farm sheep in Wales. But whatever it was, we'd talk about it. We'd sit down with a bottle of wine between us and talk, something I'd been so afraid to do in case something else came out. Yes, maybe he could retrain? Teach, perhaps, like Daniel. Daniel.

I glanced back across the table. Eleanor had drifted away and was gazing out of the window too: away from Alex and me and our relatively minor problems, and back to her own misery.

'I've made it so much worse for you,' I said suddenly. 'Shouting in the street like that. In a village this size it'll get around in minutes.'

I went hot with horror. Why hadn't I gone the whole hog? Painted 'Slut' or 'Harlot' on the front door, demand that she be tarred and feathered, dipped in the village pond?

'Let it,' she said quietly, gripping the stem of her glass. 'Let it get around. It's what I want now. And I'd already decided that, Imogen. Decided I was going to tell Piers. I just didn't want anyone to tell him first.'

'Really?' I was startled.

'Really.' She gave a funny, sad smile. 'One of the reasons I wanted you and Alex to come here, Imo, to take the cottage in the first place, was because in my heart I knew I was going to tell him and I wanted friends around. Wanted moral support, somewhere to run to. I was scared. Oh, I have friends round here of course, masses of them, but they're all Piers's, really. They've known him since he was born. They're not *my* mates. Can you understand that?'

'Yes. Yes, I can.'

'And I count you and Alex as two of my best.'

I bent my head and nodded shamefully, realising how stupid I'd been, how I'd maligned her. She'd always tried so hard, and I'd always been so

394

suspicious, questioned her motives, thought the worst. Yet . . . there had been moments when my scepticism hadn't been based on mere suspicion; moments when I'd been convinced . . .

'The other day, when I saw you two together in the drawing room,' I said suddenly, 'and you sprang apart when I came in. I'm sure you did, I'm sure I saw you in his arms, in the mirror.'

'I was telling him,' she nodded, 'about Daniel. And he hugged me, was comforting me, and then I saw you get up from the terrace and come towards us and I leaped for the phone. I thought you might get the wrong idea, I just hoped you wouldn't think it was odd to be ordering silk flowers on a Sunday. And then later, when I pretended to show him the spare room upstairs, I was telling him the rest of it, because you'd interrupted us. I just wanted to tell *some*one,' she said desperately, 'so that someone other than me or Daniel knew. I wanted to make it more real, but I was so afraid of being overheard by Piers. And then Hannah had her baby and distracted everyone, and—'

'And I thought I was going mad,' I cut in. 'Thought I was imagining the two of you together because I was so paranoid, thought my mind was playing tricks on me.'

'I asked Alex not to tell you immediately. I knew he would eventually—he said he would—but just not yet. And not because I don't trust you or anything,' she said quickly, 'but because I didn't think it was fair on Piers if everyone knew before him. But I had to tell someone. I was going crazy with it.'

'But why now? Why are you telling Piers now, after three years of keeping it a secret?'

395

I saw the fear in her eyes as she looked up. And suddenly I knew.

'Because I'm pregnant,' she breathed.

## CHAPTER TWENTY-FOUR

'Oh Lord.'

She nodded. 'Exactly. Oh Lord.'

We sat in silence for a moment as the ramifications sank in. I gazed at her.

'That's . . . actually what I was telling Alex,' she said. 'When he was holding me.'

'Right,' I whispered. 'And . . . I suppose I don't have to ask if—'

'Yes. I'm keeping it.' She held my eye. 'I don't blame any young girl who's never had a baby for having an abortion, but when you've had four like I have, the idea of getting rid of it is—'

'No, I know,' I said quickly, looking down at my hands. Unthinkable. I wouldn't be able to do it either. Not now I'd had Rufus. But for the baby's brothers and sisters . . . oh God. There was real terror in her eyes as I looked up.

'I know,' she said, going pale, 'the others.'

I licked my lips. For them it would be *so* ghastly. And much as I hadn't always warmed to Piers, my heart went out to him too.

'So you'll leave him? Piers?'

'Yes, I'll leave him. Hopefully he'll give me a quick divorce and I'll move in with Daniel. The children are all at boarding school now anyway, apart from Theo, and he goes off in September.'

Ah. So that was all right then. I swallowed.

396

She shrugged miserably. 'And I suppose we'll just share their holidays. A week with Mummy and a week with Daddy. After all, other couples manage it, don't they? I mean, look at Alex.'

Yes, look at Alex. Who hadn't seen his daughters for six months, who invited them in the school holidays, but found, increasingly, that boyfriends and parties took precedence, and that even though their mother, Tilly, came to London quite regularly to see family—was over here at the moment, in fact—the girls stayed at home. Was he sad about that? About the fact that they seemed to call him slightly less these days? Unbelievably, I didn't know, because—oh God, my chest tightened with guilt—I didn't ask him. Didn't go there, because in my paranoiac state I'd been afraid that if it *didn't* upset him too much, then my goodness, it could be me and Rufus next, couldn't it? After all, he'd left one wife and family, why not another? So I hadn't brought it up: hadn't been supportive, said, how d'you feel, my love? Do you miss them, the girls? Oh, there was *so* much I had to make up for, I thought, ashamed. I glanced at Eleanor. Yes, she was right, divorced couples did juggle their children, but she must know it wasn't ideal. Must know too that Piers may be dull, but that that was all he was. To Poppy, Sam, Natasha and Theo, he was Daddy. Beloved Daddy. He wasn't a cheat, like Mummy, an adulterer, and neither was he having a child with someone else. Eleanor was in for a very bumpy ride, particularly from her teenagers. I wondered if they'd ever forgive her. It seemed to me she was gaining one child and in danger of losing four others.

'I know,' she said quickly, reading my mind, 'it's

going to be unutterably bloody, and I can't tell you the number of times I've lain awake at night thinking about it, knowing a time bomb is growing inside me. And yet, if anyone said to me, what if you miscarried tomorrow?—d'you know, Imo, I'd be devastated. Just devastated. I want this baby so badly. I've never wanted something so badly in my life. I got pregnant with the others to cement my marriage, but this baby was conceived through love and I'm having it.' There was something desperate yet fierce about her eyes and I knew she meant it.

'How many months are you?'

'Three. So please God I'm over the dodgy stage and it sticks. And if it doesn't, I'll still leave Piers. This has made up my mind. I can't live a lie any more. Not even for the children.'

That was quite a decision to come to as a mother, and she knew it. We fell silent for a moment, lost in thought.

'You'll have to tell them soon,' I said breaking the silence. 'I mean, that you're leaving. Or else you'll start to show.'

She gave a twisted smile. 'Except that they'll still do the maths when it appears, won't they? Think—right, so six months ago when she said she was leaving Daddy because he didn't understand her, and that marriages weren't always made in heaven, in fact she was three months pregnant with another man's child and it was all a load of crap. No. There are no hiding places here, Imo. I've got to tell them the truth. And actually,' she looked at me squarely, 'you'd be surprised how much straight talking children can take. They're very resilient, you know.'

Were they now? I caught my breath at her

pragmatism. It seemed to me she had the weight of the world on her shoulders and didn't seem to feel it. She was about to shatter so many lives, just as, I realised with a jolt, she'd once shattered Tilly and the girls'. Only this time it was her own family, her own children who'd end up in pieces. I wondered if it could be right to cause so much pain just to achieve personal fulfilment. Did we really have such a divine right to be happy? Did it rank above duty and compassion and loyalty? I wasn't convinced. I wondered too if she ever *would* truly be happy. If her 'in-loveness' would last. Would Daniel—without the added frisson that an affair gave a relationship—eventually become dull and stupid like Piers? And would the headmaster's semi that she would undoubtedly have to swap Stockley Hall for, become, not an exciting love-nest, but a miserable, poky little place? Time would tell. In Eleanor's eyes, she'd made one simple mistake: she'd married the wrong man, and now she was rectifying it. But an awful lot of people were going to have to be sacrificed on the altar of Eleanor's happiness.

'Will you stay around here?' I asked, swimming to the surface of my reverie. 'I mean, presumably with Daniel's school being up the road . . .'

'We'll have to, yes, to begin with. But Daniel's already applying for a post elsewhere. The head of a primary's coming up in Shropshire. He's going to go for that.'

Strangely, I felt something like relief at this: to know that they'd be moving away, and yet . . . she was my friend, wasn't she? But a friend, I thought uncomfortably, who'd never sought me out in London, never come to tea with me and Rufus, only my husband, for lunch in the City. And a friend who'd wanted me to come down here because she'd needed my moral support, had wanted somewhere to run to. I wondered if I'd ever trust her entirely, her and her relentless quest for happiness. Where might she look to find it next?

'And anyway, I'll have to say something to the family soon, otherwise Piers's mother will do it for me,' Eleanor said darkly.

'She knows?' I said sharply, coming back to her.

'Suspects. I'm pretty sure she has no idea who it is, but she cornered me a few weeks ago, upstairs in my bedroom. Said she had a shrewd idea I was up to something and she didn't trust me.'

I gazed at her. 'Oh! Was that when we first arrived?' I said, suddenly remembering when we'd come to Stockley a day early, and Eleanor had run down the stairs into Alex's arms, crying.

'Yes, she was absolutely foul. As only she can be. And now she's suddenly decided she needs the flat in London too.'

Yes, she had, hadn't she? She was protecting her son. Fighting for his interests. As, I'm sure I would protect Rufus's. Go to any lengths. Was that so wrong?

I shifted in my seat; a regrouping gesture. Not uncomfortable, exactly, but—

'I'll get the bill,' said Eleanor, quickly, noticing. She raised her hand and Molly appeared from behind the bar in her long apron.

'Oh!' I looked up in surprise. 'I thought you weren't here this afternoon. I looked for you when I came in.'

'I was upstairs sorting out my flat. I've got the

400

decorators in so it's pretty chaotic, but at least the kitchen's ready now. You must come and see it some time, come and have supper one night.'

'I'd love to,' I glowed. The true hand of friendship. 'Oh, d'you know Eleanor Latimer? This is Molly, the owner.'

Eleanor smiled. 'I've seen you around but I don't think we've met.'

'We haven't, but nice to meet you.' Molly smiled and took away the ten-pound note Eleanor had put on the saucer.

Eleanor leaned across the table. 'I've seen her around, because she's one of Pat Flaherty's visitors,' she hissed.

'Really?' My heart, inexplicably, thudded at this.

'Constantly in and out of his cottage. I've often spotted her creeping in last thing at night and then leaving early in the morning.' She grinned.

'Oh. Right. Well, good luck to them.' I reached for my drink and drained it too quickly. Some missed my mouth. I wiped my wet chin as I stood up, gathering my coat hurriedly from the back of my chair. 'I must say, he seems to lead a complicated life,' I said lightly.

'Just a bit,' Eleanor rolled her eyes, as Molly came back with the change. 'Thanks.'

So. Pat and Molly were an item. Right. I shoved my arms into my coat sleeves. Well, why not? She was a very pretty girl. I shot her a quick smile as she went to the door and held it open for us. Tall and slim, and with that shining bob of hair and creamy complexion, she knocked Pink Jeans into a cocked hat. I wondered if they knew about each other. Or did he run them in tandem? How did it work, exactly? For some reason, I was disappointed. In her, I think.

'I've got someone else interested in your pictures incidentally,' she was saying as we went out under her arm. 'A family came in for lunch earlier and liked the one of the church. They're local, so I reckon I can work on them!'

'Great!' I grinned, but my heart wasn't in it. It was elsewhere. Why, I wondered? Why did my balloon feel so pricked, when it had recently been so buoyant?

Confused, I drove Eleanor back to her car. We travelled the short distance in silence. When we'd bumped down the stony track and drawn up outside the cottages, she got out. I turned to look at her as she was about to slam the door.

'Goodbye, Eleanor.' Even as I said it, I felt it had a note of finality to it.

She smiled but her eyes were already somewhere else, darting up to the bedroom window. Daniel was up there, by the curtains, waiting.

'Bye,' she said distractedly, before shutting the door and nipping away. No, correction, before *strid*ing away, up the path, golden-brown curls blowing in the breeze, head held high, not caring now who saw her.

I drove thoughtfully to Sheila's and picked up Rufus, who bounced out of the trailer with round eyes and vertical hair; full of E numbers and artificial colouring, no doubt. I thanked Sheila who was busy hosing down the Alsatian and drove away with him pinging off the seat beside me.

'Can we go and see the baby now? You said we could, and I'm the only one who hasn't seen him!'

'Oh Rufus . . .' I raked a hand through my hair,

'I think we might do that another day. I'm shattered, actually.' I was. Although I felt about two stone lighter for knowing that Alex wasn't part of the Latimer family drama, I still felt emotionally drained by all that I'd heard just now and my head was aching. What I really wanted was to lay it on a crisp white pillow in a darkened room, preferably in the Swiss Alps, prior to sipping beef tea on the veranda. I certainly wanted to be alone.

'Oh come on, we practically go past their house!'

'Yes, but I don't know if Hannah's back from hospital yet,' I lied.

'She is! I heard you talking to Eddie on the mobile earlier!'

I sighed and swung the car into their road. Sharp lad, this. Too sharp for me. But actually, maybe this was a good idea, I thought as we drew up and saw Eddie, pushing a brand-new pram around the front garden. Maybe a dash of old-fashioned family values was just what I needed right now, after Eleanor's sledge-hammering of them so very recently.

'Well, how lovely!' Eddie hailed us, leaving the pram and coming to meet us as we picked our way across the wet grass and soggy remains of daffodils, through low shafts of evening sunshine. He scooped Rufus up and swung him round in an arc in the air. Rufus squealed with delight.

'Just practising,' Eddie wheezed as he set him down, 'for when the babe's a bit bigger. Older father, you know, got to keep young. Ooh, me back.' He hobbled off to the pram, rubbing the base of his spine. 'Shouldn't have done that.'

'Still "the babe" then, is it? No name yet?' I followed and peered in the pram.

'Tobias,' said Eddie, straightening up proudly. 'Means gift of God. Tobias Martin Sidebottom, after his grandfather.'

'Oh! Dad will love that.'

'He does,' Eddie assured me. 'Ask him. He's round the back putting the finishing touches to his work of art. Have you seen it yet?'

'No, but I've heard about it, Hannah told me on the phone.' Dad was a bit of a whiz at carpentry and was apparently making a cradle for the baby.

'Can we wake him up?' asked Rufus, peering at the little orange face in the pram.

Eddie looked shocked. 'Good Lord, no. It's taken me twenty minutes to get him off!'

'Maybe he'll wake up later,' I said, seeing Rufus's disappointed face. 'And if he doesn't, we'll come again tomorrow, but Rufus, it'll be a while before he's playing conkers with you.' I could see that Rufus had envisaged something a little more entertaining than this blob of pond life.

'At least he's a boy,' he said at length. 'At least he'll want to do the same things as me.'

'Course he will!' agreed Eddie. 'Golly, before you know it the pair of you will be running round the garden kicking a football together!'

'Really?' Rufus brightened, Pond Life already morphing, in his suggestible mind, into a little tyke in Man U strip.

'Yes, well, let him get out of nappies first,' I advised. 'Is Hannah around?'

'In the house. Tell you what, Rufus. You can push, and we'll take him to the corner shop for an ice cream. It'll still be open if we hurry.'

'Cool! How fast can I push?'

'Fast as you like, as long as you don't actually

404

catapult him out of it. Hannah's inside, by the way,' he directed this at me as he shadowed Rufus, who was already off with the pram, anxiously across the grass, out of the gate and on up the road.

I watched as they went, shading my eyes with my hand into the evening sun. For all his big talk, Rufus was actually pushing very carefully, taking this new responsibility very seriously, handling his cousin with care. His cousin. Lovely. Another member of the family, making Rufus not such an only, cherished child. And if only there were more. If only I could *have* more. For a moment I felt a pang of jealousy for Eleanor. Why wasn't I like that, pregnant at the drop of a pair of trousers?

I sighed and went in to find Hannah. She was on the top of a stepladder, cleaning the windows.

'Should you be doing that?' I asked in alarm.

She looked down. 'Why not?'

'Well, you've just had a baby and—good God, look at this place! You've had a tidy up, and—blimey, the flowers!'

I gazed round in wonder. The piles of dusty books, bundles of newspapers, chairs with broken legs stacked in a pagoda awaiting mending had all gone, and instead, space prevailed: glorious, glorious space, with freshly hoovered blue carpet, gleaming skirting boards revealed for the first time in years, and all around the room, vases and vases of flowers.

She came down her ladder, looking slightly sheepish.

'I know, aren't they lovely?'

'Who are they from?'

'Oh, all sorts. Locals in the village, teachers, kids at school.' She fingered some delicate wild flowers

405

in a bowl.

'Oh, how sweet—sweet of everyone! You see?' I rounded on her accusingly.

'I know,' she agreed ruefully. 'Everyone's been so kind. And of course I had to have a tidy-up. I can't have a baby in all this clutter and dust, and anyway, most of the so-called projects I had on the go were never going to be finished.'

I eyed her beadily. Ah, so she knew that too, did she?

'Yes, all right,' she muttered, folding her arms. 'Too much talk and not enough action, and too much running round being bossy. Too many committees. I'm staying on at Sea Scouts, but I've resigned from the Brownies.'

'*Have* you?' Hannah had battled her way furiously to the top of that particular little empire. 'Who's going to be Brown Owl, then?'

'Tawny Owl, no doubt. She's frightfully ambitious, been snapping at my heels for years. Or pecking at them, should I say.' She grinned.

'Well, quite,' I blinked, stunned that she'd made a pecking order joke. The rest of the family had for years, but secretly of course, never in front of her. Quite a lot of giggling about ruffled feathers. 'But you're still going to teach?'

'Oh, yes, but part time,' she said happily, balling her J cloth and aiming it at the bucket. 'The school's agreed to me doing four mornings a week, and I get all my maternity leave too, since I obviously didn't take any while I was pregnant!' She grinned and I marvelled at how well she looked. Shiny hair, rosy cheeks and *slimm*er. Well, obviously slimmer, since Tobias had come out, but still, she was in better shape than I'd expected. She saw me looking her up and down.

'Breast-feeding,' she said proudly. 'Tobias sucks for England, and after every feed I reckon I lose a couple of pounds. I promise you, it's the best diet ever.'

'But you're eating?' I said, concerned. 'You've got to eat properly, to feed.'

She laughed. 'You sound like Eddie. Yes, I'm eating, but instead of a couple of rounds of sandwiches and a whole chocolate cake, it's one round of sandwiches and a piece of chocolate cake. I don't need all that food any more.'

'Because you're happy.'

Tears filled her eyes. 'Because I'm happy. You're right, I was misery eating before. Pretending everything was fine, but feeling hollow inside. I know it's unfashionable to admit it, Imo, but all I ever wanted was to get married and have children. To have the roses round the door, the baking, the babies. I never wanted to be a success.'

'Who says that's not a success?' I said softly. 'And now you are. Now you've got it.'

'Now I've got it!' she echoed, and a big beam spread across her face as she opened her arms to me.

I walked into them, my eyes like saucers. Hannah and I never hugged, *never*. Tears sprang to my eyes too. For her, for her hard-won, unexpected happiness, but, I suspect, for myself also. For my peace at last, my own family's sanity and security, free from the tyranny of Eleanor. Never again would my heart flip with fear when she rang and asked to speak to Alex; never again would I hold my breath when he mentioned he'd had lunch with her. I wished I could tell Hannah, but I'd promised to stay silent until Eleanor had broken it to Piers, and I would.

'You look well too,' she commented, linking my arm—*linking my arm!*—as she led me towards the back door and the garden.

'I am well,' I agreed, trying not to wonder who'd unlink first. As it happened it was me. My hands shot to my mouth in surprise as I stepped out on to the back steps. 'Oh golly—look at this!'

'I know,' Hannah agreed, leaning against the door frame, folding her arms. 'Didn't know your father was a master craftsman, did you? He was up all night making that.'

Dad, looking tired but unbowed, straightened up from his carpentry in the middle of the lawn, and stood back to admire his handiwork. I blinked.

'That's amazing.'

I drifted down the steps and across the lawn. An immaculate wooden cradle, complete with curved wooden hood and a pair of rocking feet, stood proudly on the grass.

'Dad, I can't *believe* you made that. It's fantastic!'

'Well, the bottom's a bit of a cheat—it's an old drawer—but the hood I'm pleased with.'

'I'm not surprised!'

'Isn't it great?' yelled Hannah, before turning and going back to her windows.

Dad beamed. 'Only the best for the Marmalade Bishop.'

'The what?' I frowned.

'Tobias. Haven't you noticed his hair?' he said gleefully. 'Definite touch of ginger, and that profile: noble yet pious. Made for the ministry.'

I giggled. 'If you say so.'

'And hopefully it's built to last.' He patted the hood. 'Can accommodate any number of grandchildren that might come along.' He winked at me, and although my tummy twisted, I smiled gamely.

'Well, you never know.'

It occurred to me that Dad was looking very unlike his usual self today. Instead of the lurid shirts and tight jeans, he had on a pair of ancient beige trousers and a blue sweater. Even the white Gucci shoes had been replaced by comfortable old deck shoes covered in glue and putty, and his hair was a bit mussed, not slicked back as usual. He looked like a regular grandpa, putting the finishing touches to his grandson's cradle. I smelled a rat.

'Dawn gone to Newcastle, yet?' I asked lightly.

'Yes, luv. Went Monday.'

'I thought you said she was in the car, outside the hospital?'

He grinned. 'Poetic licence. Didn't want you all thinking I'd been deserted, did I?' He crouched down to avoid my eye, packing away his tools in a tin box. 'And she's staying put. We've called it a day, as you probably know.'

'I didn't actually, not for sure, but . . . well. There was talk you might not go the distance, as it were.'

He glanced up. 'It's not just the travelling, luv. She's too young for me. Needs someone her own age.'

I gaped. Too young? For my dad? He straightened up and whipped off his jumper, chucking it on the grass. Then he dropped his trousers. I didn't flinch, since my father had been taking his clothes off at a moment's notice for as long as I could remember, claiming that as an actor he was used to people wandering in and out of his dressing room and seeing him in the buff—although privately I thought it had more to do with the fact that he was keen to show off his small but perfectly formed physique, his muscular chest and toned stomach. But I did wonder why he was doing it here, now, on Hannah's lawn. He reached into a rucksack on the grass and buttoned himself into a crisp, pinstripe shirt; then he pulled on a pair of mustard cords and some brown leather loafers, looking for all the world like a country squire.

'Where the hell are you going?' I asked in wonder.

He looked at me with round, innocent eyes as he shrugged on a tweed jacket, shooting out his shirt cuffs complete with gold crested cufflinks.

'Out to dinner with Helena Parker. Why?'

'Helena Parker? Helena Parker! Why?'

Helena was one of Mum and Dad's oldest friends; a lovely, elegant lady, widowed tragically early and now in her late fifties.

'I met up with her at that dinner party Tessa Stanley gave at The Hurlingham a while back. Tessa was all over me,' he grinned, 'tried to snog me in the rose bushes, a real gay divorcee on the prowl, but Helena's much more my type. She's a lovely woman.'

Yes. She was.

'Does Mum know?' I asked anxiously, following him up the garden path and back through the house as he searched in his natty little leather pouch for his car keys. He shrugged. Frowned back at me.

'No idea, why?'

410

'Well, I . . . just wondered.'

'I don't see what it's got to do with your mother,' he said as we went down the hall. 'And anyway, she likes Helena. It's Tessa she can't bear.'

'Yes. No, you're right.' I chewed my thumbnail.

'I thought I'd take her to that new Marco Polo restaurant in Chelsea. It's got a garden, apparently. Had fantastic reviews in the paper. Blimey,' he glanced at his watch, 'better get a wiggle on.'

'Marco Pierre. Yes. Yes, it has.' Cost an arm and a leg too. I swallowed. 'Helena Parker's not your usual type, Dad. Isn't she a bit—you know—old for you?'

'Oh, but have you seen her recently?' He turned in the narrow hallway, eyes wide. 'She looks about thirty-five! Fan*tastic*ally toned body, gorgeous long legs, honey-coloured hair and she's got terrific bone structure too. Honestly, she knocks a lot of young girls for six. And anyway, fifty's the new thirty, didn't you know?' He flashed me a grin.

'But what about discoing, clubbing, all that sort of thing?' I went on doggedly. 'You'd miss all that, wouldn't you? You love that!'

'Oh, so does Helena. We thought we might go to Raffles afterwards. She's a member. How do I look?' He turned to me at the front door and stood to attention, beaming.

'Terrific.' I swallowed.

'Wish me luck?' He looked a bit anxious, for Dad. A nervous man on a first date. I smiled.

'And good luck.'

'Bye, darling!' he called to Hannah, who was back up her ladder in the front room.

'Bye, Dad, and thanks!' she shouted back.

As he went down the front path, Rufus and

411

Eddie were coming back up it.

'Bye, Bishop!' he sang, giving them a jaunty wave as he strutted past, shoulders back, to his BMW at the kerb.

Rufus and Eddie laughed. 'Got a date, Grandpa?' Rufus called.

'That's it, laddie. Onwards and upwards. Onwards and upwards!'

I turned and walked thoughtfully back inside, still chewing my thumbnail. Stopped at the foot of Hannah's ladder.

'Helena Parker!'

'I know, isn't it lovely?' She paused in her wiping to glance down. 'They've always got on so well. Remember when they used to go out as a foursome, when Geoffrey was alive? Oh, I think it would be marvellous. He's terribly keen, you know. Says she's got the best legs in London, which she probably has. And so intelligent too. Imagine, Dad acting his age for a change, with a suitable girlfriend. Wouldn't it be great?'

'Great,' I agreed shortly.

As she resumed her scrubbing, I gazed out of the window, past Rufus and Eddie, who were manoeuvring the pram back under the tree, watching, as Dad's shiny blue convertible purred expensively off down the road in the evening sun, en route to London.

## CHAPTER TWENTY-FIVE

Later that evening, when Rufus had gone to bed, I rang Alex. His mobile was off, so I tried the office.

412

'North American Desk?'

'Alex?'

'Oh, hi, darling.' He sounded tired. 'How's tricks?'

'Alex, it's half-past nine. You're not still working, are you?'

' 'Fraid so,' he yawned. 'But nearly finished. Christ, is it half-past nine? I had no idea.'

'Darling, pack up and go home. You'll be exhausted.'

'Yeah, I'm about to, actually. Just putting the finishing touches to this wretched pitch for the Cable and Wireless account that Baxter has been bellyaching about. It's not bad actually, d'you want to hear my closing para?'

'Go on then.'

He cleared his throat and put on a pompous voice. 'And that, ladies and gentlemen, in conclusion, is why the corporate finance team at Weinberg and Parsons is so uniquely placed, with Charles Baxter at the helm, to lead Cable and Wireless's fortunes further into the twenty-first century. Infinity and beyond.'

He gave a snort of laughter. 'Baxter will love that. Massages his ego and plays to his hubris too. Wanker.'

I laughed, and felt a sudden rush of love for him; working away late into the night for his family, for me and Rufus, but I felt indignation, too. Why *should* he be kowtowing to Charles Baxter, a man ten years younger and infinitely less experienced than he? Alex had been brokering deals when Baxter was still puking into loos at teenage parties, still picking his spots. As I heard him turn off his computer and scrape back his

413

chair, I resolved once again that I'd persuade him to chuck it in; tell Baxter and his ego to take a running jump. We'd sell up in London and use the money to start our own business, a joint venture— not salmon farming perhaps; that had been a bit far-fetched—but, well, ordinary farming maybe, I thought wildly, looking out of the window at the cows. Golly, there was nothing to it, was there? I knew that now. A few bales of hay and a bit of chicken feed—yes, it was a doddle. And anything to get Alex out of this loop of misery. I felt a fierce wave of protectiveness towards him, something I'd never felt before, always believing him to be so strong, so inviolable, which, I realised with a jolt, was what he'd wanted. He hadn't wanted me to see this soft, vulnerable underbelly, but actually, he was all the more lovable for it.

'How's the flat?' I asked.

'Well, sumptuous, as you might imagine. Kate doesn't skimp on the décor, even for a nanny flat. I should think it all came from designer showrooms in Chelsea. Have you not seen it?'

'No, because Sandra was always there. Maybe I'll come up.'

'Do! Leave Rufus with Hannah and come up for the night. We could see a play or something, have dinner.'

I glowed with pleasure. 'I will. And maybe Kate and Sebastian could come with us?'

'They could, but it's you I want to see. I don't see you all week, don't want to share you. Anyway, as you know, Kate and Sebastian's social whirl dictates that nothing can go into the diary without three weeks' notice. I tried to ask them out for supper this week, to thank them for the flat, and

414

Kate said, "This week? Oh, no, Alex, we can't do anything until the end of the month!"'

I laughed. 'I shall have words with her. Tell her she's turning into a real card-carrying member of the glitterati. So what will you do for supper tonight, my darling?'

'Oh, I don't know, pick up a curry in Putney High Street and eat it in front of Sky footy, I expect.'

I smiled. 'Bachelor life has its compensations.'

'Not many,' he said gloomily. 'Sleep well, my love.'

'And you.'

I put down the phone in a glow of warmth and happiness. Clutching the tops of my arms I went to the window, threw back my head and gazed out at the clear night sky with its sprinkling of stars. Oh, the relief. The *relief* to be natural and light-hearted with him, without a shadow lurking over us. Without Her between us. Think of the time I'd wasted! The time I'd spent *not* feeling light and carefree like this!

I drew the curtains and pulled my dressing gown around me as I went up to bed. It would have been nice if he'd asked after Rufus, I thought ruefully as I climbed the stairs; nice if he'd asked how his day had been, but hey, that was being picky, I told myself hurriedly. He was so busy, and anyway, all that would come, in time, when my plans for our new life had been instigated. He'd have more time for Rufus then, be more of a father to him. I poked my head around my sleeping son's bedroom door and smiled. And anyway, it wasn't as if Rufus was missing his daddy. Wasn't asking when he'd be back, how long he'd be in London, but all that

415

would come too, I reasoned, going across the landing to my room, come the start of the Cameron family's new life together. Come the revolution. I got into bed with a smile and turned out the light.

At three twenty, I was awakened by Rufus shaking me vigorously.

'Mum. Mum! Wake up!'

'Hmm? Wha'?' I peered at him blearily.

'Mum, the cows are out! The cows are out of the field!'

I frowned. 'Don't have any cows,' I mumbled. I turned over and went back to sleep.

'MUM!' He shook my shoulders violently. 'Come on, get up!'

He threw back my duvet, and in that instant, stark naked and curled up in the foetal position, I came to. My eyes widened at the wall and I sat bolt upright.

Shit! The cows were out!

I ran to the window. Down below, Marge was casually snacking on a few tea roses in the front garden, whilst Princess Consuela was busy tap-dancing on the lawn.

'Christ! How the hell did they get out?'

'I think I might have left the gate open,' Rufus cowered. 'I gave them some grass cuttings 'cos Tanya said they liked them, and I must have forgotten to tie up the gate!'

'Jesus wept! Well, come on, we've got to get them back in again!'

Seizing my dressing gown, I flew downstairs, shoving my arms into the sleeves as I went.

'Wellies on,' I panted, scrabbling around and finding mine by the front door.

'What—in my jim-jams?'

'Yes, in your flaming birthday suit, if need be. Now come on!'

We flew outside, me waving my arms and shouting like a banshee, whereupon Marge and Consuela, alarmed by a mad woman in a Chinese silk dressing gown complete with dragon motif, lolloped out of the garden, past their open gate, and on down the track.

'You frightened them, Mummy!' yelled Rufus. 'You need to be calm, and controlled, that's what Tanya says!'

I'd give him calm and controlled. I'd give him Tanya too. 'Get behind them!' I screeched. 'Run round the back and we'll drive them back in a pincer movement!'

'But hadn't we better shut the gate? Otherwise the others will get out?'

'Then how are we going to get this pair in?' I screamed.

'I could stand guard at the gate and open it at the last minute! When you've got them lined up to come through!'

Good plan, good plan. Wish I'd thought of it myself, although what I really wished I'd thought of was being the gate opener, I decided as I hustled off to get behind them. I wasn't too keen on being the herder. I was reasonably au fait with cows now, but only from the pretty end. Wasn't sure about Going Round The Back. One hand clutching my dressing gown, since it had lost its cord, I nervously nipped around the beasts. Marge and Consuela eyed me with interest as Rufus ran to shut the gate—just in time, before Homer and Bart came ambling out. He shooed them away, and they

417

shuffled off into the darkness. Good boy, good *boy*. Got his father's brains.

'Right. Ready?' he yelled, standing by at the gate.

'Ready!'

'Then drive them towards me!'

Easier said than done, actually. As I ran behind Marge's large brown bottom, she flicked her tail and ambled forwards amiably enough, but then the other one slipped away in the opposite direction. As I ran to chivvy that one, the first one slipped off too. For all their bovine bulk, these beasts were like bleeding quicksilver.

Finally, though, with much swearing and cursing, I'd got them lined up sufficiently to yell, 'Right—open it, Rufus! Open it now!'

He did, and Marge went straight in. Rufus whooped with delight and went to shut the gate but, flushed with success, I yelled, 'No, keep it open! I can get the other one in too!'

'No, Mum. Wait till you've lined her up properly.'

'Keep it open!' I shrieked. 'I've got her!'

Unfortunately, I hadn't quite, and when Rufus opened the gate, she darted in the other direction. Instinctively we both lunged after her, and as we did, Marge and Bart slipped past Rufus and began galloping joyously after Consuela, who was lolloping down the hill, even giving little bucks occasionally, thrilled to be out in the open country, the moonlight on her back, her disciples behind her.

Rufus and I watched in dismay.

'After them!' I hollered, careering down the chalk track.

418

'No! Take the car!' called Rufus.

I stopped. Good plan. Good plan.

I came tearing back, ran inside for the car keys, then back to the car. Rufus was already in the front seat.

'If we get the other side of them, we can use the headlights to drive them back in the right direction,' he explained. 'I've seen it in films.'

I nodded, mute with admiration, but also, fear. Oh, thumping great fear because—what would Piers say? His prize herd, his exotics, disappearing into the next county, injuring themselves perhaps, on barbed wire, keeling over in ditches, dying even—what would he say? He'd say get out, that's what.

'Maybe we should ring Piers?' said Rufus, bouncing up and down on the seat beside me as we bumped down the track. 'Ask him to help?'

'No!' I yelped. 'No, we can manage this together, Rufus, just you and me. Here they are!' Three broad bottoms with whisking tails trotted plumply ahead of us in the headlights. 'Right, I'll drive up on this verge, get round the other—oh shit, SHIT!'

'They think you're racing them!' squealed Rufus.

They surely did. As I drew up alongside them, they put their heads down and charged, Consuela rolling her eyes and shooting me a flirtatious, catch-me-if-you-can look, thrilling to the chase.

'Slow down, Mummy, slow down. They're heading for the road!'

I hit the brakes as the cattle stampeded on. They'd clearly decided this had become a big night out and were heading for the bright lights—as bright as they got around here, anyway—the beckoning twinkle of the A41. Oh God, I thought in terror, now someone would *die*! And it wouldn't just be a cow, it would be a human being, driving along—a nurse perhaps, returning from a night shift, a very nice, innocent person anyway, not a drunk returning from a pub crawl—and SMACK! into the cows she'd go, swerving off the road, into a ditch, dead in seconds.

'This isn't working!' I yelled. 'The car's frightening them. We'll leave it here and get out!'

As we stopped, the cows, placid, inquisitive creatures by nature, stopped too and turned to look at us, sides heaving. Then they promptly put their heads down and grazed, greedy for the uncharacteristically lush pasture. We crept up on them, Rufus and I, like Red Indians, and there then ensued much scampering about in the fields, much waving of our arms and cajoling, but we were outnumbered.

'It's no good, Mummy, we need someone else! Every time I get Consuela, Bart goes running off again!'

In the moonlight Rufus was scarlet behind his freckles, and I could tell from his voice he was close to tears.

'Pat's house is just there.' He pointed to the brick and flint lodge, the proximity of which hadn't escaped me. 'Why don't I go and get him?'

Holding my sides and panting hard, I hesitated. The last, the very *last* person I wanted to involve, aside from Piers, of course, was that man. But actually, things were getting out of control here, and if I wasn't careful I'd have an accident on my hands. I swallowed my pride, which was about the

420

size of a baked potato, and nodded.

'Wait here,' I muttered. 'I'll go.'

I ran across the fields and down the lane beside the little stone wall, clutching my dressing gown to me as I threw open his front gate. We'd move, obviously, after this. Yes, move house. Somewhere far flung, somewhere remote, where no one knew us. Yorkshire perhaps. Yorkshire had farms. No, no farms. No cows. Liverpool, then. No cows in Liverpool. I rang the bell. He didn't answer. Well, of course he didn't; it was nearly three in the morning. Shutting my eyes for courage, I rang again, leaning on it this time. Scotland, I decided. Right up in the Highlands. Back to the salmon farming.

Eventually there was a shuffling sound down the passage: a light went on in the decorative fanlight above the door, and then it opened. Molly peered at me, clutching her own dressing gown and looking dazed.

'Oh, I'm so sorry,' I breathed, taken aback. 'It's me, Imogen.'

'Imogen,' she mumbled, rubbing her eyes.

'Um, Molly, our cows have escaped and I just wondered—is Pat in? Only I'm rather hopeless and I've only got Rufus.' It all came babbling out in a rush. 'You see the thing is, they're almost on the road now and I'm so worried there'll be an accident!'

My voice sounded as small and cracked as Rufus's.

'Oh Lord,' she said sleepily. She turned. 'Pat . . . oh.'

A pair of tanned legs in boxer shorts and a bare bronzed torso emerged down the hallway behind her. Instinctively, I glanced away.

'I'm so sorry,' I gasped, keeping my eyes firmly on the architrave around the door, 'but our cows have escaped, and I just wondered . . . only there's only me and Rufus—'

'Hang on.'

As I glanced back, he'd turned and legged it back down the hallway. He reappeared seconds later, thrusting his legs into jeans as he hopped along, a fishing jumper over his head.

'I'd offer to help,' mumbled Molly sleepily, 'but I'm afraid I'm terrified of cows.'

'Such a townie,' said Pat affectionately, ruffling her hair. 'How many are there?' This to me, not so affectionately.

'Oh. Three.'

'Fine. With Rufus we can handle that. Go back to bed, Moll.'

Needing no further prompting she turned, gave us a weary backward wave, and floated back inside.

Pat grabbed a handful of walking sticks from the umbrella stand in the hall and a torch from the table and we hurried off down the path. I couldn't resist turning at the gate and looking back at the house. I saw her, by the light of the bedroom window, shrug the dressing gown off and slip naked back into bed, before turning the bedside light out. I gulped and snuck a glance at him. Blimey. Quite a coolie, wasn't he? Bedding one beautiful woman after another like that? And here I was dragging him away from it all.

'I'm really sorry,' I mumbled, flaming face trained to the ground as we hurried along in the darkness. Thank God for the darkness. 'I didn't know what else to do, and Piers will freak.'

'He will,' he agreed grimly. 'Where are they?'

'Just down the track, over by the water meadow. Luckily the river runs between them and the road and they were grazing quite happily beside it. I told Rufus to stay with them, not to try and move them but—oh!'

As we rounded the bend, I swung about in horror. The track was empty; no Rufus, no cows, just black fields laced with dry-stone walls.

'RUFUS!' I screamed, terrified now. 'WHERE ARE YOU?'

'I'm here!' an equally terrified voice screamed back out of the night. 'I couldn't stop them, Mum!'

I swung round the other way, and as Pat shone his torch, we saw Rufus, in his red checked pyjamas, pointing desperately as the three shaggy Longhorns ambled into the distance. They'd crossed the stream and were heading for the road, for the ribbon of halogen glowing in the night, for the action of the A41.

'Oh Christ, that's exactly what we don't want!' said Pat, already running in the general direction. 'Come on, we'll have to cross the stream and head them back.'

He was fast and sure-footed, much, much more sure-footed than I, and it was dark, damn it, and the terrain was rough, and he had the torch. As he leaped the stream at its narrowest point, Rufus following, I tried nimbly to follow suit—and slipped and fell.

'All right?' he called back over his shoulder, still running, I noticed.

I wasn't at all—my ankle was killing me—but I struggled, soaked to my knees, and scrambled up the bank on all fours. As I got to my feet I was almost annoyed to find my leg was not broken.

'Yes!' I bleated, completely sodden, both boots full of water, plastered with mud and pond weed.

'Right.' He paused a moment, swinging round to give us orders. 'Now we need to take a cow each and get behind it, got it?' His dark eyes flashed in the moonlight as Rufus and I stood panting before him like the poor bloody infantry. 'And then, with outstretched arms, like this—' he demonstrated a crucifix position—'and with a stick in each hand, like so—' he showed us, then handed us some sticks—'we drive them forwards. *Calm*ly, OK? But if they cut up rough, don't be afraid to whack them on the backside. Rufus, you take the brown and white one, and, Imogen, that one's yours. I'll take this stroppy little madam.'

For a moment I thought he was looking at me, then realised he meant Consuela. Expertly wielding two sticks, like a Kung Fu fighter, he began to turn her around, and head her back across the stream, towards home. Rufus got the idea and Bart followed suit, but Marge, clearly a good-time girl, was still intent on partying, and shot off in the opposite direction. Multiple pile-ups swam before my eyes.

'Run around her!' yelled Pat, still shepherding his cow, 'and spread your arms out like this!' I knew exactly what he was demonstrating, but pretended I hadn't heard because obviously I couldn't do that. I had to clutch my dressing gown because it had no cord and I was completely naked underneath. I waved a stick feebly with one hand and ran after Marge, but every time I got behind her and tried to drive her forward, she dodged and doubled back on herself.

'STICK IN EACH HAND!' Pat hollered. 'ARMS OUT!'

'Yes I KNOW!' I screamed back, still clutching my Chinese silk to me. Marge ducked round me again, grinning almost, it seemed, tongue hanging out, and galloped joyously towards the road. Headlights came towards us.

'IMOGEN!' roared Pat, furious.

Fuck. Oh fuckity-*fuck*!

Sticks held aloft, I charged after her, zoomed around her rear end, turned her expertly, and with my dressing gown streaming out behind me, came running back towards Pat and Rufus, arms high. A good look, I felt; naked but for sticks and Wellingtons.

'Happy?' I screeched, as the cow obediently trundled towards them.

Pat's eyes were on stalks. 'Very,' I think I heard him say, but I expect I was mistaken.

As Marge fell into line with the others, the cows crossed the stream in unison and we followed. They were going at a fair old lick, though, and we struggled to keep up, but at least they were going the right way. I'd managed to clutch my dignity back again too, much to my son's relief.

'Mummy! You're naked!' he hissed as he came up beside me.

'Well spotted, darling,' I panted, gasping for breath.

To my relief, I saw that the cows were stampeding up the track to our cottage now, and if Pat sprinted ahead . . . I struggled up the hill, almost on my knees now, exhausted beyond belief, holding my side, watching as Pat put on a spurt to overtake them—and to swing open the gate. Rufus ran on gamely in his red pyjamas, but he was going to struggle to get all three in on his own so . . . I gritted my teeth, and with one last superhuman effort and a mighty roar, 'GOO ON!' I urged, running up beside him and whacking Marge's backside.

She shot in, followed by the others, and the gate swung shut, with a decisive click, on Bart's bottom. The three of us clung to the top bar, panting hard. I thought I was going to pass out, actually. Either that or vomit.

'All right?' gasped Pat at length, quite breathless himself, I was pleased to see.

'Yes!' I wheezed. 'Rufus?'

Rufus had collapsed, spread-eagled on his back on the grass. 'Bloody knackered!'

'Rufus!'

We gave ourselves a moment, there in the moonlight, panting, wheezing, and coughing, to recover.

Then, 'Come on.' Pat reached down and pulled Rufus to his feet with both hands. 'Let's get you to bed, cowboy.'

'Yes, bed, Rufus,' I agreed, putting a hand on each of his shoulders and propelling him weakly towards the cottage. We staggered up the path, the two of us, and through the front door; Rufus, completely spent, and on automatic now, heading up the stairs. As I followed him, it occurred to me to wonder if I should make him wash his hands, which were black, before he got into bed, or just wash the sheets in the morning. Just wash the sheets, I thought as he crawled in under the covers, exhausted.

'Sorry, Mum,' I heard him mutter as I went to

426

shut his door. 'I mean, for letting them out.'

I turned and gave a weak smile in the doorway. 'These things happen, darling. All part of country life.'

When I got back downstairs, Pat was in the sitting room, slumped in an armchair, legs splayed out in front of him.

'Oh—sorry,' he muttered, hauling himself wearily to his feet. 'Collapsed for a moment, there. I'll be on my way.'

'No, no, don't. It's my fault for getting you up in the middle of the night. D'you want a cup of tea or something? Or even something stronger?'

'Now you're talking,' he grinned, flopping back again. 'Mind if I help myself to a brandy?' He nodded to the sideboard where the bottles were arrayed.

'Do, I'm just going to take off my—well, to change.'

I flushed and disappeared again, flying up to my room. God, I must look a complete fright, and if we were having a drink, I must change. A glance in the mirror confirmed my fears. Mud and slime covered my face, my dressing gown was ripped at the shoulder, and my legs were filthy and grazed. I tore the wretched garment off with a shudder and dropped it in the waste-paper bin—never liked it—then quickly washed my face and pulled on jeans and a jumper. I'd got as far as the landing before I ran back to rake a comb through my hair. Well, I looked *such* a mess, I reasoned. As I went past Rufus's door, I peeked in. Fast asleep again, good.

Pat was crouched down by the hearth when I got downstairs and I realised he'd lit the fire.

'Oh!'

'Well, it's so bloody cold I felt I had to,' he said, straightening up and handing me a brandy. 'And I thought you could do with some warmth after that dip in the river.'

'Thanks.'

I realised I was shivering, despite having changed. I kneeled down by the fire, which hadn't really got going yet, trying to absorb its heat.

'I don't usually drink this,' I said, wrinkling my nose into the glass. I sipped it cautiously. 'But actually, it's quite nice.'

He crouched beside me. 'Ah, well, brandy tastes different under different circumstances. It's mercurial stuff. I can't be doing with it after dinner, but after a shock, it's always very welcome.'

I heard the lilt in his voice as he said this. His face flickered in the firelight.

'It was a bit of a shock,' I admitted. 'I don't often wake up with a jolt and run a steeplechase at three in the morning. Not sure I'm fit enough.'

He grinned into the flames. 'You looked pretty fit to me.'

I blushed, aware he was referring to my streak through the water meadow and was grateful he wasn't looking me in the eye. 'Yes, well. Thanks to you, it didn't end in disaster.' I took another sip of my drink. 'I don't know how I can begin to thank you.'

'Then don't. Anyway, I'm used to getting up at all hours. It's an occupational hazard. In fact I thought it was Jack Hawkins, about his bull again.' He eased down on his haunches to sit on the rug.

'Yes, I suppose broken nights are nothing new to you. Not so funny for Molly, though,' I said, deliberately mentioning her to see what he said.

428

He grinned. 'She'll live.'

Right. Not much.

'Still,' I went on, 'you could have told me to sod off and gone back to bed.'

'I could,' he agreed.

'I mean,' I went on doggedly, surprised I was pursuing this, 'I haven't exactly been a model client, have I, dragging you out to look at dead chicks and not even being able to feed my own cows?'

He smiled. 'I'm not sure I've ever thought of you as a client, Imogen.'

There was a silence as we both digested this.

'And anyway,' he went on, 'we all have to start somewhere. You're new to the country. I dare say I'd be crap at commuting to the City, probably end up in Croydon or somewhere.'

I smiled. Somehow I couldn't see him in a pinstripe suit behind a *Telegraph*, trundling off on the misery line to Liverpool Street. I looked at him, leaning back on his elbows by the fire, legs stretched out in front of him now, crossed at the ankle, his tall, broad frame encased in jeans and an old navy fishing jumper; at ease, happy in his own skin in that relaxed Irish way.

'Have you always lived in the country?'

'No, I lived in Dublin when I was at university, and then for a couple of years in Belfast when I was at veterinary college. I'm not entirely a country bumpkin. My family are from West Cork though, and that's where my heart is.'

My own heart, inexplicably, stalled at this.

'Is that where you'll go back to, then? Eventually?'

He shrugged. 'Who knows? When is

429

"eventually"?'

He stared into the flames. I wanted to say, is that where your wife and child are? But didn't dare.

'At the moment, I'm happy being elsewhere,' he said quietly.

Elsewhere. It sounded as if he was running from something. Ties, perhaps. Responsibilities.

I licked my lips. 'My mother always says you can change your skies but you can't change your soul.' I looked at him defiantly.

He smiled. 'Sounds like a very wise woman, your mother.'

'She is,' I agreed.

A silence fell between us.

'And anyway, it's people that make a place,' I went on boldly.

'You're so right. And I think . . . because of that, this place is becoming more than just Elsewhere.'

Ah, I thought. Molly.

'Anyway,' he shifted round on to one elbow, putting his back to the fire to face me, 'enough of me. What about you? What brings you down here to the sticks away from the glamour of London?'

I smiled wryly. 'We couldn't afford to live there any more. Couldn't afford the glamour. Had to downsize, change our lifestyle. So money, I suppose. The root of all evil.'

'Not always. The human condition accounts for quite a bit too.'

I wondered what he meant by that, but something about the set of his jaw and a flinty look in his eye dissuaded me from asking. He sipped his drink then glanced up at me.

'And is that where *your* heart is, then? London?'

'Well, up to now, I suppose. I'm a born-and-bred townie, and I never thought I'd take to country life, but actually, I'll be sad to leave this place.'

As I said it, I realised it was true. What, go back to London? To Hastoe Avenue? Back to the house I loved, opposite Kate? Surely that would be bliss? But . . . we weren't going to London, were we. We were going to Scotland, salmon farming, or—or Yorkshire. Liverpool, even. Yes, that was it. Anyway, we were definitely on the move. I swallowed. So, I wouldn't be setting up my easel in the buttercup meadow any more, or walking with Rufus to the stream to watch the ducks after school . . . but presumably there were ducks everywhere . . .

'What are you thinking?' He was watching me.

I smiled ruefully. 'That I've let this place get to me. And I said I never would.'

'Ah, well, places have a habit of doing that. They creep up on you. Steal into your heart when you're not looking. People too. Just when you don't want them to.'

He looked into the fire as he said this, leaning back on his elbows, but it seemed to me he looked straight into my soul. I hardly dared breathe. I watched the flames lick around the logs, knowing it was imperative not to take my eyes away from them. From those embers. And suddenly, I knew too I wanted to bottle this moment for ever. Wanted to freeze-frame this snapshot of the two of us: Pat, stretched out with fluid grace on the rug, me beside him on the hearth, my legs tucked under me, brandy glasses by our sides, the firelight flickering on our faces. As the implications of this thought trickled through to my consciousness, it

431

simultaneously horrified me. I began to scramble to my feet, but as I did, he laid a hand on my arm.

'Where are you going?'

'Well, I just . . .'

'Come here.'

And with those words, he rolled over and took me in his arms. His weight wasn't heavy against me, just warm and solid, not pinning or constricting: and his lips, when they touched mine, weren't hard or forceful; they were gentle, tender. I could easily have pulled away. But I didn't. I surrendered entirely to his embrace, and as his fingers swept through my hair, cradling my head in his hands, I arched my back into him; felt a flood of uncomplicated passion surge through me, then lost all sense of myself in the utter abandonment of the moment.

## CHAPTER TWENTY-SIX

Seconds later, I was on my feet, my hands clutching my mouth. I stared down at him, appalled.

'I can't believe I did that!' I gasped.

He propped himself up on one elbow and regarded me. 'Joint effort, surely?'

'What must you think of me!'

'Would you like me to tell you?'

'No!'

I dropped the hands, aghast, and began to wring them instead, pacing the room in an agitated fashion.

'You must go,' I breathed, stopping at the

window and spinning round to face him. 'Go on, quick!'

It seemed to me I needed a duster to shake at him, to shoo him away like a dirty fly.

'I'm going, I'm going.' He got to his feet in one fluid movement, grinning and still looking absurdly handsome.

'You must think I'm appalling!'

'You said you didn't want me to tell you what I thought of you.'

'No, no, you're right. Quite right.' I gaped into his amused eyes.

'I—I don't do this sort of thing,' I flustered, hastening him down the passage way to the door.

'Of course you don't.'

'I mean, God, if Rufus had come down—'

'He didn't.'

'No, but if he had!'

He turned and I boggled into his twinkling eyes, inches from mine in the narrow hallway 'What were we *think*ing of?' I breathed.

'Well, I know what I was thinking of.'

'Yes, but I'm *married*!'

'You are. But you're lonely.' The eyes that held me now were steady, less amused. I stared into them.

'Don't be ridiculous,' I spluttered.

'I'm not being ridiculous. It happens. Good night, Imogen.' He reached up and ran a finger lightly down my cheek. 'Take care.'

And then he went, letting himself out of the front door, sauntering down the path and into the night, or the dawn, actually: a tall, broad figure in a navy fishing jumper, hands in his pockets, moving with casual grace down the zigzag track,

433

silhouetted against the cold pale light that filtered over the distant hills. When he got to the end of the track, he turned to look back at me. Oh God—now he thought I was *watch*ing him!

I slammed the door shut and spun round with my back against it, wondering, for a gaudy moment, if perhaps he were coming back. For more? I held my breath. But when it became clear he wasn't, I crept through the hall and across to the sitting-room window. I twitched the curtain and peered out. Yes. Yes he'd gone. I clutched the neck of my jumper and stole across to the fire, like a criminal. What had come over me? What on earth had possessed me to behave like that, like—like a *teen*ager, down there on the rug? I gazed at it in horror. It seemed to zoom towards me, magnified, like a shot in a horror movie. One brandy? No, surely not. Surely I couldn't blame that.

On an impulse, I hastened to the downstairs loo, switched on the light and stared in the mirror. My eyes were overbright, my hair was mussed and I had—oh God—I had *snog* rash round my mouth! *Just* like a teenager. I touched it tentatively. But also . . . well, also I looked younger too, I decided, moving closer to the glass, fascinated, as if perhaps my reflection might reveal other clues to my new personality, my new-found wantonness. But the moment it threatened to, I snapped the light off. Turned and hurried from the room. On second thoughts, I didn't want to know.

I went upstairs, my arms wrapped around myself, holding tightly. It was hardly worth going to bed now, I reasoned, but maybe I'd just crawl in under the duvet in my clothes, just for an hour or so. I wouldn't sleep, not after all that drama, but I could just lie down. Yes, that was it. Too much excitement; that's what my mother would have said when I was younger. Running round after cows in the middle of the night—golly, it was bound to lead to trouble. Bound to end in tears.

I awoke to find bright sunlight streaming through the thin cotton curtains. Rufus was shaking my shoulder.

'Mummy—Mummy, wake up!'

'Hmm?' I peered at him through bleary, half-shut eyes. 'Wha's wrong?'

'We've overslept. It's ten o'clock!'

'Bugger.'

I sat bolt upright and grabbed the clock. He was right, it was.

'Oh God, we're going to be so late, Rufus!' I threw back the covers, happily already fully dressed.

'Much too late,' he said decisively. 'No point going in now, Mum. Why don't I have the day off?'

I paused, midway through scrabbling for my trainers under the bed, midway through shoving my still grubby feet into them, and looked up into his wide, innocent brown eyes. Then I flopped back on to the bed.

'Good idea. Why not? God, we've been up half the night cattle rustling. I think we deserve it.'

A big grin broke over Rufus's face and I could tell this was no impulse plan. He'd been dreaming it up over his cocoa-puffs downstairs in the kitchen for the last ten minutes.

'But this is a one-off, Rufus,' I warned, sitting up again. 'We won't be making a habit of missing school just because the cows get out, OK?'

'OK,' he agreed, sitting with a bounce beside me

on the bed. 'It was fun, though, wasn't it? Seems really weird now, to think we were running round the countryside in our pyjamas. Like a dream.'

Wish it had been a dream, I thought darkly as I got to my feet, snatching up a towel from the floor and heading off for a shower; particularly the latter part of the evening, the steamier end; but actually, Rufus was right: in the bright morning light, the whole episode had taken on a faintly surreal quality. Perhaps Pat would see it in the same light, I thought nervously as I padded round the bathroom finding my shampoo, conditioner. Perhaps he too could imagine it had never happened?

It was a glorious, bright spring morning, tiny clouds scudding around after each other in a sailor-blue sky, and as Rufus skipped outside to feed the chickens, revelling in his unexpected day of freedom, I resolved to set to in the house. Yes, I'd give it a jolly good going-over, I decided, getting out the Hoover and roaring around, enjoying the noise as it blocked out thought. I found a feather duster and got up on chairs, flicking efficiently at pictures. Really—you know—get it gleaming, really lose myself in it.

An hour or so later, I took my head out of the oven and sat back on my haunches, Brillo Pad limp in my hand, shoulders sagging. This wasn't working. Wasn't working at all. I wasn't in the least bit lost. Not remotely. I sighed. It was no good, no amount of elbow grease and sparkling chrome was going to exorcise the memory of . . . you know. I bit my lip. Well, of course it wouldn't. When had housework ever, ever solved anything? Painting— that was it, I thought feverishly, throwing down my

Mr Muscle. Why wasn't I painting? Well, because Rufus was around, that's why, and I wasn't sure I could immerse myself in it properly with him badgering me for a biscuit every ten minutes, but, on the other hand, I'd managed it in London sometimes, when the evenings had been really bad, so why not here?

When the evenings had been bad. That brought me up short as I went to get my easel. Yes, painting had been a balm, a salve there, but I'd been happier here. *We'd* been happier, Alex and I. My chest tightened. Why was I trying to ruin everything, then, by grappling with the local stud? The man who exercised women the same way some men do polo ponies, who had a string of them, and clearly regarded me as a challenge, a bit of married totty to be added to that string—*flaming cheek*!

Face burning and hands fluttering, I fell on my oils in the cupboard under the stairs and hustled them outside. I hastened to the buttercup meadow. Here. No, here. No, actually, over *here*, in the lie of the hill, in the sunshine. Too hot—back into the shade. Under the trees. I set my easel up quickly, trying not to notice my hands were still quivering. This would do the trick. And Rufus was happy in the hay barn. I could see him out of the corner of my eye, whittling sticks with a horribly dangerous-looking knife. Now. That barley field over there, with the old hay wagon in the distance and those scampering clouds above—perfect.

Somehow, though, I couldn't get started. Couldn't capture it. My brushstrokes were tense and agitated, and nothing flowed. It felt all . . . wrong. All disjointed. After a couple of hours, I stood back in dismay. All I was doing here was wrecking a canvas, I decided grimly as I unscrewed it from the easel. Pouring good money down the drain.

I went inside for something to eat. Yes, food. That's what I needed. Hadn't even had breakfast. Rufus appeared to have made himself a sandwich, judging by the cheese and pickle left out on the side and the uneven fly-walk on the loaf of bread. God, he'd be in care soon. A nine-year-old boy, playing truant from school, getting his own meals, experimenting with knives. Social Services would have something to say about that. I picked up the loaf and the knife. But I wasn't hungry. Wasn't hungry at all, I realised in horror as I put them down. Now that was a first. Well, not entirely a first. I'd gone off my food once before, when I'd first met Alex; but that was because I was in . . . oh Lord.

Hands trembling, I reached for the coffee jar. Caffeine. Yes, caffeine would help, and actually, I glanced at the phone—a chat. With Kate. My heart leaped. Yes, *that* was who I needed to talk to, to spill the Pat Flaherty beans to. She'd be horrified, of course, appalled, but then, being intrinsically on my side, would laugh it off too. Tell me that these things happen, particularly in the middle of the night on a glass of brandy, and not to get it out of proportion, to move on, de-dah-de-dah.

I took the phone in the sitting room and rang her number, but her answer machine was on. Damn. Knowing Kate, it could be days before she picked up a message, and likewise it was hopeless ringing her mobile, which only sat in her car in case of a breakdown. I glanced at my diary. Thursday. Where was she likely to be on a . . . oh God. I went cold. The play! There it was, in my diary, in red, on the evening of Thursday 25th—*As You Like It*—underlined in red too. I went hot. From cold to hot in moments. Lordy. I'd completely forgotten. What sort of a friend was I? But then again, that date had been put in my diary months ago, I reasoned wildly, while I was still in London: she wouldn't expect me to come all the way from here for it, would she? I got up and paced across to the window. And there was Rufus to think of . . .

I rang Alex. My voice was unnaturally high when he answered. I hadn't envisaged speaking to him quite so soon after . . . I gulped, my eyes darting across the room to the rug.

'Um, darling, you couldn't possibly scoot along to Kate's play tonight, could you? I completely forgot, it's a charity thing, at that Little Britain theatre in Kensington, near the Albert Hall.'

He groaned and I heard him push his chair back. 'Imo, I would, but I've got the ghastly Cronin brothers over from the States today. I've got to entertain them this evening. I dare say I shall be ploughing through Yorkshire pudding at Simpson's yet again, indulging in some good old-fashioned English nosh. They'll explode soon, the pair of them.'

'Oh God, poor you. No, well, don't worry, I'll leave Kate a message. She'll understand. Are you very busy, my darling?'

'Sadly, yes, and I've just been told I've got to head back to New York next month to clinch this wretched Cable and Wireless deal. Charles Baxter's just arrived to crunch some numbers, actually.' His voice suddenly became more formal.

'Ah. Right oh.'

I took it as my cue to say goodbye and put the phone down.

I walked slowly back to the window, arms folded, and gazed out. Well . . . OK, hang on. I narrowed my eyes at the sheep sprinkled decoratively on the hillside. Why was it so impossible for me to go? There was always Hannah. I mean, sure, she'd just had a baby, but Rufus was no trouble: could even be a help, fetching and carrying nappies and things . . . Yes, why didn't I go to Kate's play myself? We could maybe have supper together afterwards—or a drink, if she had to eat with the cast—and then I could whiz back here. I felt my shoulders unknot. Suddenly, I felt better. I had a plan. I *always* felt better with a plan. Yes, I thought, my heart quickening, I'd talk it over with Kate, and she'd say, Don't worry, these things happen, heavens, Imo, we've *all* behaved disgracefully in our time— although actually, I thought cringing, I couldn't imagine Kate *ever* doing that, or saying that, but no matter. I'd come back feeling it was just a silly nonsense to be passed over and quickly forgotten.

I rang Hannah, who said she couldn't be more pleased to have Rufus helping with bath time. I quickly got changed, chivvied him out of the barn and into the car—persuading him to leave the knife behind—and then dropped him off on the way. I watched as he ran up the path, hardly giving me a backward glance; thrilled to bits to be with his new cousin, to be an invaluable helping hand.

I roared off down the lanes. Yes, this was a *good* plan, I decided, straightening my back and smiling as I joined the slip road that led to the M40. I zoomed up the hill to meet it, checking my lipstick in the rear-view mirror. A night out in London was just what I needed, to remind myself that there was a world out there; a world beyond my bucolic little village, my rural idyll, beyond snogging a local vet. *Snogging a vet!* I gripped the wheel as I almost swerved under the wheels of a passing juggernaut. Oh God. I bit my lip, feeling very sticky-mouthed. There was no doubt I needed to get out more.

There was surprisingly little traffic on the roads, and I reached London in record time. I should do this more often, I thought, as I swung confidently around the Hammersmith roundabout and headed off towards Kensington; after all, Alex did it regularly, so did Eleanor, and even Mum popped up and down at a moment's notice. It was sheer laziness that made me not bother.

It was only six thirty, early still, and the play didn't start for an hour, so on an impulse, I parked on a meter behind Kensington High Street, and then, dodging and weaving through the crowds, nipped into Jigsaw. I'd dressed in something of a hurry this afternoon in my rush to leave that cottage, and felt a bit dowdy in my boring navy-blue jacket now that I was up here. Adopting the serious shopper position—head down amongst the rails, tail up and sniffing—I got to work, and emerged, forty minutes later, proudly sporting a new sparkly pink cardigan, a pretty shell necklace, and a long velvet scarf, my old clothes in a Jigsaw carrier bag swinging jauntily from my arm. There. Marvellous. I strode off confidently towards Kensington Gardens. Now all I needed was a side-splitting play to lose myself in and I'd forget all about the little hearthrug incident. In fact, I'd almost forgotten it already.

I walked off towards the park, ducking down into a side street under the gaze of the Albert Hall, and joined the queue for tickets outside the theatre. Quite a glitzy throng had gathered, I noticed. I glanced around. They were well-heeled, these young things, because this was very much an upper-middle production. It wasn't your usual am-dram, produced on a shoestring with rehearsals in some chilly town hall. No, it was well funded and professionally produced. These thespians were City bankers and lawyers by day—or high-maintenance wives like Kate—folk with no money problems, but who dreamed of treading the boards, and, once a year, thanks to knowing the right people—a director here, a producer met at house party there—got to live their dream and act on a real stage before a proper audience, most of whom, of course, were friends and family. I recognised a few people in the queue: Amanda Quentin-Smith, who was quite a party girl, Tamara Hogg, and a couple of exotic friends of Kate's. On balance, I was glad I'd ditched the navy jacket.

We trooped in amongst much laughter and chatter, and took our seats, but because I'd bought a ticket on the night, I was badly placed: right at the back, behind a pillar. Damn. I'd need my glasses for this. I rooted around in my bag, but clearly hadn't brought them. Double damn. Although actually, I decided, closing my bag and looking around, the theatricals going on off-stage were entertaining enough. Confident, fruity voices rang out: 'Bumble! Bumble over here!' 'Oh God, we're in the wrong *row*. Oh, Ludo, you're *such* a prat!' Jewellery rattled and pashminas swept and I sat, like a country mouse, drooling and lapping it all up. Lovely.

When the curtain went up with a flourish, I realised I'd been so preoccupied with my people-watching, I'd failed to buy a programme. Stupid. And I couldn't for the life of me remember who Kate was playing. Was she Rosalind? The main part? Or that other girl, the sister, in the green dress? I couldn't really see from here, but actually, it didn't take long to realise she was neither. Right, so she must be one of the more minor characters at the back, some sort of spear carrier. Trouble was, they all had wigs and gowns on and were tittering coyly behind fans, and I was blowed if I could work out which one she was. I leaned across to a pinstriped type beside me.

'Excuse me, could I possibly borrow your programme?'

I was met with the pale blue, uncomprehending stare of the seriously overbred and stupid. I watched as slowly, the penny visibly dropped, the eyes cleared, and eventually a programme was duly passed, together with a toothy grin. Smiling my thanks, I scanned the cast list in the dark. Then I scanned it again. No Kate Barrington. Or even Katherine Barrington. I glanced up at the stage. She wasn't in it. I frowned. Perhaps I'd got it wrong? Perhaps she was helping backstage, or something.

I tried to follow it anyway and laugh at the right bits, but Shakespeare wasn't really my thing, particularly the supposedly comic kind, with very unfunny jokes about cross-dressing and lots of thigh slapping and 'lawks a mercy, my liege!' although the audience seemed to lap it up, roaring with laughter and haw-haw-*haw*ing away. Blue

Eyes beside me looked fit to bust his pinstripes. I was glad when it was the interval, and being at the back, was able to muscle my way pretty promptly to the bar—something I'd got down to a fine art after years of watching Dad's productions—where I ordered a gin and tonic.

'Hello, Imogen.'

I swung round in surprise. A tall, handsome young man with long, poetic chestnut hair curling over the collar of a blue velvet jacket was smiling at me. His dark eyes were shy, and I knew him, definitely knew him, but couldn't quite place him. Then, as he reddened under my gaze . . . it dawned.

'Oh, good grief, *Casper!*'

I reddened too, and he went an even deeper shade of claret as we collectively remembered our first meeting together, ostensibly as gallery owner and prospective artist discussing a forthcoming exhibition, but actually—if he'd had his way—as older woman and young blade about to embark on a marathon session of afternoon delight in a double bed in the Markham Hotel.

'What are you doing here?' I said stupidly, for something to say, because actually, why on earth shouldn't he be here?

'Well, watching the play, like you.' He laughed, embarrassed.

'Yes, of course!'

'Can I get you a—'

'No, no, I've ordered. But let me—'

'Absolutely not, my shout.' He caught the barman's eye, ordered a beer for himself and paid for my gin too, which gave me a moment to collect myself. Casper. Good heavens.

'I saw you when you came in, actually,' he admitted, passing me my drink, 'but didn't quite have the nerve to talk to you.'

'Whyever not?'

'Well, you know . . .' He made a face. 'But I wanted to,' he went on quickly, 'to apologise for my appalling behaviour that day, which I do, unreservedly. I seem to remember attempting to rape you, then weeping all over you. Not my finest hour.'

'These things happen,' I murmured into my drink. God, I'd forgotten how young he was; how sweet-looking, with his long wavy hair.

'But I also wanted to thank you,' he went on determinedly, obviously keen to spit it out. He looked at me earnestly under dark sweeping lashes. 'The advice you gave me that day was spot on. I did lie low, and I did play the long game, and in the end, it all blew over between Charlotte and Jesus.'

Charlotte and . . . for a moment I couldn't think what the devil a girl called Charlotte was doing with Our Lord, then . . . oh yes. His wife, and the personal trainer.

'She eventually got bored with him and saw him for the shallow slab of beefcake he was. Came back to me.'

'Oh, Casper, I'm *so* pleased.' I really was. I beamed delightedly at him.

'And you were so right to dissuade me from pursuing older women round hotel bedrooms,' he went on as I gawped into my gin—*old*er women— 'and chopping up Charlotte's clothes, which I was so close to doing. I even dragged them all out of the wardrobe, put them on the bed. I can't quite

445

believe it, now. Can't believe that was me.' He gazed into his beer.

I smiled. 'Love, or the removal of it, makes us do strange things, Casper. Turns us into people we don't recognise, or like. And the more it's withdrawn, the more we behave abominably. It seems impossible to stop.'

'I know. But I did stop, thank God. And thanks to you. It was as if you had an insight, as if you'd been there.'

I smiled. 'I thought I had. But I hadn't. I'd made a stupid mistake. Happily.' I rested one elbow on the bar. He seemed about to ask me what I meant, so I rushed on. 'So now you're back together? You and Charlotte? With the children?'

'Yes, all back together. In fact, I'm watching her tonight. She's in the play.'

'Oh, *is* she! Gosh, how brave. Well, that's why I'm here too, I thought Kate was in it, but I can't see her.'

'Oh, no, Kate left the show a while ago. It was all too much with the children and Sebastian's work and everything. He felt she was doing too much so she dropped out.'

'*Did* she? God, I didn't know.' I felt awful. God, I hadn't even *asked*.

'She has so much to juggle you see, but she's always got time for her friends. Charlotte and I went to dinner there the other night.'

He went a bit pink and I smiled into my gin. This was clearly a social triumph. I used to tease Kate about being a society hostess and collecting admirers; I'd forgotten Casper was one of them.

'Yes, she has got a lot of time for her mates,' I agreed. 'In fact, she got us together in the first place, didn't she?'

'She did. In fact, she was the one who suggested I go for a little bit more than just lunch with you.'

I blinked. 'Sorry?'

'Oh, no,' he said quickly, 'not—you know—like that. I handled it very badly. She didn't mean for me to jump on you in the restaurant or anything—that was all my stupid idea—she just . . .' he hesitated. 'Well, actually, she said she thought you might be lonely.'

I stared at him for a long moment. 'I'm married, Casper.'

'I know,' he said quickly. 'But,' he shrugged, 'well, so was I. And I cocked it up, of course. Should have just made a mate of you.'

'Or even just considered my paintings,' I said sharply. This conversation was getting a little too personal for me. 'I seem to recall that's why we met in the first place.'

He reddened. 'Yes, quite. Um, how is the painting going, by the way? Are you still sticking with it?'

'Yes. Yes I am,' I said vaguely, but I was miles away. Lonely. Two people, one of whom was my best friend, the other, a man, whose opinion for some obscure reason I valued, had both levelled that accusation against me within the last twenty-four hours. I began to feel hot. Prickly. The theatre was very warm, and the loud, self-confident voices less entertaining now. More oppressive. I needed some air.

Casper was still talking, enthusing about my work, which he assured me he had genuinely liked and admired, but I wasn't listening. I needed to go, to get out, and when the bell went for the second

447

half, I did. I said goodbye to Casper, parting amicably and pretending I was going back to my seat, but actually, slipping away down a corridor and some clattery back steps, and out of the side entrance on to the street. It was dark now, and the night air was sharp and cool on my cheeks; welcome. I took a few deep breaths. I was indifferent to the play, and if Kate wasn't in it, well, I wasn't going to sit there. Also, I had a sudden urge, a sudden burning desire, to see Alex. I walked quickly up the main road. I was cross. Cross with everyone making assumptions about my life, trying, quietly, to make things better for me. A quick bonk by the fire perhaps—or, or a young man estranged from his wife for me to befriend in a restaurant—there, that would do the trick; that would make it better. Poor Imogen, stuck with a busy, distracted husband, with just her small son and her painting for company, poor, *poor* Imogen. The blood rushed to my face as I walked quickly to my car. Did people really pity me? Think I had a sad, solitary life? We'd soon see about that.

I glanced at my watch. It was half-past nine now, and Alex would still be entertaining the Cronins at Simpson's, but I knew he liked to be in and out of that place, popping them smartly in a taxi and back to their hotel, and he'd be on to the pudding by now—coffee, even. We'd meet up, I decided, getting into the car and snapping my seat belt on. I pulled away from the kerb. Maybe we could go to that piano bar in Burlington Street, the one he'd read about in the *Standard* and told me about; said we must go, where they served cocktails till midnight? Yes, OK, it was a bit late for cocktails, but we could have a brandy, couldn't we? The car swerved violently in the road. No—not brandy. Cointreau, then, I decided. Yes, because now I was up here, in town, I still very much wanted my night out, but I wanted it with my husband.

I rang him, but his mobile was off. Annoyed, I left a message, then suddenly, on an impulse, found myself pointing the car towards the Strand. In the direction of Simpson's. Yes, why not? I could leave a message at reception. Or even get one of the waiters to take it in, hand it to him at his table on a silver tray, a billet-doux; very old-fashioned. I smiled to myself. 'Darling, I'm up in town—long story. Will meet you in half an hour at Romano's.' Yes, that was the name of the bar, I thought eagerly, Romano's.

I drew up and parked, rather punchily, right outside Simpson's, on a double yellow line. Then I got out, had a quick shufty round for the police, and leaving the hazard lights on, nipped up the wide stone steps and through the front door. I glanced briefly through the open door into the dining room full of identical-looking businessmen, wearily wining and dining clients, then put my head down—crikey, I wouldn't want to be seen, that *would* be embarrassing—and made a beeline for the supercilious-looking Latin maître d', guarding the front desk.

'Excuse me, could you possibly give this to Mr Alex Cameron, please?' I breathed, handed him my hastily written note. 'He's eating here this evening.'

He looked at me a moment, then: 'With pleasure, madam.' He inclined his head politely, put it on a tray, and went to take it in.

I watched him go. Good. No questions; no—Mr

Alex who? Oh no, he was well known here. God, he flaming well *should* be, the amount of company money he put the restaurant's way.

I nipped back to the car and drove off via Regent Street, down Conduit Street to Burlington Street. Alex had heard about this place, kept telling me we ought to go and check it—ah, here it was, Romano's.

I approached it slowly, no traffic behind me, and paused for a second, double-parked but engine still running, to look. I peered in. Through a brightly lit plate-glass window, a bustling bar was getting up a nice head of steam; a man in a tail coat was tinkling away at a grand piano at the back of the room, and some really rather beautiful people were reclining on white sofas, or perched on stools at the bar, chatting and sipping champagne. Lovely. I shivered. I'd buy an evening paper, I determined, excitement fizzing in my veins now, find a quiet corner and wait for him with my cocktail; nab one of those white sofas. Might even get picked up! God, that would be funny, seeing his face when he walked in. I imagined his amused, quizzical look as I frantically rolled my eyes over some professional lounge lizard's head. I grinned and shunted the car into first, about to drive past and find a parking space, when suddenly, the door opened, and out into the street, came my husband, Alex. He was laughing, and throwing back his head, and then turning to smile delightedly at a beautiful girl in a pink sheath dress, with long blond hair. On an impulse, he took her in his arms on the pavement and pulled her in towards him, kissing her thoroughly on the lips. It was Kate.

# CHAPTER TWENTY-SEVEN

There are moments, often brutal, invariably tragic, when one becomes aware that life as we know it is never going to be the same again. In a film, such a moment would be accompanied by a rising crescendo of stirring music, by violins screeching; in life, it's usually by a silent stopping heart. This was my moment. Glimpsed in a second, yet destined to change years. The catalyst for unravelling aeons of time that had gone before, and aeons to come. And I couldn't take my eyes off it. I sat there, transfixed by my moment, a spectator on my destiny, caught in that mixture of billowing blond hair and tailored grey flannel as it came down the street, frozen like a wild animal in headlights, by the horror that was unfolding before me.

They crossed the street, yards from my car, and came down towards me on the opposite side of the road, holding hands, laughing into each other's face. As they got closer, I felt a sharp stab of panic, as if I was the one that shouldn't be seen; as if I were the interloper. I hit the accelerator. I remember not being able to breathe, or at least, only shallowly, as if through a straw, and as if my lungs were deflating fast, like a burst balloon. Somehow, I steered the car through the traffic, through lights, through a cacophony of beeping horns, which seemed to follow inexorably in my wake, across London. No coherent thoughts formed in my head, just crazy white ones—Alex and Kate, Alex and Kate—chasing around in

451

nightmarish circles, with the rhythm of a train, like a poem I'd learned as a child—faster than fairies, faster than witches, Alex and Kate, Alex and Kate. The only thing I knew with any certainty was that I had to get away.

I drove around the streets, anywhere, round and round in circles like the ones whirling in my head, but eventually found myself at Hyde Park Corner. Then I was in Knightsbridge, and then, in the blink of an eye, it seemed, driving much too fast through Chelsea going towards Putney, towards home. I drove mechanically, hypnotically, over the bridge, as if being pulled by a force I was unequal to, down familiar streets, taking familiar short cuts. Eventually I turned the corner into Hastoe Avenue. I skidded to a halt outside Kate's house, and opposite mine: I turned off the engine, and sat there in the darkness staring straight ahead, like someone who knows they've reached their journey's end in so many senses, my heart pounding.

I glanced down. My hands were sweaty, clenched tightly in my lap. Alex and Kate. Alex and Kate. At one point, a car swept past, illuminating the interior of my car, and as I looked in my rear-view mirror, I saw my face, chalk white and ethereal, my eyes huge. I realised there was blood in my mouth. I must have bitten the inside of my cheek. I swallowed it, and looked at Kate's house. There were a couple of downstairs lights on, the curtains were drawn, but otherwise, it was in darkness. The children would be in bed by now, and perhaps Sebastian too, if he was at home. Did he know, I wondered? Or suspect that Alex and Kate—oh, Alex and *Kate*. The bile rose in my

452

throat and I opened the door just in time, bending low to vomit in the gutter. I stared as it dripped away down the street. Flowed down a drain. Then I found a tissue, wiped my mouth, and shut the door. In the glove compartment was an old bottle of Evian water. I took a slug, gulping it down.

The water, fresh and cool in my mouth, rushing down my throat, seemed to clear my thought processes. How long? I wondered suddenly. And where? And how often? My mind, up until then a shocked, blank canvas, was suddenly ambushed by questions, which jostled feverishly for position, like protesters at a rally, shooting up their hands. Lots of times? Once? We must be told! I shut them out, all of them, squeezing my eyes tight, slamming the door in an heroic effort at self-preservation.

My eyes snapped open as I heard a taxi trundle up. It stopped in the middle of the road. Kate got out, her long tanned legs flashing, blonde hair getting stuck on her lipstick as it blew into her face in the breeze. She unstuck it and turned to pay the driver. I saw her face, radiant and smiling in the moonlight. My stomach gave a sickening lurch. Kate. Dear Kate. I watched as she said a cheery good night to the driver, turned away, and walked quickly to the pavement, skirting the bonnet of my car as I shrank down, feeling like the guilty party again, the shadowy figure in the dirty mac. She went up her path, ducking under the magnolia tree, a spring in her step, and I heard her call out, 'Hi Maria!' as she turned the key and went inside. I sat there, trembling, watching, as more lights went on in the house. Then Maria came out of the front door: I recognised the elderly Spanish lady who lived down the road and baby-sat occasionally, the collar of her old camel coat turned up against the night air, her head bowed as she shuffled off down the road. So Sebastian was away.

A few minutes later, as I knew it would, another taxi drew up. Out got Alex. Like Kate, he looked buoyant, cheerful, excited even. He joked with the driver as he paid him. My heart began to pound. Suddenly I remembered other evenings, long ago, when I was in that house across the street, in bed, or painting, long into the night, and the same thing would happen. A taxi would rumble up, bearing Kate—and, I'd assumed, Sebastian—and then another would arrive, a few minutes later, with Alex. I used to smile to myself and think how uncanny it was that everyone unerringly arrived back just before midnight, before the witching hour, everyone doggedly aware of the working week ahead. I never put two and two together. Why would I? Alex would come up the stairs and crawl into bed, too tired after a bellyful of the Cronin brothers to make love to me, and I'd go back to sleep. And on more than one occasion I'd known that Sebastian was abroad, so I'd known that Kate was alone in that taxi, coming back from her play rehearsals . . . every Wednesday, which was usually the night Alex entertained clients.

Breathe, breathe, I told myself fiercely, realising I was hunched up over the wheel, fists clenched, no neck. I straightened up and watched Alex go—not into the main house as I'd expected, but down into the basement flat. I stared. For a moment I wondered if I'd been seeing things in Burlington Street, hallucinating, rather as I thought I had at Eleanor's house when I'd caught him embracing her in the mirror, but then—no. Clever. Very

454

clever. Always separate taxis, and always, even if Sebastian was away, separate entrances: for the neighbours' benefit. Always scrupulously careful in their movements, which, of course, was why they'd never been caught.

As a light went on in the basement, I got out of the car and walked up the path to the front door of the main house. I rang the bell, thinking how often I would have bent down and called through the letter box, 'Only me!'

Kate's quick, light footsteps came down the hallway. There was a pause as she looked through the spy hole, and when she opened the door, I saw she was still in her pink dress, but barefoot. She looked startled to see me.

'Imogen!'

'Hi.' I smiled.

'Good heavens. What on earth are you doing here?'

She had the grace to flush. I laughed. A shrill, unnatural sound ringing out in the still night. 'Oh, it's a long story. Can I come in?'

Normally I'd be in already, right in, but she was still standing, sledgehammered by my presence, squarely in the doorway.

'Oh! Of course you can.' She collected herself, gave me a quick kiss, the same one Judas gave, and stood aside to let me through. I went on down the hallway to the long creamy kitchen.

I knew that room intimately: every willow-pattern plate on the oak dresser, every cup, every pan hanging over the wooden island, the National Trust calendar hanging on the wall, which Kate would flip through impatiently when the phone rang—I knew every inch. Tears threatened. Don't think, no, *don't* think. Kate was behind me.

'Actually,' I turned, 'I came up to see your play.'

'My play?' She looked rattled.

I smiled and sat down on a stool at the granite breakfast bar. 'Yes, you know. *As You Like It.*'

'Oh!' Her eyes were wide. Scared. 'Oh, the play! Oh no, I dropped out of that ages ago. Haven't done that for a while.'

She fluttered around the kitchen, folding a dishcloth over the taps at the sink, putting a glass away on the draining board, her hands, it seemed, unable to stay still.

'Oh?'

'Yes, it all became too much. The rehearsals, you know, every week. And Orlando always seemed to have loads of homework on a Wednesday and—well, you know how it is.'

'Yes. I do,' I said softly.

Tears scuttled up like a ball in my throat as I watched her fidget around her kitchen. Kate. Watched her open the huge, pale blue American fridge that I'd envied and opened and shut so many times, to get the milk out, to grab something to make the children sandwiches as she made us a pot of tea after school—'Ham, shall I make, Kate? Or cheese?' Calling out to make myself heard over the noise the boys were making in the conservatory. I knew the exact, soft, expensive click of that fridge door shutting, as it did now. Kate had a bottle of white wine in her hand.

'Drink?' She attempted a smile.

'No, thanks, I'm driving.'

She looked surprised and poured herself a large one.

'So . . . you just stopped going?' I watched her,

as a cat would a mouse.

'What? Oh. Yes. I felt terrible about letting them all down, but the juggling just became too much.'

I nodded. 'Yes. Casper said.'

'Casper?'

'Yes, well, I went, you see. And he was there. You remember Casper, Kate, the art dealer. The one I had lunch with, who jumped me.'

'Oh. Yes, I—' Her eyes were big with fear.

'We had a drink together in the interval. He was there because his wife was in the play. Charlotte. They're back together again, which is nice, but we were recalling our disastrous lunch, which of course you instigated, but not with a view to selling my paintings. I gather you thought I was lonely! Thought I might like a companion. Anyone would think I didn't have a husband of my own!' I didn't recognise my voice, didn't know how it could carry on. Kate was in trouble now.

'Well, I—I thought you could use a friend, you know . . .' her voice was almost a whisper, her face grey, lowered to the counter.

'But I've got loads of friends! I've got you for a start. Tell you what, I might have a cup of coffee before I drive home. Instant will do.'

She turned, very shaken, but gladly went to the sink to fill the kettle. I'd seen her seize that kettle so many times, cheerfully, confidently, in irritation, cursing her tap, which splashed, setting it down on the Aga, the pale blue one, which matched the fridge, the one she'd fought Sebastian for as her nod to a farmhouse kitchen, and which we'd sit either side of on a cold winter's afternoon, while Rufus and Orlando played, the lids thrown up for

457

warmth, Kate laughing that her mother, a country woman, would be horrified at the heat loss from the oven. But then she'd laugh, 'It's not as if I've got jugged hare in there—all this ironmongery for a solitary baked potato for Sebastian when he finally gets home!' And we'd gossip about Carrington House, about the mothers, about how Ursula Moncreif had the hots for Mr Pritchard, wondering if Miss Tulliver, the school secretary, was a lesbian, and whether the odd German chap two doors down who shuffled around with a coat over his pyjamas was actually a mass murderer with bodies under his floorboards, and—oh, all manner of silly, silly things as we picked at bars of chocolate, whiling away the hours until it was time to get the boys into their baths, time for our husbands to come home. I sucked in my breath. Oh God, please tell me this started last week. Not then. Not way back then. But in my heart, I knew.

'I'd forgotten Casper,' Kate was saying as she shakily measured out the Nescafé. Her face was wretched. She looked about ten years older.

'So had I, until today. Good heavens, there's someone at the back door, Kate.'

Alex, fresh from the basement steps at the back of the house, and fresh from a shower too, by the look of his wet hair, had half opened the French windows, got his foot inside, before he saw me. His face went from delicious excitement to dismay in a trice.

'Imogen!'

'Hello, darling.'

'Wh-what on earth . . . ?'

'I came up to see Kate's play. Did you run out of sugar, or something?'

His eyes darted to Kate. She met them briefly, in fright, then hid her face in the sink.

'Yes, um, coffee. I fancied a coffee. Hadn't got any. I just wondered, Kate—'

'Of course.' Her voice was only barely audible as she passed him the jar of Nescafé, not looking at him.

'Oh, well, have it here, now we're all here!' I smiled. 'Very jolly.'

I reached up to where the mugs were kept and got one down, taking the Nescafé from him and spooning some in. Thought processes visibly whirring, he gingerly came into the kitchen and perched on a stool at the breakfast bar opposite me, as Kate tried to pour boiling water from the kettle. She kept missing the mugs on the granite surface.

'Here.' I took the kettle from her, so tempted to feel sorry for her, dear, dear Kate, her face crumpled with shock and pain, and so, so tempted to pour it on my husband's groin. I nearly did. Nearly moved my hand just six inches to the left of his mug. Would it drop off, I wondered? His penis? If I poured for long enough? I was pretty sure he'd never be able to use it again. No, he'd probably have to have it amputated.

'Milk?'

'No, thanks,' he muttered.

No, of course, he took it black at night, but then I'd forgotten. Hadn't shared a coffee with him at night for so long.

'So, you came up for the play, then straight here?' he said lightly, conversationally, much better than Kate, who was mute, sunk in misery, but then he'd had more practice, hadn't he? With

459

Eleanor, when he was married to Tilly.

'No, I watched the first half, then realised Kate wasn't in it and left. Then I went to Simpson's to see if you wanted to have a drink after your dinner with the Cronins. I left a note with the maître d'.'

He frowned. 'That's odd. I didn't get it.'

Because you weren't fucking there.

'Then I drove on to where I thought we could meet, that new wine bar you'd read about in the *Standard*. You know, the one in Burlington Street? Romano's?'

There was a highly charged silence. Alex glanced at Kate, who, for the first time, raised terrified, beautiful blue eyes from the counter. Both pairs then swivelled to me. They knew.

'Imo . . .' began Alex.

'And what should I see,' I went on, my voice trembling with emotion, 'as I sat there in my car, thinking how fun and happening it looked, this bar, this night spot, but two fun, happening people emerging, their bodies entwined, high on excitement, high on the promise of what was to come, kissing in the street. My husband and my best friend.'

Kate sank down on to a stool, shoulders sagging, arms limp, holed below the misery line. Her face buckled and tears streamed down her cheeks unchecked, as Alex struggled to exact damage limitation.

'Now look, Imo, this is all my fault—' he began softly, but my eyes were on Kate.

'Too right it's your fault. You're a serial womaniser, Alex. You can't stay faithful to one woman for any length of time. You couldn't to Tilly and you couldn't to me. You have no moral compass, no notion of honour or duty, you're like a little boy in a sweet shop. You see something glittering and pretty and you've got to have it. I knew you were having an affair, I've known it in my heart for a long time, but Kate . . .'

My voice broke. It was odd. I felt more grief at her betrayal. Much more. Kate was sobbing.

'I'm so sorry,' her hands covered her face now. 'Imo, you have no idea—'

'Of course I had no idea. I had no idea when I asked you if Alex could live in your basement, had no idea how perfect that would be for the pair of you, how joyfully you would receive that request, how neatly I'd played into your hands.'

'No!' she shrieked, jerking her wet face up. 'It wasn't like that! I tried so hard! I was the one who tried to put an end to it, who kept telling Alex it had to stop. I even wanted to move out of London to get away from him, and when Sebastian wouldn't, it was me who persuaded Alex to move instead. I thought that putting distance between us would help us to stop.'

'You orchestrated my move to the country?' I boggled at the ramifications. A tiny cottage. My son changing schools . . .

'Yes, and I told him it was over when you left, finished, but I was so *so* miserable without him, and when you rang and asked about the basement, initially of course I recoiled, but the more I lived with the idea, and the more I missed him, the more I knew I couldn't resist it.'

Alex was over by the French windows now, his back to us, hands in his pockets, looking out into the dark night. It was almost as if he were peripheral, almost as if we weren't talking about him at all, as if he were incidental to proceedings.

'I could feel him drifting away, you see, which was what I'd wanted, of course; could feel him going back to you, so our plan was working, the distance was working, but it was horrible. I—wasn't strong enough. And I was so unhappy. *So* unhappy,' she said fiercely. 'I panicked. Said yes.'

I remembered how short-tempered and snappy she'd been on the phone when we'd first moved out. I'd thought she was jealous of me being in the country. And I remembered a brief, happy time for Alex and me, when he'd made love to me more frequently. I remembered counting the times. Then the tiredness returning.

Alex had opened the French windows now and walked out into the garden, head bowed, gazing down at the damp grass. Literally absenting himself, like a small child who knows the adults need to talk.

'I couldn't do it!' Her eyes were bright with pain. 'I missed him so much, you have no id*ea* how much I love him, Imo,' she hissed fiercely, shocking me. As if she were entitled to love him. '*No* idea.' She clenched her fists. 'It eats at me all day. It's all I think about, care about.' If he could hear her in the garden she clearly didn't care about that, either. 'I would do anything to keep him, it's all-consuming.'

Her pain was raw, tangible. It brought me up short. Oh, she loved him all right. She was in real trouble. She was in the sort of trouble I'd been in when I'd worked for him, when he was married to Tilly; when I'd sat outside his office dreaming about him, giving up two years of my life, two years of my painting career to be a secretary; stroking his diary, the chair he sat in, his Anglepoise lamp . . .

she was in that sort of trouble and it came to me, as a great wave of relief, that I was not. I didn't feel that horrible obsession any more, didn't feel my whole personality ebbing away, evaporating, as I forgot everything and everyone I'd ever cared about, my whole existence focusing on him. Didn't feel myself disappearing without him. No. Because I didn't love him as much as she did. It made me catch my breath. Made me almost feel sorry for her, my best friend, her face crumpled with anguish, shoulders hunched, hands clenched.

'Does Sebastian know? Or suspect?'

'No. He's away so much, he hardly notices anything.'

'Are you going to tell him?'

She glanced up, fearful. 'Why would I do that?'

I shrugged. 'Well, I don't want him. Alex, I mean. You have him, Kate. Tell Sebastian, and go and live with him. Take your children with you. Tilly and I would naturally advise against it, but feel free, he's all yours.'

She stared at me, shocked. She was trying to work out if I was mocking her, or telling the truth. I was surprised to discover the latter.

'Go on, do it. I've suffered for years, wondering where he is, what he's up to—you have a go. See if you make a better fist of it.'

Yes, OK, I was mocking her now. But I didn't feel bitter. Or angry. I felt pity. Pity for everything she'd go through. Pity for how it would wreck her life, her pretty, enviable life: this gorgeous house, this surgeon husband, these well-adjusted children, these friends they'd shared, but I knew too that Alex's gravitational pull was greater than any of these, and that she would do it. She would go down that route. I saw the flash of hope in her eyes that she tried to mask, but couldn't, as she entertained the possibility. I looked out to Alex in the garden. One man. That one man could do all this—and such an insubstantial man, at that, I thought in surprise. Not a man like Sebastian, a clever, serious, talented man, a man who did great things, who healed people. No, a man, who was not clever, but cunning. Not a nice word. A man the wrong side of forty, with a mediocre job, precious few assets, slightly on the lanky side, and whose teeth, if we're being picky and I was right now, were not great lately, either. I saw him with brand-new eyes.

Kate followed my gaze. She was looking at him too. And I saw in her eyes what my mother and sister and flatmates must have seen in mine all those years ago, and despaired. They were ablaze; full of an almost messianic light, a zeal, that nothing and nobody was going to get in the way of. Not a husband, not three children, and certainly not a best friend. I swallowed. Felt something approaching awe. I got up from my stool.

'Take him,' I said softly. 'Really, he's all yours. Marry him, Kate, if you like. I'll give him a quick divorce. Become Mrs Alex Cameron. Here.' I took off my wedding ring and tossed it at her. It bounced on the work surface. She looked at me, astonished.

'But never forget, Kate, that from his point of view, marrying the mistress only starts another chapter.'

She gazed at me, uncomprehending.

'It creates a vacancy,' I said quietly.

This time our eyes communed, silently and for the last time. I picked up my car keys, cast a final look at my husband's silhouette in the garden, and then I turned and walked away.

## CHAPTER TWENTY-EIGHT

I drove back to the country in a trance. Well, clearly in a trance because the tears were not coursing down my cheeks and I wasn't hyperventilating or gripping the wheel, struggling to keep the car on the road. I felt calm, controlled even. Shock, I decided as I listened to the windscreen wipers swish away a light drizzle then thud quietly as they hit horizontal; that was it, I must be in shock. Or denial. The tears would come later. Well, they were bound to, weren't they? I'd lost my husband, lost him to my best friend, two strikes in one. I held my breath, waited for the floodgates to open. They didn't. They would, though. And after the tears would come the depression as my empty life yawned before me like a chasm: I'd hide away like a recluse, pulling up the drawbridge; a gaunt, grief-stricken figure in a headscarf and dark glasses, who emerged from her cottage only to take her son to school, everyone talking about her, worrying about her—how thin she looks, how pale—well she's distraught, poor thing, dis*traught*. But somehow . . . I gazed beyond the wipers to the Catseyes shining in the wet road, listened to the hypnotic swish—thud, swish—thud . . . somehow, I didn't think that would happen.

I ransacked my feelings. Why? Why didn't I think that would happen? I *did* feel grief, but it was for Kate, not Alex, I realised with a jolt. I felt her betrayal much more keenly. After all, men did cheat on their wives, we all knew that—brains in their trousers, can't help themselves, poor buggers—and I'd been waiting for Alex to do it for years, been rehearsing this moment in my head for God knows how long, but that Kate should cheat on *me* . . . It was unnatural, against all the rules; she was my friend. Suddenly I experienced that thin air feeling again as my lungs appeared to shrink. Yes, my best friend, who'd not only taken my husband, but made a farce of my life too—that was the shaker, I decided. That a great slab of my life was completely different from how I'd imagined it to be. Like a movie shot on two different rolls of film, from two different angles. I was living one version, and all the time another was showing at a different cinema. You could watch both and find them similar—same characters, same houses in the same street in Putney, same children playing in the gardens—but spot the difference. There's Kate in her kitchen making a cup of tea for her friend, but—no, on the other screen, she's making a cup of tea for her lover's *wife*. Offering her lover's *wife* a piece of chocolate as they sit by the Aga together. The deceit was breathtaking. It made me so sad I almost stopped the car. Kate. My best friend. But . . . was I hers? Kate had lots of friends, I knew that—Lucinda, Betsy, Amanda—and I was her friend across the road. She used to say that: 'This is Imo, my friend from across the road.' Close, geographically, but . . . I swallowed. Anyway, all that was academic. Beside the point. Because, of course, all along she'd been Alex's friend, not mine.

466

This did make me breathe through my teeth, make my nostrils flare, as I wondered how on earth they'd managed it? Obviously Kate's play rehearsals and Alex's late nights at work had been their cover, but—what, had they met for supper? In town? No, no, of course not, they'd have gone straight to a hotel. Wouldn't have been brazen enough to sit in bars like Romano's until I was safely in the country. Which one, I wondered. Which hotel?

I pictured Kate, getting ready across the road from me while I bathed Rufus, and Sandra bathed her children, a-flutter with excitement as she put on her make-up, tied a scarf around her neck—the pink one? No, this turquoise one, shows off the blue eyes better—slipped her feet into pretty jewelled mules. Once, I remember, I was at the window as she ran across the road to get a taxi—yes, always a taxi, and yet one didn't really drink at play rehearsals, did one? Anyway, I'd stuck my head out and called, 'Break a leg!' and she'd called back, 'I'll break Ferdinand's if he still doesn't know his lines!' I was awestruck by that, now. That took some doing, didn't it? To lie, so comprehensively. Not just to laugh and look embarrassed. And then, trying to fix me up with Casper, trying to get me laid, in order to have a clear run at Alex. Did he know about that? Yes, of course he did. They'd cooked it up together—'Let's see if she takes the bait.' The wickedness threatened to overwhelm me as I hunched over the wheel, my head down in my neck, because—yes, my overriding emotion now was fury. I could feel it surging up inside me, oozing over the deep gashes in my heart, flooding me to the core.

And yet, still I hadn't thought about Alex. Hadn't considered his part in this treachery. Well, I'd dismissed him, I realised with a start. Dismissed my husband. What he'd done was so irredeemably dishonest, so disgusting, I'd mentally washed my hands of him. He hadn't been a teensy bit naughty with Old Lover Eleanor—let's face it, I've bonked her before so perhaps I'll get it past the wife—no, he'd picked Kate. Taken Kate to bed, caressed Kate's—no, don't go there, Imo. I exhaled shakily. There was no decision to be made, no—should I forgive him? Keep the family together? It was a clear, unequivocal *no*. Our relationship had been hanging by a thread, and now that it had snapped, now that I'd finally plummeted to the dark waters below, the ones I'd dreaded, I was finding them surprisingly buoyant. I wasn't drowning. My head was above water.

But my guts wrenched when I thought of Rufus. When I thought of him not having a mummy and a daddy who lived together, of just having me. And Alex—well, when he could fit Rufus in, I supposed. Around all his other commitments. His other children. Oh, he'd be pleased to see him when he was older, I'm sure, when Rufus was tall and good-looking, take him to his club and say, 'Have you met my son?' Put an arm round his shoulders as he introduced him, as if he'd played a major part in his moulding, his shaping. I changed lanes to let a Porsche go past. And, after all, he didn't see much of Lucy and Miranda, did he? That didn't appear to break his heart. And he and Rufus had never been particularly close . . . I caught my breath. *Not particularly close?* A man who wasn't close to his children? Was this *really* who I'd married? How

468

*could* I? Where was my judgement? Why, against all the evidence, had I done it?

But I knew why. Because, in a secret, shameful corner of my heart, I'd believed it must be her fault. Tilly's. Believed she'd gone wrong somewhere. Handled it badly. But I'd do it differently. Better. Be a better wife. He loved me differently too. Loved me more. He'd said he did. I filled my lungs shakily. Let it out huskily. Oh, Imogen. The scales were falling from my eyes with such a resounding clatter I was in danger of being deafened as they hit the dashboard. What had I seen in him? This wicked man? No, I struggled with the truth, not a wicked man, a weak man; a man who was easily swayed, who couldn't help himself, who wafted this way and that, as if blown by the scarves of beautiful women, like the one around Kate's neck. I realised I hadn't even formally ended it with him—he hadn't exactly begged me to stay—that I'd walked out on Kate, not Alex; thrown the ring at her, not him; told *her* it was over. But there was no need. In my bones I'd known it was over long ago. I'd known his heart didn't belong to me, that it belonged to someone else. I'd just got the wrong girl. Details.

When I got back to the cottage I went to the sideboard and swallowed two mouthfuls of whisky straight from the bottle, tipping my head right back. I'd never done that before and I've never done it since. As I wiped my mouth with my sleeve, I realised the answer machine was flashing. It was Hannah.

'I presume you'd like us to keep Rufus for the night. You left in such a rush you didn't quite clarify that. Anyway, he's asleep now, and Eddie

469

will take him to school in the morning. Hope the play was fun! Lots of love.'

I mounted the stairs, alone in the quiet house. I stopped, halfway up. And he'd never come back here, Alex, I mean. I'd never live in this house, or any other house for that matter, with him, my husband, ever again. Never hear his key in the door, his footsteps in the hallway. I waited for this to devastate me, for my heart to plummet, sobs to rack me. But . . . it was an oddly liberating feeling. I went on up to the landing. It meant Rufus and I could live where we liked. We could even go back to London if we wanted, although, 'No, Mummy, here,' was what I knew Rufus would say firmly. He loved it so, we both did, I thought in surprise. We'd made it our home. So, if not in this cottage, then around here somewhere.

I undressed and got into bed thinking, now, now I'll cry. Now it'll hit me and the tears will fall, soaking my pillow, but I just lay there, listening to the quiet outside, the night owls calling to each other. I hoped they called to each other like that all night, because I certainly wouldn't sleep. I needed some company on what was bound to be a very dark night of the soul. Morpheus combined with the Scotch, though, had other ideas, and before long I was being easily led down the long dark passages of sleep, to oblivion.

The next few days passed in something of a blur. I kept waiting to be shattered. I felt as if I were holding my breath, that any minute now I'd drop the scoop of chicken feed, or my paintbrush, and raise shaking hands to the heavens, wail with anguish like Middle Eastern women do, and fall prostrate to the ground. It's true I didn't walk so

470

tall; tottered, rather than strode around our smallholding, and it's true too, that eventually, I did weep. But quietly. Silent tears slipping unexpectedly down my face as I washed up, or read the paper. Nothing violent. Nothing prostrate. I felt the cold a lot too; lit a fire in the evenings and sat by it, staring into it, no television, wrapped in huge cardigans. By day I painted, but my paintings were darker, I noticed, more sombre, less vibrant. But quite good too. Yes, I painted, I looked after my child, I even ate, albeit erratically. The world, I discovered, had an extraordinary habit of turning, irrespective of personal fortunes, and I turned with it.

A weekend slipped by. On the Monday, Rufus went to school as usual and I went to pick him up as usual, chatting to the mothers at the school gates—no headscarf, although I did keep my sunglasses on. As I drove him home that afternoon, it occurred to me that since he hadn't mentioned his father, hadn't asked where he'd been this last weekend, I could just never mention it. Just carry on as usual, and then, one day when he did say, 'Where's Daddy?' I could say, 'Daddy? Oh, Daddy. Well, we've sort of decided it's better if he lives in London for a bit. Because of his work. See how it goes.' Yes, I could just let it drift. But that would be cowardly, and actually, there were enough cowards in this family.

That afternoon, I made him a Nutella sandwich and sat down with him at the kitchen table. I started my preamble with the usual claptrap about not all mummies and daddies being able to get on well for ever because people grew apart and sometimes stopped loving each other and blah

471

blah blah and just as I'd got to the bit about it being better, sometimes, for mummies and daddies to split up, even get a divorce, he said, 'Is it because of Kate?'

The saliva dried in my mouth. 'What?'

'Is that why you're splitting up, because of Daddy and Kate?'

I stared. 'What do you know about that?'

'I saw them kissing in Orlando's back garden.'

'You did?' I gasped. 'When?'

'At Orlando's birthday. You know, the one he had in the conservatory with the funny man. Magic Malcolm.'

I thought back feverishly. Yes, and I'd come across the road with Alex to help Kate and the nanny deal with twenty overexcited children, pour orange squash, hand out sandwiches. But that hadn't been Orlando's last birthday party, because last year he'd gone to the Planetarium. That had been his birthday two years ago.

'I needed a pee,' Rufus said, 'and someone was in the downstairs loo, so I ran outside to the bushes. They were kissing down by the rabbit hutch in the orchard, but they didn't see me.'

Whilst Magic Malcolm was entertaining the children. Entertaining me too. I remembered laughing with Sandra at the back of the room, as he pulled hankies from his trouser legs, did his tricks. Meanwhile, Alex and Kate were turning theirs . . .

'Why didn't you say something?'

'Because I thought you'd be upset,' he said simply, brown eyes large.

I gulped. 'Yes,' I whispered. 'Yes, I would.'

'And then I thought, maybe it was nothing. But I

472

kept seeing little things after that. The way they looked at each other, and the way Daddy kept his hand on Kate's waist when he kissed her hello.'

I stood up quickly. My son had known. My nine-year-old son. Seven, at the time.

'And you didn't say anything to Daddy?'

He frowned. 'Like what?'

Yes, like what? Watch out or I'm telling Mummy? But he'd been cool towards him, towards his father, hadn't he? I'd seen it. Alex, I was sure, had noticed it, and at the time, I'd been cross with Rufus. 'Daddy would so love you to enjoy rugby, to watch it with him on the telly.' A shrug. 'So? I just don't.' 'Daddy's coming to see your nativity play!' 'He doesn't have to, I'm only a shepherd.'

And I'd been upset for Alex. But all the time, my poor boy had been suffering, and I hadn't known. I bent to hug him. He didn't burst into tears, but he did lay his head on my shoulder.

'I'm glad you know,' he said, in a small voice into my neck. 'That was the worst bit. You not knowing. You thinking he loved us.'

I drew back. Held his shoulders. 'He does love you, Rufus. This has nothing whatever to do with you. It's me he stopped loving.'

He shrugged. 'Whatever.'

My heart began to beat fast. And not for Alex's sake, for Rufus's. I had to mend bridges here, had to let Rufus know he still had a father. I kept hold of his shoulders, looked into his eyes.

'Rufus, Daddy loves you very much. It's me he's leaving, not you.'

He picked up a stick he'd been whittling for a while and his Nutella sandwich, slipped off his chair, and made to go outside. He turned at the door and gave me a wise look.

'Actually, Mum, I prefer to think we're leaving him.'

And then he headed out for the barn.

*     *     *

The following afternoon, when Rufus was at school, I went to see Piers and Eleanor. I badly wanted to stay in the cottage, as I knew Rufus did, but they needed to know the score. After all, it was Alex who was their friend, Alex who'd been invited to live on their estate. I was also aware that the rent was due soon and since I didn't have a bean and had spent all the painting money settling my debts, I wasn't entirely sure how I was going to pay it. Would Alex carry on forking out even though he wasn't living here? Unlikely, I thought uneasily as I rang the bell. If I'd had a cap, I'd have put it in my hand.

Eleanor wasn't there, and Vera took me through to see Piers in his study. Now I really did feel like a forelock-tugging tenant, I thought, as I went in and saw him sitting at his desk in his tweed jacket, half-moon glasses perched on his nose. He did stand up, though, and give me a kiss, before waving me into a chair on the other side of his leather-topped desk. I outlined the situation in the baldest terms and asked if it would be possible for Rufus and me to continue living in the cottage.

Piers took his glasses off. He pushed his chair back, got up from his desk and turned to look out of the long Georgian window behind him. His hands were in his pockets, his profile to me. He looked tired. Old, even.

'You and Alex are going to separate?'

'Yes.'

'He's leaving you?'

I smiled. 'That . . . hasn't been discussed yet, believe it or not.'

It hadn't. I'd just left, that night at Kate's, and thus far, I'd had no contact with him. He hadn't rung me, written to me, attempted to discuss Rufus with me. Did it surprise me? No. Not really. I think he was waiting for me to make the first move.

'But as far as I'm concerned he's never coming back. I'll change the locks if I have to.'

Yes. Yes, I would. And even if Kate stayed with Sebastian, I still wouldn't want him. I found this thought remarkably cheering. Perhaps Rufus was right, perhaps I *was* leaving him, after all.

'And I know you and Eleanor are very fond of him,' I rushed on, 'and that it was he you invited to live here at a peppercorn rent, so I just want you to know—well, you *need* to know—that the situation's changed.'

He nodded. 'But then I'm sure you'll know that my situation has changed too.'

I took a deep breath. 'Ah. I'd wondered.'

'Eleanor's gone. She went last Friday. She's living with Daniel Hunter.' A muscle went in his face, betraying him.

'I'm sorry, Piers.'

He didn't reply for a while. Stayed staring out of the window at his rose garden, working his mouth a bit, jutting his chin for composure. Then: 'I always knew she would, actually,' he said in a low voice. 'Knew in my heart I wouldn't keep her.'

I blanched with recognition. 'That's . . . rather how I felt about Alex. But never really admitted it.'

475

'No, you don't. You can't believe your luck when you marry someone like that. Or when someone like that marries you. Just thank your lucky stars and hope it will continue. Hope it's for ever. But Eleanor was always discontented with me.'

'Was she? Why?' I knew I was being disingenuous, but it would be rude not to.

He turned from the window to face me. Smiled sadly. 'I'm a dull chap, Imogen. Set in my ways, wedded to this house.'

'Yes, but Eleanor loved this house, didn't she?' I said, confining myself to the latter part of his remark.

'She did. Too much, initially. And my bank balance. But that's never enough, is it? As my mother always says, if you marry money, you pay for it. She should know too. But luckily for her, my father died relatively young.'

Right. Which was clearly a good thing. Blimey. The family skeletons were clattering out of the closet now, weren't they?

'People think it's an asset, a house like this, lord of the manor and all that, but it's a bit of a poisoned chalice, actually,' he said ruefully. 'Women don't see me at all, just the trimmings.'

'Rather like Alex,' I said suddenly.

He frowned. 'How d'you mean?'

'He's almost too handsome for his own good. Women fall for it too easily. But actually, there's not much substance to back it up. I don't mean like you,' I said quickly. I didn't. I was warming to Piers. He didn't seem quite so arrogant and aloof today.

'I've always been rather scared of you, Imogen.'

'Me?' I yelped.

476

'Yes. You and Alex were such a glamorous London couple, and you're so clever and talented. I thought you looked down on us rough country folk.'

'But I thought you looked down on me for being common!'

'Common?'

'Well, you know, my family and everything.' I blushed.

'Oh, I think they're great fun. Your father's a hoot and your mother's frightfully amusing. My father was a turkey farmer, you know. A self-made man.'

'No, I didn't.' Blimey, that closet door just wouldn't stay shut, would it? 'I thought he was Sir Somebody-something?'

'He was. Got knighted for services to food and industry. Started the trend for reconstituted poultry. Probably get his head chopped off now— Turkey Twizzlers, and all that.'

'Right.' I looked at him with new eyes. So, all this, via trade, and in only two generations. Three, counting his children. His children. I almost daren't ask.

'Are the children . . . ? I mean, is Eleanor . . . ?'

'They're staying here,' he said, meeting my eye. 'Eleanor agreed to that. Obviously she'll have them in the holidays, but she and the teacher man are moving to Shropshire. He's got a job up there, you know.'

'Yes, I heard.'

'And the children don't want to go. Can't say I blame them. We gave them the choice, you see. All frightfully civilised.'

'And they chose you.'

'Yes.' He blinked, surprised. 'They chose me. Well,' he countered, 'they chose their home.'

'Yes, but with you in it. That's quite a vote of confidence, Piers. Even Theo?'

'Even Theo.'

I breathed in sharply. Heavens. Quite something when an eleven-year-old chooses to live without his mother. So she'd gone without any of them. She'd said she didn't want to lose them, but she had. I wondered how that had felt. It didn't bear thinking about. And yet, still she'd gone. I wondered if the children had been told about the baby. Wondered if Piers knew.

'I knew she was pregnant long before she told me,' he said quietly, reading my face. 'You don't live with someone for fifteen years and have four children and not know things like that. Not notice she's gone off coffee and eased off the wine and that her periods have stopped—what does she take me for?'

'And yet you never said anything?'

'No, I never said anything.'

'Why?'

He smiled. 'Because I had a vain, foolish hope that it might be mine. I am married to her, after all,' he reminded me, sadly.

'Yes, of course.'

We looked at one another, and it seemed to me we'd learned more about each other in the last five minutes than we had in all the years we'd known each other. And I liked what I saw.

'As to the cottage,' he went on, 'of course you can stay. I'd like you to. Theo would like it. And it might be good for the two little chaps in view of their rather similar circumstances.'

478

'Yes, you're right, it might. Thank you, Piers. But I'm not sure when I'll be able to pay you. Alex and I haven't worked out finances yet—haven't worked out anything yet—so I don't know . . .'

'Oh, don't worry about the rent.' He waved his hand. 'Pay me whenever. You need somewhere to live, and if it suits you, it suits me. We'll sort out the finer nuances in due course.'

I got up suddenly and crossed the room. Reached up to kiss his cheek impulsively. 'Thank you. Thank you so much. You've been very kind.'

He looked taken aback, but not too displeased. As we moved as one towards the door, the interview seeming to be at a natural close, I thought, yes. Yes, that's what he is, a kind man. A good man. And what, after all, is a little dullness, set against that?

As we got to the front door, his ancient black Labrador lumbered up from the Persian rug in the middle of the hallway to say goodbye. I patted her.

'She's huge,' I observed.

'She is. About to pop. This house is full of pregnant females.'

'Oh!' I looked at him, but his face gave nothing away.

'And she's far too old to be giving birth—like someone else I know—but she slipped away while she was on heat. No doubt found some rough trade in the village.' This too delivered deadpan. 'Can I interest you in a puppy?'

'No, thanks. I've got enough animals.'

'Well, quite, me too. I'll have to keep one, though, to placate Theo. But Pat will deal with the rest.'

'Oh—you mean . . . ?'

479

'Better than a sack at the side of the M25.' He saw my face. 'It's kinder, Imogen,' he went on more gently. 'A humane injection. They won't know about it. I suggested the same to Eleanor, but she wouldn't hear of it.'

He had a way of delivering these black lines that made me keep glancing up at him.

'Sorry,' he said softly. 'It's my way of dealing with the situation. Got to get through it somehow.'

I gave him a hug and, to my surprise, he held on tight. There were tears in his eyes too. I patted his tweedy shoulder.

'We'll get through this, Piers, you and I. We could even form a club for abandoned spouses,' I grinned.

He chuckled. 'Well, we'd better find some more members, or we'll be the talk of the village. They'll think we're Finding Solace in Each Other.'

I laughed, only a trifle nervously. Drew back. 'Thank you for the cottage, Piers.'

'Ah, yes. Back to the landlord-tenant relationship. My pleasure, wench. That'll be two guineas and a spot of deflowering on the first of every month.'

I giggled and turned to go, tripping lightly down the steps, crossing the gravel to the car. Gracious. He'd come out of his shell, hadn't he? Positively sparky.

Yes, it was odd, I reflected as I drove off towards Rufus's school. Once the barriers had been broken down—or crashed down, by circumstances—you saw people for what they really were. The same as oneself. Insecure, fallible, but not without humour, if one bothered to look for it.

On the road to the village, I flew past the

480

turning to Winslow, where Dad lived. It was a good eight miles away, but . . . I glanced at my watch. I still had an hour to kill before I picked up Rufus. I hesitated, then on an impulse, performed an emergency stop and reversed dangerously up the lane, swinging the car left and driving off towards the bypass. Twenty minutes later I was threading through some backstreets to the middle of Dad's little market town, coming to a halt outside the wisteria-clad exterior of his pale blue terraced house. I turned the engine off and gazed up at it. I'd dreaded telling my family, but now that I'd told one person, actually, it wasn't so terrible. And maybe if I told Dad, who was the least likely to fall apart at the news, well, then maybe he could tell Mum and Hannah, and I wouldn't have to?

He came down the passage to the glass front door wearing a broad grin and a blue towelling dressing gown. Tom Jones was crooning away in the background and Dad was why-why-why Delilah-ing along with him in his broadest Welsh accent. Something in his swagger and the way he slid his hand seductively up the doorframe as he swung back the door with a flourish, told me he had company.

'Ah. Bad moment.'

'Not the best.' He grinned.

'I'll come back later.'

'Could you, darling? Marvellous.'

I smiled. 'Helena Parker?'

He inspected the paintwork on the architrave and attempted to look demure and sheepish, but actually, more like the cat who'd got an entire pint of cream. If he'd had a moustache he'd have stroked it. 'Well . . .' his bare chest swelled under his dressing gown, 'you know how it is.'

I did. You had to hand it to Dad, didn't you? I'd only seen him motoring off to London to wine and dine her a few days ago, and now, here she was, flat on her back in his king size.

'You all right, luv?' He gave me a quizzical look as I turned to go.

'Yes. Fine.'

'Sure?'

I took a deep breath. Actually, this would be ideal. Dad only had a few moments before he'd want to get back to prancing round the bedroom, shrugging his dressing gown off theatrically and twanging his thong to Delilah, prior to launching himself headlong at the bed and ravishing Helena. Why not?

I turned. 'Not great, actually. Alex and I have split up.'

'Ah.' He nodded.

I blinked. ' "Ah"? Is that it—"ah"?'

'Well, I had an idea it was coming. Can't say I'm surprised. Rufus told me.'

'Rufus! But when have you seen Rufus?'

'Oh, not recently. But he told me when it happened. Alex and Kate.'

I breathed in sharply. 'Did he?'

'Yes. About two years ago.'

'Two years!' I had to clutch the drainpipe. Dad had tried to screen it with pyracantha, so it was horribly prickly. 'Ouch!' I sucked my finger as it bled. Looked at him aghast. 'I had no *idea*! Why did he tell you?'

'Well, I suppose it was a big thing for a little chap to be carrying around. He had to tell someone. Couldn't tell you, obviously, and I

482

suppose he thought I'd had some experience in the field.'

'What . . . did you tell him?' I gazed, horrified.

'I told him that in all probability it was a one-off. That drunken adults did things like that at parties, and that it didn't mean anything. That's what I hoped too.'

'It wasn't that sort of party. It was a seven-year-old's birthday.'

'I know, luv,' he said softly. 'Anyway, I told him to forget it, but when he saw them use tongues one night, he said he couldn't forget it.'

'Use what!'

'Rufus said Kate returned some eggs she'd borrowed. You weren't there, and he was in his room, but he saw them over the banisters. Alex closed the front door for a second and kissed her with his tongue.'

I had a sudden mental image of Alex, daringly pressing Kate up behind the door, pushing himself against her, kissing her again and again, running his hands over her body; Kate, the eggs in her hand, aroused, murmuring for him to stop, loving it.

'Right,' I muttered. 'Well. You obviously know. No ground-breaking news here, then. It seems the wife, as ever, is the last to find out.'

'I couldn't tell you, luv. It seemed to me you wouldn't want to be informed. Wouldn't want the truth.'

I thought about this.

'You were wrong, actually, Dad. I wouldn't have wanted to know about Eleanor, who I thought it was, but Kate . . . oh, yes. I'd have liked to have known. We all have our breaking point. Our

483

saturation level. And that would have been mine. Has been mine. He's gone, Dad. For ever, as far as I'm concerned.'

He nodded. 'And I applaud your decision. There are rakes and there are bounders, but Alex . . . well, I hate to say it about one of my own, but he was a bit of a . . .'

'Shit.'

'Hmm.' He looked uncomfortable.

I straightened up. Collected myself. 'Anyway, I'll let you go. I've got to go and get Rufus.'

'Give him my love.'

'I will.'

'He's all right?'

'He's fine. He . . . what are those doing there?'

'What?'

He turned as I pointed to the hall table behind him.

'Mum's reading glasses. I recognise the case. I bought it for her in Bath when I . . . oh my God.'

I'd seen his face. He was blushing. My father, who never blushed, who had so much neck he could challenge an emu, was turning the colour of the geraniums in the pot on the step.

'Dad! I don't believe it. Have you got Mum in there?'


## CHAPTER TWENTY-NINE

Dad's bravado staged a dramatic comeback and he began to whistle softly as he pretended to dead-head a rambling rose around the door.

'Mum?' I shoved him bodily aside and poked my

head round. 'Mum, are you in there?'

My father cleared his throat. 'Um, Celia, my dear, we appear to have been rumbled. I hope you're decent.'

'Perfectly decent, thank you. I was just throwing away these ghastly coasters—oh, hello, darling.'

By now I'd pushed past Dad and made it down the hallway into the sitting room, where Mum, looking elegant in a buttermilk silk robe, her hair pinned up but falling down attractively à la Napoleon's mistress, was disdainfully dropping Carlsberg beer mats into the waste-paper bin. I planted both feet apart, more for balance than stance.

'Mum! What the hell are you doing here?'

She tried to maintain her composure but I saw her neck redden. 'Well, aside from ridding your father of some ghastly mementoes he's picked up over the last ten years, what does it look like?'

I sat down, stunned, on the arm of a chair. My legs simply wouldn't support me any longer.

'But I thought . . .' I turned to Dad, who, whilst pretending studiously to realign a raft of silver photo frames on a table, was also trying—not terribly hard—to suppress a smile. 'I thought you were seeing Helena Parker! Thought it was all going swimmingly!'

'Oh, it was. It worked a treat.'

'Worked a . . . what d'you mean?'

'I wasn't really seeing Helena Parker, Imo, but when I met her the other week at Tessa Stanley's dinner party, it occurred to me she was just the sort of woman to drive your mother crazy. As, of course, the others haven't.'

'The others haven't? You mean . . .'

485

'Imogen, your mother and I split up ten years ago, when, due to a mid-life male wobble, I had an affair with another woman. A stupid, silly mistake, but these things happen, or so I thought. Unfortunately, your mother saw it differently and chucked me out—quite rightly—and then put the seal on things by moving lock, stock and barrel to the South of France. So that was the end of everything. The end of our marriage. *Finito*.'

'You never questioned it,' said Mum softly, perching on the piano stool and crossing her legs, arranging her dressing gown around them.

'Because you never gave me a chance! You made it very clear from the outset that I would not be forgiven, and that you were starting a new life without me.'

I glanced at her. It was true, she had. She'd never left the door ajar; was far too proud. But then, no one had thought Dad wanted to come back in.

'You were firmly ensconced with Marjorie, or so I thought,' pointed out Mum.

'Marjorie was a pain in the tubes,' he said irritably, 'as you well know. She doesn't draw breath and she nagged me the whole time.'

'Well, I could have told you that. She nearly pecked poor Derek to death.'

'And anyway, she went back to him—after a fairly hefty push from me—and I came out to see you in France.'

'Yes, but you brought that magician's assistant with you! Mandy something-or-other.'

'Only to make you jealous. I thought if I went younger and prettier it would do the trick!'

I put my head in my hands and rocked from side

to side, groaning. 'I don't believe this,' I whispered to the carpet.

'Younger and prettier?' Mum gazed at him incredulously. 'But she lasted two years!'

'Well, what was I supposed to do? I was on my own, spurned, deserted!'

'And then came Audrey, and then Marissa—'

'And all the time,' I jerked my head out of my hands, turned to her, 'you found it more and more amusing, as each new model appeared.'

'Well, it was! Seeing your father making an absolute fool of himself is, without doubt, hilarious.'

'And as long as he was doing that, you could cope with it. But when he presented you with Helena Parker . . .'

'Inspired,' murmured my father, drawing himself up and retying his dressing-gown cord. 'An inspired choice. Elegant, sophisticated—'

'Well, I wouldn't be too pleased with yourself,' I snapped. 'It took you ten years to think of it. I can't *believe* you've wasted so much time!'

My parents looked down at their feet like a couple of chastened, naughty children. 'And all because you were too proud and stupid to talk to each other, to communicate. I've always wondered why pride was one of the seven deadly sins; well, now we know!'

Further contemplation of the carpet ensued.

'So—then what happened? You broke up with Dawn,' I turned accusingly to my father, 'and while Mum was eagerly awaiting Trixie, or Jordan, rubbing her hands with anticipatory glee, you had a rush of blood to the head and realised—and what kept you—that you were on the wrong tack, and pretended you were seeing Helena. I seem to remember you even got the dress code right, the choice of restaurant.'

'And then your mother rang her up!' roared Dad, eyes huge, voice full of awe. 'Gave her an earful about honouring old friendships and ties, and about divided loyalties, and how she should keep her hands to herself, until Helena finally managed to get a word in edgeways and told her to get her tanks off her lawn, because aside from sitting opposite me at a dinner party the other night, she hadn't seen me for four years!'

'Yes, that was slightly embarrassing,' admitted Mum, inspecting her nails ruefully. 'Had to do quite a bit of back-pedalling and apologising, but Helena was very sympathetic. She's always been a good friend, and in fact, she gave me a lecture. A slightly lengthier version of what you've just said.'

'What, about never leaving the door open?'

'Exactly. And that if your father could go to the lengths of thinking up such a ridiculous ruse he must care very deeply about me, and wasn't it time we stopped behaving like children and sat down and talked. So we did.'

'Bit more than talked,' grinned my father, unable to suppress himself.

'Thank you, Dad.' I shut my eyes. 'Please. It's enough of a shock to find my parents canoodling in their dressing gowns without getting the gory details.'

'But you're pleased?' said Mum, anxiously. 'I mean, you're not too shocked?'

'Oh, I'm *delighted*. Oh God, haven't I said?' I jumped up and went across to hug her. Hugged Dad, too, who, when I let go, leaped up in the air scissoring his legs together sideways, always his party trick.

'I'm thrilled to bits for you both, I'm just so cross you wasted so much time!' I looked at them despairingly. 'Does Hannah know?'

'No!' They both gasped in unison, eyes full of fear.

'Well, you must tell her.'

'Oh no, we can't tell *her* the whole story. She'll be furious!' Mum quaked.

'Have to make something up,' agreed Dad. 'Say—you know—we just coincidentally, and rather bizarrely, started fancying each other again.'

'Oh, she'll really fall for that,' I said drily.

'Yes, she might think it's a bit odd,' agreed Mum. 'After ten years of hating each other.'

'But you never *did* hate each other.' I turned to her, exasperated. 'That was what was so unusual. Most divorced couples do, most are at each other's throats, but you've always been good friends, always got on. I feel so stupid that I didn't think of it, didn't sit each of you down and say—now look, Mum, you still like him, and—come on, Dad, you certainly can't want to spend the rest of your life with bimbos.' Dad blanched but I swept on. 'But I was too tied up with my own life, I expect, to notice.'

'You had a lot to be tied up with,' said Mum, putting a hand on my arm.

I looked up at her sharply. 'Dad told you?' I said alarmed.

'About what Rufus saw? Yes. And I think he should have told you sooner. I would have done, there and then, but I take the point that he thought Alex might not be serious about her.'

'Well, *I* never was about Marjorie, or Mandy, or Dawn, so I thought perhaps he wasn't. I've only ever really loved your mother,' Dad said sadly. As he did, he looked across the room at her and his eyes filled. That didn't surprise me—Dad was an emotional being—but I was overcome when Mum gazed back and hers filled up too. Mum wasn't tough, but she certainly wasn't a soft touch either. She pretty much kept a lid on things.

I stood up. Time to go.

'Well, I'm delighted. And so will Hannah be. And now you can both go and tell her.'

'Oh, no!' they chorused again, looking horrified.

'Oh, yes,' I insisted. 'You can do it. But make sure Eddie's there,' I added as an afterthought as they followed me down the hallway. I could already hear Hannah's horrified tones: 'How *could* you be so stupid? Ten years. Ten *years*!'

Her outrage would be short-lived, though, because I could also hear her joy at having them together again, as loving grandparents for little Tobias, and for Rufus too, I thought as my heart gave a leap. Oh, this would go a long way to healing his hurt. A long, long way. I turned at the door in realisation.

'Rufus will be thrilled.'

They both beamed until I thought their faces would crack.

'That's what we thought,' purred Mum.

'And we also thought,' went on Dad excitedly, 'that we'd keep your Mum's place in the South of France, use it as a holiday home. Have you all down in the summer—Hannah, Eddie, Rufus and Tobias—put a pool in.'

'Lovely,' I agreed faintly. And it would be. I

490

wasn't uttering faintly for any other reason than I wondered . . . well, I suppose I wondered who I'd be with. By the pool, in the sun, the cicadas croaking in the grasses, Eddie mixing a tray of cocktails under an umbrella . . . I straightened up. Well, I'd be with my son. And my sister and brother-in-law, and my nephew, and both my parents. I looked at them, standing together in the doorway: Mum, looking younger and softer, her hair mussed, cheeks glowing; Dad, well, Dad perhaps a little older, a little wiser. But then, he'd needed to grow up, hadn't he?

I embraced them both again.

'I'm so pleased,' I whispered in their ears. 'So, *so* pleased.'

And then I turned and went down the path, leaving them alone.

\*     \*     \*

When I picked Rufus up, I had difficulty keeping a foolish grin at bay. Rufus spotted it immediately.

'Why are you smiling so much?' he demanded as I put his cricket bat in the boot.

'I've just had some rather good news.' I shut the boot with a satisfying click.

'Oh?' Rufus looked up at me, hopeful, and for a moment, for all his bravado about us being better off on our own, I wondered if he thought his father was coming back.

'It's about Granny and Grandpa,' I said quickly as we got in the car. I wondered if it would be an anti-climax now. 'They're going to get back together again.'

Rufus stared at me, astonished. Then his face lit

up. 'Wow!'

'I know,' I said, relieved. 'Wow. After all these years, they've suddenly remembered why they loved each other in the first place, and why they got married.'

'Are they going to get married again?'

'Oh,' I laughed as I let out the handbrake, 'I don't know about that. They might, I suppose.' God, Dad would love that. I could just see him in a frilly shirt and tuxedo in Las Vegas, retaking his vows, although Mum might prefer to be barefoot on a beach, flowers in her hair.

'Grandpa must be so pleased,' Rufus mused as we drove off. 'He was a bit lonely, wasn't he?'

'Was he?' I shot him a look, surprised. 'But Grandpa was the one with all the girlfriends. Granny was the one on her own.'

'Yes, but Granny's good at being on her own. Grandpa didn't have a soul mate.'

I smiled. 'What do you know about soul mates?'

'What he told me, when I told him about Dad and Kate. He said, "Silly arse. I'd give anything not to have made that mistake. Not to have alienated my soul mate." I looked up "alienated", but I couldn't find "soul mate". What is it, Mum?'

'It's . . . someone you feel very deeply about. Someone you feel instinctively is right for you, for ever. Part of you, almost. Like the missing piece in a jigsaw.'

'Did you feel that about Dad?'

I considered this. 'I thought I did, but looking back, I wonder if it wasn't a bit one-sided. If I wasn't a bit . . . well, obsessed with him, when I met him, to see clearly.'

'What's obsessed?'

492

I paused. 'Keen.'

'Oh. And have you ever met anyone else who you thought could be a soul mate?'

I didn't answer.

'Rufus, there's an ice-cream shop over there, would you like one?'

'Oh, cool. Yes, please, Mum.'

We pulled up on the edge of the village. This conversation was getting just a little too adult for my liking.

'That's where your pictures are, isn't it?' Rufus pointed to Molly's bar, a few hundred yards down the road.

'Yes. That's right.'

I realised I'd been avoiding it for the last few days, for reasons best known to myself. Avoiding her. But that was silly, I decided. I couldn't do that for ever. She was selling my paintings, for heaven's sake.

'Rufus, you go and choose your lolly, and I'll pop in and see if anything's been sold.'

'OK. I'll come and find you.'

I gave him some money and he was off at the double, loving that little bit of independence that made him feel so grown up, to be buying his sweets, at nine, on his own.

The bar was closed and in darkness, but I could see movement in the shadows. When I rang the bell, Molly wove her way briskly through the tables and came to swing back the door.

'Hello stranger! We haven't seen you round these parts for a while.'

'I know. I've . . . been busy.'

I'd forgotten how beautiful she was. Her heart-shaped face was wreathed in smiles and her green eyes danced. Her sheet of silky dark hair shone like a mahogany halo in the bright sunlight. No wonder he loved her.

'Come in, come in. You'll have a quick coffee?'

'I won't, thanks,' I said stepping inside. 'Rufus will be back in a mo. He's just gone to get an ice cream. I just wondered how the pictures were doing?'

'Well, look!' She reached for the light switch and illuminated the dark cavern. Flung her arms around the bare red walls. 'I was going to ring and tell you—I need more!'

I gasped. 'You've sold them all?'

'Well, not all of them—there's still a couple down there.' She pointed to the room through the archway. 'But I've sold eight out of eleven. Not bad, eh?'

'Not bad? My God—it's brilliant!'

All sorts of dizzy emotions jostled within me—excitement, pride—but mostly, an entirely practical one: paying my rent, properly, without going cap in hand to Piers; paying my bills, being independent, perhaps entirely independent of Alex, which, I suddenly realised, was what I craved.

'How much?' I couldn't help it.

'Well, I haven't completely totted it up yet, but I've got it written down somewhere . . .' She made towards her pad of paper behind the bar. 'Just got to take off my commission and—'

'No, no, it's OK, Molly.' I blushed and stayed her arm. 'I can work it out at home. It's just . . . well, I'm not used to having money. Of my own.'

She grinned. 'And there was I thinking you were a bored housewife doing it to Find Yourself. Hadn't realised you were a proper struggling artist

494

needing the dosh.'

'Well, I am now.' I saw her curious look but didn't want to elaborate.

'But who bought them all?' I went on quickly. 'D'you have a list?'

'I do, and they're mostly locals. Even Piers Latimer bought one!'

'Piers!'

'Yes. We had a kind of official opening party for the bar. It was last week, very impromptu, and I tried to get hold of you, but someone said you were in London. Anyway, he came and bought one, and my parents came and absolutely *loved* them and they bought one, and all three of my brothers came, and one of my brothers even bought three!'

'Good heavens.' I was stupefied. That people would actually want to part with hard cash for my paintings . . . hang them on their walls, above their fireplaces, show their friends—'Yes, a local artist. Rather talented, we think.' I gulped, overcome. And it was mostly the large canvases that had gone, the recent, sweeping landscapes, not tiny loo pictures. Only three, the ones I'd painted in London, remained.

'Well, I don't know what to say. I'm staggered. Thank you so much, Molly.'

'Don't thank me. You painted them,' she grinned, as Rufus came running back in with his lolly. 'I just provided the wall space. Hello, you.'

'Hi.' Rufus smiled politely, then, not so politely: 'Mummy, can we go now? I want to see if Biscuit's had her puppies.'

'The Latimers' dog?' asked Molly.

'Yes.'

'She's just about to. Pat was here a minute ago,

having a cup of tea, and he got a call from Piers. She's having a few complications, I gather.'

'Oh! Mum, can we go?' Rufus looked up at me, anxious.

'We can, my darling, but I'm not sure Piers will want you up there.' We made for the door. 'Thanks, Molly, we'll speak soon.'

'Oh, he will,' urged my son, 'he said I could. And he said I could have a puppy too. Theo's having one. Can I, Mum?'

'I'm afraid I've already said no Rufus. We've got too many animals.'

'I knew you'd say that,' he grumbled as he hurried to the car. 'Anyway, quick, I want to see her have them. And if we don't hurry, Pat will have delivered them.'

'I'll drop you off,' I told him firmly.

*       *       *

We drove up to the Latimers' and I deposited Rufus round at the back door. I half expected to see Pat's beaten up Land Rover already in situ, but the back yard was empty. Nevertheless, in case he'd parked around the front, I kept the engine running as Rufus got out, only lingering long enough to see him run through the back door and into the depths of the house, a regular who knew the way, knew the ropes. I sighed and drove home, knowing Rufus would ring when he wanted to be collected.

Back at the cottage, I went straight up to the bedroom where I was forced to keep my paintings in the wardrobe. Maybe I'd earn enough to build a studio, I thought wildly, dragging them all out of

496

the cupboard, just a little wooden one, like a summerhouse. And maybe I'd paint on real canvas now, and maybe . . . maybe I could approach the chap who ran the gallery in town. Have a proper exhibition. If the locals liked them, he might have heard about my success at Molly's. I crouched down and sifted eagerly through them, wondering which ones I should pick to fill the gaps at the bar. I wouldn't desert Molly. Oh, no, as long as she was selling them, I'd keep putting them on her walls. Gosh, I had plenty, so—what about this seascape above the bar? I propped it up on the bed, standing back to view it critically with narrowed eyes. Or—this Parisian street scene that I'd done in London? It had a certain café society feel to it— perfect for the ambience. But they weren't framed. None of them. And framing was so expensive. About sixty pounds a throw. But I had money now, I determined, and I must plough it back in. If I was going to be a success, I had to reinvest.

Fizzing with excitement, I carried the seascape and the street scene downstairs. I'd take them into the framer's tomorrow, I decided. The one in town. I'd heard he was good—in fact, I'd take six or seven. My heart pounded. I'd never had so many pictures framed in one go; usually did them one at a time, never had the confidence. But I'd worked the money out in my head in the car, and I realised I had over two thousand pounds. Two thousand pounds! My heart flipped with excitement.

As I propped up the paintings by the front door ready to put in the car—carefully, always back to back so as not to scrape the paint—and made to dash upstairs for more, I realised there was post on

497

the doormat. I picked it up and instantly felt sick. Two envelopes, one cream, one blue, both written in hands I recognised. One from Alex, and one from Kate. I dropped them; had to sit down on the stairs I felt so wobbly. I stared at them on the mat for a long while. Couldn't touch them, just sat there, staring at them. I could feel my fizzy excitement dripping off me, soaking into the carpet, like so many raindrops.

After a while, I stood up. I collected the letters, and also a pen from the hall table. Then I sat down on the stairs again. I narrowed my eyes and gazed out of the tiny hall window to my cows, all lying on their sides, slumbering peacefully in the sunshine. Dad had once told me it was the ultimate insult, but also the ultimate in personal dignity. I carefully crossed out my address on each envelope, and then readdressed them, back from whence they came. No. No thank you, Alex and Kate. I don't want your fawning apologies; don't want to think about either of you right now, don't want my bubble burst. Oh, I knew I'd be speaking to Alex about Rufus soon enough, organising access, but I'd contact him. I'd write to him, in my own time, on my own terms, when I was good and ready. And when Rufus was good and ready too. But Kate? I gazed out of the window. No. Never.

I thought of the hours of agonising, the hours of writing and rewriting that had gone into those letters, the collaboration, perhaps. Kate's full of, 'You don't know how many times I tried to stop myself, don't know how I've hated myself, how dreadful I feel'—trying, as if she hadn't taken everything else from me, to steal feeling dreadful as well. And Alex's, full of much the same, but with possibly some 'Can you ever forgive me?' thrown in, or possibly not, but either way, it didn't matter, because I'd made up my mind. No, I couldn't. And wouldn't forgive him.

As I put the letters on the hall table to send in the morning, I thought of the expressions on their faces as they received them. I went back upstairs for my next two paintings, feeling slightly less sick, feeling my spirits returning, my equilibrium making a heroic comeback. Good, I thought as I managed to spring up the top two stairs. As my dad would say, *nil desperandum*—or, don't let the bastards grind you down. Well, I wouldn't.

I made two more trips up and down the stairs until I had seven boards in all stacked in the hall, and was just chewing my thumbnail and dithering over whether or not to make it eight—that still life, perhaps, of the fruit and flowers, but then at sixty pounds a frame that would swallow up nearly a quarter of my earnings—when the phone rang.

I leaped in alarm, for some obscure reason thinking it might be Alex, having miraculously received his redirected mail, ringing up in high dudgeon, but of course it couldn't be. I picked it up. Was about to say hello, when Rufus's voice, without waiting for mine, came down the line. It was shaking with emotion.

'I can't believe you knew they'd be killed! I can't believe it! You knew Pat was going to put them down. I'm never speaking to you again. Never!'

# CHAPTER THIRTY

'Rufus. Rufus!'

But he'd gone. The phone had been slammed down. I hastily dialled Piers's number but the line was engaged. I tried again. Still engaged, presumably Rufus had slammed it down, missed and run off. Damn! I thought for a moment, then grabbed my car keys and ran outside. Rufus didn't get like that, didn't *sound* like that. He was such a calm, controlled little boy. I hadn't heard him so upset for ages.

I dived into the driver's seat and turned the ignition, crunching the gears. And how come it was all my fault, I thought as I lurched out of the yard, pushing hair out of my eyes. How come I was the villain? I mean, of course the puppies shouldn't be killed, but what was I supposed to do about it? Give seven or eight mongrels a home, a start in life, like something out of *The One Hundred and One Dalmatians*? And if I didn't, well, then I was Cruella de flaming Vil, all swirling fur coats and cruel red lips—Jesus!

I roared up the hill, bouncing along the chalky zigzag track and then along the lane and down the back drive to Stockley. I went round to the back yard again, knowing that the dogs all slept in the boot room, and hastened in through the back door, half expecting to interrupt the murder scene: half expecting to find Piers and Pat, plucking puppies from a basket by the scruff of their necks, Pat poised with a bucket of water for drowning purposes, two small boys hanging on to his arm

500

pleading piteously whilst Biscuit barked and circled frantically, but—the boot room was empty. Just the usual serried ranks of Wellingtons, Barbours, fishing rods and shooting sticks prevailed.

I ran down the corridor and pushed open the kitchen door. Piers's lurchers, lying under the table, raised their heads and bayed a welcome, thumping the floor with their tails, but no Biscuit. And no Piers either, sitting at the table picking his teeth, or Vera washing up, and certainly no Rufus.

I ran on—'Rufus. *Rufus!*'—throwing open the laundry door, the playroom door, but there was no sign of anyone. Perhaps they were all upstairs? Feeling a little uneasy about charging around someone's house—but not that uneasy, I decided, recalling Rufus's hysterical tones—I flew up the back stairs, taking them two at a time, ran across the landing, and down the passageway to Theo's room. The door was wide open and piles of Lego and Playmobil castles littered the floor, but no little boys. As I was about to leave, I spun about, spotting Piers out of the window on the terrace below, admiring his roses. I flew to the window and flung it open.

'Stay there!' I ordered, as Piers glanced up, astonished, before dashing back downstairs, out of the French windows, and tracking him down in his flowerbeds, secateurs poised.

'Piers!' I gasped.

'Oh, hello, Imogen. I've been trying to get hold of you but your phone just rang and rang.'

'I'm looking for Rufus,' I panted, clutching my knees, trying to catch my breath.

'Yes, that's why I was ringing. I'm afraid I've

rather upset him. One forgets how sensitive these small boys are, and I told him—'

'Yes, yes, I know, but where is he?'

'Well, I told him Pat had taken Biscuit away because she might need a Caesarean section, and then I, you know, told him what might happen to the puppies—and he shot off on Theo's bike after him.'

'On a bike!'

'Yes, I know. I'm terribly sorry, Imogen.' He looked distressed. 'I tried to stop him, didn't think you'd want him cycling into town, but my office line went and it was my stock man with a problem about some gypsies in the lower meadow, so I was distracted, and when I turned round—he'd gone.'

'OK,' I nodded quickly. 'Not to worry, Piers. I'll find him.'

Piers was still calling his apologies after me, but I waved them aside as I ran off to the car. Cycling into town alone! At nine! Rufus didn't know the first thing about roads and traffic, particularly windy country lanes with thundering great hay lorries and tractors. He'd enjoyed a degree of independence since we'd been here, but not to that extent.

I sped to the vet's surgery, but not too fast, I thought suddenly, slowing down dramatically. I didn't want to be the one to knock him off his bike, I thought in panic as I glanced left and right—he could easily be on the wrong side of the road—but there was no sign of him. At the vet's I parked creatively outside, front wheels on the pavement, and ran up the steps and through the open door. Pink Jeans was sitting behind her desk in reception, looking poised, blonde and bored. Her face darkened when she saw me.

'Where's Pat?' I gasped, clutching her desk, no pride now.

She raised her eyebrows. 'Panting for him now, are we, dear?'

'Just tell me where he is, dear.'

'He's out on a call,' she said shortly. 'Someone's bitch was in trouble. Wasn't you, was it?'

'No,' I ground my teeth, 'it was the Latimers', but he's not there now. I assumed he was here. My son's following him.'

Her pale blue eyes widened. 'Oh, so the entire family's chasing round the countryside after him now, are they? You'll be laying traps for him next.'

I wanted to slap her. 'Do you or do you not know where he is?'

'No idea,' she said crisply. 'If he's got any sense he's barricaded himself into his home. Away from desperate women like you.'

'But he's got a sick dog with him—wouldn't he bring her here?'

She looked under a pile of papers. Then under her desk.

'Can't see him, can you?'

'Can't you ring him on his mobile?'

'He's turned it off. Don't blame him either, do you?'

I glared at her and made for the door.

'My pleasure,' she murmured.

As the door swung shut behind me, I pushed it open again and poked my head around.

'Oh, by the way, d'you ever change those jeans?' I flashed her a sweet smile and left.

So where the hell was he, I thought as I ran down the steps and back to the car. He'd picked

503

Biscuit up from the Latimers', Piers had thought he was bringing her here for a Caesarean—was there another surgery? Somewhere closer? I should have asked, but then again, I was hardly likely to get a civil answer from the She Devil, was I?

I roared back down the lanes, wondering, if, in fact, Rufus had simply cycled home and I'd missed him. So off the lane I turned and down the bouncy zigzag track—to an empty cottage. I swung around helplessly in the yard, narrowing my eyes into the distance. Right. Don't panic. Just . . . don't panic. I jumped back in the car and slammed the door— one way and another my door-slamming arm was getting a lot of exercise today—because there was now only one obvious place they could be and that was Pat's house. Perhaps he'd decided a home birth would be best. In a paddling pool, complete with womb music. Christ alive. I took a deep breath, braced myself, and headed off towards the lodge.

I realised, as I roared down the narrow lane banked either side with cow parsley, that mentally I'd been rather hoping I wouldn't have to do this, to go there, but now, here I was, turning into the main gates to Stockley and approaching Crumpet Cottage, and there, sure enough, in the front garden, casually discarded on its side, was a bright red Raleigh bike. I heaved a monumental sigh of relief. Thank God. And by the look of it—it wasn't tangled and twisted, or even mud-spattered—he was in one piece.

I hesitated on the doorstep. Maybe I should get back in the car and just beep the horn? Keep the engine running and shout, 'Come on, Rufus!'

through the open window. Maybe I didn't have to go in? Too late. The door swung back, and Pat stood framed in the doorway.

'Oh. Hi.' He looked surprised.

'Hi!' I gulped, and rocked back slightly in my trainers.

He looked gorgeous. Tall and bronzed from the sun, wearing an old checked shirt over a white T-shirt and jeans, sleeves rolled up to reveal broad, tanned forearms. Suddenly I was aware of the attractive apparition I must present: hot and sweaty with my fringe plastered to my forehead, the rest of my hair frizzing nicely, no doubt, no make-up, grubby old jeans.

A quizzical look came into his eye and he stretched a lazy hand up the door frame, leaning casually on it, a slightly droll smile playing on his lips.

'Looking for your son?'

'I was, actually.'

'Come right in. He's in the sitting room, along with Biscuit, and, apparently, HobNob, KitKat and Jammy Dodger.'

'Or Garibaldi,' warned Rufus as I went in. He was sitting cross-legged on the rug by the fireplace, a tiny puppy cradled in his arms. 'I'm not sure yet.'

'Oh!' I crossed the room and sank to my knees beside him. 'She's had them!'

'About twenty minutes ago.' Pat came across and stood over us. 'I picked her up from Piers's, thinking she might need a Caesarean she was in such a bad way, but she went into labour in the back of the car. I quickly pulled in here thinking, shit, I've got no apparatus, but before I knew it, she'd popped out four pups on the rug in front of

505

the fire.'

'Four?'

'One died.'

'Of natural causes,' put in Rufus pointedly. 'It was stillborn.'

'Rufus, I'm so sorry, I didn't think. When Piers said he was going to put them down I just assumed that was what country people did. I thought objecting was a bit like squealing when you saw a pheasant shot, then tucking into it for Sunday lunch.'

'Some country people do behave like that,' agreed Pat, 'and Piers is one of them. A lot of farmers drown litters of kittens rather than have the place overrun with unneutered cats, but I wouldn't have done it. We can usually find homes for puppies, especially if we put cute photos on the notice board in the surgery.'

'And anyway, these have all got homes,' said Rufus. 'Theo's having one, Pat's having another, and I'm having this one, Jammy Dodger. Dodger for short.' He eyed me defiantly.

I swallowed. 'Right.'

There didn't seem to be any answer to that. Under the circumstances I didn't appear to have a leg to stand on, and I certainly didn't want to make a scene in front of Pat. I glanced up at him.

'You're having one too?'

He crouched down beside us, a hand resting on the floor between his knees to steady himself. 'Your son has some very persuasive arguments. Apparently I need a dog. Apparently I'm not a proper vet if I don't have one. I can't imagine what I've been thinking of all these years. Can't imagine why I've even got a practising certificate.'

506

I laughed. 'Yes, he's good at getting his own way.'

'I might draw the line at KitKat, though. People might think I've got a screw loose if I call that in the park, think I can't distinguish between a kitty-cat and a dog. Might get struck off.'

I giggled. He was very close to me now. His knee, as he crouched, was brushing my arm. It felt as if it was on fire. I was jolly glad to see Rufus safe and sound, but right now, I wished him a million miles away. Couldn't he run into the garden and play with the tiny scraps? Throw them a ball? No, clearly not. One of them hadn't even opened her eyes yet. Couldn't walk, let alone chase a ball. Biscuit nuzzled them proudly as they suckled.

'She'd done jolly well for an old girl of seven,' Pat observed. 'That's about forty-nine in human terms.'

'Good for you, Biscuit.' I stroked her silky ear. She looked knackered.

'And I'm pretty sure they're half Collie. Old Geoff Harper has got a very randy sheepdog that's always sniffing around. That's a good cross. They look nice, and they're intelligent too.'

I wished I looked nice and felt even remotely intelligent. I couldn't think of a thing to say. I was conscious of him being very close and that my breathing was getting a bit heavy. I could hear it whistling in my ears, billowing and blowing around the room. Anyone would think I was the one in labour.

'And of course, there are some Labrador crosses you really wouldn't want. A poodle, for example, or a dachshund.'

'Wouldn't that be a bit difficult anyway?'

507

'What, you mean the copulation?'

I blushed. Oh, splendid, Imogen. You've brought up doggy sex and the problems associated with canine penetration at this very spine-tingling moment. Well done.

'Oh, you'd be surprised.' He laughed. 'Where there's a will—or a libido—there's generally a way.'

He looked at me, quite . . . you know . . . smoulderingly. Intently. His eyes were like two dark, glittering chips of coal. I knew I was pink already, and I felt myself going even pinker. Would I combust soon, under his gaze? Go up in flames? I didn't know where to look, so I glanced at the walls.

'Oh!' My mouth fell open. 'My pictures!'

I stood up, astonished, almost tripping over KitKat, who happily, Rufus shielded from my foot. I stared in amazement. Over the fireplace was the billowing hayfield I'd painted a couple of weeks ago, and opposite, above the sofa, was the same field but earlier on in the year when it was still pasture, with the cows in the foreground. They were big pictures. Expensive pictures.

He stood up too and looked embarrassed. 'Er, yes. I bought them at Molly's. Had to buy both of them because I felt they kind of went together.'

'W-well they do,' I stuttered. 'They're two studies of the same view, but . . .'

'There's another one in the bedroom,' piped up Rufus. 'I saw it when I went to the loo. In here.'

He grabbed my hand. Wide-eyed and open-mouthed, I let myself be dragged back through the hall, through another door, and into the bedroom, where I found myself looking at the very first

508

landscape I'd ever done here, that first day I'd painted, of the weeping willows dripping in the stream. That day . . . well, that day, actually, when he'd come to see the chickens that I was starving to death. He'd have driven past my easel, seen the painting from the track. And here it was, bold as brass, above an equally bold brass bed.

'You bought three!' I said astonished.

He ran his hand over the hair on the back of his head awkwardly. 'Four, actually. There's one I bought earlier in another room. But yes, I bought three in one go. Obviously had a drink too many at Molly's party.'

I dragged my eyes away from the picture to stare at him. Tiny fragments of sense were flying round my head like so many particles of dust in space, trying to cohere, to adhere, to find a home. Three pictures. Molly's party.

'You're Molly's brother,' I breathed.

He looked surprised. 'Yes, of course I'm Molly's brother. Didn't you know that?'

'Well . . . no, I . . .' I licked my lips. Swallowed. 'I knew she was living here.'

'Because she's decorating her flat above the bar. And I must say it's been great having her. We've had a blast, but she's bloody messy. About time she moved on,' he grumbled. Then he grinned. 'And she will, next week.'

'But I . . . I never knew . . .' I was still staring at him, gaping openly. 'I mean—she's not even Irish!'

He threw back his head and hooted at the ceiling. 'She bloody is! But she did come to boarding school in England when she was twelve,' he admitted. 'Ironed out the accent a bit. My brothers did too. I, on the other hand, was expelled from Ampleforth for driving the headmaster's car on to the cricket pitch.'

'Oh!'

'Went to All Saints in Dublin instead, and got the brogue. We were laughing about it just the other night in fact, with Mum and Dad, at Molly's bar—they all came over from Cork for the party. About how Molly sounds like the Duchess of Devonshire, and Tom and Michael like Prince Phillip, and I still sound like Paddy O'Reilly.'

'You don't.'

'Oh, don't worry, I'm rather proud of it.'

'Yes. I like it. The lilt.'

'Thank you.' He gave a mock bow. Then looked at me with those dark, sparkling eyes. 'And I like you too.'

I held his gaze for a moment, then cracked. I moved away, twisting my hands about.

'You . . . bought all my latest pictures, I notice,' I said, for something to say. 'Not any of my London ones. That's interesting.'

'Well, they're not as good.'

I blinked. Swung round. 'I'm sorry?'

'They're not. They look as if they've been painted from photographs.'

'They were,' I spluttered.

'And there's no passion in them. These look like you've really been swept away by something. Or someone.'

I was silenced. He seemed to know more about me than I did.

'This one in particular,' he opened a door into an en suite bathroom and there, hanging on the wall facing the end of the bath, was the very first one I'd sold in the bar, the cornfield flecked with poppies.

'Oh! That's the first one I sold! Molly said she didn't know who bought it, said Pierre sold it on a Sunday, but—he'd have known you, surely?'

'Ah, yes, but I bribed him with a bottle of Merlot. Bought his silence,' he grinned.

'Why?' I asked. Couldn't help it.

'Didn't want you to think I was too keen, I suppose.'

A silence hung between us. The room seemed very still. Very quiet. Poised on a knife edge.

'All . . . those girlfriends,' I stuttered.

He frowned. 'Which girlfriends?'

'Well, Piers said,' I mumbled, feeling stupid, because of course one of them had obviously been his sister, 'well—you know, Pink Jeans.'

'Who?'

'The receptionist at the surgery.'

'Oh, Samantha.' He nodded. 'Yes, you're quite right, I did have a quick ding-dong with her when I first came here. She flung herself at me and I was feeling raw and angry so I flung back. Why, should I be celibate? Were you expecting a virgin?'

'N-no! Of course not.' And I felt nosy and intrusive asking about his girlfriends, but what I really wanted to get back to was the raw and angry bit.

'Was it . . . were you feeling that way, because—because you'd left your wife?' I ploughed on clumsily.

His face changed. A shadow crossed it and the light went from his eyes. He turned, went back into the bedroom, crossed to the book shelves, and picked up a china ornament from a shelf.

'I left my wife? Is that what people say?'

'Well, I think Eleanor, or maybe Piers said it.' I'd followed him through. He didn't speak for a moment, his back still to me.

'Yes, I suppose I did leave her. I could have stayed.' He looked down at the china object in his hand. It was a small pink rabbit, incongruous in this no-nonsense masculine bedroom.

'You . . . have a child, too? A little girl?'

He turned and smiled. But it was an odd sort of smile.

'She's not mine.'

'Not yours? But I thought—'

'Yes, I did too. Well, who wouldn't?' He laughed quietly. 'You marry the girl you love, have a child, assume it's yours. But it wasn't.'

'Oh!' I sat down hard on the bed. My legs seemed to insist upon it.

'She—Marina, had been having an affair. With our best man.'

'Your best man. Your best friend!'

'It's not unheard of.'

'No. I . . . know.'

He sat down beside me. 'It started after the wedding, apparently. She hadn't met him before. He's an Aussie. I met him when I was out in Melbourne, just after university for my year off, ranching cattle. We ended up touring New Zealand together. He was a laugh. A good mate. He was also tall, blond and very attractive. Anyway, when I got married, he came across to be my best man. He liked England, found a job in a bar, and found my wife.'

'Crikey.' That sounded rather inadequate. 'How did you find out about the child?'

'Isobel? Marina told me. When the baby was

three months old. Couldn't keep it in any more, I guess. And she wanted to be with him, Pete, the father. So she told me one dark November night, just as she was coming downstairs after putting Isobel to bed, washing the empty bottle at the sink, sterilising it with shaking hands.'

I gulped. 'Did you believe her?'

'I did, actually. I think . . . you can pretend you don't know your other half is having an affair, but in your heart you know.'

I nodded. Lowered my eyes to the carpet. 'Yes. You do.'

'I did insist on DNA, though. I wanted to be sure. But she was his all right. Pete's.'

'So . . . you left?'

'Yes. I left.' He turned his face to mine. His eyes were raw with pain. 'I just couldn't do it, Imo. Bring up another man's child. A better man might have done, but I couldn't. But it was hard, because I loved Isobel. Loved her very much.' He gave a cracked laugh. 'As if she was mine.' He sighed. 'But I couldn't even look at Marina. So I left Ireland. Came over here.'

'And they're still together?'

'No, they split up. Marina chucked him out. I don't know why, but I know Pete's always had a wandering eye. Perhaps that was the trouble. Anyway, he's gone back to Melbourne.'

'Right.'

I considered this tall, wise-cracking man who'd been through so much pain. So much anguish. To lose a child like that.

'That's why I couldn't face the maternity ward when Hannah had her baby. The last time I'd been in one of those it was under very different circumstances. My darling wife had just given birth to my darling daughter. It was the happiest day of my life. Or so I thought.'

I paused. 'You still think of her as your darling wife?'

He looked surprised. 'Oh, no. I use that term in the heavily ironic, historical sense. I got over Marina long ago. Getting over Isobel was harder.'

'Will you . . . still see her?'

He put the china rabbit down on the bed beside him and narrowed his eyes at the wall. 'I don't know. Let's see how her life pans out. Marina has a boyfriend now, I gather from my brothers. A nice chap, a local GP. I wouldn't want to complicate things if he became Isobel's stepfather. It wouldn't be right.'

No. No, it wouldn't. And at the end of the day, we have to do what's right. My own heart lurched for Rufus. I'd make sure he saw as much of his father as he wanted. And actually, I realised with surprise, seeing Alex wouldn't bother me. I wouldn't feel the need to glam up on the Sundays he came to pick Rufus up, slick on the old lippy and blast the perfume behind my ears. No, I could be feeding the cows in mud-splattered jeans as his car rocked up. The sound of the engine coming down the track wouldn't twist my heart, wouldn't screw me tight. I'd just feel rather cross and exasperated.

'I heard about your own sadness, Imo. I'm sorry.'

'You did?' I glanced at him, surprised. 'Who told you?'

'Rufus.'

'Oh!'

'We were tending the puppies, and I, rather casually, but with sheer, scheming self-interest, asked if Daddy was coming back this weekend. He said, no, Daddy's not coming back at all. He's gone off with Mum's best friend. I think she's going to divorce him.'

I gulped. Blimey. Tell it like it is, son.

'There's obviously a lot of it about,' I muttered.

'The best-friend scenario? Oh, I believe it's a well-worn theme. And it's no real surprise, is it? If we like someone a lot, chances are our husband or wife will too. After all, we've got similar tastes.'

'I suppose. And . . .' I struggled, 'Rufus's reaction. Cold and matter-of-fact. It makes him sound like a tough, hard-nosed kid, but he's not. It's just that he's known about it for a while. Two years, in fact.'

'Ah. So his heart's been hardening gradually.'

'Yes.'

'And you? Did you know?'

I looked at him. 'Like you say. You always know in your heart. Just depends on whether you want to hide from it, ignore it. Yes, I knew.'

We were side by side on the bed. Our elbows were touching. Our legs. Just.

'It—won't do the paint any good, you know,' I breathed, looking through the open doorway to my picture in the bathroom. 'The condensation.'

He followed my eyes. 'No, I know. Needs glass. But I like to lie and look at it, you see. When I'm in the bath.'

I caught my breath, imagining that, then frantically tried not to imagine. Tanned knees sticking up through the bubbles. A bucketful of adrenalin shot through me.

515

'Glass might steam up too,' I managed, in a squeak.

'No more than I do.'

We turned to look at each other. He raised a hand and tucked a bit of hair behind my ear. I almost stopped breathing. Almost passed out. I could hear Rufus in the next room.

'Oh, KitKat, *don't* sit on Dodger!'

Pat leaned forward and kissed me, very gently, twice, on the lips. I shut my eyes and felt my pulse race.

'Rufus,' I breathed.

'I know.' He kissed me again.

'Oh, hi!'

We sprang apart. Leaped up from the bed like two deflecting magnets. Molly was wheeling her bicycle past the window.

'Oh!' She got the picture. Her face broke into a broad grin. 'Oh, *good*. How marvellous. *Just* what I had in mind.'

'Thank you, Molly,' said Pat evenly, 'for that vote of confidence, and since you've clearly masterminded this whole thing, perhaps you'd like to baby-sit a nine-year-old boy and some puppies. They're in the next room. Imo and I are going for a walk.'

'With pleasure!' She parked her bike against the wall, smiling widely, and slipped inside through the front door. Pat and I, hand in hand, left by the back.

We walked out of the tiny garden via a little wooden gate and on towards the water meadow, through the long grass dotted with cornflowers and buttercups, their nodding heads brushing our knees.

516

'I thought you were going to ravage me on the bed back there, in front of my son.'

'Would you have let me?'

'Certainly not!'

He grinned. Squeezed my hand. I felt weak with longing.

'Anyway, what would be the point? I've seen it all before.'

I stopped. 'What?'

'Sure I have. First time I met you you fell out of your dress at a dinner party, then you took your knickers off and threw them in a flowerbed, then you ran after a herd of cows stark naked. You've never stopped revealing yourself to me.'

I cuffed him lightly on the shoulder. He laughed, caught my hand, kissed it hard, his eyes dancing into mine. As they did, I remembered what it was like to look at someone who looked at you the same way back. Who liked me back. Something very close to heaven was happening to me. A dark, lonely place hidden deep inside that had been sad and dormant for a long time was opening its doors, letting its captive go free, and this man, this lovely, kind, caring, funny man was doing the opening; not with a creak, but with a flourish. I had a very certain feeling, one I was almost too scared to identify, but was equally sure I was right about. We turned and walked on, towards the water meadow, the sun getting lower in the sky, sinking into a rosy glow over the horizon.

'Pat, we appear to be walking off into the sunset.'

'Relax. Thousands have done it before us, and thousands more will do it after us. Just keep smiling and don't look at the camera. As I told you before, there's no new material. Nothing ground-breaking here. It's a well-worn theme, love.'

Love. Ah, yes, that was it.

As he slipped his arm around my shoulders, I smiled up at him, and then we moved on together, as one, into the pink light.

# CHIVERS LARGE PRINT *-direct-*

If you have enjoyed this Large Print book and would like to build up your own collection of Large Print books, please contact

## Chivers Large Print Direct

Chivers Large Print Direct offers you a full service:

• Prompt mail order service

• Easy-to-read type

• The very best authors

• Special low prices

For further details either call Customer Services on (01225) 336552 or write to us at Chivers Large Print Direct, **FREEPOST**, Bath BA1 3ZZ

Telephone Orders: **FREEPHONE** 08081 72 74 75